God Was Bored

CHRIS OSWALD

NEWMORE PUBLISHING

First edition published in 2020 by Newmore Publishing.

ISBN 978-1-9160719-7-1

Chris Oswald has lived in America, Scotland and England and is now living in Dorset with his wife, Suzanne, and six children. For many years he was in international business but now has a little more time to follow his love of writing. His books have been described as dystopian but they are more about individual choice, human frailty and how our history influences the decisions we make, also about how quickly things can go so wrong.

In memory of Kenneth McKinney and
many happy stays on Bent Mountain.

And dedicated to Pattie McKinney, aunt
to our children and friend forever.

Contents

God Was
Bored

Start of Term

"God was bored." His deep, rich voice carried across the room of sober-suited students. "So God created the world. It did not take long, even with all the bits and pieces to take care of; the little things like ants, cricket bats, colours and long evenings with a gently declining sun." The sun outside was far from gently declining. It was at its high point for mid-September, beating down on the thick clay roof tiles and yellow travertine walls, but with no impact on their ground floor lecture room, leaving it as cold as a morgue. The occupants sat on benches across the room, the warmth restricted to the fringes where the sun broke in and danced against the interior.

"It took God only six days, for he was a mighty God. But at the end, instead of taking a rest (for what god needs to rest?), God started on another world, and then another and another.

In fact, God created infinity worlds, each one sitting alongside the others, and into these worlds were put different situations, every situation and every decision catered for with its own world. Even this did not take long, for with God there is no time. All time is one – past, present and future amalgamated into one blasting, searing sensation of nowness. When this work was done, God sat back and observed his infinity worlds.

Then God was not bored anymore. "

He had always wanted to start his teaching career in this way.

With a jolt to make his students sit up.

And now he was doing it.

"Into one of these worlds was put a man called Adam. And Adam had a wife called Eve. Adam was thickset, hairy, strong with sandy, almost red hair, and a grin that spoke of the future. But the future was nothing to God. For God, everything was now but he let his people have their future, just as he let them have their present and their past. For that way led to infinity worlds and, with infinity worlds, choice was possible. Each world could sprout a new infinity as it faced each decision, every fork leading to new creation." His approach was working, rapt attention from the whole class.

It was his way of imparting the beauty of free will under the umbrella of the Almighty.

"And Eve was his wife. She was petite with the richest black hair you have ever seen and wide, open eyes that echoed her husband's honesty. Adam lived with Eve in this world, the world we call ours, where they worked their happiness as if they were king and queen, favoured above all."

Was he making sufficient impact? Certainly, 34 pairs of eyes were glued on him. He chided himself for pride, but then forgave himself; he was doing God's work.

"For God had made one rule when the worlds were created. The rule said each world should have the same sum total of happiness. God made no other rules, for no other rules mattered. For happiness was measured in terms of love.

And the only thing that mattered to God was love. And… not being bored." The pause in this sentence was artificial. It prompted the expected outburst of laughter, rippling across the cold room like a physics experiment into acoustics.

"But there were others for whom love was weakness. And to them only strength mattered. They had once cared about love. Indeed, once they had cared only for love, just like God, their creator.

But, gentlemen, there is a whole story before the story I tell today." Now he was getting poetical. There was a danger he would become too lyrical, smashing the atmosphere he had created. He paused and looked around the room, saw his new devotees, 34 of them. He was safe.

But what was that movement at the edge, where the light from outside broke in? The disrespectful movement was confirmed in that late summer stillness by the sound of a door closing. Somebody had left. And he was sure he had seen long golden hair move in a semi-circle, flaying out as she turned, kinetic energy abounding.

Physics again.

As 'she' turned.

He was sure now that he had seen a woman. And she had left his lecture halfway through. The faint aroma of rich perfume came to him, spreading across the air molecules to leave an identity.

He had paused too long, savouring the sweet smell in a masculine world, disturbed by the departure of someone who should not have been there. He continued, but some of the fire was gone now, destroyed by the golden hair swinging as it left the room.

And the click of the door closing behind her.

"These others set one rule; that each world should strive to have the most misery. They could not change the level of happiness, for that was prescribed, so they worked instead to maximise the amount of misery.

Tomorrow we will examine this story and consider the implications for free will. Class dismissed."

It was a pitiful end to a glorious start. The class shuffled, broke slowly. Individuals emerged from the benches of grey and black. He looked down at his notes, saw salvation in his briefcase. He did not want to answer questions.

"Father Barrow?" It was no good. He had to be there for them.

"Yes, my son." That was pompous. The voice was almost Barrow's age, an older recruit.

"My name is Pierre Pascal. I've read all your books. I have always wanted to meet you."

"Thank you." But his mind screamed 'not now, not in my moment of failure, not when that long golden hair has wreaked havoc in this sea of neat brown cuts'.

"I would like to ask you about some of your theories."

"Of course, Pierre. Perhaps we should get some coffee?" He owed it to his students. It was not Pierre's fault that the yellow abandon had destroyed the moment.

"That would be delightful, but perhaps another time?" Pierre was sensitive as well as intelligent, seeing the disturbance in Barrow's eyes, the uncertainty in his expression.

"No time like the present, because there is only the present in the eyes of God!" The joke broke the barrier; it was his duty manifested.

But that night, Father Humphrey Barrow dreamed of golden hair swinging wildly and bringing chaos all around. He woke several times in a sweat, walked once to the window and opened it for air, breathing deeply. But he returned to the fleeting vision in his dreams, her character, her beauty developing as the midnight hours ticked by.

In the morning he went to confession before saying early Mass.

It was at communion he saw her again. At least it might have been her.

He smelt her perfume first. It was the essence of a long hot summer's day; sweet, lazy but brim-full of life, like insects buzzing above a pond.

"Corpus Christi," he muttered.

"Amen," she replied.

"Amen," she repeated, a little louder for he had not moved, had not placed the host in her cupped hands.

He could not be sure that the veiled figure before him was the same girl, but something said it was; the way the hair reflected the light, although still now and not in motion, veiled in black.

"Ti vedro dopo la Messa," she whispered.

He did not answer but moved to the next person kneeling in front of the altar.

"Corpus Christi."

"Amen."

She stayed behind after Mass, just as she said she would, kneeling in the front row.

"You are the English priest?" She did not remove her veil, nor stand up, switching easily to English, although obviously a native Italian speaker.

"I am Father Humphrey Barrow." He did not like her lack of reverence. "I am newly attached to the English College." He replied in Italian, thinking she would prefer it.

"Jesuit?" She looked up. He detected disdain in her enquiry.

"Not everyone at the English College is a Jesuit by any means." He checked himself, aware that he was sounding pompous, wanting to be friendly. "But it so happens that I am a priest ordained into the Society of Jesus. I am a Jesuit."

She made the sign of the cross, stood up and turned to go.

"I have a message from the Cardinal. I am his assistant. He sent me to summon you at 11 a.m. today."

There was the slightest flash of light on her hair as she turned to leave the chapel, darkened by her veil, tinted by the stained windows, but evident nonetheless.

He wanted to say he had seen her in the lecture room, but she was gone. It seemed undignified to chase her up the aisle.

It was only afterwards, at breakfast of tea, porridge, eggs and bacon that he realised that she had not said which cardinal he had been summoned to.

The administration office was the place to go to. It was run by an English woman, Signora Silversitrinni, but to everyone at the English College she was known as Old Ma Silver. They had met on Humphrey's arrival the week before and, after showing him around, she had told him to come back with any problems. Then, to answer the unspoken question, she gave her story, speaking in English rather than Italian.

"I applied for temporary work during my year off before university." Her story had been told a million times over the years, her English accent somehow grown stronger with each passing year in a foreign country. "That was in 1978 and I'm still on a temporary contract!" Her face was wrinkled and lined with laughter over the years.

She had met Signor Silversitrinni in December of that year. The wedding had taken place at the English College in June 1979, followed a year later by his funeral.

"We were left…"

"We?" Humphrey could not help interrupting.

"Yes, my son and me. Simon was six weeks old. He's almost 55 now." Pride was wrung through her voice. "He's a successful stockbroker on the Borsa Italiana. But he's still my little boy!"

Old Ma Silver was in her 75th year but still put in a hard days' work and, many said, held the whole place together. At 34, she had started to streak grey, giving credence to her nickname. Now, for as long as anyone could remember, she presented with a thick abundance of hair: vibrant, healthy but distinctly silver.

Humphrey knocked on the door of the admin office and was told off gently, there being no need to knock, 'just wander right in'. He thanked her and then explained the situation. Old Ma Silver rose to the challenge.

"It can only be one of a handful. You say she was Italian, this girl?"

"Yes, long blonde hair, almost as tall as me. She came to Mass this morning."

"Ah, so she has access to the college? Well, that narrows it down a little. Do you have any classes now?"

"Yes, from nine to ten I'm giving a lecture on 'Morals in the Modern World' and then nothing until after lunch. My full workload has not started yet."

"We always try and phase it in with the new teachers so that they can get to know the other staff and their surroundings. I will make some enquiries if you would like to come back at ten. Are you otherwise settling in alright?"

"Yes, Signora Silversitrinni."

"That is quite a mouthful, just call me Old Ma like the others do." She smiled, broadly and warmly. For a moment Humphrey was back with his mother, sitting at her feet in their tiny front room, listening to her story-telling before she clapped closed the big book and said 'more tomorrow my little one, bedtime now.'

"Thanks…Old Ma." He grinned, as did she. He had been so lucky to be selected for this teaching assignment. Everything felt right. The other teachers were friendly, the students respectful, the accommodation comfortable. And the food was spectacular.

"Enough," Old Ma had said when she had showed him around, "to make quite a roly-poly of your stick-like frame!"

He had prepared for 'Morals in the Modern World', wanting to make an impact from the start, just as in 'Core Theology' that had started so well the previous day.

"Good morning class, my name is Father Humphrey Barrow S.J., which, as most of you know, stands for the Society of Jesus. I am thus a Jesuit priest and have the good fortune of hosting this class with you."

"Good morning, Father Barrow." The chorus floated back to him.

"Tell me, you in the front row, what do you see when you look at the podium."

"I see you, Father."

"No, that is who you see. I asked what you see."

"Oh, well…I see…a theology professor, a priest, a mentor, I mean someone to look up to."

"Wrong answer, young man. You see a sinner." That produced an intake of collective breath. "Let me tell you what you see. You see a vain man who appears good but hides many weaknesses. Yes, Pierre?" Pascal, the man he had bought coffee for the previous day, had his hand in the air. Humphrey briefly wondered who would notice his use of a Christian name, not bad for the first week of the new year.

"Father, I think I know the answer."

"Go on, stand up Pierre so we can all hear you." It would be even better coming from one of the students.

"Father," Pierre stood up in the fifth row of the banked seats so he was taller than Humphrey on his podium in the front, "I see a man, an ordinary man, cursed or blessed, I know not which, with original sin."

It was the perfect answer.

And the perfect opening to his series of lectures on 'Morals in the Modern World'.

The hour wound on in similar vein, free-flowing ideas, bartering concepts as if in the market place. Humphrey's role was to guide in a general direction towards a purpose but certainly not reaching it in the very first lecture of this class; he had the whole academic year to achieve that objective.

He felt good as he packed away his notes while the discussion continued into the hallway and, no doubt, into the students' common room as well. This was what education was all about.

And there had been no invasion of long blonde hair, flaying out as she turned.

Old Ma Silver had the cardinal pinpointed when Humphrey returned just after 10 a.m.

"The one you want is Cardinal Forrundiker. He's the Prefect Emeritus of the Congregation for Catholic Education. I expect he would like to meet you as a promising young educator!"

"You flatter me," he replied but was a little relieved that it was work related and nothing more.

"Be warned, Father, he is an ambitious man. Now, you better take the college car or you'll be late."

"I've not driven in Rome before."

"That's not a problem. I'll drive you and you can drive back."

Sophie LaNeve was in a foul mood. And her boss was the reason why. Once tall, now slanted over, forwards and to the right, her boss walked with a shuffle that seemed endearing.

Only Sophie knew otherwise. She knew exactly what he was like, his ambition, his clinical detachment, his total lack of humanity.

And most of all, his complete lack of interest in Sophie LaNeve.

She slammed the papers onto the table that made do for her desk and kicked the metal filing cabinet shut with her foot, scuffs on the lower drawer indicating the same action repeated many times. It hit the lock mechanism and bounced back open. She kicked it again, sighed and bent to close it properly.

The main offices had mahogany cabinets with matching chairs and desks. Her office had a plyboard table on aluminium legs, an unwanted coat stand and a linoleum floor with a crack running like a ravine diagonally from corner to corner.

She had asked for an office makeover last year.

It had been refused.

She slumped into her chair, wondering again why she endured this job.

But she knew why.

It was for her father.

Her thoughts were interrupted by a knock on the door. Father Barrow's body came into the room, the top half at speed as he stumbled on the lip of the linoleum and crashed into Sophie's table, breaking a section with a snap of plyboard. Papers took off, caught by the breeze from the open window so they soared like birds of prey before floating gently downwards.

"I'm sorry, I'm so sorry," Humphrey blurted from the floor, grasping at papers all around him, but most seemed to avoid his grip, making neat dodges sideways before resuming their gentle progression down. He grabbed some, scrunching them in his fists to secure them.

"Don't damage my papers," Sophie shouted as one caught in the ragged edge of the broken plyboard and tore. "What have you done now? Get up and help me gather them from the floor."

He tried to rise but fell backwards.

"I think I've injured my foot. It's the ankle."

As she helped him to his feet and into her chair, he again smelt her perfume. It took him to the sunny harvests of his deepest memory, hedgerows of middle England, busy insects above still ponds in which he had fished with his friends and talked of girls on his way back from school.

That was before the vocation had hit him like a train at full speed.

But it had a large dose of Italy too; the urban Rome he had known as a student ten years earlier, now returned to as educator. It was simplicity from the past meeting sophistication from the present.

"It's swelling like a melon," she broke into his thoughts. "Or more like an aubergine!" she laughed.

She was right; the bruising was spreading like purple gangrene.

When she helped him hobble out of her office and back down the stairs, he could feel the rhythm of her body, pumping beneath her fair skin.

"You'll need to get someone to drive you back," she said, not offering. "I'll explain to the cardinal that you became indisposed following an accident." There was anger in her voice. He did not understand why but left it too late to question, instead just said.

"It's ok, I have someone here, Signora?"

"Signorina LaNeve." She was not married.

"Signora Silversitrinni drove me here. She is waiting outside, Signorina LaNeve."

She seemed like snow yet was burning hot against Humphrey's skin.

Strategy Meeting

The room above the chip shop had steeply sloping floorboards so it seemed like the eight occupants were likely to slide into the street outside. Grouped around the square table, two to each side, those on the lower elevation had to grip the edge to prevent their chairs slipping backwards.

But it was a base.

All eight were concentrated on the four iPads linking their room above the chip shop to headquarters three thousand miles west and south in the northern regions of the Bible Belt.

Headquarters was a pleasant clapboard building in the Cave Springs area of Roanoke, Virginia, six acres skirted by newly planted maples and spiked-leaf oaks, now surging skywards with the vigour of new growth. The land and the capital to build both the headquarters and the adjoining church had been donated by their first president, Jay Burton Sideley, now resting in the tiny graveyard beside the church.

His premature death after 22 years devotion to the New Moderation Church had left all 1200 members in shock. It had been his church, built on his beliefs. He had been president, pastor and chief fundraiser. He had made the rules and then enforced the rules.

It left a void.

And into that void came Tammy Shroton. Tammy was unremarkable, yet surprisingly remarkable. She had moved to Roanoke four years before the death of Jay; four years working in an insurance claims department. She was young and single, height and weight on the fiftieth centile. She wore her light brown hair up for work but let it spill down her back at night. She was regular in her habits. Every Saturday in season she coached softball to the kindergarten girls. Every Saturday evening, she worked in the mission, helping the homeless, before driving out early on Sunday with friends along the Blue

Ridge Parkway where they would get a late breakfast in one of the lonely eateries north or south of Roanoke.

When she applied for the job of assistant to Jay Sideley, struck with pancreatic cancer and given months to live, she owned up to the fact that she did not go to church.

"My life is my church," she had said.

It was enough for Jay, or perhaps he saw something that nobody else saw. Certainly, what others saw was the stricken right side, almost like she had suffered a stroke. Her right arm needed support to operate fully. She had a metal and leather brace on that arm that looked medieval in its construction. She had a limp on the right side, while the same eye twitched to an irregular beat.

It had been a panel interview but, towards the end, Jay dismissed the others and walked out into the car park with her. It was then he offered her the job.

Her last day at the insurance company was Friday 30 March 2029. It was Good Friday but still a workday. Her first day at New Moderation was Monday 2 April. Her first day at church was Easter Sunday.

She took notes throughout the service, scratching with a broken pencil into a tiny notebook.

Jay Sideley died four weeks later.

His will made Tammy, at 28 years old, life president of the New Moderation Church.

Five years on, most of the original members had fallen away. Many had been older and had died, following their leader to the afterlife. Others had sensed the shift and, feeling slightly uncomfortable, had switched allegiance to other local churches. There was nothing to home in on; certainly no doctrinal disputes, unholy schisms or power struggles. Tammy just took the church in a different direction.

And membership rose enormously. In the summer of 2030, they celebrated 5,000 members. Two years later they reached 100,000 with churches sprouting like fast-food restaurants across America. In 2033, they opened their first overseas church, only it was not so much a church as the room above the chip shop, owned and run by Miles Standish, their first British member.

And, thus, back to the strategy meeting held across the airwaves, headquarters in Roanoke and outpost above the chip shop. Tammy, now thirty-three, still single but radiant in her success such that her disabilities seemed inconsequential to those that met her now, had a particular purpose in including Miles Standish and the team at their first overseas church in this meeting.

In fact, she had two purposes if she was honest about it. The first one kept her awake at night, shivering in the quiet ranch house she owned up on Bent Mountain, a place where America was still America, where people meant what they said and did the right thing regardless. She had first met Miles last April. He had knocked on the office door in Roanoke and asked if there was a hostel nearby.

She had felt the attraction immediately.

He had stayed ten days in her spare bedroom, politely not getting involved but staying long past his schedule and into the time he should be back at the chip shop, long after all possible excuses to stay had run their course.

They had talked late into the night about their lives, their values, almost a two-way verification process before they could get intimate. He was lost, had come to America to find something, almost anything such was the depth of private despair.

He attended their Wednesday evening service, introduced as 'my friend from across the pond'. She sprang something on him then, saying to the 250 people gathered, "Miles, stand up and tell them why you are here".

He had to repeat his talk the following Sunday in front of a much larger congregation.

He did so with a remarkable mix of eloquence, passion and intellect.

By the following Wednesday he was gone, back to England, back to start the first overseas branch of the Church of New Moderation.

The whole congregation missed him but Tammy woke each night thinking of him. She wandered the bare floorboards searching for a breeze in the dead still of night, wondering when she would see him again. When she closed her eyes, she saw his stubby black beard and his jet-black hair, not a strand gone grey after 36 years. And she saw his green-blue eyes and heard his earnest, soft, calm voice as it echoed across the ages, ranging from mountaintop to riverbed, always on the move.

Despite her past, this seemed so right, so natural, so loving.

The second reason was far more complicated, anchored in that past. And it hurt immeasurably to admit it.

So, she pursued it without owning up to it.

"We now have 331,000 members, with an estimated increase well in excess of a thousand a day." Tammy spoke through the iPad to the eight people seated around the table in Miles' flat above his fish and chip shop; her deep southern accent ensuring everyone paid attention. It was dusk in England, early afternoon in Roanoke. The background noises contrasted and, in a strange way, complemented the two settings. The quiet hub of a large office at work both mixed and clashed with the raising and lowering of voices from the chip shop below the British contingent. "I want to discuss a radically different approach tonight, but first I need your absolute commitment to secrecy. You first, Miles."

"I swear not to reveal anything we discuss tonight without your prior approval, Miss President. My allegiance is to the Church of New Moderation and my obedience lies with the church's leadership." It was a good form of words, so the others above the chip shop repeated it, going around the table clockwise.

Then each of the twelve board members in Roanoke, seated in the conference room with her, recited the same words, each speaking to both their colleagues in Roanoke and, through the big screen on the wall, to the British section 3,000 miles away. Tammy fought down her rising pride. The church was not about her. She was simply an instrument of its delivery.

But it was a great feeling nevertheless.

"As I said, we are growing rapidly. But this is not enough for me. I hope it's not enough for you too. Because I believe in this wonderful church, I want to bring it to the attention of the whole world. I see it as our duty to do so." She was not being wholly honest with herself, but the words carried import nevertheless.

And they provoked much discussion, at times two discussions at two ends of the meeting. Some in Roanoke were not sure that growth in membership could be accelerated.

"We can barely keep up with new members as it is." That was true, the membership team was working shifts around the clock; three people processing 1,200 to 1.300 new applications a day.

"Surely it is better to be steady and slow?" But that did not fit with Tammy's ambition.

"No," she replied firmly, "it is our God-given duty to bring the New Moderation movement to as many people as possible across the world."

"But we only have 16 churches outside America."

"Precisely my point, Mr. Farringdon. We need 16,000 churches outside America. Nobody should be denied the chance to become a New Moderator."

Eventually, as the smell of fish and chips made the British contingent anxious to be on their way home, Miles asked Tammy what she had in mind.

"We need to do something to bring the church to the attention of every single one of the eight and a half billion people on earth."

"We have Facebook, Instagram, Twitter and a pretty good website." This was Ernest Justice, probably the most difficult of the Roanokers. He was one of the few early and remaining members. Heavy spectacles, moderate paunches to both face and stomach, not out of line with his sixty something years. He had expected to become president when Sideley died. His wife, Sara, had persuaded him to bide his time. He had remained in nominal support of the new life president, but nominal only.

"Not enough," Tammy replied, seeming a bit weary of the struggle. This rallied Ernest.

"I think we should hold this discussion over until the next general board meeting on, let me see now, December 19." That was three months away. Also, a general board meeting would be just the twelve in Roanoke plus Tammy as president. There would be no British contingent, no other participants. "I suggest a show of hands. All those in favour please raise their hands: good. Now all those not in favour please do so."

Most of the British contingent looked embarrassed and did not raise their hands for the motion or against. This left the vote to the headquarters party and they split down the middle, six to six. Now Tammy would have the casting vote.

And she knew she would have to compromise.

There was a short silence while she pondered her options. Into that silence came a voice singing through the floorboards from the chip shop 'Cor, if I eat another bleedin' chip, they'll have to plant me in the bleedin' vegetable garden!'

The laughter broke the ice, giving Tammy her opportunity.

"We'll compromise", she said as the chortles gradually died, "we'll postpone for now but hold a special meeting in three weeks to decide what to do. So please raise your hands if in favour of postponement to October 1, same participants, same time."

Every hand was raised, including that of Ernest Justice.

It was a tactical victory when faced with defeat.

It left the strategy unchanged but stalled for the time being and Tammy was in a dreadful hurry.

Two separate conversations took place in the minutes following the strategy meeting. The first was between Ernest Justice, Howard Farringdon and two other close followers.

"She's overreaching herself."

"We need to get her to commit further," Ernest replied. "In fact, I believe she is making a trap for herself by pushing this new strategy of hers."

"It's hardly a strategy," said another. "She doesn't know what to do."

"The key thing is she needs to resign," Ernest continued. "We need to get her totally embarrassed so that she feels no option but to resign."

Suddenly it dawned on Howard. He gave a little hop and skip in the car park and said "I have it! Notice how she favours that Brit of hers who stayed with her?"

"Sure, I see where you're going," replied Ernest. "If we expose them as involved in some form of seedy relationship, she won't be able to cling on to the presidency. We need to get him over here pronto so they can get 'involved'! But how do we do that?"

"We eat humble pie," said a new voice, Sandy O'Connor, one of the twelve.

"Sorry?"

"Or rather Ern, you eat humble pie. Go to Tammy and tell her you've come around to her way of thinking. Then suggest she gets Standish over here before the next meeting, as early as possible. When they are together and he's staying with her, they're bound to get down to something improper!"

It was an excellent plan, even more so because of the second conversation taking place at that moment. For shortly after the meeting concluded, iPad lids clicking off for the day, Tammy picked up her phone and called Miles on his mobile.

And he switched to speaker so that he could check flights to Roanoke on his phone while they talked.

Background Checks

"It's as well that the new priest could not make his appointment yesterday," the Cardinal said. "It gives us time to check into his background." He slid a large folder across the table to Monseigneur Bizique while Sophie poured coffee for them both.

"Leave us please, Signorina LaNeve."

"I think perhaps the girl should stay," Bizique said. "She won't be in the way if she stands quietly by the window. And, of course, she heard the lecture directly I believe." The suggested position by the window would give the fat priest an excellent view of her long legs and shapely body.

"Thank you, Monseigneur." Sophie moved to the window and was rewarded with bulging eyes above a salivating mouth, a tiny dribble of spit down the right side, glistening as it slid slowly towards his multi-layered chin. The dribble reminded Sophie of the 104-year-old man she had visited in a care home as a young teenager. Except the centenarian had been stick thin, sitting upright in his chair rather than splayed backwards like a beached whale. The man had died suddenly one night and she had not been able to go to the funeral because it conflicted with her confirmation class.

When the monseigneur died, or the cardinal for that matter, she would definitely go to the funerals. She would want to make sure that they both were gone to the other place.

But she was daydreaming when she should have been listening to their discussion about Father Barrow. For a moment she daydreamed further, wondering why the tall, slim priest had seemed so clumsy and awkward the other day.

Suddenly she realised that they were talking to her.

"Sorry, please repeat the question."

They were asking about the lecture. She repeated what she had heard, then wished she had not, for they sighed and groaned and shook their heads.

"It won't do. We must have strict orthodoxy in the education of our seminarians."

"Your Eminence, I think he was just trying to get their attention. It was like a marketing tool…"

"Well, there is no place for theatricals here. We must stamp it out."

"He has an excellent academic record," she said in his defence, then wondered why she was defending him, one more priest amongst the many. "He has published serious theological works." She had quickly scanned his confidential file the afternoon he had stumbled in her office and twisted his ankle.

"If he is a theologian he should appreciate the importance of orthodoxy. I strongly recommend, Your Eminence, that you bring him in for a severe talking to. There is far too much of this going on these days…" Sophie stopped listening. She suspected her boss was not listening either. It would be several minutes before the cardinal could break into the monologue and steer the conversation towards a conclusion. She wished for a moment that she had lied, reporting back that Father Barrow had followed the prescribed text to the letter and was unlikely to deviate. She wished she had reported that 'Orthodoxy' was Father Barrow's middle name.

"Signorina LaNeve, be so kind as to summon Father Barrow for a meeting with myself and Monseigneur Bizique next week."

"Yes, Your Eminence." She made to leave but was called back.

"Signorina, you forgot his file." He held it with only a half-stretched arm so she had to cross the room, directly past the monseigneur, to retrieve it. "How is your new filing system coming along?"

"Quite well, Your Eminence." This was a lie. Sophie was most certainly not suited to secretarial work. Order meant nothing to her, witnessed by the stacks of paper in her office. She took the file from the cardinal, flinched as the Monseigneur's hand stroked her leg as she passed, then turned abruptly, holding back any retort, and left the room.

Tonight, when she got home, she would beg her father to be allowed to seek another position. Surely he could see that she was unhappy in her employment? She thought she would make a good tour guide, except for her disorganisation; that would let her down.

But then she thought of her father's dedication to the Roman Catholic Church. She knew of the struggle that had framed his early life as a poor bookseller; she had heard it from others over the years. Then they had moved, just before she was born, into the lovely, quaint narrow house she loved so much and the square it sat on. When Sophie had left school, her father had been insistent on her working in the Vatican. She knew there was a connection but had never bothered to work out what it was.

She could not let him down now, not when her employment was giving him so much pleasure. Instead, when she got home that evening, she would report that it had been a fine day, assisting the cardinal in a small way as he toiled at God's will. Her own will was nothing compared to God's will and her father's contentment at the end of his life, when sickness crept up on him, drawing tight the reins of the chariot that would take him on.

Back in her scrappy office, she flicked open Barrow's file and saw again that he had four degrees, culminating in a Doctorate of Philosophy at Cambridge. She would like to study, if only she could. But that would mean breaking with her father, plus several years at night school.

Better to dream.

Dream and read on.

Two hours later, the phone broke the concentrated silence in her office. She had spent those two hours reading Father Barrow's file, a bristling hostility rising like the froth on the lattes she bought each morning on the way to work.

"Cardinal Forrundiker's office, Signorina LaNeve speaking", she spoke into the receiver without thinking. How could Father Barrow have done that?

"It's the cardinal, you dolt. Surely you know the difference between internal calls and external ones?"

"I'm sorry, Your Eminence. I was not thinking." Had Barrow acted in the name of the church or through his own prejudice?

"That's the problem with you, LaNeve." No 'signorina' now as there was no audience. "You do not think."

In fact, she had been thinking, and thinking hard. How could Barrow have stooped so low?

"I'm sorry, Your Eminence. It won't happen again."

"Have you made the appointment for Father Barrow?"

"No, Your Eminence, I placed a call but he has not responded yet." This was a lie. She had made no call, nor yet consulted the cardinal's diary; her right hand held the phone so she used her left for a quick sign of the cross. She had been lost in Father Barrow's personal file.

Not the bit about his education, his postings in his native England, his recent transfer to Rome. Even the sections on childhood and background she skipped through. Normally these would have held her interest. She would have read about the lonely time in the tiny council house on the edge of a north Lancashire mill-village, the mother who clearly loved him, the strong relationship between mother and only child. Her imagination would have filled in the gaps when reading about the father who left after three years of a stormy marriage, gone back to Preston, back to the drug abuse that had seen him homeless, begging and stealing; young Humphrey just another statistic on a government report into one parent families.

Under different circumstances she would have loved to learn of his intelligence and how he was singled out in primary school, of the scholarship he got to Barnhurst, a Catholic boarding school sitting as a dignified pile in a remote Northumbrian valley on the other side of the Pennines from home. She would detour to read his final school report, chuckling over the headmaster's concluding remarks. Young Barrow, just turned seventeen, had, apparently, 'great intellectual abilities but lacks the rounded qualities of a young gentleman. His interest in the church is noted, his vocation appreciated, but the collective opinion of his teachers and pastoral staff is that he needs to be a part of the wider world for a time in order to confirm or otherwise his intentions with regard to the priesthood.'

Usually at this point, she would pause to picture in her mind the fresh-faced youth, pimples still evident, as he tried to make sense of the headmaster's recommendations. Seeking reassurance, he had gone to the parish priest of his home village, sitting in the lee of the Pennines. She would imagine the hills playing strange games with the light, slanting it this way and that, sometimes as dark as evening at midday, other times light well into the night, as if the hills owned the sun and did with it what they will. And she would have wondered what the elderly parish priest, Father Gerald, would have known of the wider world?

But all this did not occupy her, nor Father Gerald's advice of a year at an African mission that confirmed his vocation. Nor the ten years and four degrees on the way to becoming a Jesuit priest. Nor the reputation those four brilliant degrees endowed upon him as an expert in Catholic theology, most specifically with regard to the practice of celibacy in the Catholic Church.

The only thing that caught her attention that afternoon was the first job he had done following his ordination. Father Barrow's personal file contained a typed initial report of his first short assignment when he was sent to America.

When Sophie finished the report, she turned over the page and swore.

There were no more pages. Just the back cover of the folder with a glued note to say all reports and entries from October 2025 were held in the newly-established Online Vocational Personnel System, the OVPS.

She had no access to the online system.

Instead, brought by frustration to reality, she called the English College and was glad to speak to Signora Silversitrinni rather than be put through to Barrow himself.

"Signorina LaNeve, I have his schedule here and can make an appointment for him. Tuesday afternoon is fine, shall we say 3 p.m.? I must say Father Barrow has been a joy to have these last two weeks, such a breath of fresh air!"

Sophie did not respond, other than to confirm the appointment and replace the receiver.

Instead, she removed the report from his personal file, ran it through the antiquated photocopier on the landing outside her office, then returned it to the folder.

She put the copy in her handbag. She would read it again that night.

Would she show it to her father?

Initial Report

Sophie leant back against the cushions, swirled the red wine remaining in her glass and reached into her handbag for the report she had copied.

It was just light enough in her cubbyhole with the reading lamp. There was the bare bulb overhead that lit the whole place with a uniform brilliance, but she had always preferred the angular shadows caused by the small light. It invited the imagination. As a child she had made conversation with the fairies inhabiting the darker regions, but they always fled with the main light switched on.

This had always been her hideaway, her secret place. She thanked God that she had somewhere private, somewhere her own. Warmth and mystery came from the hot water pipes running around the walls, gurgling with purpose like happy spring water as they chugged on.

The report took four pages of standard printer paper. The copier in its antiquity had stained and coloured the print, as if telling the world there was far more to this report than mere words on the page.

She was sure this was the case.

She topped up her glass from one of several bottles behind the little bookcase holding her childhood books. She looked at her soft toys perched on top, glad that she had company. This was her world.

Then she read, glad that it was in Italian. She was proficient in English but much preferred reading her native language.

Confidential Initial Report Concerning Project Containment

Author: Father Humphrey Barrow Society of Jesus

Written onboard a flight to Charlotte, North Carolina, on 22nd September 2025.

1. Remit

On 16 September 2025, I was assigned the task of flying to America to investigate matters at the Convent of the Sisters of the Cross, situated outside a place called Vigilance in Virginia. My particular remit concerned recent allegations of a young nun, Sister Mary John, with regard to the fact that she is apparently with child. It is understood that allegations she has made could, if upheld, be severely damaging to the reputation of the church and, thus, my further task is to limit this damage as fully as can be done. Furthermore, I am to advise on the future of Sister Mary John after discussions with her. I understand that I am authorised to offer up to $100,000 in return for her silence in these matters. At all costs, the lay authorities are not to be involved.

After my briefing in London, I flew by special charter to the Vatican for a further private meeting, then by scheduled airline to Charlotte. It is during this flight that I am writing an initial scoping report.

2. Background (as known at present)

Sister Mary John joined the Order of the Sisters of the Cross immediately after leaving high school in the summer of 2021. In fact, she finished high school on the Friday and was admitted as a postulant on the Saturday afternoon. In following her vocation, she broke with her family, both immediate and wider, who have a long heritage of following the Baptist faith. She was questioned heavily during her final year at Davy Crockett High, the Catholic Church quite rightly wanting to ensure the sincerity of her calling.

She chose the name John because it was the name of her parish priest who had, in rapid order, baptised her, given her First Holy Communion and then prepared her for confirmation.

It should be noted that during this recent period in which certain allegations have been made and are to be investigated by me, Father John Truly has remained a friend and confidante of Sister Mary John. I understand he has written to her and she was allowed to visit him in hospital on one occasion. I fully intend to meet Father Truly and aim to enlist his support with regard to damage limitation. However, Father Truly is 89 years old. His health has deteriorated recently and he is currently hospitalised. I will have to move fast to gain any benefit.

Sister Mary John's family has lived in Jonesboro, Tennessee for several generations. The father inherited a second-hand car sales and service operation just outside town. It was started by his grandfather. The mother is a nurse at a local doctor's office. They have been happily married for 34 years and have four children, of which Sister Mary John is the youngest. She has two brothers, both of whom joined the military. The oldest is still in the Navy. The younger one was in the Army but then went to university and became a lawyer. He practices in Jonesboro. She has an older sister who is a dental nurse. They were all shocked by Sister Mary John's decision to become a nun, mainly as she was turning her back on the Baptist religion. When they heard about her conversion, it provoked a family row of epic proportions. Most of the family would have nothing to do with her. Only her lawyer brother stuck up for her. I understand that she is particularly close to him and my intention is to meet him in order to attempt to prevent any legal action. He would appear to be the most obvious candidate to go to law on her behalf. Hence, he must be tackled early on in the investigation.

Sister Mary John has an extensive wider family in Jonesboro and the surrounding area, including grandparents, aunts, uncles and cousins. By all reports she was a quiet, serious and studious girl without any notable friends but with a large and previously supportive family. I do not believe she has had any visits from her family, other than the one brother, throughout the four years she has been a postulant at the convent. This means she has been very much on her own in making the decision to devote her life to Our Lord.

The Order of the Sisters of the Cross was founded in 1697 in Maryland and is one of the oldest North American orders. Interestingly, it was founded with a particular aim in mind, that being to house the illegitimate children of priests and other clergy, thus giving them a little education and a grounding in religion in a safe but austere orphanage environment. For my first PhD, I wrote a thesis entitled 'The Church's Treatment of their Offspring'. The argument effectively was that our Church actually treated their illegitimate offspring with responsibility and due care rather than disowning them. I suspect it is for this reason that I was selected to undertake this delicate task.

The convent in Vigilance, Virginia was built in 1821 as an offshoot of the original house. A very plain and functional building, it was substantially rebuilt during the 1960s following a fire that gutted the church, the refectory and the dormitory. I understand the rebuild did nothing to add to the beauty of the convent. The original thinking was to handle such matters in as down-to-earth way as possible. Hence there is little decoration or adornment other than their special book (see below).

It is a strict order, following a regime of individual and communal prayer, work in the gardens and fields, and charitable work amongst the local community. It is noted, however, for having a wonderfully adorned book that is ongoing and depicting the life of the community. This book, 'A Life with Christ', is renowned for its beauty and Sister Mary John, as a young postulant, would have contributed by mixing inks and making pencil sketches for the more experienced nuns to copy into the book. The founders of the order believed that every convent should have one – and only one – item of ongoing beauty. In the mother convent they chose a garden. Apparently, it is still of great beauty. In Vigilance, they chose a book.

The Order of the Sisters of the Cross is, as I said, a strict order. The nuns follow a daily routine that does not vary much and spend a lot of each day in silence. Their dress and practices would be considered old-fashioned by many in the 'modern church'. For instance, the nuns wear a partial facemask, with a cross cut into the front of their heavy habit. The horizontal allows for limited vision, while the vertical beam gives the ability to talk and also opens the forehead to exposure. Each morning at matins the foreheads are marked with a cross of ash by the Mother Superior. She in turn is then marked by the youngest postulant in the convent. It is fairly certain, therefore, that Sister Mary John would have marked her Superior's forehead many times after the cross was first traced on her own skin. As the Mother Superior places the cross with her thumb she utters a derivative of the words we all use on Ash Wednesday. Their abbreviated version goes 'Remember child of God that thou art dust'. When the youngest postulant has her turn she says 'Remember Mother that thou art dust'. The book they keep, 'A Life with Christ' indicates that the young orphans did a parallel cross marking ceremony each day with the most senior postulant marking each child.

It seems to me a remarkable and beautiful tradition, reminding each and every member of the convent that they are God's people. I had studied the Sisters of the Cross for my PhD but carried out that study from my desk in Cambridge. I wish now that I had asked to go to America to explore their practices in depth at that time.

But I digress and need to move on.

3. The Key Players

Sister Mary John – background already given
Father John Truly – background already given
Mother Mary Francis – Mother Superior of the Convent of the Sisters of the Cross in Vigilance. Mother Superior is 76 years old and has been in the order for fifty-nine years. She has been Mother Superior for twenty-eight years and to my knowledge there has never been a whiff of potential scandal under her leadership until now.

Sister Mary Paul – an experienced nun who has been a leading light in the convent for almost 20 years. She is Sister Mary John's mentor and provided pastoral care during the four years Sister Mary John has been at the convent.

Father Peter Davies – the priest about whom the allegations have been made.

4. Tactics

My objective is to keep whatever may have happened as confidential as possible, while finding a way forward that will make everyone reasonably content. I will make no judgements until I have met the key people, but it would seem likely that Sister Mary John is pregnant and was, quite possibly, forced into intercourse. I have reviewed her files and there is nothing in her background to suggest any promiscuity or forwardness in any way. I intend to avoid paternity tests as these will prove beyond doubt what is best left as an uncertainty. In all likelihood, Sister Mary John will not stay in the order but, at any rate, the baby should be given up for adoption to a good Catholic family (Note the Order of the Cross stopped running orphanages in the 1940s). At this moment, I do not think it a good idea for Sister Mary John as an ex-nun to look after the baby. There will be too many associations with the recent past and too many reminders of any injustice she feels she has suffered.

The adoption should be arranged immediately and the baby taken straight after birth. I do not see it as my task to choose the family, more to get acceptance from Sister Mary John that this is the best course of action for all involved, including her and the baby. I believe Mother Superior should be aware of a good Catholic family who will take the baby as their own. The available money will be offered to Sister Mary John sparingly in order to help her start a new job as an office girl or some similar occupation.

To achieve this, I will have to listen carefully but be forceful in my personality. The key thing is to sweep Sister Mary John and any other key people who could be difficult along with me from the start.

5. Conclusion

I thank Your Grace for this practical opportunity to further the interests of the Church, protecting its reputation while repositioning the people involved, thus ensuring their long-term happiness in, and continued devotion to, Our Lord.

I will write follow up reports as I make progress. The next one will, in all likelihood, be when I have done initial interviews with the key players.

This was the end of the typed report. Sophie saw handwriting on the last page, now smudged. Clearly the report was a draft only, a work in progress, later amended with handwritten notes. She turned her attention to the last page and sighed again. The writing was in English this time, rather than her native Italian, and was hastily written with a fountain pen, smudged all those years ago. It was going to be a strain. She reached up, taking the weight of her body on her calves, and turned on the main light.

Immediately her cubbyhole was turned from mysterious hideaway to spacious under stairs cupboard. She could see the wine stains on the floorboards, bathed in light, like darkened lakes in bright sunshine. The pipes, source of heat and comfort, took on a brown utilitarian look that was reality, giving only a dull shine in response to the bright light from above.

But with this light she could make some sense of the scrawl.

I have now met Sister Mary John and have no illusions as to the truth of her words, nor the honesty of her character. Moreover, she is angry – this last word was underlined and in much heavier print, gone over and over with the pen, as if the author had dwelled on the word, pondering what to write next   *- but she does not display her anger in any obvious way. It is near impossible to read her mind when she can only reveal a tiny part of her face. True, the habit front is cut in the shape of a cross to reveal the eyes, mouth and forehead, but the habit projects forward from her face and puts all exposed facial features in deep shadow. In two hours of questioning, I do not think I saw anything of her face, just the faintest movement of cloth as she talked. Moreover, she spoke as she was trained to speak – that is very quietly and minimally as well, only replying to my questions and never volunteering anything.*

I expect you wonder how I could deduce that she was angry with the low level of communication from her. She asked me to hear her confession. I said I would but only if she gave me permission to include in my report any sins revealed, as I am principally an investigator and would be her confessor in a secondary capacity. I did not think she would agree if she had something to hide.

She agreed straightaway, clearly anxious to confess, but then asked that I agree to reveal only those sins that pertain to the case I was investigating. I was astonished and deeply impressed that this meek child of God could have the foresight to consider this at a time of great anxiety.

The truth was she only confessed three sins. The first was a love of her body. In her own words she said 'Father, I take inordinate pride in my body which I know to be beautiful'. This further convinced me of her innocence because who but an innocent would raise this with an investigating officer? The second was the anger. She said this was terrible and was eating away at her. We spoke about this anger and Sister Mary John said she was deeply upset because a man of God had defiled the body she was trying to give to God. She asked me how to cope with this anger and all I could say was 'pray sister, pray for deliverance, for forgiveness and for God's grace'. I like to think it helped her a little.

The third sin is, well actually it falls outside the remit of this investigation so I cannot mention it.

There is another reason I thought Sister Mary John angry when I first met her. However, I was mistaken in that anger was not the cause of the infliction she has down her right-hand side. Later, I asked Sister Mary Paul about it and was told that she developed this disability over the last four years in the convent; Sister Mary Paul thought it was an acute form of anxiety. A year ago, Sister Mary John was fitted with a brace on her right arm, hidden, of course, beneath her robes; without this brace she was unable to move the arm. I immediately thought that for one to be so nervous suggests that maybe the closed religious life was not suitable, hence it would be easier to suggest she departs the order. This sounds mercenary in the extreme but I feel the need to be honest about my thoughts and actions, bearing in mind our objective in Project Containment.

My first impression is that, despite her obvious innocence, and the abuse she has suffered, this must be kept quiet at all costs. Sister Mary John must be pressed/ encouraged/ dare I say bribed into silence. The damage this could generate to the Church, coming on top of the Cassidy case last year, is incredible and does not bear thinking about. The only other option is to sully her character and – again first impressions – I do not think this would work. It would also be clearly wrong.

Underneath were a few more scribbled words, scored through countless times. She thought she read the words *'Davies'* and *'bastard'* but the last word could be bastion or breaking or any number of variants.

She read it through twice more, then switched the overhead light off and went back to how she preferred it.

She was in shock. She had been interested in Father Barrow, had tried to defend him in front of the cardinal and monseigneur yet Father Barrow had done this to a poor young nun. He had ascertained her innocence and yet had immediately decided to cover it up.

One thing she was sure about. She could not tell her father this terrible story. He could not bear criticism of his beloved church.

But, somehow, she would make Father Humphrey Barrow SJ pay for the damage he had done. He would not find her meek and mild, like a lamb to the slaughter. She would fight for the poor nun who had only tried to follow Christ.

It was clearly her duty to do this.

In Transit, Mind and Body

Miles saw his name on the poster and stopped to read it, stepping backwards on the moving walkway.

Last year we flew over a billion passenger miles more than the year before. We are growing because we put our customers first.

He often saw his name in print, was often disappointed but always stopped for a second look. He did not fully read the small print at the bottom of the poster, something about periods of measurement and average miles flown. His left eye had caught a large family, many young ones, two crying, several others running up and down the walkway. They were coming up on him rapidly. He needed to get to the gate and select a seat in a quiet corner before they took over.

Then he relaxed, for he remembered he was flying first class. He was not going to the plastic orange chairs, coupled together, seat pads of cheap foam in a darker colour, the whole an uncomfortable eyesore they called airport-style.

Instead he was going to the first-class lounge. He had once been upgraded to business class but never dreamed of flying first class.

"Welcome, sir," the lady at the desk checked his ticket, "please take a seat and a waiter will be right with you. The bathrooms, including showers are behind this screen. Would you like to read a newspaper?"

Miles had showered four hours earlier but could not resist the lure of luxury.

"I'll take a shower, if I may."

"Of course, sir, I'll arrange it right away. Frank, please show Mr. Standish to the bathrooms and get him everything he needs."

An hour later he sipped a malt, relaxed, at ease. Following the shower, he had been offered a massage with body oils. There was still 30 minutes to boarding. That meant time to try a different Scotch after this one.

Tammy had been insistent about Miles flying first class.

"I'm paying, well, the church is, and I want you to be in maximum comfort so you can use the time to think on our strategy. Have a few drinks and let the imagination flow!" She had laughed this last bit.

But it had made Miles think. For the leader of a new church in the modern world, it was surprising that Tammy drank, not excessively, but she appreciated good wine and beer too. It seemed like a release to her, a liquid version of letting your hair down and tucking your legs in so you sat on them. He had commented on it once, but her reply had been vague, ruling out further discussion.

Quite a lot about Tammy was lost in vagueness. Perhaps he would get to know her better this time.

Tammy's strategy worked, as Miles felt he had to earn his first-class passage. He pondered subsidiary matters while in the lounge: why he was being summoned and Tammy's leadership style. But once on board, a glass of champagne on the little table in front of him, his mind turned to the main task.

How was the New Moderation Church, membership 300,000 and rising, to make an enormous splash? What could he add to make it happen? He asked the stewardess for paper and pen. He would list the possibilities.

But first, lunch got in the way. It was ready to be served.

"What would you like, Mr. Standish?"

"Anything but fish and chips!" Then, in response to the query this produced on the air steward's face, he explained. "I own a fish and chip shop."

"Ah, I see, sir. Well, as it happens we don't have fish and chips on the menu today." The steward was thinking, if he's travelling first class, his fish and chip operation must be a whole chain.

Miles chose steak with rice and vegetables, with liver pâté to start: no fish and no potatoes. It was laid out on the table in front of him with a flourish, as he imagined it would be in a top restaurant.

"Thank you, yes the Merlot will be very nice, thank you."

With a fine meal inside him, three quarters of a bottle of Merlot and a third whisky, his notepaper lay untouched for the next few hours. Instead, he watched a film about Wall Street and a young executive who falls for the receptionist who has a secret life as a dancer. There was a neat twist when he ruthlessly takes over the firm that owns her dance school, closes the school because it is 'non-core' and occupying real estate ripe for development. Then he spies her in amongst the protesters and a furious row is followed by cold silence on the love front. Needless to say, they come to understand each other better through their trials, and the school reopens in a new building, better and bigger than before, with his receptionist girlfriend as co-owner.

Both money and love triumphed. It was a depiction of modern fantasy-capitalism in a formulaic movie, helped along by attractive and highly-paid protagonists, and a writer who had a knack for turning the ordinary into something pleasing. For a moment, Miles identified with the Wall Streeter, especially when he explained to his girlfriend that what he was doing did not so much enrich himself but the whole community and nation. But as the closing credits flew by, accompanied by a song he should be able to name but could not, reality hit again.

He owned a heavily mortgaged fish and chip shop and was far from magnate material. So why had Tammy made him head of the first overseas branch of her church? What had she seen in him when the church was in such expansion mode?

More to the point, what did she expect of him?

The Boeing aircraft started its slow descent into Charlotte. He went to the bathroom, tidied up his spacious seat and then spotted the blank paper he had asked for at the beginning of the flight.

"Do you want me to take that for you, Mr Standish?"

"No thanks, actually I still need it."

"Right you are, Sir." The neat stewardess moved up the aisle, chatting casually but respectfully with the few passengers in first class. Miles watched her for a moment, wishing he had that easy-going capability that some seemed to have in abundance. Then he forced himself to concentrate on the blank piece of paper.

But nothing came, no ideas, no concepts, no possibilities.

An hour later, through immigration, bag collected and re-deposited the other side of customs, sitting in the Captain's First-Class Lounge, waiting for a flight to Roanoke, still nothing by way of ideas.

He had been sure something would come to him during the flight. Instead he had drunk slightly too much and wasted time on a mediocre movie.

"Penny for your thoughts, young man."

"What, oh sorry, I mean…"

"You were miles away!" The speaker was old, white hair around wrinkled skin, impeccably dressed but in a distinctive way. His brightly checked jacket with white sailor's sweater underneath, his tan leather lace-ups, hint of the moccasin, and his designer jeans, all spoke of studied individuality; pieces of personality picked out from a selection box.

"Do you mind if I sit here?"

"By all means." Miles was polite, then wondered why with so many spare seats this old man wanted to sit with him.

"The name is Chesington Bloakes III." Miles thought the name too like the name of a character in a rushed novel to be true.

"Miles," he said in return, "Miles Standish." Miles offered a hand.

"I know who you are, Miles. You see I came here to meet you."

"Meet me?" Miles felt like prodding the old man to see if he was real.

"Yes, Sir." But there was no explanation at that moment. Instead he ordered a large bourbon with 'one for my friend here, no, I won't hear rejection'.

They sipped from their glasses, darting their eyes over the rims of their whiskies. Every time their eyes met, Chesington wrinkled up in good humour, while Miles looked awkward, looked away, focusing instead on the mid-distance where the flight announcement board watched over them with an occasional flicker like the odds moving at the races.

Finally, drinks half gone, waiter hovering to offer refills, Chesington pulled out a dollar bill and slapped it on the table. The waiter made a beeline for the cash, then sensed it was not for him and swerved off, quickly adjusting the neat stack of untouched magazines on the table.

"There!" said Chesington, chuckling at the waiter's pretence.

"What is that for?"

"A hundred pennies for all your thoughts!"

Miles met his eyes, this time more boldly, English reserve shaken off. They smiled together, then laughed, relaxed, a metaphorical kicking off of shoes.

"I was thinking of who I'm going to visit" he replied, suddenly wanting to talk.

"Tammy Shroton," Chesington replied.

"You know her?" Miles' voice raised several whole tones, body jerked like the great big strings of a double bass.

"Sure, she's my boss."

Tammy had been looking for someone to go to Charlotte, meet with Miles, brief him on what to expect. Chesington had volunteered.

"We, that is Mrs Bloakes and I, are committed a hundred ten per cent to the Church. I'm Director of Catechism, sounds fancy but it's just a full-time position dealing with the theology behind the New Moderation. My wife, Melissa, is Youth Director. She runs all the programmes to do with our youngsters."

Suddenly the names meant something. Both had appeared on official paperwork from the church over the last 18 months since he had started the British branch. Both had been just that – names on paper advising of this and that, printed at the bottom of the page as if an afterthought.

"But Mr. Bloakes…"

"Call me Ches, all my friends do."

"Well…Ches, but why the need to meet me here? Surely there's no…"

"There's a lot to brief you on, Miles." Ches leaned over to talk more confidentially, their bourbons almost breaching the gap between them.

Chesington Bloakes III knew and liked his bourbon. He started Miles on Four Roses Yellow Label.

"A standard in the trade. It's smooth, tasty and with a great aroma. Do you get the hit of spice at the end?"

Then they tried an old staple, Jim Beam, but instead of White Label they went straight to Black.

Fighting Cock they had with soda water, "a good strong one, best mixed but too sweet for anything like coke".

Finally, as the flight for Roanoke was announced, Ches chose old Grand Dad Bonded, a real treat, strong with a sharpness from the rye mixed in. It was as they sipped the Grand Dad Bonded that Ches told Miles of the drinks distribution business his grandfather had started during prohibition.

"It was pure gangster stuff to start with. Grandpapa was adept at staying one step ahead of the police." The word 'police' was elongated with the stress in the wrong place, making them seem a formidable force, whether for good or bad Miles did not know. "We beat off the competition and supplied hundreds of speakeasies from top joints to common bars. The stories from those days! One day when we have time I'll tell you a few of them. Then with the repeal of prohibition we went legit. Soon Bloakes covered twenty states across the south. We employed over two thousand people with retail stores as well." Miles thought of his fish and chip shop; including him it numbered six full time equivalents.

"Did you sell the business?" Miles had picked up the use of the past tense.

"Sort of. Well, we went public in my daddy's time. We sold 49% of the shares. I inherited 34% and 17% went to my cousin. He sold most of his holding in dribs and drabs to fund his wasteful lifestyle. He ended up with no shares and bankrupt – such a waste. The consequence of that was suddenly we found we did not control a majority of the shares. Then we got approached by the International Drinks Group. They wanted to buy us out. I wasn't interested. That year we made over $20million profit and I wanted to continue."

"But presumably you changed your mind?"

"Far from it, Miles. The takeover bid turned hostile and it was a brutal time. I was bought out whether I liked it or not."

"I'm sorry to hear that."

"Don't be," Ches said with a big grin. "I got $80million dollars for my shares and I've never looked back! Best thing that ever happened to me!"

They were interrupted by the last call for their flight.

"We'll see what bourbon they have on the plane," Ches said, standing to reveal six foot three of muscle and fat in equal proportion.

But Miles drank nothing onboard. Instead he slept from take-off to the jerky landing, the small propeller plane struck sideways by a rising wind.

"This will be the last flight in to Roanoke with the weather like it is. We better get a scoot on if we're going to get you to Tammy's tonight. She's up on the mountain as you know."

Miles fought with sleep, more drunk than he had been since university. Trying to cope with Ches' joviality was one thing, but he had another problem to contend with.

He had just had the most brilliant idea. It came to him as a half-thought, like the best sublime advertising, registering somewhere in his drink-messed mind. He had, somehow, to keep up with banter from Ches while struggling to hold the thought. With mental fingernails, he dragged his idea, slowly and painfully, across Bourbon Mountain to brain central.

Only then was it secure. Only then could he let it explode into every avenue, lane and expressway of his mind, multiplying, dividing like cancer cells, growing in dreadful strength with every second.

He could not wait to see Tammy again.

Office Manoeuvres

Sophie's friend clicked on her mouse rapidly, far too fast for Sophie to register the screens her old work computer was running through.

"What are you doing? I've never got it to go that fast!" she asked.

"Sshh," was the only answer Sophie received. It was not the first time she had asked.

The door opened. It was the cardinal. He was not supposed to be there today. They had planned their enterprise for a day he was scheduled in offsite meetings.

"I want…who is this LaNeve?"

"Computer Department," Sophie lied, blushing, looking down, thinking of the confessional.

"Why has she no badge for security?" The cardinal's eyes were keen, his attention to detail astounding for a very old man.

"Waiting on security, they take forever these days," her friend added to the charge sheet. "You are not Cardinal Forrundiker, are you?" Sophie's friend stood up and politely offered her hand. "I've wanted to meet you for the longest time. I admire your work so much. For instance, the discipline you bring to the church and to its education department. I've always wanted to ask you what you think about…"

"I would be delighted to answer your questions, my dear, come with me. As it happens I have some free time as the meeting I have been attending is adjourned until later today. You have the advantage of me, of course, as I do not know your name."

"Eliza Brizotto," she replied, giving the name of an Italian film star. She was sure a cardinal would not recognise the name.

"As in the actress? What a coincidence that you share her name. I was with her recently, let me see when it was." He closed the door on Sophie's office, having guided Eliza out. Then it opened halfway, just a voice floating through. "Bring some coffee into my office." His briskness was stark against the accommodating tones towards Sophie's friend.

"Yes, Your Eminence," but said to the back of the tatty door.

To get her friend back, Sophie had to remind the cardinal of his meeting reconvening. She went forty minutes on her own, then could wait no longer.

But Eliza, real name Mia, had virtually finished her illicit work that day.

"I've got you access," she said, grimacing and chuckling alternatively after her forty-minute slot with 'that old man', "but you might be disappointed. You see they changed the computer system about six years ago and were charged with progressively moving all the files onto the new system. It was one of the projects I worked on when at The Computer Firm." That had been Mia's job before she had set up on her own.

"So I have access but there is nothing there?"

"I didn't say nothing! The Computer Firm was contracted to do it all but then the dispute started and they got fired. It was something to do with a high-level breach of security. Suddenly, we were not allowed any access and we went out of business shortly afterwards. That's when I started up on my own. It seems like the job was never finished, judging by the size of these folders."

"So, what is there?"

"Well, let's take a peek and find out!" Mia turned quickly from computer to Sophie and back to the computer again. Her hair flared out as she moved, catching itself as she changed direction. It was similar to Sophie's, only jet-black to Sophie's white-blonde. They were both tall, but Mia was older at close to thirty and had gathered about her an air of sophistication. She dressed, spoke and acted like she belonged. She had large, endearing brown eyes, set against a lightly tanned face. She wore expensive clothes, makeup and perfume, thus announcing herself as someone to be considered. She seemed to Sophie like a female spy in a Bond film; sophisticated, sexy, highly talented, full of life.

By contrast, Sophie, although prettier and more classical in her beauty, seemed like the younger sister still in school; clumsier, less together, more open.

It had been Mia's idea to hack the work computer. Sophie had told her of the handwritten report and that all others had been filed electronically and she lacked access to them.

It had been Mia's idea, but Sophie had been hoping she would come up with it.

"You want to find out more about this Jesuit?" Mia had asked her.

Sophie had confirmed with a nod but did not know why. Thankfully Mia had not asked.

"I can get into the system. Just get me into your office for a couple of hours."

So Sophie had. And now she waited as Mia flipped through the names in alphabetical order. Only Mia did not do anything slowly so the screen was a blur.

"What name did you say?"

"Barrow, Humphrey Barrow, you've gone too far, look see Dunrovo! You're in the Ds."

"Here it is, two records. Let's open the first. A report dated 22 September 2025, written onboard an aeroplane. It starts 'Remit', then 'Background'."

"That's the one I've already got!" She was disappointed, not thinking of the handwritten postscript to the hard copy. Instead she turned away from the computer, suddenly realising that today was also 22 September. It was nine years to the day that Father Barrow had written the first report of his assignment, the dreadful task of forever silencing the complaint of a young nun abused in her place of prayer. The sun outside, now fairly low in the sky, as befits an early evening in September, seemed to be playing a game with her, bouncing its rays in rapid splurges of energetic light to wash out the shade. But then it retreated, allowing the darker shades back in. The contrast between light and shade on the move was like two football teams, trying to catch and retain the ball. But, ultimately, no team cared enough to make progress.

"This is obviously the follow-on report," Mia said, wondering why the window so distracted her friend.

"The second report!" Sophie had forgotten about the second report. She turned from window to screen, one oblong to another, her eyes full of expectation.

She skimmed it and asked Mia to print out both reports. Then Mia logged out and closed down the computer. They left a few minutes later, light cotton scarves fluttering over their shoulders like the banners of a small army.

It was payment time. They went to a bar they liked. Sophie ordered muscles with tagliatelle while Mia had sea bass braised in lemon and herbs. Afterwards the dancing would start.

They both loved dancing.

Much later that evening, Sophie settled in her cubbyhole. Flushed with martinis, she declined the red wine she offered herself, put on the reading lamp and opened the second report.

Written by Humphrey Barrow SJ in the Guest Suite of the Convent of the Sisters of the Cross, Vigilance, Virginia on the evening of 25 September 2025.

The last three days have been nonstop interviewing and exhausting work. I am drained by the experience, not least because I am making slow progress.

I determined that the best way to proceed was to elicit the absolute truth from all involved. Then I would be in the best position to decide how to achieve the objectives set by my superiors, namely to limit the damage done in a highly sensitive situation, to ensure maximum secrecy and then to decide a suitable future for Sister Mary John.

Sophie bristled in anger at the audacity of a newly-ordained priest thinking he could decide the fate of a young American nun, a girl who had clearly been sinned against. She accepted that glass of wine she had earlier refused, adjusted the cushion at her back and read on.

In this regard, my early efforts have met with intense frustration. I have interviewed four people at length and met with four wildly different accounts as to recent events.

In my enthusiasm, I decided first to speak with Father Peter Davies. I thought priest-to-priest, man-to-man, was the best way to start. He is, of course, as a priest, the most senior of those involved. Afterwards I would tackle the women, who I imagined might be more prone to emotion and hysteria.

I made a mistake, for all seem turned resolutely against me while Father Davies gave me little more than repeated denials plus the statement that Sister Mary John had always been a troublemaker.

Father Peter Davies is not a pleasant man, dare I speak ill of a man of the cloth. He is 54 years old and has a grubby appearance. He wears a full cassock, which is unusual these days. I suspect it is to hide the fact that he is considerably overweight. My impression was of someone who has indulged not excessively but consistently over the decades. Moreover, he seems to expect such indulgence as his right. He was eating chocolates as we spoke 'given to me by a devout parishioner'. I also disliked the way he looked down his nose at me, as if I had no right to question him.

A summary of his story is that he knows nothing of the alleged events. He expressed considerable surprise, something I am inclined to take with a pinch of salt. After I explained the accusations to him (although of course he had to be fully aware of them), he claimed the very opposite, namely that Sister Mary John made inappropriate advances on him after Mass one morning. He rejected the advances and says she then took spite and made up a claptrap of lies about being attacked and raped by the priest. In my opinion, he was feigning indignation and is not a good liar.

However, unless I can penetrate further into this situation through subsequent interviews, my instinct is to accept the Father Davies version of events. He is, after all, a priest.

Sophie gasped, poured more wine, read on. She was two pages into four; there was a lot more to come. She turned to the next page, gave a cry of exasperation as she found the page blank, or rather consisting of two faint lines down the edge; this was the standard notification that her printer ink was low and the cartridge needed replacing. She would have to get a chit from the cardinal and take it to central stationery, explaining to the tight-fisted stationer why she had not yet converted her office into a paperless one.

But then her father called her, his thin voice bouncing down the stairs like a Slinky. She put the report away, sliding the four pages between 'In Imitation of Christ' and a translation of 'The House at Pooh Corner' that her godfather had given her when she was six. Then she glugged down her wine, opened the door and turned off the light.

She would read the rest tomorrow evening after work if she could get some printer ink in the morning.

Meeting of Minds

Humphrey Barrow stood awkwardly in Cardinal Forrundiker's office, facing the cardinal, wondering what on earth was behind the blasting he was receiving. Outside rain and wind beat against the building, applauding the cardinal in his outrage. Were even the elements against him now?

In an easy chair in front of the desk sat a fat monseigneur, beaming with pleasure. They had been introduced, but the name had not registered with Humphrey. His mind focused on Sophie in the untidy sprawling office with just table, chair and hat stand plus half a dozen metal cabinets with tabs on the drawers that had been scored through, written over time and time again.

Why had Sophie LaNeve been like ice towards him? Was it merely because of the damage when he had fallen in her office the previous week? He had broken one leg of her table-desk, now propped up on a pile of old folders. But it had to be something else. That alone did not warrant such extreme frostiness.

Perhaps it was something to do with what the cardinal was saying, but he had not been listening, rather dwelling on Sophie.

"And another thing…," the cardinal certainly knew how to make a point. Humphrey tried to concentrate on what he was saying, thought he should understand in order to be able to rebut. But each time he failed, came back to Sophie's strange anger.

"I really expect better of you in future. Now, be off with you. I expect you have a lot of lessons to rewrite. Remember, think orthodoxy." So that was what it was about. He was being hauled over the coals because he had dared to tear up the lesson plans and think what might fire his students' imagination, get debate going, some real learning. Sophie must have reported him. But even this did not ring true as an explanation for her sudden cold attitude.

Was that a wink from the cardinal as he delivered the dismissal? Perhaps it was just a twitch. But there it was again.

Was this a blasting or not? If only he had been attending to the detail, he would have some idea. Instead his mind could not move off Sophie's anger.

"Oh, Father Barrow, one more thing." Large shaggy white eyebrows looked up at Humphrey; those eyebrows overhung his crinkly face, dominating the deep hollows in each cheek like frozen whirlpools. "Go first to LaNeve's office and tell her to get in here."

No first name, no 'signorina', just 'LaNeve' and said with disdain, or was it something else? The emotion was recognised but Humphrey could not name it; that part of his brain drunk with injustice, splaying thoughts like badly managed fireworks.

He was being played in some way and he did not know why or how.

"Yes, Your Eminence."

Then either Heaven or some little-used part of his mind kicked in with damage control.

"Your Eminence, I just want to say how sorry I am to cause you so much anxiety through my thoughtless actions." Was he really saying these words? Was he towing the line like a soldier told to turn about? What of the grand ideas he had laid out as this hoped-for appointment had become reality?

"You are forgiven, Barrow, provided there is no repetition." The cardinal waved him away, but again the slightest of winks. It reminded Humphrey of one of his old school monitors. The boy had wanted to play both sides at the same time – in truth he was, representing authority, yet still a schoolboy.

Was the cardinal playing both sides now? Telling him off for the sake of authority, but winking his approval at the same time?

Clearly the cardinal was ambitious, manipulative too. But did he have some role in mind for Humphrey? Or was this how he was, preparing for all possibilities, setting up placemen wherever he went?

Which led Humphrey to ask himself, where was the cardinal going?

And why was Signorina Sophie LaNeve so angry with him?

Ten minutes later he was no wiser on either count.

Once out of the cardinal's office, he had gone directly to Sophie's room, taking care not to trip on entering.

"Made it!" he joked.

"Made what?" There was no reciprocal humour in her words, rather the deadpan of disinterest.

Or distaste.

"Into your office without slipping, Signorina LaNeve."

"Oh, I see, well, what do you want?" Sophie's voice was infuriatingly flat, as if Humphrey was of no consequence whatsoever.

"The Cardinal wants to see you in his office. He asked me to tell you." He wondered how much of the blasting she had heard. For just a moment, he imagined her, ear to the cardinal's door, relishing the ticking off he had received. But no, that was not her style. She would not have listened at the door. Instead she had probably used these quiet moments to get on with filing or copying or whatever else she did from nine to six.

Sophie had indeed listened, then scuttled back to her chair when Barrow was dismissed. She looked at her desktop, shuffled some papers that did not belong together, aware of his thoughts and concerned he may detect her guilt. But all Humphrey saw was someone angry with him, very angry and he did not know why.

"I'll be off then." He could not ask why.

"Okay."

They parted in silence; a silence that said everything but gave nothing away, nothing for Humphrey to grasp on to.

Just like the scowling, winking cardinal.

"Ah LaNeve, any messages?"

"Just one, Your Eminence. The Archbishop of New York called and wanted you to call him back." Sophie, lost in her private rage, would not have remembered had the cardinal not asked for his messages. "I have his number here. He said it was urgent."

"Close the door then, LaNeve."

"Yes, Your Eminence."

Twenty minutes later, as Sophie was thinking of what she would say to Father Barrow once she had summoned up the courage, her boss burst into her office, flustered red, trembling. Sophie had never seen him like this before.

On instinct she opened the drawer to a filing cabinet, selected the cleanest looking glasses and poured two Scotches. He did not refuse and sank into the only chair, spinning it around to face away from Sophie. But she could see over the top of him, like a nanny supervising a toddler's suppertime.

His face was as white as his hair.

"What is it?" but no answer. "Have a sip, Your Eminence." Like a nurse dispensing medicine, she stood over the old cardinal and guided the glass to his lips. And like a wounded soldier, barely conscious, the first drops dribbled down his chin.

He did not speak.

All he did was touch her hand, the hand that would like to slap him. Then slowly he looked into her eyes. Two pairs of eyes met that were unrelentingly hard towards each other: the uncaring boss and the hating-to-be-there secretary.

Only something had changed. Was it the pale face, like the blondest of bare pine in a cheap furniture store? Or was it the slumped shoulders, or the perspiration making his old skin shiny?

Whatever the past, whatever the reason, she felt sudden tenderness for this very old man. Her eyes softened. She crouched down and took his hand in one of hers, then lifted his caved-in chin because his head had slumped again.

"Tell me what happened so I can help." He did not look like an eminence now. She thought of the old man she had assisted when a teenager, but he had never looked like this, never so dejected. Here was pride smashed, replaced with fear. Or maybe terror.

Or knowledge.

Through persistence and refills of Scotch, she gradually got the story. At first his mutterings made little sense, but after a while she could piece parts together. It was like the jigsaw puzzle she had as a child, still had for it was on the bottom shelf of the bookcase in her cubbyhole. It was a scene of a 19th Century picnic on a hill overlooking an unknown city. There was pink everywhere; pink in the flowers and the blossom overhead, pink in the girls' dresses and pink tinged clouds in the sky, hinting at sunset on its way. She had found it infuriating. Half the pieces had pink splashed across them, making it impossible to put the whole puzzle together. She had only done it once on her own. When she was twelve, she had become determined to do it and had sat up after bedtime weeks in a row until finally it was complete.

The following day she had sorted out her clothes, removing any that contained pink and put them in a charity pile for the housekeeper to take with her. She had told her father that they were too small. Then she had gone to confession.

Now she was piecing together a different picture and there was nothing pretty about it.

"It was the archbishop," he had started, repeating this introductory phrase several times over. "New York's in turmoil. It will be on the news."

"What caused the turmoil, Your Eminence?" She used an old duster to wipe a mixture of sweat and whisky from his chin, noticing that the few teeth he had were like individual worn-down monoliths in a pink-tinged cave. There was the pink again.

Then, as she raised his head with her fingers, she noticed for the first time his eyes, uncluttered by the glasses dangling from his left hand. They were warm and brown, an attractive shape, a little familiar. They were not the eyes of a hard man.

So why was he always hard with her?

More to the point, why did he want her to work for him, yet treat her so harshly?

All these thoughts came to her in a flash of time, surpassed instantly by concern for this very old, suddenly fragile-seeming, man.

"Please tell me what is troubling you. I may be able to help." She tried again, some instinct deep inside her wanting to assist.

The replies were single words, separated by blocks of silent sobs, very old body shaking as if in birth pain.

Sophie pieced the words together, like her childhood jigsaw puzzle. The trouble was in America; that much she could tell. She heard 'aggressive takeover' and wondered if it was something to do with the church's investments.

But that made no sense. Cardinal Forrundiker had no involvement in money matters. He had made a point of telling her when she had started working for him three years previously. "I am responsible for spending money, not watching over it!" It was the nearest he had come to a joke with her during her employment.

"I still don't understand," she said, stroking his cheek gently to calm him further. She had come closer to him in thirty minutes than the whole of the last thirty-six months since her father had brought her in for her first interview after school one evening.

"Our church is threatened. The rock of St. Peter is shaken to its base." This was more valuable information, but begged the question why?

"Takeover of the church. Have you ever heard such a thing? The upstarts…" Some of his usual caustic self was returning, probably the way she stood behind him and massaged his sunken shoulders; up, down, around, up, down, around.

Thus, she learned the whole story, although it took until the sun went on across Iberia and into the Atlantic, chasing itself around the globe. She learned of the Church of New Moderation, whatever that name meant. And she learned of the idea that had come to Miles Standish in the little propeller plane on the way from Atlanta to Roanoke where Tammy awaited him.

"My God!" she said when it all came out. "The whole Catholic Church?"

"The whole Roman Catholic Church. But that is not the way it works with us." Whether it was massage therapy, the Scotch, or both, some of Cardinal Forrundiker's vigour was returning. "We are not some seedy democracy. We don't bow and scrape to the popular vote. No Siree!" He ended with a mock American accent, giving strong emphasis to his words. The irony of ridiculing democracy in an American accent escaped them both.

There was fight left in the old cardinal. That was a certainty.

And where there is life, there is opportunity.

But there was also something else, now that Sophie had stood by him in his half-hour of need.

It was something she had never thought to see.

It was a connection with her, just the briefest acknowledgement with his brown eyes to hers, no speech, no words, just a look.

As the cardinal had predicted, it was all over every news channel that evening. The New Moderation Church had launched a hostile takeover bid for the Roman Catholic Church. The newspapers were full of it, crowding out the troubles in the Far East for a change, bringing Rome and Europe back to centre stage after a long absence.

"Your Eminence, how do they plan to bring it about?" A senior priest with shaggy black hair sitting on his sombre face like a hat at the races asked the question on everyone's mind. Sophie had developed a crush on Father Ellsworthy when she had first come to work for the cardinal. She had confessed, received an extraordinarily light penance, and afterwards realised that it was Ellsworthy himself in the confessional. But that had been before the arrival of…well, she had certainly changed her mind about that arrival.

But there was no time for idle thoughts. The cardinal had called a department-wide meeting, a 'council of war' as he had described it. Sophie was delighted to be included, saw it as a sign of changing times.

"That is the interesting thing," the cardinal replied, 'first they want to convert us into a democracy and then…"

"One person, one vote!" Sophie cried so that all eyes turned to her.

"Precisely, Signorina. Now, quiet please." It was not an admonition, more that there was pressing news to tell. "I had an audience with His Holiness this morning and…"There was a pause while he looked around his department: 56 priests, 41 assistants and three nuns on secondment as they were experts on education. One hundred and one including himself. He continued, speaking slowly to reinforce each word. "His Holiness has asked me to run the defence against this ridiculous challenge to the true church. Over the next 48 hours, I am going to be calling upon several of you, and a few from outside the department no doubt, to form a war cabinet. For this is no less than a full-scale war to save the true faith."

"It's a crusade," Sophie cried, her enthusiasm and imagination pumping the words out, bypassing her brain. "I'm sorry, Your Eminence."

Sophie saw knights in armour, clean white tabards despite the dust, with strong red crosses front and back. Then she imagined Cardinal Forrundiker calling her into his office to sit with a handful of others in the easy chairs by the window. Perhaps she would be the only girl selected. 'Sophie, we desperately need a female perspective on this serious situation.' She would have a leather-bound notebook and a propelling pencil to scribble down ideas before pronouncing to the assembly who would nod and murmur 'Yes, excellent idea, Signorina LaNeve'.

She waited but that call to arms never came.

At least not in the format she envisaged.

"LaNeve, I mean…um…"

"Please call me Sophie, Your Eminence, at least when no-one else is around." Sophie looked down at the old man, seeing just that, not something to hate and fear.

"Um, yes…Sophie. I wanted to ask your advice. Please sit down." It was starting, she thought. She took a seat by the window, had never sat in his room before, wondered where the others were.

"You know a good number of the priests around here, both within the department and outside it." So, she was going to be the Chief Personnel Officer for the war cabinet, helping the cardinal to slot the best people into their roles. That made her the architect of its success. It would work only if she made the right selections.

"I need a priest who has experience of America. I need someone who has completed sensitive and difficult work over there, dealing with Americans. Do you know of any we can rely on?" The first selection! When would he announce her position? Perhaps she had to prove herself first with this first recommendation? She opened her mouth.

But nothing came. Her mind was suddenly empty, or rather full of half-ideas. She shook her head, trying to loosen her thoughts. But all remained in deep fog, simple ideas fighting their way through but failing and falling into the dark ditches where nothingness lived.

"Can you recommend anyone, Sophie?" He had given her several minutes, wondering at the look of panic that spread like flames across her ashen face, causing bright red patches of heat on her cheeks, her neck, her forehead.

Why she said Father Barrow she would never know. She supposed afterwards that he was topmost in her mind because of the scandalous way he had dealt with poor Sister Mary John. But surely that proved that he was the last person for the job?

But she was saved because the cardinal would never select someone he was so dissatisfied with, someone who had been severely told off for a lack of orthodoxy in his teaching approach just last week. She would have to justify the selection, something about being all-inclusive, thinking outside the box, pushing the boundaries, but the bigoted priest would not get the position.

And it seemed she was right. The cardinal looked aghast, mouth formed for words but none escaped. Instead there was a sucking and pumping of air, as if the old man was playing a wind instrument badly. For a moment, as she thought she was alright, she pictured the cardinal worrying away at the bagpipes. But then the puzzle lines on the old man's face eased a bit, turning up at the corners, becoming more certain features.

"Excellent, Sophie. Please ask him to come in immediately. And…"

"Yes, Your Eminence?" He had accepted her crazy choice. Whatever next? At least her promotion was about to happen. Perverse suggestion indeed, but maybe in an odd way it had worked with the old man.

"I am assigning you to assist Father Barrow."

"Assist?"

"As his secretary. Please do everything he asks promptly and courteously. Well, I know you will. You have always been a good office girl for me." His words were soaked in condescension, but innocent condescension only. When Sophie thought about it afterwards, she could not detect a note of the hostility that had made sour music of her days before.

"But…"

"No more 'buts' my dear, my mind is fully made up." He looked away, then back to the folder on his desk when Sophie fixed him with a stare. But his eyes were full of watery depth now, no sheen of hardness projected.

The interview was over.
And Father Barrow was her new boss.
And Cardinal Forrundiker was deep in thought. This bid threatened his church but, like clouds and silver linings, it could be worked somehow to his advantage.
He just had to find out how.

On Bent Mountain

First you need to get there. And that depends where you are coming from. The 'big' city of Roanoke lies a few miles to the north, in the valley that Bent Mountain leans over. It boasts the regional airport so, first off, assume you are flying in.

From the airport, take I-581S until it ends a few miles down the road. By that time, you've gone past what Roanoke has to offer by way of downtown; a few semi-quaint streets that mix tiredness with a faint attempt at the cosmopolitan. But it is slight, for Roanoke is a conservative town full of churches, baseball pitches, friendly people with cheery voices and worn out shopping malls with trees pretty well everywhere.

Then after a few miles around Electric Road you hit Cave Spring Corners, south on 221 and you head up steeply through twists and turns that almost send you back on yourself. This is the start of Bent Mountain.

But Bent Mountain is more than a tiny town outside Roanoke. In fact, it is barely a town, rather homesteads spread across the top of a leafy mountain. It has a different personality with its fresh air, cool nights and straightforward people. It somehow mixes conservative with alternative in a way you only find in America and only then from time to time.

This is where Tammy Shroton set up home when she came to the Roanoke Valley. She purchased a rundown ranch house for cash. It perched on three acres that sloped up steeply and threatened to let its trees slide down onto the house below. This was probably why it had not sold for three years and why it went for a song to Tammy as a cash buyer. But she got two workmen in, brothers who had a dying dairy farm in Floyd County; healthy fat cows but antiquated machinery that kept breaking down. With their digger they shovelled out the hill for 30 yards then built a wall to retain the tall trees that fringed the clearing. Thus, she created a shady yard at the same time. It was cool in summer, funnelling a steady breeze around the house, but kept some warmth in winter. She then built a wraparound porch with red flagstones from a demolition site and half a dozen rocking chairs to furnish it.

The house had a basement garage and workshop, three bedrooms and an open plan living area combined with a small kitchen. The place was filthy, torn newspaper, mice droppings and layers of dust hiding ingrained coffee and cigarette stains, making a statement about its previous occupants. Tammy did all the internal cleaning and decoration herself, working into the evenings after her day job. She took the smallest bedroom to be the one for her, just ten feet by seven and at the opposite end of the house to the bathroom. She painted it white and scrubbed the floorboards until they were a smooth pale yellow like just ripened corn.

Then she sat back and surveyed her work. It was pleasing to see cleanliness and order where before there had been filth and debris.

"Hard work never killed anybody," she said, reflecting that quite often hard work had probably been the direct cause of death. But the sentiment behind the phrase was what was important. Good, hard work caused no harm.

There is a big difference between seeing someone in the flesh on the one hand and their representation on a screen on the other. Tammy had seen Miles many times since he had returned to England. Sometimes, for instance, on the big office computer with the superfast broadband and pixels in the thousands, he was almost as clear as real-life, yet somehow unlifelike. Physical proximity lends so much to the other senses. As well as adding depth to sight, there is smell, touch, hearing and intuition. A screen can never rival this; put 3,000 miles and a dependency on modern technology between two people and something is lost.

Hence Tammy was nervous as she waited for Ches to bring Miles to her mountain retreat. How would the stay go? Why had she asked him? Why had he agreed to come? What was going on with her? She had been in complete control since her early twenties. Why did this tall man make her nervous, yet she desperately wanted to consult with him?

She sat on the porch, sheltered from the heavy rain that splashed around, drumming against the roof, looking for a way in, rebounding up the wooden planks that raised the porch above ground level. She rocked twenty rocks, then twenty more. She was on her fourteenth set of twenty when car lights flooded the rough drive, catching raindrops like butterflies in a net.

"Hello Tammy."

"Hello Miles, it's real good to see you." She stood on tiptoes so he could kiss her on the cheek. It was a polite kiss. They had never got beyond that stage; never let passion out. Yet they were drawn to each other. "You must be exhausted after your journey. Can I get you anything or do you want to go straight to bed? A glass of wine perhaps?" She was suddenly aware that she was talking nonstop, kept quiet, looked down at the floor, felt that her heart was pumping.

"No wine," he laughed, looking at Ches, "I've had enough booze for a lifetime!"

"Some water perhaps or…?" They settled on water and a large slice of melon. Ches left in the taxi that had brought them both. Tammy poured herself a glass of red wine and put everything on a tray. On the porch there was an old oak beer barrel, sawn in two and placed upside down to make two round tables. They sat on rocking chairs, a barrel table between them.

The rain had stopped, the wind dying with it, as if in league to batter the ranch house that stood against the hillside they claimed as their own but now exhausted from their combined attack. It was suddenly still. It was 8pm, darkness settling like a worn-out blanket, a few stars appearing through the holes; shiny earrings hanging in the sky.

And Miles started talking about his idea.

They were still there at midnight. Tammy rose a few times to replenish their glasses, once lighting a fire in an old tin milk churn donated by the dairy brothers, cut to allow the air to flow. The spout became a chimney and a trail of smoke and sparks fluttered off into the black night. But it warmed their souls, or at least something did, for their rocking chairs rocked steadily closer until Miles pushed the barrel table back behind them. He felt they were two ships in a black sea, rocking to a gentle current. Somehow, they moved closer as the minutes clocked by, yet were subject to the same tide. He wanted to ram her rocker-ship and lead a boarding party up the side and into the seat of her vessel. The two arm pieces were now very close, almost touching. One more sideways manoeuvre and he would be able to leap the closing gap and be on her deck, looking for her.

But he did not. He would not. There was something that held him back, some reverence perhaps, or maybe hesitation from confusion.

He wanted to hug her, grip her, kiss her, but did not.

And the sad thing was she felt the exact same thing.

They made do with conversation. It started with the mundane, the ordinary. Had he had an enjoyable flight? Was the weather very different? She would so like to go to England. Well, one day she would take him up on that kind offer.

But then he mentioned his idea. The clock in the sitting room-come-kitchen had just chimed a quarter to nine. It sounded like a gong banging for everybody's attention, but there was only Tammy in the audience; only Tammy to appreciate the genius, to feel pride at her choice of lieutenant.

"Sweet mercy," she said when his idea was first aired. "What a brilliant idea. We launch a takeover bid for the entire Catholic Church. It is breath-taking in its audacity. Miles, it's just exactly what we need. Wow!"

They sat up beyond midnight, working the ideas, developing plans with that crazy late-at-night sensation that makes all things possible.

Eventually, exhaustion took over Miles. The yawns punctuated every sentence.

"I'm sorry Miles, I have kept you up too late. What time is it now in England?"

"5:47 a.m." he replied, stretching then standing up. "Yes, I have to hit the sack."

She led him to his room. It was the largest room, overlooking the slope down the mountain, with a door straight onto the porch. It had an ensuite bathroom of enormous proportions with a giant bathtub.

Miles nodded goodnight, shared a quick kiss. Then he brushed his teeth and slipped into bed, while Tammy stepped quietly back to her own plain bedroom.

She lay awake a long time that night, planning and praying, then planning and praying some more.

This was exactly the type of move she had been looking for.

Tammy woke early, as she did every morning, despite the fact that her sleep had been fitful. She sat on the other side of the house, where the morning sun slanted through the trees and poked into the porch, making the flagstones seem on fire with dancing flame-like movements. She had a pot of coffee. She had become used to coffee again in recent years, after a long spell without it. She savoured the aroma it gave of exotic places where she imagined the sun beat down more strongly than Bent Mountain.

The same sun that seemed to work around the world each day, ticking off the days with each revolution of the spinning earth. She never tired of the wonder that God had put into His creation. She was far from a creationist, understanding the part science played. But, to her mind, God and science were together, joined at the hip. God used science. Instead of thunderbolts and clicks of his fingers, He had employed science and evolution to create His world, His universe, over billions of years.

It was not a popular theory in some parts of the south. Many at her high school, attending more fundamentalist churches, would damn her to hell for her views.

She had with her a brand-new notebook and a set of pencils in different colours. She poured more coffee, looked again at the flames of sunlight across the floor and opened the notebook at the first page. She wrote in capitals and in red:

PLANNED TAKEOVER OF THE
ROMAN CATHOLIC CHURCH

She underlined the word 'ROMAN' several times, then went over it with the red pencil as if anchoring it on the page and in her mind. Then, thinking it looked too much like a newspaper headline, she ringed TAKEOVER several times in blue and drew balloons coming out of it. Into one she wrote, lower case this time:

How is it to be done?

Into another she printed:

NEED ADVICE!!!!

Into the third she wrote some names. These were the people she knew might be able to help.

Top of the list was Chesington Bloakes III.

Second was a woman who had come three times to her church on visits to Roanoke for business. Her name was Fi D'Alianti. She came from New York and worked on Wall Street, not the actual street but somewhere in the vicinity. She was ruthless but brilliant. Fi had stayed behind to talk to Tammy on each visit, finally going to lunch together the last time she visited. Fi had drunk champagne, ordered a second bottle, then a third as Fi's driver took them up the mountain to sit on the same porch she now sat on.

They had both known that their paths might never cross again so they condensed into five hours a lifetime of communication and experiences, hopes and fears. They talked in turn, spilling out everything honestly and fully.

Tammy knew about the tricks Fi had utilised to gain such enormous wealth. She listened and wondered at such a world. It was a world that would always be alien to her.

"But your motives are not all honest either," Fi had said, shocking Tammy. She protested of course, but her defence rang slightly hollow, like knocking damp plaster on the walls of her ranch house. For weeks afterwards she had sat alone on her wraparound and thought on those few words. How could Fi be so perceptive on such casual acquaintance? Finally, she admitted some truth to it and was able to move on, surprised and pleased and shocked that her conscience did not hold sway.

The third and last name was Ernest Justice, one of the ruling council of the Church of New Moderation. He had worked all his life as a corporate lawyer before retiring to help run the church. He would know a lot of the legalities.

It was a good list, a start. Add to it the name of Miles Standish, the originator of the idea, who was asleep at that moment in her house. That would be her core team.

Together they could make this work.

As if summoned by her thought process, Miles stirred at that moment. His bedroom looked onto the porch where Tammy sat, where the morning sun presided. She turned at a slight noise, saw through the unblinded door a man standing completely naked and looked away immediately.

But the vision stayed with her, whether eyes were open or shut.

Later, they had breakfast together, again on the porch.

"You really live on this porch, don't you?"

"Yes, for sure. It's real nice and peaceful out here. Do you see the trash cans?" She pointed to a small enclosure outside the kitchen.

"They're all over the place! Was it the storm?"

"No, we had a visitor last night, a bear."

"A grizzly?"

"No," she laughed, "they're all out west. This was a small brown bear, but enough to create a real mess!"

After breakfast of bacon and eggs, cooked 'for the Englishman', only Tammy was no cook and the eggs were hard and the bacon so brittle it snapped on the fork, Miles helped Tammy put the trash cans back. They laughed when he called them 'bins' and she imitated him with repeated mentions of the word.

It was Saturday; no office to go to. They had the day free. They went for a long walk, checked on an elderly couple who could no longer drive, ran down to the store to fetch them a few things, then repaired a broken window at their house that was letting in water badly. They had lunch of apples, cheese and milk bought from the store, talking of everything and anything. It was polite talk, not intimate. Typically, Miles would ask a question about Tammy then listen to a long explanation. Miles was aware that she talked when nervous, but now she was talking more than ever before; fidgeting also. She had a delightful way of placing her left hand on the back of her neck as she spoke, then manipulating it around and up and down, as if operating a pump that pumped out the words. When their eyes met, she smiled warmly but quickly looked downwards. At one point he dared to break the convention.

"When our eyes meet you always look away. I think you're studying the flaws in your porch tiles!" It was meant as a joke and she smiled, caught his eyes, looked down again at the tiles. Suddenly, they were both laughing on their individual rockers, back and forth, back and forth, in time to the laughter.

But the next time they made eye contact, she looked to the far horizon, to the trees in the distance.

Miles desperately wanted to take her to his big bed, but something in her manner made him stay away from that suggestion.

Instead, she pulled out her notebook while Miles put on more coffee.

Then they started their planning.

New York, New York

"It's so ginormous!" Tammy said, looking out of the window to the blocks of skyscrapers below, dissected and bounded by wide roads crammed with vehicles. "Everything is concrete."

"Wait until you see Central Park." Miles found it hard to believe that Tammy had never been to New York; moreover, she had never been on a plane before.

"We went everywhere we needed to by automobile," she declared, but then would not answer more questions about her childhood.

There was a car the size of a bus waiting outside LaGuardia Airport. They sat back in luscious leather individual armchairs.

"Ma'am and Sir, the drinks cabinet is to the right in front of you." The voice was piped back to them, making Miles think of old black and white movies.

They poured themselves drinks, both opting for a Shiraz from a delightful vineyard named Wild Horses somewhere in Oregon, for it had a map of the state on the back. Apparently, it was still a horse ranch but the owner's wife had planted 500 vines back in 2020 and that had grown to over 10,000 now. Miles looked up on his phone and saw that a bottle of Wild Horses Shiraz retailed for $79.

"Can you take a detour for a few minutes, please?" Miles asked the chauffer as they passed 98th Street on FDR Drive. "I would love to show Miss Shroton Central Park."

"Of course, Sir." He swung onto 97th Street and headed directly for the park. "Shall I pick you up here in, say, 30 minutes?"

Fi D'Alianti had the 74th and 75th floors of a skyscraper on a road Tammy did not catch but which was one turning off Wall Street. Her office was full of incredibly smart people in expensive clothes, looking clean and hard. They were met at the elevator doors by a male secretary with large round glasses like Superman before he changed. He was very polite.

"Welcome to D'Alianti and Associates, Miss Shroton and Mr Standish." Tammy had not known that Fi owned the firm. "My name is Al Faraday and I am the personal assistant to Miss D'Alianti. May I take your coats?" He stepped forward to help Tammy and somehow managed to assist Miles at the same time. "Miss D'Alianti asked me to inform you that regrettably she has been delayed a few minutes. A meeting with the Stock Exchange has overrun. She asked me to entertain you with a brief history of the organisation, if you are interested?"

They settled down with coffee in a conference room that was big enough to be a small theatre. And they heard how Fi had made her fortune. And then they learned just how big that fortune was.

"So, let me get this right, Al," Miles needed to double-check his understanding. "You're saying that Fi, I mean Miss D'Alianti, made $7billion by selling stock in a company she did not own a single share in?"

"That's correct, sir. Then she made another $4billion by buying them after they collapsed."

"Because she had sold all that stock, I suppose."

"That's correct, sir. She created a massive misalignment in the market and then capitalised on it. It was a remarkable coup. In all, she made over $12 billion profit from Xertgy Inc. and she still owns 20% of the company. With a new management team and lots of focus, it's making real good profits now." The esteem for his boss was evident in every word Al spoke. Then he added something in a smaller voice, almost daring them to hear him. "That is our reason d'etre. We find underperforming, undervalued companies, sneak up on them and then 'Pow! Kerplunk! Wham!', we jump all over them! It's a licence to print money!" Al was now a boyish superman, punching the air with his fists, in all but the costume.

Miles caught Tammy's eyes. She smiled and whispered that it was all in an excellent cause. Then she looked down again, as was her habit, eyes weighed by mini anchors to keep them firmly on the ground. But this time, before she looked down, Miles saw something else in her almost black eyes. He saw the shine of fear at the unknown but also the flicker of thrills, of jumping into another world; shine and flicker revolving. He also saw something for him, although it was not until hours later that he worked out what it was. He woke in the night when it came to him. He got out of his bed and did a dance on the floorboards, singing far too loudly for 2:30 a.m.

What he saw, what gave him so much nocturnal joy, was simply her love for him.

But wind back to the 75th floor of the elegantly thin building that housed the firm of D'Alianti, with Tammy and Miles waiting patiently for Fi, with her PA, Al Faraday, trying to fill the growing gap in time.

When Fi did arrive at 4.47 p.m., she was full of apologies, flung herself down in a large chair with metal arms twisted like snakes, and called for a bottle of the 'right stuff'.

The right stuff turned out to be two bottles of Krug Grande Cuvee 2018.

"It's so good to see you, Tammy." Somehow with Fi you knew she meant it. "And who is your friend?"

Introductions done, only a modicum of flirting from Fi, who looked ten years younger than her 44 years, "thanks to the great guys down at 'Look Good, Feel Good', my local 'all under one roof' therapists", they settled down to business.

They were still there three hours later when the September sun knocked on their window and reminded them she was off duty in a moment and would be sinking below the horizon for a well-earned rest.

"Let's go eat," Fi said. They went to her favourite seafood restaurant, 43 blocks up Manhattan and a stone's throw from her apartment looking onto Central Park like a mother watching her children play. Eating involved more champagne, always champagne with Fi.

"I like the bubbles," she giggled as she signed the cheque, and they stood up to walk the short distance to her apartment.

For Fi had said 'stuff and nonsense' to Tammy's insistence on finding a hotel. "You will both stay with me and that's final."

The truth was she relished the company. Fi had many billions in the bank but very few friends and no husband or boyfriend. She could not get close to anyone, hence she drank. Not close to anyone until she had gone to the Church of New Moderation, taking a few hours off from a viscous takeover of a defence business headquartered in sleepy Roanoke. She had made over $2billion on that deal.

But she had gained something else. She had straight away sensed in Tammy someone she could trust with everything, thus the frank disclosures on the porch of Bent Mountain.

And if it took every penny of that, she would keep her only friend.

The next morning Tammy and Miles both overslept, heavy heads coming out of their bedrooms well after Fi had left for the office. They ate breakfast, served by the housekeeper, then went to their separate bathrooms to get washed and ready for the day.

The car was waiting just outside the foyer. Two dozen yards across 5th Avenue was the start of Central Park, brown invading green after a long hot summer. A group of cyclists on hired bicycles jostled with each other, getting ready to plunge in. Several stared at the stretch limo with darkened glass and the uniformed porter holding the door for them both. Miles started chuckling.

"What is it, Miles?"

"If only they knew. I own a fish and chip shop back home. Last week I was cleaning chip pans, now I'm climbing into the biggest car ever made to be driven down to some bigwig meeting."

She kissed him lightly when they were safely in the car, thinking if only he knew what changes she had been through.

In return he held her hand, then felt slightly awkward. He drummed his fingers against the back of that hand, tapping out a rhythm in a jokey way. It was a relief to laugh when she laughed, to smile in return, to have a modicum of physical contact but to remain safely contained.

Fi had assumed they would share a bed together, had been embarrassed to be corrected. Then she rushed to find extra sheets and quilts late at night because the housekeeper had gone to bed. Tammy wanted to take the box room, seemed happier that way, so Miles had the guest suite. But in their joint denials that they were lovers, they had raised the question in both their minds.

Howard Farringdon did not mind playing second fiddle, for at least it meant he was in the orchestra. With half a tedious lifetime behind him as the general manager of a chain of grocery stores, he craved something more exciting, anything that would give some fizz when he told his grandchildren what he was about. Already they were asking questions that he evaded with a chuckle, but another year or two and they would see right through him.

As he said the immortal words "follow that car, cabbie, there's an extra 20 in it if you don't lose him," he felt a thrill travelling up his spine like a lift shooting up its shaft.

The cabbie hid his astonishment behind a "yes, sir," and pulled out two back from the limo, causing a shuddering echo of horns as he jerked into the traffic stream.

Howard had volunteered to go when Ernest Justice had pulled him aside in the parking lot, under the same huge forked oak that Tammy had stood when she accepted the position of New Moderation leader. He had been delighted to be selected, so much so that Ernest decided to change his script from, 'you are our last chance, all the others have refused' to, 'I thought of you immediately'. It was not strictly a lie; Ernest had thought of him first and then dismissed him, going for a younger, more spy-like look at first.

He was the seventh person Ernest had asked and the first to say he would.

His task was to track Tammy and the Brit, to find out who they were meeting with and why. And he thought he was doing well.

The doubts crept in when the limo, after bending its long body around numerous corners, pulled into a workshop. The chauffeur got out, newspaper under left arm, chucked the keys at a mechanic and walked into a coffee shop.

Meanwhile, Tammy and Miles were sitting in the vast conference room on the 75th floor, sipping the richest coffee they had ever tasted.

"It was your chauffer's idea," Miles laughed, fingering a tiny chocolate biscuit that matched the coffee for richness. "As soon as he realised we were being followed, he called up to arrange an oil change."

"And then we had a lovely tour of downtown Manhattan!" Tammy added, her laughter spreading to Fi, who needed little encouragement to see humour at any time.

But pretty soon the laughter was put away. Tammy and Miles had a lot to learn and little time to do it in.

'Fi, start by telling us how a typical takeover works."

"Wait a minute, you're the leader of a church and you want to get involved with buying a business?"

But Tammy would not be drawn, prodded Miles under the table when he started to explain.

"All in good time," was all that Tammy would say.

So Fi used old case files quickly grabbed from the archives by Al Faraday.

"First, you need to be crystal clear about your objectives, that is, exactly what you are trying to achieve. You need to sketch out the finances; how you're going to pay, what stock you can issue, what you can borrow etc. At this stage, that can be top level as the detail will come later. Then you need to do a SWOT analysis to…"

"What?"

"It's an acronym for Strengths, Weaknesses, Opportunities and Threats. It's a tried and tested way of looking at a deal and I swear by it, except I think of it a little differently. Find a weakness in the target and pounce!"

"It sounds like the jungle,"Tammy commented. "Why can't people sit around and talk calmly about a future together?"

"There's a simple answer to that, Tam. While you're sitting talking calmly, someone else will see the opportunity and pounce instead of you. And they may even pounce on you as well." She looked at the two empty faces staring back at her. It was clear to Fi that she was going to have to take both her students through the basics.

She did just that. When they broke for lunch – seafood and champagne brought in by a team of caterers in stiff white – their heads were overflowing with the fundamentals of takeovers.

And a lot of it was sticking.

They reached Fi's apartment at midnight after an exhausting day followed by a tour of the Village, Fi's favourite part of her hometown. It seemed as if she was known all over her city.

"It helps when you tip generously," she said, being strangely modest. But it was not just the waiters and door staff who reacted to her; more the clientele.

"We made real good progress today." Fi was hovering over the two of them with a bottle of malt, tipping large amounts into the glasses with very little control. "But now you need to let me in on your big secret. What exactly are you two misfits planning?"

By the time they had told her, she was absolutely sober.

And her mind, sober though soaked in alcohol, screamed at her. It was, without doubt, the greatest idea of her 20-year career.

Campaign Headquarters

Humphrey Barrow did not know how to behave in front of her, so copied the cardinal, matching the brusqueness he had seen him employ.

But he could not bring himself to call her by her last name.

"Sophie, we need to set up a campaign headquarters in the suite of offices the cardinal has donated." They were away from the main building, in a small network of ground floor dusty rooms set in a large rose garden tended by two old men who had been on the payroll forever. "I will take this office," he led her through the maze of rooms, "and want you to move into this little one next to me."

"It has a glass door."

"What is wrong with that? In fact, it will make communication easier." She would be visible to him all the time.

"And there is only one place for the desk to go." That was right in front of the glass door.

"You only need one place to put a desk." His logic was perfect but there was something missing.

"What about all the files we will make. Where will they…?" She could not imagine all day under the gaze of this bigot.

"Ah, I've thought about that. I want a central place for all the files making easy access. Your job will be to collect the files the team needs and then put them back again after each meeting. The file registry is going to be on the other side of your office so it is very convenient. Now, you will also need to keep the refreshments on the go as we will probably have lots of long meetings. I would like us to offer water, coffee, tea, fruit and biscuits, all on proper china, of course."

"Yes, Father Barrow."

"Father," he said in reply.

"Sorry?"

"Father Barrow is too formal. Just call me Father."

"Yes…eh…Father."

"Now, how are your dictation skills?"

Sophie had taken pride in her dictation at the evening school she had gone to for her first two years of work for the cardinal. She had consistently been top of the class.

"They're not good…Father."

"Too bad, we'll have to get another girl for dictation. Your job will be to welcome participants, provide refreshments and locate the files and paperwork we need. Now, as to the participants, I want each one to have…"

But Sophie was not listening. Instead she was hating everything around her. Just as she had found a degree of tenderness for her old boss, so all rage was focused on the new one.

But it was not her fault. He was a patronising shit who put women down at every opportunity. She only had to read his reports from the American convent to see that.

Well, she would show him.

Whatever her personal feelings, however, there was simply not time to develop them over the next few weeks. Sophie came in at 8:55 a.m. on the first day of the new regime to find Humphrey already at his desk, piles of papers and notes building up around him like the walls of a new castle. On the second day she made it by 8:30 a.m. to find him working steadily. She went by irregular jumps back from there until by the Tuesday of the second week, she found the door locked and could, at last, use the keys she had been presented with. It was 6:55 a.m. as she switched on all the lights, then turned them off again, all except her desk lamp. It spotlighted her when Humphrey walked in twenty minutes later.

"Sophie, you are early today!"

Suddenly, she decided to make a move, kicked back her chair, rose to her full height, came around to the front of the desk and sat on it, legs dangling down at a slant across the face of the oak veneer.

Her skirt was slightly too short.

Humphrey had to look away.

"I just want to be helpful, Father. I want to do as much as I can for the campaign." She forced herself to use his chosen term of address.

His eyes were drawn back to hers, only then they had to drop.

But that was a mistake. She had the most gorgeous legs and Humphrey needed to get out of her office.

"Very good, Sophie, carry on," he said hastily, backing out, red blush rising like the tender pink of sunburn, compressed; a day under the glare in just a few seconds.

He was gone, closing the glass door, only, in his haste, it did not close fully. It swung back open, as if inviting her to launch a further attack.

She did not move, legs still dangling in front of the desk, swinging back and forth in a mini-victory parade.

From that position two feet from the open door, she clearly heard his muttering, could make out the words 'Please God, save me.'

Well, he needed saving from his spiteful, ignorant self.

And Sophie LaNeve was not the lady to do that saving.

Days followed days as September sped around the track and October took the batten. Sophie faced competition to be the first one in and the same competition to be the last one to leave, often as deepest night skies sent pinpoints of light from another age across space.

On her way home, she would look up at that night sky, reflecting that God had not spent six days making the world, more like six billion years, carefully folding every tuck and tear to make a platform for something else, nurturing every suckling, worm, flea and human for His pleasure, His purpose; for love of life and choice and everything that was possible.

She wondered at the glory of it all as she pushed her bicycle across the cobblestones, before mounting at the street corner. She saw window shoppers, late at night, admiring leather shoes and handbags, shawls and hats that looked alive. The shoppers had eaten well, probably seafood and the lightest of crispy wines. Sometimes, although it was late, she would stop and have a glass at the café on the corner of the square where she lived, leaving her bicycle in an untidy heap with several others. Every sip held another world of taste, smell and sensation, sweeping away bile like a gentle river thrown down by God to cleanse the very earth it travelled through.

She often thought of Father Barrow, then shook him out of her mind. She found herself alternately angry at some dismissive remark he had made, or secretly admiring the mastery with which he worked.

"You should have been in corporate finance," she had joked once, not caring that she was angry with him, not caring for that moment at least.

"I serve God not mammon," he had replied, somewhat dismissively and with an unintended pompous tone, transforming her joke into another turn of the humiliation screw. Her anger returned, of course. All the rest of that day she was robotic, severely efficient, slamming folders shut with a clap that could be heard by the gardeners outside, if they had not gone half-deaf with age, working their roses to dowdy perfection.

"I hear the opposition is on the move," Father LaPetite said one yellow morning on the cusp between September and October. He was an oddly named Frenchman, being vast. When he stood in front of the window to stretch and yawn during the interminable meetings, as was his custom, he blocked out the sun, turning the contrast from glow to shade. Everything about him was in proportion to his body bulk, as if every periphery, every feature had continued growing as his stomach had expanded over the years. He was jovial, warm but with a look in his eye and his manner that said, 'only take me so far because inside all the blubber and fluff is a rod of steel'. Sophie liked him immediately and, thus, he was one of the principal beneficiaries of her 'biscuit distribution policy'. This same policy put broken, plain biscuits on Father Barrow's plate, rich chocolate on LaPetite's.

It was the only power she had so she used it unapologetically.

"What do you mean?" one of the pointless crew asked. Sophie had given them this nickname for their lack of contribution, just punching pointless questions into the air from time to time so that they could go back to their lodgings and say they had made an impact that day.

Sophie sighed at the question. It was completely pointless because they all knew that LaPetite would tell everyone what he meant without prompting from the wings.

"They're moving from New York to London," LaPetite said, leaning back on his chair legs, waiting for the appreciation.

"Are they really?" Sophie heard the next query with disgust. If she were in charge she would ban all such trivial questions, come down like a ton of bricks on any such feeble-minded utterances.

Better than that, she would have Father LaPetite sit on them during the long, long meetings that stretched from now to some distant future time.

"Why?" someone asked. That was a little better, a little further up the scale. She would allow that question this time, but they really needed to think first. They could have worked it out for themselves.

"To be closer to the action, closer to us, of course." She did not realise that she had spoken until the words were out, hanging over the central table, finding routes into the 40 brains stretched around the table perimeter. She was standing, silver coffee pot in hand, while the only other woman in the room was scratching at paper in shorthand, head bent over her project.

"Precisely," LaPetite spoke up. "Very perceptive, Sophie. Sometimes I think you have more brain power than the entire Catholic clergy!"

LaPetite had earned his mid-morning chocolate biscuits, rich brown cream spilling out of the sides when he squeezed them between his pudgy fingers.

Sophie did not know but LaPetite went further that day. He went further in actions but also in perception. He asked for a private meeting with Barrow when the main meeting eventually petered out. Barrow, recognising intelligence and seeing also that his perpetual, all-inclusive meetings were getting nowhere, suggested they go out to eat together. LaPetite had no objection. He chose the restaurant.

Mussels and clams with tagliatelle, washed down with a lemon-fresh Frascati, went together perfectly, eased away frustration within Barrow and freed his mind for a greater purpose.

"Whoever said alcohol blunted the imagination? They have never sat in a Roman square, under an awning advertising some obscure beer, drinking Frascati and sunshine in equal proportions," LaPetite said to open the conversation.

"What are we doing wrong?" Humphrey asked.

"You've gone for quantity not quality."

"Explain please." It seemed more business-like to speak in clipped sentences, something Barrow imagined the other side would do.

"Certainly. You had a big task placed on you. Naturally you responded by assembling a big team. It makes you feel secure. It is entirely understandable."

"Go on."

"Well, putting it bluntly, my dear friend, you have surrounded yourself with a bunch of nobodies, no-hopers, useless bodies with useless minds. You would do better to strip away the deadwood and just retain me and a half-dozen others. And, another thing."

"Yes?"

"For goodness sake, you need to promote Sophie. I know she is young but she has the best brain in the room, excepting maybe yours."

"I can't, Francoise. I just cannot."

It was then that Father Francoise LaPetite displayed his brilliant perception.

"Go to confession, spill it all out and then get on with the job," he said, roughly but not unkindly. "The truth is your job will get a whole load easier with Sophie on the team, regardless of whether you are in love with her."

Humphrey did not deny, nor argue. Instead he sat, twirling his glass round and round, tipped slightly to make a drunken whirlwind of wine. He sat without saying anything, watching the green-yellow-white liquid climb up the glass with each revolution, then breaking free and spilling over the rim to land, splat, on the russet tablecloth embroidered with blue bowls of steaming soup and stylised champagne flutes. The first splash landed on the soup bowl; the second, as if a range officer was giving orders to raise the gun elevation, went straight into a cotton glass, mixing liquid wine with cloth champagne.

Then he nodded, said like a boy being told to apologise, "I expect you are right."

"Say again, Humphrey," said with exaggerated Gallic accent on the second syllable of his name.

"I said I think you are right."

That was enough talk. LaPetite demonstrated that his skills repertoire ran broader than perception by employing both tact and charm, switching suddenly to the Vatican soccer team and their abysmal performance, laughing in unison with his new friend.

But he had made his point.

If Sophie had thought her days were busy before, they were far busier now. At first there was little change, but the numbers in the meetings slipped a few each day. Forty plus attendees gave way to 35, then a day later there was only 29. By the end of the first week it seemed like every second chair was empty. Sophie suggested a smaller table, then found Barrow had moved the meetings to a back room that could only take a dozen with comfort. It was a statement of how things were changing.

She wondered how long she would be needed with the new slimline team. Whereas forty or more needed secretarial assistance, surely a couple of handfuls of bodies could cope for themselves? Every day she was expecting a summons that would send her back to her old job with the cardinal.

"Sophie, rather than standing at the back, why don't you sit down for this meeting? You could tell us what you think of the youth church across the world." It seemed as if Father Barrow had read her mind.

More likely he had picked up an ounce or two of wisdom from Father LaPetite, spilling off the bigger man as they shovelled their clams.

"I see the young people as having a different church," she started. At first, she looked only at the china coffee cup in front of her but steadily found eyes, then faces behind the eyes, then connections beyond the faces. "It needs to be far more flexible, far more open to accept different ideas and attitudes."

"Explain." When LaPetite gave one-word commands everyone knew two things. First, he wanted a no-nonsense answer and second, he had at least a drop of respect for you. Everyone else got less than one word.

Sophie screwed up her courage, daring herself to sound articulate and considered, as if she were one of them. But inside, her calm genes were tossed from side to side, like a small boat taken stupidly into a rising sea.

"I think you have to consider what is fundamental to the church. These are the abiding principles we all follow. All other things can be considered fashion or fads. I mean no disrespect by this, but surely there is a distinction to be made between the fundamental truths of any religion and the practices and customs that are followed? For instance, it was not unknown in the medieval church for priests to get married. Celibacy is an example of how the church has created a rule out of thin air, a fashion to suit a particular circumstance or time." She stopped then and thought of her father, old long before his time, worn out by some unexplained dedication to the church, by sacrifice. Had he traded who he was for a place in Heaven? Would not the all-seeing God see through that? But then rather than anger, would He not shake His body with laughter, perhaps a little like LaPetite's uncontrollable mirth, usually at his own jokes? Was all man's effort just such a joke to Him? Or did He care like she did and want things better, but also more exciting, more sensual?

But as she made her points about celibacy, she had not been thinking about her father. She had to be honest about that because honesty was the fibre running through her, keeping mind and soul and heart and body connected, as one.

She had been thinking of Humphrey Barrow and her keen desire to strike a javelin into his skinny belly. She would do it with sufficient force to see the sharp point out the other side.

And then, as he lay writhing on the ground, in those last moments of life, she would say, like her warrior ancestors would have said, 'this is for Sister Mary John'.

In the Rear-View Mirror

The taxi driver sat low in his seat, thoroughly disinterested in his surroundings. He had seen it all before; Heathrow to the City, between 64 and 79 minutes with normal traffic. He hoped mid-morning on a weekday would be closer to the 64 as the American lady sitting in his cab looked like a heavy tipper. He was expert at using the rear-view mirror to size up his passengers and this one seemed wealthy and gorgeous with it. She would, no doubt, be fascinating; life, achievements and friends all A plus.

Depending on the size of that tip, he might take a detour by the betting shop on his way back to Heathrow. He lived in dreams and many were acted out in the bookies of South London.

His real life was Heathrow to somewhere in a black moving box, usually moving slowly, then back again to wait at Heathrow; a cycle of monotony that he yearned to break.

"Young man?" That was the American woman in the expensive coat. He guessed hers was the designer luggage set, the other passengers owning the normal suitcases.

"Yes, darling." It came out without thinking. She looked shocked, about to break into rebuke, severe words forming up in correct sequence. Then he saw in the rear view mirror a slight disturbance. First, he noticed it in her left eye, then the right. A current of humour erupted from first sight in the eyes towards her mouth, first engulfing her pretty nose so that it wriggled, up and down, with cute dance movements. A million electrical signals passed in that split second; many remained within the American, but quite a few burnt their way across the six feet and through the Perspex screen that separated driver and passenger, leaving scorch marks in the broken air between them.

"Watch out driver!" That was the Englishman in the back.

He slammed on the brakes, but not quite fast enough to avoid ramming the car in front.

"Bloody hell!"

A man got out of the car ahead dressed in a suit, phone jammed in the crook of his neck like a growth.

"What the hell?" he shouted, "I've got a job interview in twenty minutes. What am I going to do?"

Fi came up with the solution.

"Where're you going?" she drawled.

"The City."

"Hop in."

"But my car?" He looked at his old Toyota, battered even before the latest knock. But it was undrivable now, the bumper was hanging like the belly of an obese man, the rear lights lay in pieces on the road around two very flat tyres. The car was an old, overworked donkey.

"You need a new one, that's for sure. Miles, help this gent push his vehicle into that layby then we'll be on our way."

The day worked out fine for a number of people. The young man got to his interview in time, got the job too. Fi had given him a business card and he had the manners to call and thank her for getting him to the interview. She responded with her blessings and a large bank draft "for a replacement car".

It worked out for the taxi driver too.

"Say, Bill, I need a driver while in town. Can you take a busman's vacation and take us around for a few weeks, maybe two months tops? You can lay the taxicab up for the duration. We'll get you a proper automobile to drive. Only you've got to agree to keep your eyes on the road, no more diversions in the rear-view mirror."

They both knew what had diverted Bill Mannings. They kept that for later.

And it worked out superbly for Fi. She was welcomed at the modest London office of D'Alianti by her London branch manager.

"Welcome, Miss D'Alianti, to this little outpost of your empire. While you're over here I would love to outline my plans for expansion. I know it's early days as it's only been three months since you hired me, but I hope very much you will like some of my ideas. But first things first, I've rented a three-bedroom house in Mayfair, exactly as requested. It comes with a small household staff, one of whom is waiting downstairs to take your luggage right to the house." Sidney Franco was not British but tried hard to be so. Nobody who met him ever took offence at this dalliance with make-believe. Both Tammy and Miles liked him immediately.

"That's great, Sid. I've got a driver and car arranged already. He's quite dishy as it happens! Can you put Bill Mannings on the payroll for the next couple of months?"

"I most certainly can, Miss D'Alianti."

"Call me Fi, all my friends do."

The smile that rose on Sidney's oval tanned face took off and bounced around the room, either mimicking or leading the early October sun that climbed the walls before retreating in a dance that spoke of constantly changing fortunes.

Bill's new car was a dream. In typical Fi-style, he was sent to a distant rundown industrial estate to pick it up, somewhere instantly forgettable with a sorrowful convenience store on the corner. Expecting a utilitarian vehicle, 'built for comfort not speed', his breath was taken away on being led behind an abandoned warehouse and seeing the silver Aston Martin Rapide S, rented for an initial six weeks. It stood out like a beautiful stallion in a desert of weeds, broken concrete, crushed cans and cardboard boxes from when the warehouse had served a purpose.

"How much does this beauty cost new?" he dared ask.

"With these accessories I would say retail price is around 300."

"My God!"

Bill drove gingerly at first, running quickly through the gears without accelerating too much so the car wallowed on low power. Then he got on a clear patch of M25 and pushed the pedal down.

He had never experienced anything like it before. He swore then that one day, hopefully not too far off, he would own an Aston Martin.

"You enjoyed that, didn't you?" Miles said to Fi when he and Tammy learned of her fun and games with Bill and the Aston Martin.

"So what if I did?" but said without aggression, her grin capturing all parts of her thin face. "Frankly, there isn't much point in being a billionaire if you can't spend a few bucks on creating a bit of happiness here and there."

"I wouldn't know," both Miles and Tammy said in unison, like a comedy duo getting their timing all wrong, or perhaps getting it perfectly right. But it got a good long laugh despite itself.

"Now, down to business" Fi called their first British-based meeting to order. "First off, does anyone mind if Sid sits in on these meetings? Good. Now, as you all know we've announced our intention to make an offer for the Roman Catholic Church. We've come to London to be at the centre of things, similar time zone and all that. Plus, I wanted a little holiday!" Tammy, Miles and Sidney laughed dutifully but genuinely. It was time to get down to the real purpose.

"Now, we need to announce our terms," Fi added as the chuckle lay down. "Miles' original idea was to launch a bid as if each Catholic was a stockholder, free to make the decision whether to sell their stock or not. Thus, if we succeed, we create a democracy at the same time; a neat twist considering the patriarchal nature of the church."

Tammy replied with a grim smile, twisted up then down as she tried to control it. But she did not speak, would have done but Sidney spoke first.

"But…"

"Yes, Sid?"

"I don't understand. I mean…where does payment come in? Who pays who?"

"Nobody pays anybody," Fi replied, loving the sense of mystery. "It is a takeover without money."

"But the fees? How do we...?"

"We don't. Our percentage will be paid in glory." She did not need to add that the enormous publicity of a successful bid would keep them in work for decades to come.

And their names would be in all the history books.

Sid leaned into this project, adding 16 stone, of which who knew how much was brainpower? He leaned in to that meeting, adding his views with vigour, displaying what Fi had seen in him during the interview earlier that year; controlled aggression, someone determined to make it, but not by cutting corners or walking over others.

As Fi listened to the back and forth, she knew she had made the right decision in coming to London.

And afterwards, when all meetings were put away, she could look at the back of Bill Mannings' neck as they slid over to Mayfair for a quiet night in with some damn good champagne.

But their session went on far longer than Fi had anticipated. With the jetlag, they were asleep on their feet when they finally headed for their London home. The meeting lasted into the small hours because Sid took centre stage, organising and delegating.

In the morning, after a steamy hot shower and strong coffee, she made Sid the project manager.

It was the first time she had delegated a major job.

"I'll be right here, Sid, for when you need me. And Tammy and Miles need to approve each big step, but within those constraints you need to run with it as you will. This is the Sid Show, so go to it!" She picked up her pastel pink raincoat, grabbed her bag, stood up.

"Where're you going then?"

"Shopping. I'll be back later. Can you call Bill for me?"

The shopping expedition took four hours, including lunch at the Ritz, after which they left the car and took a cab back to the flat.

"But we got the shopping done perfect," Fi said as she turned the oversize key in the oversize door.

"Too right," said Bill, "thanks for the new clothes. They are spectacular."

"I like my men looking smart," she replied, then turned in the doorway, reached up the wooden door frame with her hands, like a fox unfurling, then looping her hands over Bill's neck and kissing him urgently on the lips.

A maid appeared, hastily straightening her hair.

"Madam, I was not expecting you. I was on my break."

"Go back to it, Elsie. We're going to a conference upstairs. We don't want to be disturbed."

"Yes, Madam, of course."

"Oh, just one thing, Elsie."

"Madam?"

"Run and get us a bottle of champagne, no, make it two bottles."

It would be a long afternoon.

Tammy, Miles and Sidney made progress of a different kind. Sidney provided a whiteboard and a large pad on a tripod. First, they scribbled ideas on the whiteboard, then transferred those that made the grade to the tripod.

"What we've done," Sidney summarised as a member of staff went out for sandwiches, "is essentially a SWOT analysis. Look at the pad, lots of ideas down there. Now we do four new pages and parcel them out into Strengths, Weaknesses, Opportunities and Threats." They spent a few minutes pushing the ideas onto the right page, sometimes arguing, sometimes duplicating, but a picture emerged. "Right Tammy, why don't you encapsulate what we've come up with? We can do it as we eat because lunch is here."

"Okay," Tammy spoke between mouthfuls of smoked salmon and lettuce in a seeded roll, "first, Strengths. We have the big one at the top. Let's call it Moral Stance. Put simply, the New Moderation Church has a different moral stance with regard to certain sins. These sins are ones of the flesh, by and large. But we don't get on our high horse like a 17th Century puritan. We simply take away the temptation and resulting guilt that haunts the Catholic Church. This is what we've termed 'Artificial or Man-Made Temptation'; essentially, we are sweeping away rules surrounding certain aspects of sexuality that, through their enforcement, cause sins to exist. Take away the rule and you take away the sin."

"Well said, great summary." Sid was a natural leader. "This is our principle strength and I think it puts us leagues ahead of the opposition. It is almost like a purifying."

"Or a new Reformation," added Miles. "But we aren't going to get enough response from this to make a difference. We need something else, something that really grabs people."

They debated Miles' point as the sun changed its angle of attack, getting lower, striking longer and deeper through the windows that surrounded three sides of the large conference room. The players shifted their chairs to avoid the glare. Specs of dust played bumper cars in that light, reflecting the clash and merging of ideas amongst the human occupants of the room.

But those dust specs danced and played in vain, for no new ideas came that day.

Nor the next day, or the day after that.

It was Bill Mannings who came up with the breakthrough. They were in the Aston Martin on day four of their London stay, heading for Windsor Castle for some 'downtime'. Tammy and Miles sat in the back seats where they enjoyed a sense of closing off or hiding away, like children playing sardines and squeezed into the perfect hiding place. Bill drove, with Fi next to him and they played a smiley-twisty game with hands and mouths and eyes, screened partially from behind by the seat backs, but not totally so flashes came through to the rear passengers who smiled and dared to touch fingers, a watered-down imitation of what was going on in front.

The conversation ranged across the car, sometimes in zones, rear and front, sometimes a whole car experience. It also ranged across the mundane, the playful and the serious.

It was at a point when the scale was on super serious that the idea came to Bill. They had been discussing the edge they needed in the planned takeover, the illusive edge that jogged on the horizon but never came near.

"We need something to really bite," Fi said once again.

"The other day I had a cab load of young trainee priests, seminarians I think they are called. I picked them up in Farm Street and took them to Westminster Cathedral, you know the Catholic one." Bill poked himself in to the conversation, seemingly meaningless chatter, but Fi knew him better after four days together. There was some purpose in what he said; just because she could not see it did not mean it was not there.

"What did they talk about?" It was a question worthy of Father LaPetite. It opened the way for Bill to develop an emerging idea.

"There were four of them. I watched them carefully in the rear-view mirror."

"What did you hit that time?" It was deliberately light, showing intense fondness through teasing but added to the moment rather than detracting from it.

"Nothing. I was not so distracted!" That was a compliment to Fi. She acknowledged it with a squeeze of his hand on the steering wheel.

"They had two main conversations. Both struck me as strange."

"Go on." Everyone was listening now; the zone had moved out to total vehicle, Tammy particularly alert, leaning forward as if she could drag the words, or their meaning, from Bill's mouth.

"It's normally only a ten-minute journey, but only three got in at Farm Street. They asked me to pick up the fourth at another house north of the park, Hyde Park I mean."

'So, what was strange?" Tammy asked, leaning so far forward she could operate the gear stick if she chose, only it was alien to her as she had only ever driven an automatic.

"The first conversation was just the three of them. They were talking like young men, twenty-somethings."

"But that is what they were. You said they were young trainees."

"Yes, but they were talking about women. It was the kind of chat I would not think twice about with most young men, but not seminarians. They are preparing to take a vow of celibacy, after all!"

It was a good point. Tammy wanted to pursue it further.

"Bill, did anything else happen?"

"Did you speak to them?" Fi said. She had been studying Bill since arriving in London.

"Yes, I said 'why are you talking like that when you are preparing for the priesthood?'"

"And?"

"They laughed. One said it did no harm. Another said it didn't mean they didn't have natural feelings. Then they started talking about the weather and their studies."

"So that was it?" Tammy asked.

"Yes, but it set me to thinking. I grew up Catholic and I always thought the priests were a breed apart, different to the rest of us. Yet their banter in the back of the car dripped with lust."

Bill told them that he had driven on a few moments in silence. He appeared to have killed the conversation with his intervention. "But the truth was the conversation would have ended soon anyway for they were close to picking up the fourth passenger."

One of the seminarians had jumped out when Bill pulled down a tired Victorian street resting on its past splendour. The other two shuffled up to make room. The new arrival was big, overweight, middle-aged. He dominated the second conversation as the black cab slipped back into the traffic.

"The new one was clearly senior; they looked up to him, deferred to him. And he was vitriolic in his misogamist views. They were like spilling out of him the moment he got in the car. And the others…"

"Go on," said Tammy, urgently.

"Well, the others were agreeing with him. They seemed to lock their lust away and turned on the fair sex. It wasn't a pleasant time. I didn't want to hear any more so I turned up the radio and said I had to listen to the traffic news. I closed the window between us."

"They were like teenagers," Tammy said, seemingly stuck with the first conversation between the trainees. But her next words showed that perhaps she saw more than the others; saw the connection. "We've created a system that promotes this. We have to reverse it before it's too late."

She sat back. Bill adjusted his rear-view mirror, his old habit, and saw her lost in contemplation, unaware of Windsor Park with its great big trees and expanse of grassland like a savannah stretching to the horizon, unaware of her friends, of the splendid castle they were driving to, lost somewhere in a place only she knew. She had gone to another time, he decided.

They were parked, doors open, stretching, getting ready to visit the castle when Tammy next spoke.

"Let's get coffee," she said, "I've got it! I think I've got the edge we need."

They did not see Windsor Castle that day, nor any other day. They were too busy building turrets in the sky to worry about walls and moats on the ground.

Monopolies and Mergers Notice 1.231
Notification of an Intention to Bid

The Monopolies and Mergers Commission released the following document at 4:17 p.m. BST on October 24 2034.

Form 1.231 is required (Monopolies and Mergers Act 2029) to be submitted whenever a party (the bidder) has the intention to bid for another party (the target).

Notice 1.231 is required despite the fact that the bid in this case is a proposed non-cash merger of two non-business entities. This principle was tested in the courts in the case of Care Homes of England and Welsh Historic Monuments, both registered charities.

The bidder is the Church of New Moderation, headquartered at 2274 Cave Spring Lane, Roanoke, Virginia, a religious entity organised under the laws of the Commonwealth of Virginia.

The target is the Roman Catholic Church, headquartered at the Vatican, Vatican City, a religious entity organised under the laws of Vatican City and Canon Law.

Monopolies and Mergers Commission rules set up by the 1929 Act require each party (bidder and target) to set out a brief statement arguing their case within form 1.231. The bidder's case is to be followed by the target's response.

Bidder's Case (Maximum 2,500 characters. One attachment can be scanned for additional information).

The bidder has gained an estimated 263,000 converts from the target over the last 12 months and has reason to believe that the proposition it now makes is of fundamental and critical interest to all members of the target.

The bidder has issued a charter in two parts. Part one guarantees every member of the target a free and open vote on the future of the target, something not currently allowed for members of the target.

Part two is a manifesto for changes on completion of a successful bid. It is attached to this document and also summarised as follows:

On gaining control of the target, the bidder will immediately put into place steps to eliminate all gender bias with regard to the clergy. The fact that clergy members are intensively trained is recognised so a parallel track will be followed. All seminaries will be opened up for female candidates, while committees will determine individual applications for special advance promotion to the priesthood. This will depend on the level of experience and commitment to the church.

In addition, vows on entering any part of the religious life will be reformed as follows:

1. The vow of poverty for individuals will remain.
2. A new vow of institutional poverty will be taken collectively for each organisation within the church. Holy treasures and assets held for the general good are to be excluded.
3. The vow of obedience to be amended to reflect personal conscience.
4. The vow of celibacy to be revoked entirely and absolutely, subject to the point below for closed religious orders.

All members of the priesthood will be free to marry and have children. Closed religious orders will be required to vote on celibacy and single sex status every three years.

Any future changes to these rules and all such regulations to be debated in a general meeting founded on democratic lines and held at least annually on a rotating geographical basis.

We stress, however, that the fundamental central tenet of the Christian faith will remain unchanged:

Thou shalt love the Lord thy God with all thy heart, and with all thy soul, and with all thy mind. This is the first and great commandment. And the second is like unto it, thou shalt love thy neighbour as thyself. On these two commandments hang all the law and the prophets.

The principle behind this takeover bid is that only this central tenet (and the Ten Commandments that flow from the central tenet) is constant. All other rules are governed by individual conscience and morality expressed in a collective democratic way and it is recognised that these will change with time.

The Target's Case (Maximum 2,500 characters. One attachment can be scanned for additional information).

The "bid" by the New Moderation Movement is opportunistic. It attempts to make sweeping changes to the Roman Catholic Church that has been in existence very successfully for over 2,000 years.

Your church is not intended to operate as a democracy because it is designed to be a permanent rock through changing times. It is built on absolute truth, namely that God created the world and Jesus Christ came down from Heaven to earth to redeem mankind's sins. Its authority comes from God and, crucially, it is passed through the Holy Father, the ruler of our church, to the priesthood and clergy at large, in order to dispense the holy sacraments to the people who have faith.

It is very tempting to speak of change, especially when the word 'democracy' is employed. But our church is not one that twists and changes to every new fashion. Rather its essence is one of endurance built on the confidence of morality and the teachings of our priests who are all God's representatives on earth.

It is likewise tempting to hold up fallen priests (who are just men after all, therefore susceptible to sin) and cry that change is needed. But which of you goes out and buys a new car because of a flat tyre? Instead we replace the tyre, often repairing it before continuing on our journey.

That journey will take us to Heaven. The priests, under the supervision of the Holy Father, are our guides. Do not cast them off and journey alone in the wilderness without the protection of the Holy Church.

We all need criticism from time to time – your church is no exception. But the way to do this is from within, constructively and in accordance with the principles of our creed.

Reject this futile attack on your church and let us return to the normal business of leading good, wholesome lives in the imitation of Christ and with the certain knowledge that He will welcome us in Heaven after our stay on this earth.

"It's short and sweet," Miles said, on reading the church's initial response.

"Too short and too sweet," Fi said, pouring an Australian Shiraz into four oversized glasses so there was just a dribble left in the bottle. "I agree it is well written but it sounds complacent." Yet there was something that worried her; some part of their argument she had not anticipated. She read it again, trying to isolate what it was that concerned her. Her eyes rested on the word 'creed', made her think of the choir at school singing in Latin at High Mass on saints' days.

"Do you want me to drive tonight?" Bill asked. "If so, I'll pass on the wine."

"I thought we'd stay in tonight." Fi stretched back on the sofa, put her arm around Bill.

"We're going out," Miles said. He and Tammy did not want to be in the way.

"Where're you'all going?"

"We're going to a free concert in Southwark Cathedral, then on to a late supper."

"What restaurant?" Fi asked, not being able to resist the lure of a night out.

"Steve's," Miles replied, hiding his grin, but not very well.

"Steve's? I've not heard of that one. What cuisine is it?"

"Seafood."

"Delicious, perhaps we could meet you there?"

But Bill, a fellow Englishman, had picked up on Miles' humour.

"Fi, it's probably a fish and chip shop."

"It is," Miles admitted. "I tell you what, we'll bring you back my favourite; haddock and chips."

"Deal," said Fi. "Bill and I are busy early on anyway."

Bill knew exactly what Fi meant.

The Appraisal

S ophie stood like a schoolgirl in front of the headmistress' desk.

"Apparently, Sophie, I have changed your job description and should have done an appraisal first. I am not used to employing people so hope you will forgive my oversight."

"Yes, Father." *But I will never actually forgive you anything because of how you were with Sister Mary John.*

"So, we will do it now…that is if you have the time?" *Why I have to go through the agony of this, I do not know, but I might as well get on with it.*

"Yes, Father." *Perhaps this will be short if I limit my input to make it more bearable.*

"As you know, you started four weeks ago as my office girl." *Could anything sound more patronising? Yet it was the truth.*

"Yes, Father." *How ugly he is when he puts me down.*

"But you have proved yourself far more capable." *Perhaps flattery will please her, make her less angry with me, although why she is like this is still a complete mystery.* "And your role had been steadily extended and broadened to take on extra responsibilities."

"Yes, Father." *Could she get away with such minimal input to this awful process?* She shifted her weight, left foot taking over from right, looking down at her boss who sat smugly behind his desk. *Had he not thought to ask her to sit?*

"We won't do the forms as they are pretty long-winded and we are hard-pressed for time. But can you tell me about your strengths and why, in your opinion, you got the promotion?" *There it was; he had said the word 'promotion'. Now it was out there, just as real as the sunshine and rain.*

And in response he saw a moment of fine weather in her face. The heavy sultry clouds lifted like the dense mist on Loch Lomond. He remembered this from a two-week nature course years ago as part of his early priestly training. The lifting had stuck in his mind all this time because it revealed a sudden scene of beauty; water and shore pointing the way to magnificent mountains as the mist receded up the steep hillsides, all in perfect harmony as if they had spent millennia in each other's company, which, of course, they had. He had gone then to the camp toilet, an unstable contraption in a phone box sized tent. When he came out six or seven minutes later the fog had settled back down, even thicker than before, making him totally blind amongst all that incredible beauty.

"Yes, Father." *This was as far as the 'Yes, Fathers' could go.* She had pushed it as much as she could, like a child urging her daddy not to stop at the traffic lights but to keep the wheels rolling at a snail-like crawl. She had now reached the point where he applied the brakes, fully and completely, turned and grinned and said "we would have hit the car in front if we had left it any longer". "I am very organised," she started, shifting her weight again, not knowing what to do with her hands. "And I think I handle myself well in meetings. I mean, well, I take people with me." *My God, why put me through this? I hate you all over again for doing this to me. Can you hate someone and then hate them afresh? Just for who they are as a person?*

"Anything else, Sophie?" He could see that the storm clouds had returned and hated himself for causing them to descend. In fact, he hated himself all over again; could he not have forecast such a change in the weather? *It is my own stupid fault that this lovely girl glowers down at me from a height. Had she not thought to sit down? Perhaps she felt superior with her far greater artificial height?*

But, my God, or rather my goodness me, she was beautiful.

He knew afterwards that Sophie had talked on about her capabilities, confidence growing as the minutes were peppered with achievements. But he had not listened. He was mesmerised suddenly by the curves of her body, the flesh that made those curves, the way her loose hair fell around her face. *Oh, that face! Those eyes of anger and beauty! How can something be so terrible and so wonderful at the same time?* A small part of his mind considered, perversely, whether this was something to do with God's work; how else could anger and beauty hold hands?

Sophie's mind was also multi-tracked. One part of her brain trotted out the list of accomplishments. She knew these off by heart for she kept them in a notebook in her cubbyhole, updated daily in the large round handwriting she had cultivated since leaving school. Another part of her brain was looking down on Humphrey like an invading army who had just crossed the mountain range to see the undefended city below. She felt that this part was somewhere on the left-hand side, around the middle of her head. There was a little part of her brain (right rear?) deciding the location of each track of thought like a marshal at a wedding car park. Then there was the right front that could not rid itself of Sister Mary John and all the hate that involved. Strange, thought left rear, that religion should involve hate. But, pointed out right central, maybe it was her that was the fountain of hate, welling up from her impulsive heart.

Hearts and minds do not get on, as everyone knows. Perhaps it was the same as her looking down on her boss, thus the mind looked down imperiously at the emotional concoction that was the heart.

And then there was left centre, more concerned with physical appearance. It noted, quietly at first, but with growing volume, that Father Barrow was remarkably good-looking.

"What is my job title to be?" she asked, having finished the accomplishment list and bringing all the brain parts into formation. *Let it be something impressive. You know, I don't think he has thought about it? How typical of men, of him. If I were a man, I am sure his response would trot off his tongue as Director of So and So, but no, not for a girl.*

"How about Director of Defence Strategy?"

"That sounds right…Father." *Wow! What of that? But it must have been a sudden idea for he definitely had not thought about it before. Still, no matter; it is sufficiently grand and definitely a promotion.*

"And my office?" Her mind split into tracks again, discipline gone out the window to dance amongst the roses beyond. *Am I going too fast?*

"I think you should move into the large vacant one across the hall. It has a big desk and a sitting area, and also a lovely view." *She is pushing, pushing down from her height, but I don't care. Except that I will not see her so much, sitting just beyond the glass door as at present. But maybe that is for the better. I don't need distractions, but what a distraction!*

"Thank you, Father. I'll ask janitorial to help me move." *The man I hate so much has given me everything I wanted.*

It was time to summarise, only Humphrey could not summon himself. Instead, he stared at her, looking up at a 50-degree angle, creating a right-angled triangle with Sophie at the perpendicular. The desk was low enough for him to see the sweep of her thighs but not her legs, bare below the lemon-yellow skirt she was wearing. *Lord, how much I want her.*

"What did you say?"

My God, I must have spoken that aloud. His mind raced for an explanation. *Ah, that was it.*

"I just said how much I want you on the team" he said, twisting the words as they came out so that a truth became a lie.

But one lie did not matter to a man who had sinned more in the last twenty minutes than the whole of the last 20 months. *And I am supposed to be a paragon of virtue? Heaven help me for I cannot help myself.* He slipped into clichés; they had a worn, comfortable feel about them, as if someone had been there before him, testing the roads, writing a guidebook on the journey.

"Will that be all, Father?" Her words jerked him back to his office, reuniting the fancies of the mind with the physicality of the body. But thought of the word 'body' set it off again. *My God, I am a lecherous so and so!* For some reason he thought of Father Peter Davies in Vigilance, Virginia, the odious priest he had come across with that difficult case he had been assigned nine years earlier. Was he no better than Davies? Did he deserve the same fate? His mind was suddenly full of the young nun with a man's name. What was it? Sister Peter or Sister Paul? No, it was Sister Mary something, male and female competing within the same name. Why a man's name?

"John" he said suddenly.

"What?"

"I was just remembering someone I helped once, a young nun in trouble. Something made me think of her again. She had an odd name, Sister Mary John. Her order, I forget the name of it now, used men's names on entry into the convent."

"You helped her?" Sophie had no breath in her body, all expended in a great gush of rage. She found it hard to stand, wavered a bit, like a mast used to the strain of the wind but suddenly becalmed so the mast wobbled in its base. *He said he had helped her! How do you help someone by condemning them?*

"Do you want to sit down?" *Why did she insist on standing in front of him and tantalising him so?* "Yes, I helped that poor nun, but now is not the time for old stories. I'll tell you some other time perhaps."

"I've got to go," she said. *If I stay another minute, I swear I will throttle you, Father Smug Bigoted Bastard.*

Strong words but he deserved them.

Scheming and Dreaming

"Who do we know in the Vatican?" Ernest Justice asked his wife. It was early, not yet 5:00 a.m. Before retiring from the legal profession, Ernest had been at his office desk by 6:00 a.m. every morning for 40 years. For the last 34, since their marriage, Sara had risen with him to prepare his breakfast. It had not come easily to her to shake off sleep before dawn but she had been brought up in an old-fashioned household where it was expected that a wife supported her husband. Thus, she had willingly devoted her life to him from the very first moment of each day.

"Why do you ask?"

"Because, gal, we have to spill some dirt on a certain lady." When Ernest spoke in this way his voice took on an exaggerated twang, as you would expect from a poor actor given a longed-for part as a gangster. When Sara heard him, she felt like brushing down that old pinstripe suit he had with the wide lapels.

But she never did because that would be disloyal. Instead, she swung her dyed blonde but still long and bouncy hair across the bed in a way she knew he liked, telling her husband that the only person she knew who lived in Rome was a second cousin.

"She's a Brit but married an Italian. He died a long time ago. I used to send her Christmas cards but we lost touch."

"Call your mom. She might know where the lady is."

A little later, with Ernest gone, as he always did now to the church office, opening up two hours before anyone else turned up, she called her mother in Orlando.

"Mom, I know it is on Daddy's side but…"

"Don't talk to me about your father."

"Mom, it's not about Daddy, it's about his Auntie Flo's children. Do you remember one called Phyllis or something like that??

"Flo had three children. There was a boy who died in Iraq or Afghanistan, I forget which. Then there were two girls. I'm in touch with Lydia. Well at least I have her number somewhere. The other one went to Italy."

"That's the one. Was it Phyllis?"

"No, it was Phoebe. That's right. She married an Italian and he died real quick. They had a child. Why do you ask?"

"We're planning a trip to Italy and I thought it might be fun to look her up."

Sara's mother agreed to call Lydia and get the number for Phoebe. Sara felt a glow of satisfaction as she put the receiver down. Ern would be pleased with her industry.

Thus, quite out of the blue, Old Ma Silver received a phone call in the administration office of the English College, just as she was packing up to go home. Sara explained the relationship and said that they were coming across to Rome the following week. She very much hoped they could get together. She passed it off perfectly, forgetting to mention that her husband had some dirt to dish.

"I remember you well, Sara," Old Ma Silver said. "I came to your wedding and afterwards we sent Christmas cards for a few years until, well until something happened to cut us off. You must come and stay with me. It's only my son and me in a great big house in central Rome. My husband inherited it from his father and I don't have the heart to sell it. It will be grand to fill it up a bit, if only for a while. It will bring back the house parties we had when we first were married."

Ernest could run to first class tickets as he had a generous retirement plan and some good investments. And he liked the look of envy from other passengers, the way they were set apart at every stage. He insisted that they dress for the occasion so Sara wore a silk lavender skirt and jacket combination while he wore a white linen suit, as people did in hotter climes, with a broad tie dotted with mini-coliseums as if they came off a production line somewhere in the Far East.

Ernest considered they both looked just the part.

And his briefcase, expensive fawn leather with gold-like buckles, held the dirt he had to dish. At least the first phase of it.

For James Mercer, principal of the firm of Huntington Mercer and Goad, had done his work thoroughly. The upmarket private investigator's preliminary report was the principle content of that briefcase, while James Mercer had collected two cheques for $100,000 each, one to cash now for work done, the other an advance payment for the next stage. Both cheques were drawn by devious means on the bank account of the Church of New Moderation.

Ernest justified it in his mind as an insurance policy for the church.

The wide-bodied jet left Dulles and swept in a slight arc sixty-five degrees east and just three degrees north to bear down on the Leonardo Da Vinci airport outside Rome on a crisp, cold morning in the second half of October. The flight was uneventful luxury. Two and a half hours after landing, they were standing in the hall of a grand but shabby house that dominated the short street of Via Romulus.

"How wonderful to see you again, Sara!" Sara was aware of a sea of silvery-grey approaching her. The mid-length platinum dress was square cut, making a statement that the wearer was honest and no-nonsense.

"Hello, my darling." The endearment trotted out easily from Sara's lips. "This is Ern, you last saw him almost 35 years ago at the wedding."

"I can't say you haven't changed!" This in reference to the thick red hair Ernest had as a young man, reduced now to a dirty-white skirting board. "But it's so good to see you again after all these years."

It was briefly disconcerting to witness the genuineness of their host. But Ernest was deep into role-play and this particular role was so full of secrets to expose that there was no space for reality. It was all Sara could do to stop him launching into the reason for their visit immediately.

"Quiet, Ern," she whispered. "Patience in all things."

He whispered a scant apology, took a deep breath and launched instead into small talk.

Inevitably, their chat turned to the audacious bid for the Catholic Church. They sat in a grand salon of yesteryear; everything in gentle decline. No doubt there were memories in every tatty and faded piece of furniture, every ornament, every picture remaining on the walls. Sara expected that the gaps between the pictures represented past sales, necessary dispersals to keep the old home going. Perhaps there had been great excitement when a particular painting reached a good figure – enough to mend the roof or pay the taxes.

Her glance turned to the grand piano, lost in a vast bay window overlooking the herb garden that seemed as untended but as loved as the house that kept it company. The piano may or may not be in tune, she considered, but it had a secondary purpose. It hosted several dozen framed photographs perched like the fairground game where you had to send a hoop over a frame in order to win a prize. Phoebe had explained that the photographs represented seven generations of the Silversitrinni family, tiered like a giant family tree, spreading towards the broad keyboard. But the photographs faced away from the piano player and towards the room, announcing the pedigree of the Silversitrinni family to all who had sight of them.

Sara turned back to the room, looking away from the hundreds of eyes that watched her from the piano top. Her husband was saying something. She owed it to him to listen.

"Actually, we are founding members of the New Moderation Church," Ernest was not going to miss this opening.

"Well I never!" There were times when Old Ma Silver, or Phoebe Silversitrinni to use her correct name, reverted to phrases that only an English person would employ, despite her four decades in Rome. "Do you agree with this takeover bid?"

"Not one bit of it." Ern always weighed right in with his opinion, Sara observed yet again. She would have found the lay of the land first.

"Phoebe, what do you think of it?" Sara would do her bit to help her husband, to smooth out the wrinkled way he operated.

But Ernest was not listening, rather in full flow on what had become his pet topic. The two cousins waited attentively as he told them what he would do if he was leader of the New Moderation Church, headquartered under the oaks and maples 65 degrees west and three degrees south, in the sleepy bustle that was Roanoke, Virginia.

"You have very strong views, Ernest." Old Ma Silver wedged the words into his flow. "Is this why you came to Rome?"

"We wanted a vacation…," Sara started to set things right with a lie. But Ernest would have none of it.

"Yes, we want to see someone high up in the Vatican, preferably the guy who has responsibility for countering this ridiculous takeover bid."

Old Ma Silver hid her smile, simply replied that she could introduce them to the man appointed to lead the charge.

"Will tomorrow do?" This was in response to another interruption from Ernest, demanding to know when they could meet.

"I did good." Ernest assessed himself as they made themselves at home in a huge bedroom suite at the top of the grand staircase. There were gaps in the pictures here as well, the plaster cracked and battered as if the house had turned itself inside out and exposed the intricate decoration to the elements. Chunks of plaster sat in precarious positions, like amateur climbers on the Matterhorn, sheltering from a storm.

"What a lovely room," Sara had said on being shown it, marvelling at the glory it had represented. Now she expressed her opinion to her husband that only the Europeans could live happily in such decay.

But he was not listening, happily engrossed in his assessment of how he had done that morning.

"Straight to the top," he said, "we got straight to the head honcho!"

A Little History, A Little Thought

"Tell me everything you know about the main participants," Old Ma Silver said once she had poured Martinis for Ernest and Sara that evening. They sat on the left side of the terrace, overlooking a rundown orchard at the back of the house.

"There's not much to tell about Tammy," Ernest spoke first as always. "She's a regular mystery girl. But we aim to change that with a…"

"Actually, I know something of her," Sara said, earning a frown from her husband. He was about to question her assertion when she launched into everything she knew, explaining first that she had made a point of asking around, digging a little, "just out of interest, you know."

"Tammy turned up in Roanoke in 2025, took a mundane position in claims at an insurance company. For four years she led a nondescript life, daytimes in a large open plan office, evenings mainly on her own and weekends with a small group of friends, one or two I know reasonably well. It seemed she might have continued such an existence forever, perhaps getting married, having two children, later going back to the claims department and taking some exams to make supervisor."

That much was just factual and Ernest could make claim to half of it. Yet where Sara excelled was with the conjecture.

"But Tammy could only marry if she met someone to marry and, from my enquiries, she never seemed to get close to anyone, even her girlfriends. At work they called her the ice cube, which was a little unfair. My cousin, Jane, is a receptionist at the insurance company. She came down hard on this nickname, telling the originators that Tammy was no more than a lost soul.

"One lost soul amongst so many," she would say when the joking got a little intense, "everyone is lost at some stage in his or her life." I think she was spot on in her observation."

Sara paused, her audience of two quickly urged her on.

"A lot of it is speculation," she said, then asked the others why this young woman, five foot five with longish legs and a pretty face topped with lovely long hair, was so hard to understand? An analyst would probe, trying to get to what made her tick, sighing at the occasional evasive answer filled in with silence.

For nobody who knew her really knew her well enough to know the answer.

"Then came the surprise move to the leadership of the Church of New Moderation. Certainly, Joe Sideley had seen something in her, for he had been adamant about her taking over his role."

"How do you know that?" Ernest asked, annoyed at his wife's perception but wanting to find out more.

Sara replied that she did not know. She had been friendly with the founder of their church but not to the extent of him confiding in her.

"It's reason and conjecture, Ern. All I know for sure is that in her new position she was a caterpillar turned butterfly. She was suddenly all energy, all direction, all purpose."

And it worked, for the membership shot up. New churches sprang up like maple saplings in a sunlit forest. Within a year of her taking over, the New Moderation Church was on everyone's lips.

"One curiosity to note about Tammy was that the more settled in her position, the less her right side seemed to trouble her. Ern, have you seen her arm brace on in the last couple of years?"

"Can't say I have," Ern replied. To him, this was one observation too far; if he had had time to do the research, he would be centre stage right now. He hears Sara's analysis continuing but did not take in the words. Old Ma Silver did listen and made her own summing up statement.

Yet for all that purpose, all that direction, she would seem to have remained stubbornly elusive as to what she really wanted to achieve."

It was a hidden purpose; a journey that existed for others merely because it was a journey. The destination did not matter.

What mattered was that she gave a quiet reception to all those who opened their hearts to her.

"Exactly," replied Sara, "much like Jesus would have been when he was upon the earth."

While she became more outward looking, nobody got substantially closer; nobody could really claim to know her.

"Fascinating," Old Ma Silver said at the end of Sara's description of Tammy Shroton, Life President of the Church of the New Moderation, the position her husband had expected.

And desperately wanted.

Sara had more insight to come. They moved on to Fi D'Alianti. Again Sara was able to give a concise and profound character assessment, if anything even more perceptive than her words on Tammy for Fi was easier to read.

Everything with Fi was concrete. Except when she was drinking. Most of the time she dealt with hard facts; numbers, returns, margins, jobs, board meetings, resignations. Then, several times a day, for her days were long and lonely, she wondered why she was who she was. Then she would have a drink and another and another. She had a simple dream.

"She wants to be loved. And not for her money but for who she is."

She yearned to be held in a way that only a lover can hold. Every man she met she weighed up. Could they be the right one? Sure, she gave credits for prospects, for looks, for humour and a host of other categories, but the chief question was always – will he hold me the way I want to be held? It was like an addiction in reverse, this need to be held in a particular way.

"I heard that her mother asked her once whether she was gay. It was a fashionable question at the time amongst the unmarried, the uncommitted." She had answered truthfully in the negative, but it left an unpleasant element in her life, a filter with which she imagined everyone saw her. Did they not come forward and hold her because they thought she was gay?

But then the concrete world would slam back in. If that was the case, she would have been approached by a girl wanting to hold her just as tightly as a man. And that had not happened, ever.

"Fi D'Alianti dreams of a man who will hold her and love her; it's what is missing in an otherwise wonderful world."

"How do you know all this, dear?" Ernest broke in, as if bursting the balloon. His wife had gone too far with conjecture; she barely knew Miss D'Alianti.

"Simple, Ern. I talk with Tammy. She's real enamoured with Fi, talks about her a lot." She could have advised her husband to listen more and pronounce less, but that would have been disloyal, especially in front of another.

Old Ma Silver refilled the Martini glasses and asked if, in return, they would like to know something of her friend, Sophie LaNeve, newly appointed Director of Defence against the takeover bid.

She painted a picture that was beautiful and sad. Sophie wore her rage and many other emotions on the outside, like a garment that had been turned inside out in the wash. But that was a little misleading in two ways. First, she was almost all emotion, so substantially the whole of her was on display to passers-by. Second, even that is misleading, for she had a fine intellect and that was firmly locked inside its chamber. Her anger against Father Barrow was obvious for all to see, yet no-one except her friend, Mia, and, presumably, her confessor knew why.

"She's got a wild imagination. I fully expect Father Barrow has suffered a painful death several times over with more torture and agony planned. Yet I sense the plans are vague and I've no doubt that Sophie is a good person at heart, only hating when there is good cause. That puzzles me a lot because Father Barrow is, in my opinion, a good person too. What on earth has the young priest done to deserve such hatred? Moreover, there is an attraction between the two that I am struggling to fathom. I turn to you as the expert, Sara Justice."

Sara laughed while Ernest scowled. Then Sara said one final thing before Old Ma Silver went to fetch the supper from the kitchen.

"Love and hate live on the same street, often sharing the same apartment, you know."

Testing Times

This time Humphrey chose the restaurant and Father LaPetite was not happy.

"There are 50,000 restaurants or more in this delightful city and you have to bring me here?"

"It was the first place I thought of when we arranged to meet. I agree it is not up to much." The waiter scratched his face and neck as he stood at the doorway, trying to entice customers in. Flies ignored the sticky death traps hanging from the ceilings, preferring to feast like paying customers. There was an air of gloom, matched by an odour of multiple layers. Humphrey's keen nose could pick up grease, sweat, oil and tomatoes overlaid with a layer of cheap disinfectant; he imagined a quick wipe around with a heavy cloth once a day.

"Look, the table is uneven!" LaPetite put his vast weight down hard to demonstrate. The pine boards cracked but did not break cleanly, so that one side sagged down like the slope of a beach. But there was no sea lapping at the edge, just the tassels of a dirty, luminous green tablecloth.

There were few other customers; an old man with a pipe and a glass of something that matched the tablecloths, and a fat couple arguing with the second waiter over their bill.

"I need to talk to you, Bernard." Humphrey spoke quietly as if concerned the waiters would overhear his confession or whatever it was he had to reveal. He naturally shifted the emphasis of LaPetite's first name to the second syllable, giving it an immediate continental sound. "Can't we just put up with it for once? I have a lot on my mind."

"Very well. Waiter, over here if you please." The waiter whose job it was to entice new custom left his post and came over with a shuffle, as if he had learned only a strange way of walking as a boy; one large step forwards, two small to the side and one tiny one back. There was a four-beat rhythm to his walk so the stresses on the steps seemed like the beat of the blues as he crossed the room from eight empty tables away.

"Signor?" was all he said.

LaPetite took charge. "No, don't worry about bringing out the menu, my man. Bring us two of the best dishes your chef can produce. If we like it, which I doubt will be the case, we will give a handsome tip. Oh, and a bottle of your best red."

"Si, signor." One-two-shuffle-three-shuffle-four.

"Faster, Papa!" called the other waiter. As Humphrey turned, he saw that he was the same model, just 25 years newer.

"I'm coming, I'm coming." Even their voices were identical other than the effects of an extra quarter century of smoking.

Father-waiter and son-waiter disappeared through two wooden slatted swing doors, quite possibly left over from filming yet another spaghetti western and sold on to be a real door in a real bar in the capital.

The wine appeared just as LaPetite was losing patience. In the meantime, a couple came in and thumbed coins into the jukebox. Rock and roll roared out. Humphrey, hoping to have a discussion with his new friend, rose from his place and went across to ask them to turn down the volume. He was told that the volume control was broken, the sound jammed at one level, which happened to be loud.

The evening seemed to be a disaster. But then the younger waiter came out from the kitchen, no shuffle to his stride. He shouted something in furiously fast Italian and the rockers left in a hurry.

The old waiter did everything wrong with the wine. He wiped his dirty apron on the neck of the bottle, teasing the cork out with his teeth, then forgot to offer a taste first to LaPetite.

But the wine was exquisite. The flavours were like all the seasons rolled into one. Each mouthful was a sensation of taste, slightly different each sip, as if the wine was playing a game of 'guess who I am' with them.

"What is this wine?" Humphrey asked as the waiter returned with two plates of spaghetti bolognaise.

"You only get this wine here." The waiter snatched away the bottle before LaPetite could remove the dirty napkin wrapped around it. "You want some more?"

The next bottle had the label removed, scratched through with dirty fingernails. It was good marketing.

"Bon appetite," said Bernard.

"Down the hatch," said Humphrey, taking a swig of wine before daring to tackle the grimy plate.

The meal was a superb match for the wine and held both of them in concentrated silence as they ate. The beef was melt-like tender, with a sauce you could bottle and market for millions. The spaghetti was perfectly cooked, neither too soft nor too hard.

"Just like a woman's body," said Humphrey, a little drunk from his share of two bottles.

"How would you know?"

And that brought Humphrey back to reality. He remembered the reason he had asked LaPetite to dine with him.

"LaPetite," he said, either forgetting they were on first name terms, or reverting to surnames as a curious indication of familiarity known only to the British. "I have a problem I need to tell you about."

"Not now, Barrow." He returned the compliment of surnames only, despite not being British.

"What? Why?"

"You've had too much to drink. Let's get some coffee and move to an outside table to get some air. This is an excellent find for a restaurant. It's grubby, filthy, unattended, rundown but with excellent food and wine. A real treasure!"

They ordered the strongest coffee available – thick, sweetened espresso. "Keep them coming please, waiter. We'll sit outside now, if we may."

Outside was as bare of customers as inside – just a small family, parents drinking wine, two young girls in bright red identical dresses and matching red ribbons eating pastries and drinking some amber liquid, placing their straws in each other's glasses until one toppled over. They squabbled over who was to blame, then shared the remaining glass, forgetting their disagreement amidst their hopeless giggles.

After the third espresso, LaPetite prompted Humphrey to restart the conversation.

"It's Sophie LaNeve."

"I knew it would be. What exactly is wrong?"

"Several things really." Humphrey went on to describe her extreme efficiency, her anger and her coldness; the way she held herself with polite, faultless insolence or arrogance or whatever it was.

"There is something else, am I not correct my friend?"

It took a while for Humphrey to admit that he was totally drawn to her in a way no priest with the vow of celibacy like a cross on his back should ever be.

"I can't stand it!" he suddenly cried. They had moved on to a thick, dark drink that the father-waiter had brought out without being asked to. "She is the devil incarnate. She torments me so!"

LaPetite let his new friend go on for several minutes, leaning his bulk back on the chair, tipping it dangerously but adeptly, as if he had invented a new sport and was the first champion of it. His friend puzzled him. He decided to break the rules to help him.

"I slept with someone once," he lied. He had never felt the slightest need to do so but excused the invention as meaning well for Humphrey.

"You broke your vow?"

"It was a long time ago," said as if time made all things better. Perhaps it does.

A large number of partygoers passed by in a straggled bunch, making conversation difficult for a few minutes. It gave Humphrey time to think, to let the numbing churn that was his mind settle a little.

"We need to get back. It's late and we have an early meeting if you remember," Humphrey said, draining the last of his third nightcap.

Bernard paid with a generous tip that brought the first smile to the waiter's face that evening. Another neat marketing trick, LaPetite thought.

"Come again, Fathers" he said.

"We will do," they both mumbled in unison. "We will do," LaPetite said again.

"We're going to suffer for this in the morning," Humphrey slurred as they stood up.

"Too right," was the reply.

Humphrey's alarm went at 6 a.m. He shoved it on snooze, knocking the clock over the side of the bed so it buzzed like a bee stuck on its back on the floor. He slept on until there was a gentle knock on the door.

"Father Barrow?" Ellsworthy called, then turned the handle and entered. "My goodness, what a state you are in. Been partying?"

Humphrey was still in his clothes from the night before.

"What time is it?" A demolition ball swung at his temple with each word he spoke – a perfect rhythm.

"A quarter to eight. You're late for the 7:30. I said I would come and look for you."

"Father LaPetite? Is he there at the meeting?"

"He was the first in this morning, bright as a button. Is that who you were out with last night?"

Humphrey could only nod, even gentle shaking from side-to-side caused pain, a hundred hammer blows inside the head.

"I'll be along in a minute. Give them my apologies and say my alarm clock let me down." As if to prove his point, his left foot swung at the alarm clock on the floor, causing it to slide across the wooden floorboards until it hit a rug and stopped, circling briefly like a spinning top nearing the end of its run.

He had a shower, drank several pints of water and got dressed in clean clothes. Head swimming through treacle, unable to cope with changes of altitude, he carefully made his way down the stairs, across the courtyard where the fresh wind tried to blow his staleness away but failed. He then entered the rose garden; tired blooms on tired stems. He stopped and took in a few more lungfuls of air, thoughts of the paracetamol he had left in his bedroom. He could not go back now, was already too late.

"Dear fellow, would you like some paracetamol?" Bernard blocked the doorway with his huge bulk. All Humphrey saw was someone full of joy when he should have been miserable. "You look like you need them!"

The first person he saw on entering the meeting room was Sophie. More correctly he saw her long legs. She was sitting back from the table with her legs crossed, talking to a colleague. She turned as he entered, unable for a moment to hide her surprise at how he looked.

Then she turned back again to her previous conversation. It seemed to Humphrey that it was a deliberate spurning but then his head was saturated with last night and he found it hard to think clearly.

"Good morning, Sophie," he said as he passed behind her to take his place at the table.

"Oh, hello Father Barrow, after the meeting we need to discuss a few things." She no longer used the 'Father' Humphrey had requested. Her voice was level and calm, almost flat, as if she cared not one bit for the person who was behind the clerical clothing he wore. Then she turned back to Father Ellsworthy and her voice lifted decidedly.

The meeting was long, breaking Father LaPetite's rule of no meeting outlasting its usefulness, which he placed at forty minutes. It wound on until, for different reasons, both Humphrey and LaPetite could take no more.

"Meeting over." Humphrey stood faster than his blood could move, felt the sway as his head hit iron-rimmed clouds. "We'll reconvene tomorrow. Has everyone got his or her tasks? Good." He was halfway to the washroom, talking back over his shoulder, then struck the open door with the left side of his body. It propelled him around so that he was facing the table again. For half a moment, his gaze froze on Sophie's disdain, feeling it penetrate into his body like a rapier. Then he righted his direction and moved out of the room.

When he finished in the washroom, he went directly to his office, hoping to avoid everyone.

He thought he had made it as he closed the office door and walked across the room, only to find that his office chair swung around revealing Sophie sprawled across it, both legs over one armrest. She reminded him of a raffle prize, waiting to be taken home by the lucky winner.

"I was waiting for you," she said, as flat as ever. "We have the latest opinion polls to discuss."

Hangovers work in different ways, much like the original inebriation. But they almost always whittle away the veneer we wrap ourselves in. Call it politeness or civilisation or good manners, hangovers know nothing of these trite, compact words. They know only pounding and dry throats, rising sickness and wobbly legs.

Hangovers don't know how to behave. But they speak the truth.

"What are you doing in my chair?" Was he slurring? Did he sound like one of the Three Bears, making a petty claim on an article of furniture?

Could anything be his when he had taken a solemn vow against property?

Sophie, by contrast, was all business. She rose from the chair, presented a file of tiny spiderlike figures for his examination. "These are the opinion poll results correlated with those Catholics leaving for New Moderation, showing a trend of growing relevance to our defence," she said, wondering if she really knew what she was talking about.

She was all business, except for her legs.

"What are you staring at?" she asked, stepping backwards into the chair as if his stare was an approach to her. Then she sat again, needing something solid and reassuring.

"Nothing, nothing at all," he lied.

Sophie was angry but also confused. The priest in front of her was a monster. She had the evidence in her cubbyhole at home. Yet he was the most attractive man she had ever met. And she knew that the desire was mutual. Suddenly, that desire flung revulsion out of the long window that looked over the rose garden, tidily tended by the two old men. They never noticed the bundle of hate that rolled between the rose beds and came to a halt by the sundial. Perhaps one of them, towards the end of the day, would stoop down and scoop up the hate-ball, placing it in their wheelbarrow and then to the compost bins.

Or the bonfire.

But the priest indoors saw none of this, whether it happened or was imagined. For Humphrey Barrow SJ could not take his eyes from the long legs of his secretary turned sub-leader of the campaign to save the Roman Catholic Church.

Very slowly he raised his hand to her cheek, stepping forward to meet her. The first touch of her skin blew his hangover away. It sent electricity up his arm, into his shoulder, down his back; a shuddering jolt he would never forget.

It was as if he had been asleep, waiting all his life until this moment.

"I…"

"Don't talk," she said. "There are no words."

But there were words. Or rather there had been words: a vow given long ago. And there would be words in the confessional for both of them afterwards. Those words, some from the past, others from the future, tumbled into the present, just as she closed her eyes in anticipation.

They built a wall; or rather they formed the shutters in a window that looked out onto her. And as she opened her eyes again, she knew that the moment had gone.

"You forget yourself, Father Barrow." She regained her composure first, such that he seemed the more forward of the two. It was a neat trick in aggressive behaviour, claiming effrontery where none belonged. Afterwards, running it back through his mind multiple times, he swore that she had met him more than halfway.

At least for a moment before their religion had regained them.

Sophie was desperate for the seclusion of her hideaway. She stopped at the delicatessen in the next street and bought two pasta seafood suppers, piping hot.

"Early supper," she called on entering her house. A moment later, one purchased supper was on a tray, delivered with a kiss on the cheek to her father in his bedroom.

The other went cold in the kitchen. Nibbled by the neighbour's cat, it lay there until the housekeeper found it in the morning. She wrapped it in greaseproof paper and took it home for her lunch.

Sophie had gone directly to her cubbyhole. She poured herself a large glass of red wine, using one of the glasses she always meant to take down to the kitchen and wash, but never did remember. As she poured the wine, her hands shook, knocking red splashes onto her white skirt.

"Damnation," she said, thinking it would never come out.

She sat for a long time, talking occasionally to the water pipes, more to answer their questions than to precipitate her own conversation.

"Yes, he did approach me. I think he wanted his way with me." Later on, much later, she said, "I don't know what to think about him. He is such a bastard, such a misogynist. Yet I feel…," She did not finish.

Much later still, as she remembered her locking-up duties and the need to check her invalid father, honesty shone from the reading light as if illuminating an ancient and profound text on the wall of a tomb.

"I like him a lot but also I hate him."

Progress Report

Sidney checked his phone yet again, checked the wireless links to the projector. It was important that the meeting went well.

He ran through the presentation one more time in his mind. He had started with the background to the bid, running through membership numbers and objectives. Then into the tactics like fly fishers determining what fly to use on a particular stretch of river. Then…

"Morning Sid," Fi was late, as usual. The other participants were all collected in the conference room; Tammy, Miles, Bill the driver for some reason, and even Al Faraday all the way from New York overnight. "Well, are we ready or shall we pass the time of day first?"

"No, let's start." Sidney stood up, fumbled his phone but caught it mid-air like the village cricketer he had become; anything that marked him as English. "What we are going to do today is…"

"Hang on!"

"Sorry Fi, is there a problem?"

"Nothing that can't be solved." That should have been Fi's catchphrase, indicating the positivity that pumped through her veins. "I just need coffee."

Sidney scrambled for the coffee machine in the corner but was beaten there by Bill. "I'll do it," he said loudly, "need to add tranquilisers to get some peace around here."

"I heard that!"

"You were meant to hear it."

But the remarkable thing to the others was not the banter between Fi and Bill but the rays of happiness that shone from both of them, like beacons placed too close on adjacent hills so that their flooding lights met and merged, forming one brilliant sprawl of yellow.

And a mass of deepest shadow where the merged lights did not reach.

It made Miles want to hold Tammy's hand. And Tammy knew this. First, she looked at the floor, as if dealing with forbidden fruit, then stretched her arm out under the table and clasped his hand, matching fingers to fingers, thumb to thumb; a dance routine she had picked up somewhere perhaps in her mysterious past.

"Okay, shall we get started?" Sidney asked.

"Of course, otherwise we'll be here all day," Fi replied, forgetting, or not caring, that she was the only cause of lateness that morning.

"First, let me welcome Al Faraday to our little outpost of the D'Alianti Empire." It was an empire built not on kingdoms, sea-lanes or mighty armies, but on laptops, contacts and phone conversations in the middle of the night.

"We're still a way off parity," Sidney introduced the membership numbers, "but we are heading in the right direction."

"What are the numbers?" Al asked, ready to jot something down, any action to keep the jetlag at bay.

"You need to look at the trend. Last month, before the takeover bid started we had just over 385,000 members compared to over 1.4 billion Catholics."

"A drop in the ocean."

"Yes, but the next graph," Sidney added, clicking on his phone to move the slides on, "shows the trend." He clicked five times, each click adding a week's worth of membership data since the takeover had been launched.

"We hit a million in week two, actually ended the week at 1.2 million. Then it rose to two million the following week, over 4 million when we made our case to the monopolies and mergers commission." He paused before the final click, aware that only Fi knew the latest numbers. "Ladies and gentlemen, I can now reveal that the huge gap is narrowing impressively. As of yesterday, the Church of New Moderation had 12.2 million members."

"And the Catholics? What were they at?" Fi asked, although she already knew the numbers.

"Well, we don't have membership records for them, but the latest opinion polls show two interesting facts. First, 4.6% of previously declared members are disinclined to count themselves as members any longer." This provoked several minutes of debate about trends, cause and effect. Sidney was ready for each twist of the discussion so that Fi started thinking of him as the Information Man.

"And the second fact?" Fi asked.

"Well, we have the support of 7.3% of declared members for our changes. Ladies and gentlemen, our takeover bid is on track!"

The meeting moved on to tactics.

'I want to build momentum," Fi said. "We need ideas please." This produced competing voices amongst the small meeting. Ideas included regional delegations, opening a Latin American office, social media advertising and a series of online pamphlets arguing their case. But it was Bill who came up with the idea that took hold of everyone's imagination.

"A live debate," he said, as if it were just one more idea swimming with the shoal.

"What did you say?" Fi demanded, silencing the others. There was a three-second pause as everyone sought the source, turning to look at Bill. They also recorded its value in that three-second gap of time. Again, Sidney was on the ball, cursing himself for not having a slide to match.

"Brilliant idea. We must hold a live debate." Then there was no silence anymore, nor could there be with so much to talk about. It was the end of the planned meeting; the end of the way Sidney had seen it going as he made his careful arrangements. There could be no preparation for an idea as inspired as this. It simply took off, like a great big mythical bird, circling the conference room before breaking out into the world beyond.

Tammy squeezed Miles' hand. Then they both realised that they had been holding hands, under the table, throughout the whole meeting. They gave each other a knowing but not knowing look before shyness took over. Their hands unclasped and returned to their bodies by jerky movements that they desperately wanted to look natural. Tammy's hand ended on her lap, folded into her other hand as if the one was a mother, the other a wayward daughter. Miles' hand went to the table-top where it worked its passage with increasing animation.

Most of this was hidden from the other participants who saw, but did not really take in, flushes on both their faces. Only Bill had the angle from his chair to see most of it. He smiled, then looked in wonder at his own lover facing him across the table.

The meeting had been scheduled to last no more than 50 minutes. They had a hectic day ahead with press conferences, meetings and even a demonstration to attend. They should have been out of the office by 10:50 a.m. But this did not happen. Instead, hassled secretaries called hassled secretaries across the Square Mile and into the Docklands where the press offices were established. It was a rolling re-scheduling; first just the press conferences were delayed an hour, then cancelled until the next day. Finally, the whole day's meetings were postponed as Bill's idea took shape.

Normally, Fi would break it up into subsequent meetings, delegating hurried tasks before the next gathering. But Fi's modus operandi was set aside this time. It was like watching a great artist at work; nobody wanted to destroy the creative process with commonalities like other meetings or the need to eat. The assistants coped by silently placing food, coffee and water at each place, then removing and replenishing but never breaking the concentration.

"Ciao, ufficio di Padre Barrow,"The rich Italian voice with its beautiful intonation came across the speaker. It was not Sophie, for she was too senior now to answer the phone.

"Do you speak English? Can I speak to Father Barrow?"

"Of course I speak English. Who is talking please?"

"This is Fi D'Alianti."

"An Italian name," the receptionist commented. "My grandmother was a D'Alianti."

"Perhaps we are related."

"Si, one moment please." They had not expected to get through so easily.

But the next voice was also female. "Hello, my name is Signorina LaNeve. I am the Director of Defence Strategy. How can I help you?" Her voice was guarded but young; a first date tone to it.

Fi wanted to reply 'by putting me through to the guy in charge' but did not, even though the words were forming into the correct order; wadding, powder, shot.

"Signorina LaNeve, it is a pleasure to speak to you. My name is Fi D'Alianti." The introductions took a few moments; they were a formality, as each knew exactly who the other was.

"I accept your kind invitation," Sophie said.

"Excuse me, signorina. Don't you want to discuss it first with Father Barrow?" Fi said, thinking practically. She did not want a false start, especially if they kicked off the publicity and then had to withdraw.

"Father Barrow leaves such decisions to me." Her tone changed, quivering from the excitement of the situation.

For Sophie saw it as the perfect way to teach her boss a serious lesson.

The practical details were resolved in outline and contact details were exchanged so the plans could be quickly finalised.

"We envisage a head-to-head debate the week after next," Fi said.

"Perfect," replied Sophie; head-to-head was just what she needed to ensure his humiliation. He would be a lamb to the lions or tigers or wherever the lambs got sent for a bad time.

"We can handle the publicity and the arrangements our end," Fi added. Sophie agreed. She did not care if they manipulated the event in their favour. All that mattered was revenge for Sister Mary John.

Then, perhaps, she could get the arrogant priest out of her head.

"Did you say Father Burrow?" Tammy asked when the call was over. "A Jesuit?"

"Yes, I believe he is, but the name is Barrow. Why, do you know him?"

"No, just someone with a similar name," Tammy replied. There is no way the person she had known would now be so senior as to run the defence against the takeover. Besides, it was a different name.

Sophie now had a moment of reckoning.

"You did what?" Humphrey demanded.

"I agreed to a debate in London the week after next."

"But without consulting me first?"

"You left me in charge while you met that fat American. Besides, I'm your Director of Defence Strategy. This is the sort of thing you are paying me to organise."

"But I am no debater. They will make mincemeat of me."

Bring it on, thought Sophie, bring it on. She thought it but did not say it. Instead she turned a corner on the conversation by asking how the meeting had gone with the fat American. Ernest Justice was not particularly fat; it was just that stick-thin Sophie associated Americans with obesity.

"Very well indeed," Humphrey replied, forgetting the debate temporarily in his excitement. "Do you know, for instance, that Tammy Shroton is not her real name?"

"What is it then?"

"We don't know. Mr Justice hired a private investigator but he only got a preliminary report at the time he flew over to meet with us. He is staying with Old Ma Silver, I mean Signora…"

"I know who Old Ma Silver is, Father Barrow."

"Of course, of course." Humphrey looked like a little boy who had won a race against the odds only to find his parents were distracted and had missed the whole thing.

"Tell me more," she relented.

"She has some sort of past but went through a name change, almost like a cleansing process. His detective is researching it more at the moment."

"She's a criminal! Either a drug runner or a murderer!" Sophie's imagination ran to the next street and back. "Perhaps she is on the witness protection scheme. Perhaps she gave evidence against a gang of crooks."

"Well, the sooner we know, the sooner we can expose her. It will help our defence no end."

"Bring it on, bring it on!" Sophie said the words, not quite sure what she was urging for. Or whether she was urging at all.

The Trigger of Revenge

The phone rang relentlessly in Sophie's office. She now had six people answering for her, three in the wide corridor outside her office, three stuffed into the tiny room across the way that she had once occupied. Humphrey had drafted in trainee priests to man the phones and Sophie enjoyed having men report to her.

It was a furiously busy time preparing for the Great Debate, as the media had termed it.

It took seven attempts and half an hour of Mia's time to get through to Sophie. While waiting, she calculated that she had wasted 200 euros of billable time.

"Sophie, it's Mia here. You didn't turn up last night." They had an arrangement to go dancing again.

"Mia, I'm so sorry. I completely forgot! It has been crazy here."

"I'll forgive you this once, on one condition."

"Being?"

"We meet tonight, 9:00 p.m. sharp. And you are all mine until morning!"

"That's two conditions rolled into one," Sophie declared. But she readily agreed. She enjoyed Mia's company but also had another motive.

And, being how she was, she came straight out with it as they sat beneath an awning overlooking a small square, eating and drinking. Later they would go inside to dance.

"Mia, can you get me back into the computer records?" she asked, only a glug and a sip into her wine.

"Why? You have everything that was there."

Sophie explained about the printer and Sophie agreed she would help her friend on Sunday, the day before they went to London for the debate.

"And the quietest day of the week, obviously!" she added.

After Mass on Sunday, there was just a handful of people in the office. Sophie greeted them individually, mentioning casually that she was doing some last-minute research with a colleague unknown to them, before flying out the next day.

Sophie had become too senior over the last few weeks for anyone to remind her that all people entering campaign headquarters had to be vetted by security. Surely, they justified to themselves, a director would not forget such an elementary precaution?

One young trainee priest raised an eyebrow. He remembered the security briefing he had been given on starting on the phones a few days earlier. Sophie noticed and responded with a withering demand for hot, strong coffee immediately.

"And chocolate biscuits too." Breaking into the computer system made for hungry and thirsty work.

Sophie read through her private notes while Mia tapped her way into the records, cleverly eliminating the need for passwords. It was a long time to wait while November rains sent drops hurtling onto the French windows and the wind whispered amongst the rose bushes and rhododendrons beyond. Sophie read her private notes through twice; they were good but lacked something.

Something she hoped to find in the computer.

She now had her own new printer sitting on its own table beside her big new desk.

Mia barely stirred, just her fingers scratching over the keyboard as if they were responsible for Barrow's fate; the faster they moved, the greater his comeuppance. Sophie shifted constantly in her chair. She read her private notes again, then the public briefing designed to aid Humphrey in his debate. The public briefing was helpful, bland, unexciting. They established Father Barrow as an ordinary, decent man, arguing his case with a modicum, just a modicum, of passion.

But just wait until the private notes were leaked and the story of Sister Mary John was all across the newspapers on the day of the debate. She relished the complete downfall it would bring, the chaos, the humiliation, the justice of a bad man brought down, even if he was exceedingly handsome.

Her type for sure.

But to do that she needed one more thing. She needed the outcome of the extraordinary mission the newly-ordained priest had been sent on nine years earlier. And the worse it had been for Sister Mary John at the time, the worse it would be now for Humphrey Barrow SJ.

"Have you got in?" Sophie could not wait any longer.

"Yes and no." Why did Mia always talk in riddles? It gave her friend a mysterious superiority that Sophie resented.

But nobody is perfect and Mia was her best friend.

"What do you mean by that?" Sophie rose and went to the French windows. She opened one, hoping to be soaked by the enormous drops of rain that hit the panes with the dull thud of a muted bass drum. But even this was an illusion, for as she cranked open the window, turning an old brass handle to do so, the rain stopped and the sun sent down a ray to spotlight her office in a golden glow. Perhaps it was a sign that God approved of her plans.

"Come and sit down and I'll show you."

Sophie cranked the window closed again and returned to sit, overlooking the screen of the computer.

"I got straight in…"

"Good."

"Listen and don't talk. I got straight in as I said. But the documents are no longer there."

The rain started again. It had been a magical moment in November when the sun made the fallen leaves glow with pride, with the glory of God. Now it was over; the world returned to relentless rain and wind to throw those sodden leaves in every direction like a selfish person rummaging carelessly through someone else's belongings.

Would Sophie have to go to the debate in London without her private notes? Would she have to rely on the bland alternative? Would she actually have to support Barrow and his nasty ways?

"Someone has moved both the documents to the new computer system."

"So, we are sunk?"

"Far from it!" Mia replied, unable to hide her grin. "Because I have only got you into the new system!"

"What?"

"It's true, really true." Mia sounded like a small girl having to emphasise the worth of her story. "I had a flash of inspiration and guessed the preliminary access password and I was spot on!"

They did a loving, laughing dance. The noise spilled over to the trainee priests working overtime in the corridor. The one with the rising eyebrows looked especially quizzical.

"They've probably found a great argument for the debate," another said to calm his colleague, to keep him from disturbing their tedious work. "It's good sometimes to have a dose of exuberance in the work of the Lord."

"There's only one problem," Mia said as they fell back into their chairs, improvised dance over. "I said preliminary access. You need to set a password now and then wait up to 48 hours to get complete access."

"Oh, will it be in time for the debate?" The debate was set for prime- time on Tuesday evening.

"That's just over 48 hours so it should be fine. But you can keep checking it because it says up to 48 hours. Now, what password do you want? It should include capitals and numbers."

"SisterMaryJohn2025," Sophie said immediately. Let the victim be the trigger of revenge.

The End and the Means

Sara knew it was not for her, but she went along with it anyway. It was easier, she had discovered over the 34 years they had been together, for her to pretend it was give and take.

The reality was that Ernest did everything for himself. He always had done and he always would.

"Let's extend our trip," he said a week into their time in Rome.

"I've always wanted to go to Greece," she replied. It was always worth trying.

"I had London in mind."

They went first class to London. There they spent two days pretending to splash around the city seeing the sites from their base at Claridge's.

"I've booked you on a tour tomorrow." He surprised her as they sat at dinner in the most expensive restaurant Ernest could find. He had a charge card from the Church of New Moderation.

Except it was not really a surprise, for she knew him so well. Just as she could close her eyes and see the veins on his neck pulsate like a frog, so she knew his antics, his tactics and his methods.

"Where to?"

"To Shakespeare country." It was a good choice. "I booked you on a tour bus with a bunch of Americans." Perhaps she would make friends to alleviate her loneliness.

But she did not have to concern herself with that. Her loneliness was worse when she was with him, better when she was alone.

"You're leaving at 6:00 a.m. so better get your beauty sleep!" He would have all day to do whatever they had come to London for.

And Ernest thought he would need all day. He saw Sara onto her bus at 5.45 a.m. the next morning, dutifully asked for a souvenir if she had time, waved until the bus, mercifully, turned a quick corner onto Regent Street and was gone from sight. Then he took on long strides, like a man of action; hands by his side, hovering close to his imaginary holsters.

Once, years ago as a young man, his firm had sent a group of them to a long weekend on a Western ranch. It was the early days of bonding. They split into two teams, with each team's objective to catch the flag of the other.

"The team on my right are the cowboys while the left team are the Indians," the instructor had declared. Ernest was to his left, allocated to the Indian camp. He had wanted to be a cowboy, to whoop and slap his thighs like the others.

And the cowboys won easily, snatching the Indian flag from under the nose of Ernest while he had his eyes fixed on the horizon.

It had been a humiliating weekend and one that had lived in the collective memory of the firm for years afterwards, brought up at social functions, elaborated slightly with each telling.

When Ernest became a partner in the firm, he had volunteered to run the junior staff development and immediately stopped the ranch visits. Instead, they had walked the trail ways of Virginia and Tennessee, camping out in huts along the way while white water rafting on the rivers that rushed through. The competition in the activities he chose were the elements; nothing human to risk humiliation.

Sheriff Justice moved through pre-dawn London. At first, he strode, then realised he was far too early. He bought coffee and a doughnut and sat in a tiny churchyard, after wiping the sodden leaves from a bench. Two rough sleepers came to him, dog-like eyes on his doughnut. He refused them at first, stuffed the doughnut into his mouth so as to remove temptation. Then he told them to wait where they were, but they were going nowhere; the churchyard was their home.

Ernest returned with a box of doughnuts and two grandee coffees.

"Got any cash?" asked the older one, but not aggressively, more like he expected the answer to be a lie, the usual lie.

"Let me see," replied Ernest. "I've only got notes." He hesitated only a second before handing a twenty to each of them.

When he looked back, sipping his now lukewarm coffee, he saw two untidy heads bent low over a box of doughnuts. He felt like he had entered their world for a moment, was now firmly out of it again.

He found the offices of D'Alianti at 7:40 a.m., walked around the block three times slowly and rang the bell at one-minute past eight.

"D'Alianti, how can I help?" The intercom made the voice come in fits and starts, exaggerating the slight foreign accent.

"My name is Ernest Justice. I'm a director of the Church of New Moderation and I would like to see Miss D'Alianti."

There was no problem hearing the other way around. The door opened with a buzz and a click and Ernest was told to make his way to the fourth floor.

"Mr Justice, my name is Sidney Franco. I'm the manager of the London office of D'Alianti." They shook hands, circling like rival stags before the herd, eyes fixed on each other.

"Pleased to meet you." Ernest's drawl went up the gangster scale several notches. "Is Miss D'Alianti in?" He looked beyond Sidney, as if the man was screening Fi from Ernest's vision.

"She's not here yet, not expected until nine when she has a meeting."

"I'll wait."

"Can you tell me what it is about? I might be able to help."

"How much do you know of the case?" Ernest asked, not wanting to pour out the details too early.

"I'm managing it, at least the commercial side."

"Really?"

"Yes, really." Then Sidney decided to make a special effort. He reasoned as follows, all within a tick and a tock of the second hand on the clock behind him: if he is from the New Moderation Church, neither Tammy nor Miles mentioned his visit so they must be unaware of it. This is a case of no news is bad news. Because this man did not inform Tammy of his arrival, he has to be undermining her in some way. Better I get it out of him and neutralise him if I can. That will make me look good and underwrite the success of the project.

A second later he asked Ernest if he would like coffee and a doughnut. "I'll send my secretary down for some doughnuts. She'll be here in a mo."

"Just coffee, thanks."

"Well, even I can manage that," Sidney joked, trying to lift the weight from the conversation, "thanks to modern machinery," he added, holding the conference room door open for his visitor.

It was almost two hours later that Bill drove Fi to the office. Tammy and Miles had elected to stay in the house and work on preparation for the debate. It was Monday morning, only thirty-six hours until Tammy would stand behind a podium and try and change the Catholic Church forever.

But it might have been ten minutes or ten years to Sidney, for he was riveted by Ernest's lawyerly tongue. Sidney asked all around the subject, hoping to see a way through, not finding one with promise. But he knew that he had to stay detached, had to make a judgment in a cool way. His responsibility was like a lead around his neck, yanking him backwards when he looked to be indiscreet.

"I tell you," Ernest was summing up now for the prosecution, leaning forward with thumbs hooked behind braces like he had seen on television, "she is poison, that one. She comes across all shy and coy but she is naked ambition personified." Sidney got the impression that the emphasis on the 'naked' was designed for effect, like the clever title of a popular play: 'The Naked Ambition' by Noel Coward, or some such thing.

"Can you explain…?"

"And another thing," Ernest ignored the interruption, "she has a past."

"We all have pasts, Mr Justice, just some are more exciting than others." No humour was offered, no humour accepted. They were not building a relationship, not even after one and three-quarter hours alone in the conference room. How long, Sidney wondered, until they understood each other? Or would they never?

"You'll have to explain yourself more clearly, English is not my native language." Sidney made one last effort, a big sacrifice to allude to his 'non-Englishness'.

"I can't say anything more. My lips are sealed other than to mention that we are investigating right now." His script might have been written by an ex-FBI agent turned screenwriter. "But we are convinced it is something murky, shadowy. We will pass on more as the information comes to us." Ernest had a working lifetime's experience of sounding pompous without giving much away.

Sidney's mind raced. Should he dismiss Ernest Justice as a crank or let Fi make that decision? What would she expect of him? His mind was a set of scales, balancing between caution and initiative. He raced back over his career, the failures and the successes. He had done better when initiative had been on the heavy side. Yet there was so much at stake here.

"Miss D'Alianti will be here in a moment. I've just got something to attend to." Caution had weighed in heavily this time.

Fi arrived at 10:25 a.m., late again. She popped her head around the door to Sidney's office.

"Hey Sid, what's up?"

"I've got someone I want you to meet," he said, rising as he spoke. He led her to the conference room where Ernest was studying framed photographs on the walls, each one a significant moment in the firm's history.

"Fi, can I introduce Ernest..."

"We've met before," Fi interrupted.

"Really?" Ernest turned. "I don't recall."

"At the Church of New Moderation in Roanoke." His expression remained blank. "I was visiting the area on business. Tammy Shroton introduced us after the service."

"I remember now," he lied. "It's great to see you again."

"What can we do for you, Ern?" Why, Sidney wondered, did Americans shorten every name at will, whereas the English would wait to be invited to use an abbreviation.

"Well it's Tam I wanted to talk to you about." Ernest looked at Sidney, wishing him gone, fancying his chances with Fi solo.

"Talk on then, Ern. Let me just grab some coffee." Then she turned to Sidney. "You better stay, this is your project."

It was late morning when Ernest Justice finally left. Fi had tactfully mentioned a prior arrangement for lunch in order to avoid an invitation from their visitor.

"Thanks, Ern, for taking the trouble to come and warn us about Tammy. It's real considerate of you to do so. We'll bear everything in mind, especially over the next few days as this deal comes to a conclusion."

"It's a pleasure," Ern replied, a little baffled. He had been expecting a fight to establish the truth. The calmness of Fi's response sent hackles rising along his backbone, erupting one after the other as the chain of volcanoes came to life.

"Give my warm regards to Sara," Fi said as an assistant came to guide him out. "Ask her if her roses are still in bloom."

"Sure, it's been a pleasure to meet you…again, I mean." He followed the assistant, feeling like a kindergartener where the class is told to walk in line. At any moment he expected the assistant to turn around, finger to lips, with a glare that said no talking in the corridor.

But when the assistant did talk, to wish him a great day, he was surprised to hear the homely tones of a fellow American.

"You live over here?" he heard himself ask.

"No, just visiting for the duration!" Al joked. "I'm Miss D'Alianti's personal assistant, based in New York. I just got in two weeks ago."

"So, you work with Fi all the time?"

"Yes, sir."

"I only have a slight acquaintance with her." Ernest seemed to want to talk. Al had learned to listen; it was the first lesson Fi had taught him. "I came to try and persuade her about Tammy Shroton, I mean about how corrupt she is." It was a last-ditch attempt at his objective. Perhaps this young man would report their conversation back to Fi. "She has a very shady past, certainly not presidential material."

"Did you succeed, sir?"

"No. I failed, I'm certain of that."

"Never mind, sir." Al sounded like a valet soothing his panicked gentleman, perhaps after some inadvisable words with a young lady.

But the inadvisable words were in the real world, not veiled behind a curtain of drink and exuberance. And Ernest Justice was not a young gentleman of leisure, but a sixty-eight-year old retired corporate lawyer who had made partner but never the top echelon of the firm.

"I should be president of the church." Somebody outside his body said those words, stealing the tones and quirks that made his voice. Surely there was a law against voice-theft?

"I wouldn't know, Sir. That is not my business. Can I call you a cab, sir? Where are you going? I see, yes it should be nice for a walk back to the hotel provided the weather holds." The valet from Manhattan opened the front door and ushered Ernest out. "In what way would you define failure today, sir?" The question was put so casually that Ernest answered it honestly.

"I don't think Fi or her sidekick believed a word I said about damn Tam Shroton."

"Do you believe it, sir?" It was a cheeky question for a valet. It might have resulted in a reprimand, only Al had the full measure of Ernest.

"No, I mean yes, I mean…"

"Perhaps just a touch of exaggeration was there?" Al dropped the cringing 'sir' and seemed to increase in height so that he looked down at Ernest.

"No, yes…I must be off." And Ernest was gone, taking his confusion with him.

"Why did you take him seriously?" Sidney blurted out as soon as the door closed behind Ernest. "I've had his ranting all morning."

"I take everything seriously," Fi replied. "I'm famished, let's go eat. Bill's downstairs. He said he would be back at 12:30 p.m."

Al stuck his head around the door, indicating he wanted a word with Fi.

"Come in, Al," she beckoned to an empty chair, "and tell us about it. What did you and Ern talk about? No, I have a better idea, come to lunch with us and we can discuss it then."

They ate at a Vietnamese restaurant, poked down a tiny, narrow street as if it had grown up with London, rather than arriving in a removal truck two-years earlier.

"What do you want to drink?" Bill asked.

"Water," said Fi.

"Water?" All three men stopped looking at their menus, raised their stares to her as if they were doctors in triplicate, puzzled by inexplicable symptoms.

"That's what I said." She then saw that she needed to give further explanation. "Gents, we are 32 hours away from crunch time. I never drink when close to a deal conclusion." But she convinced no-one, least of all Bill who had known her the shortest period but knew her the best.

"Bring the Seafood Delight for four, plenty of shrimps." Fi ordered for all.

"Prawns, she means prawns," Bill added on seeing the blank expression on the waiter's face.

"And four large waters, lots of ice."

"So, guys, we have a problem." Fi talked, sipped her water, wished momentarily it was something stronger. Then she looked at Bill and felt a flush on her face. "Our friend, Mr Ernest Justice, means trouble."

"In what way?" Bill asked.

"Okay, Bill, you weren't in the meeting this morning. But Ernest has some dirt on Tammy, something about her past. She apparently has not always been Tammy Shroton."

"And he plans to use it against her?"

"He wants her job. Need I say more?"

They paused a moment while the waiter brought out four plates of seafood in a spicy sauce, laid on a nest of rice, four large prawns looking over the edge of the plates like chicks about to fledge.

"This is delicious," said Fi with her mouth full.

Then Al reported his conversation with Ernest. "I don't doubt that he will act and will do so quickly."

"He has the advantage over us. He knows something we don't," Sidney added, placing a prawn into his mouth and sitting back in his chair.

"So, we find out what it is," Fi replied. "Al, what's the name of that private detective firm we used in the Biofuel Industries deal?"

"Huntington something and something. I'll get in touch straight after lunch."

So it was that James Mercer received a call at 8:56 a.m. in his DC office. He smiled as he replaced the receiver. The rushed investigation was no problem. The twelve-hour reporting deadline did not worry him. All he had to do was email a copy of the report he had just rushed by courier to Ernest Justice in Rome, care of a Signora Silversitrinni. He would wait until just before the deadline to make it look better – maybe with seconds to spare like the bomb ticking down in a spy movie. He did a little dance in his chair, wriggling to imaginary triumphant music, beating his chest like Tarzan of the Apes, for the quarter million-dollar fee was already making its way into his firm's bank account.

And what chance did Tammy have of retaining any secrets with two sets of people chasing after her life story?

More to the point, Fi wondered briefly before dismissing it as a business necessity, what would Tammy make of her digging and delving into her personal affairs?

"Needs must," she said to the walls of her temporary office in the London D'Alianti building, "the end justifies the means."

Race to Make Mischief

S ara had a wonderful day with Shakespeare. No expense was spared, courtesy of the New Moderation Church charge card. The tour guides, four of them, dressed as characters from the plays, peppered their talk with phrases written by the great bard over 400 years ago, long before America was America.

The bus did not head straight for Stratford as Sara had expected. Instead, they trundled through London streets to breakfast at The George, an inn that looked, so the tour guides said, remarkably like it did in Shakespearean times. Boys hustled with stage props, directed by men in various states of costume, while maids in long skirts and aprons brought small beer, meat, cheese and bread in sledgehammer chunks to the assembled patronage.

King Lear stood and said some words. "Ladies and gentlemen, we bring you The George, a hostelry that the great bard knew well. His plays were often performed here, as they are to this day. Eat well of our fare for we have a long journey ahead of us."

The long journey was not as it would have been in Shakespeare's time. They moved against the incoming traffic and hit the M40 motorway at speed, pulling into a large coach park in Stratford a little after ten that morning.

Sara had made friends with her fellow travellers. The tour guides had made sure of this, requiring everyone to stand in turn in the coach, facing whichever way gave them greatest exposure to the other passengers. Then they were required to give a short biography, but before each one could sit down the tour guides made gentle fun, linking it back to the Shakespearean bawdy humour that always got a laugh when the audience was determined to enjoy itself.

Sara made particular friends with a couple from Massachusetts. She was an English professor at Harvard while he was a television screenwriter, mildly famous for adaptations of Shakespeare. They were in their early 60s, like Sara, and took her into their arms, providing witty and insightful sub-commentary, far better than the banter from the front of the bus.

"I feel I'm quite the expert now!" Sara said as they exchanged phone numbers and email addresses, as the bus found itself back in the bustle of central London. "Thank you for making it such an enjoyable and educational day."

"We loved it every bit as much as you, Sara," the professor replied. "We loved showing off, always do!"

"There's Ernest, my husband. Would you like to meet him?"

"Sure," they chanted in unison.

But Ernest was not in a sociable mood, passing over the introductions as if he was running a long-distance race and could only pause a second for gulps of water, lest his lead slip.

"Pleased to meet you." He interrupted Sara halfway through an amusing story about one of the tour guides who had slipped and torn his long flowing robe, revealing bright pink boxer shorts underneath. "Sara, we've got to go."

"Where to, Ernest?"

"Rome, of course. There's a package waiting for me." He was guiding her back towards the hotel, so she had to say her goodbyes over her shoulder. "It's from the P.I. firm," he added, as if that explained everything. "I got a call saying it was delivered."

Tammy and Miles sought fresh air and the hope of inspiration. They had worked at home since early morning, preparing for the debate the next day, and now, as the tired sun flopped below the building line, they needed a change of scene.

They walked closely together but did not hold hands. Miles made a few movements, touching her elbow to guide her across the street but Tammy seemed too withdrawn, too within herself, to respond.

"Big day tomorrow," he said, trying to jog her along.

"Don't remind me. I'm nervous as anything." For some reason, Miles realised just then, Tammy never swore; indeed, she flinched when someone else indulged, as if each "cuss word" was a slap around the face to her.

They wandered aimlessly, making polite chat as subjects arose around them: a bus that blew thick dark smoke into the air, a child crying in a pushchair with the young nanny clearly uncertain what to do, pushing hard on the handles as if she could drive the stroller down into the pavement and away from her.

"This is a nice park," Tammy volunteered as they walked through Grosvenor Square. It was another attempt to fill the air between them with harmless nothings. Miles thought their politeness absurd and itched to break through and laugh and rollick and tease as lovers do.

"Tammy, I want to talk to you."

"Do you see the railings? They look like the ones in church."

"There are no railings in our church."

"I meant…it doesn't matter."

"Tell me, Tammy. I need to understand you."

"Me? Understand?" She turned to him; maybe he had, at long last, bridged the gap? His pulse rose, the heat causing a contrast with the damp world around them.

But then the damp got back in. "I'm just a regular small-town girl making her way in the world. Nothing more and nothing less, what you see is what you get!" The rambling clichés were a retreat; stone bulwarks to take cover behind.

He stopped under a tall tree that leaned gently into the park like an uncle watching nephews and nieces at play. Miles could usually tell what types the trees were but this one stood an impersonal sentry under a cloudy sky; no leaves to hint at its identity. She walked on two steps, hesitated, turned to face him, eyes darting down to the bare, hard ground where roots rippled through like an unmade bed.

"Tammy, I want…"

"We need to get back, lots to do." She looked around, as if there was a great big scheduling board in the park, warning that they were behind with their timetable.

"I just want to say something…my God, isn't that someone from your church? That couple over there?"

"Yes, it's Ern and Sara Justice. We must go say hello." It was the perfect excuse and Tammy was off up Brook Street, calling "Ernest, Sara, fancy seeing you here!"

Ernest looked back over his shoulder, turned white, looked away and buried his head down and forward, concentrating on the one safe path through the minefield.

"Ernest, look it's Tammy. We must say hello!" She had her arm in his and acted like a sea anchor so that his efforts to get away turned him in a semi-circle to face his boss and the strange Englishman: rival men of war with cannon protruding.

"Hello, Ern and Sara!" Tammy greeted them much more warmly than she would have done at home, "What a coincidence! Are you on vacation?"

Sara started to reply but Ernest cut into her pleasant voice with words that sprung from deep down, born of the humiliation he had faced that morning in the D'Alianti offices and the parallel humiliation when this girl had taken the position of president of the church from under his nose.

"Well I never, if it isn't Tam. Or do you go by some other name in London? Don't worry, Miss President, there's no need for you to go into your secretive past. I am on top of that, so sit back and enjoy your time in this fine city."

"What do you mean?"

Ernest enjoyed the look that spread across her face like a weather map predicting squalls and heavy rain.

"I mean, Miss Whatever-your-name-is, that I am on top of your schemes and will expose you for what you really are sometime real soon." He did not add 'and then I will be president of our church and you will be history' but he might as well have.

They parted with no more words, no more cannonballs to skim along the waves and wreak havoc amongst the scrubbed decks and stout timbers. Miles drew Tammy away to leeward with a tender restraining arm around her shoulder. Tammy, never a proud vessel, had her masts washed overboard, hanging over the side. While Sara was in her own storm, grabbing her man as the wildest wind would, dragging him away with the strength of a capstan at work.

It was late enough to be thoroughly dark on the streets of London. A wet wind nagged at Tammy and Miles as they re-crossed the tiny park homeward bound.

"I can't do it, Miles," was all she said, spoken into the wind that pinched her face backwards and flew her hair like a streamer on the helmet of a valiant knight. But it was an illusion, for there was simply no valour left in the pot.

"It will be all finished in a little over 24 hours," Miles replied, every instinct said to hold her, yet he did not.

Instead, the move came from Tammy. She placed a single hand on his arm, looked directly into his eyes with the scrapings from the bottom of the valour pot, said, "Just please get me away for a while. Maybe I can do the debate tomorrow but right now I need to get away." Then she added, "Please, Miles."

"Okay, of course, Tammy." He had wanted to say "my dearest" or "my darling" but such strong words seemed to slash and cut when Tammy, the one he loved, needed help not hindering.

Besides, it was too complicated for an Englishman.

"We'll tell no-one." Tammy's eyes danced as she spoke, too dark to see what emotion held sway.

"We've got to tell Fi. She's expecting us tonight, to go over the debate questions again."

"Promise me you'll talk to no-one."

Miles promised. But his conscience drove him to send a text instead. It read:

Pressure on T. intense. Going away for a few hours. Make contingencies in case not back in time.

Miles then took charge, hailing a taxi.

"Charing Cross Station, please," he said, using his hand like an arresting policeman to guide her into the car.

At the very moment when Tammy boarded the taxi, the doorman of Claridge's hailed another black cab.

"Where do you want to go, sir?" he asked the American couple, addressing the wrinkled red face of the man rather than the marble-freeze of the woman.

Within an hour they were lost to London, hurtling through the first-class lounges as if Ernest could add his energy to the aircraft's, thus propelling them faster through the air to Rome.

He had smelt victory, seen vanquish in Tammy's eyes, tasted the joy of fear in another. All he needed now was the report. The report would give him the ammo he needed. It was waiting for him at the Silversitrinni house.

That same report would also justify his recent actions to his wife. He had never seen her so angry, but soon she would be enlightened and see him for the hero he was.

It was all coming together so well. He would have preferred not to come across Tammy in the street, but had he not played it magnificently given the circumstances? Was he not, undoubtedly, the lead role in this movie?

Meanwhile, Fi sipped iced coffee and clicked on her phone. She read the text from Miles, groaned, kicked the wastepaper basket across the room.

"Tammy's done a runner," she said to Bill. "That was from Miles. She flipped and he's taken her somewhere to recover."

"Where have they gone?"

"It doesn't say. It doesn't 'bloody' well say."

"Do you think she heard about the private detective we've hired?" Bill ignored Fi's adoption of a British swear word.

"No way, not unless…" Fi looked at Bill. Only he and Al knew of the commissioning of James Mercer. It was unthinkable. "No way," she said again, with finality.

"That report deadline is almost with us. Why don't you check your email?"

The first page of the report contained a gaudy crest for the firm Huntington, Mercer and Goad, laden with purple ink in a garish display of fake authenticity. But the next two pages looked detailed enough.

It would lay bare Fi's new friend for the world to see.

Twenty minutes later, Fi reached for the phone. "Al, did we make that quarter mil payment to Huntington, Mercer and Goad?"

"Yes, Ma'am. Did you get the report? It was promised for midnight our time."

"Yes, I got the report, but there's a problem with it. Come in here and see for yourself." She replaced the receiver and stared at the three pages, Bill standing behind her like a bodyguard, no-one else in the room. Al knocked and entered. She shoved the report across the desk to him.

"You see, it looks like a detailed report but it is nothing but irrelevant facts."

"It goes into a lot of detail about the last few years but almost nothing before that." Al scratched his thinning hair, put the report back on the desk and looked at the anger in Fi's eyes.

"It says she grew up as Tamara Burton in some never heard of town in Oregon. She worked as a receptionist in a hospital before moving to Roanoke nine years ago."

"That could be the truth," Al answered.

"No way! What's the most noticeable thing about our Tammy?"

"Her virginity."

"Okay, okay, I get your point, second most noticeable thing?"

Al thought hard, picturing her in his mind. She was average in many ways – weight, height, personality. She was above average intelligence and on the prettier side of the curve, but nobody could say she was stunning, other than when she wore her hair down. But Al, mostly seeing her in the office, had only once experienced her hair unbound.

"Let me help you," Fi interjected, "does she sound like she comes from Oregon?"

"No, of course not. I'd say northern Tennessee, not that I'm an expert on regional accents."

"Precisely, and nobody is going to adopt a Tennessee accent by choice. So, the story is convincing on paper but when you actually know Tammy it becomes highly unlikely to put it mildly. Bill, do sit down!" She swung around to look at him and he saw the anger too, but it was his first time. He did as he was told, dragging a chair across to the side of the desk then plumping down, much as he used to slump in his taxi.

All three sat and stared at each other for a moment, boss and assistant across the desk, boss' lover located to the side; an adjunct to the main focus between the workers. But thoughts were from every direction, multiple and colliding. In another world they might have been a screenwriting team; ideas and implications and complications jetting around the place to form a storyline that worked.

It was a short time of silence as the ideas made play. It had to end.

"What's his cell?" Fi grabbed the phone. Al read it out from the report. The first two times they got the international dialling code incorrect, got recorded messages of girls with patient voices advising them to check and redial.

"James Mercer, can I help you?" Third time lucky, Fi switched to speakerphone.

"This is Fi D'Alianti."

"Miss D'Alianti…"

"The report tells us nothing."

"It gives everything we could find after an exhaustive search."

"What do you mean exhaustive search?" Al asked, suddenly alert to something in the airwaves.

"I mean we did an extensive search, sir."

"Ten hours? I mean how extensive can it be in ten hours?"

"Well, we threw a lot of bodies at it, sir."

Al gave Fi a look, then mouthed the words 'something's not right here'. Then Fi's instinct took over.

"Mr Mercer, I believe it is in your code of practice not to accept work with a conflict of interest."

"Of course, Miss…"

"Well, that is precisely what you have done."

"No…"

"You have another client and that other client is none other than Ernest Justice Esq. of Roanoke, Virginia."

In a 'Boys' Own' story, this is where the private investigator would say 'fair cop' and come clean before being led away to the waiting police car.

Instead, Mercer continued to resist the notion, arguing fruitlessly with increasingly unlikely fabrications. His fear was that the 'quarter-mil' would soon find its way out of his firm's bank account.

"Just admit it, Mr Mercer. You have broken your code of conduct in a fundamental way."

It took 40 precious minutes to get the confession over the phone, ten more to get the wire back to Fi's bank account.

"One more thing, Mr Mercer," Al added, showing his promise to Fi, "did you send the exact same report to Mr Justice?"

"I did."

"I want that statement in writing, signed," Fi added. "That is if you ever want to work again."

"Yes, ma'am." The deflated tones spoke of complete defeat.

But defeat for Mercer only gave a hollow victory to Fi's team; they were still no closer to discovering the truth. Fi slammed the phone down.

Al excused himself, knowing what was coming. "I'll just check my email for the Mercer confirmation."

"Nothing is going right in this deal," Fi said, her fury bashing through the air between her and Bill.

"That's because it's not a deal," Bill said. "Anyone can see that."

"Yeah but look at the facts. We were asked to do this by Tammy and Miles. We throw everything at it like it was a real earner. We set up an international debate. No, don't interrupt. It was a great idea and I'm not angry at the idea." But, in truth, her anger knew no bounds, ranging over hills and farms, towns and factories, looking to pounce on whatever prey was foolish enough to be exposed. "Then we find Tammy is a regular mystery lady."

"She's your friend," Bill replied. "She's probably your best friend."

"So why is she threatening this whole project? Something I've put hundreds of hours and who knows how much money into? We're 18 hours away from the debate and the little miss has gone AWOL. How 'best friends' is that? Where the hell is the return for all this? And I don't mean dollars and cents. I mean what is she doing in return? Where the hell has she got to?"

"Fi, be reasonable. You must have weighed up the risks before taking this on. Tammy, or whatever her real name is, is obviously pretty screwed up. You must have realised this when you took the job on?"

"So now it's my damn fault?" A fury took Fi's limbs, propelling her to stand, then lean over the desk. She went over to where the wastepaper basket was lying on its side, spilling its contents onto the carpet. She kicked it again with a great big swing of her foot. It missed Bill's head by a whisker, clattering against the windowpane and falling onto a cabinet below. A paper coffee cup, the last contents of the basket, left its home and landed, upright, on the desk, just where Bill was sitting.

"Coffee?" she asked.

They laughed, then Bill locked the door so they could work on their problems.

Ernest's problem was he had no-one to ask and no-one to talk to. He scratched his head, read the two-page report again.

"What's the matter?" Sara asked, still bristling from his behaviour in London.

"Nothing, dear. It's just church business."

"You're supposed to be on vacation. Can't you…"

"The church does not run itself, Sara," Ernest snapped, then thought again. He needed help. "It's just this report does not give me what I needed. It's like a gun without a bullet. What can you do with it?"

"Easy, if you're into guns, that is."

"What do you mean?" Ernest came over to the bay window in their bedroom in Rome to stand behind his wife, suddenly sensing some import in her words. She had always been in the background quietly, now she seemed different.

"I mean, dearest," that word was a formality used frequently between them but held no water, "as long as people think it's a loaded gun, they are going to give you their full attention."

"My God, Sara, you mean play a bluff!"

"Sure do," she replied as if she were loading the washing machine at home, collecting the dark wash items and stuffing them in. "Let me read the report and together we can work out what to do."

So, together, husband and wife, worked on a plan.

Sophie checked her phone again. 'Access pending' it said as she got on the aeroplane with Humphrey and a group of black-robed priests. She was the only girl going to London for the debate. She was the only senior female in the team.

She wondered whether Father LaPetite would need two seats next to each other but was surprised by how spacious they were in first class. She settled back with a martini, checked her phone one more time but 'Access pending' stared back at her.

She would not be able to check again until they touched down at Heathrow.

She was sitting on her own in a single seat by the window. Opposite her was the cardinal, fussing over his wine and whether his briefcase was secure in the locker above his head, as if it might break loose during the flight, grow wings and buzz about the cabin causing trouble. Father Barrow was next to the cardinal; Sophie wondered whether this was by choice and, if so, whose choice it had been. Their row was behind Sophie's, so that they could see her easily, whereas she had to twist round which she could only do with good reason. Ahead of them were Father LaPetite and Father Ellsworthy. Then there was just a sea of black, like a shoal of fish, but in all shapes and sizes.

"Gentlemen and lady," Father LaPetite said once they were allowed to move around the cabin, "let us use our time wisely. We should run through the format of tomorrow's debate and the content of our main arguments. Sophie, over to you."

Sophie cleared her throat. Did they know she was a double agent, working for the enemy? Surely not, or they would have excluded her immediately.

But it was thrilling to think of her role.

"As you know," she started, "the debate is between Father Barrow and Miss Tammy Shroton. Father Barrow is the leader of the defence. Shroton is the president of the New Moderation Church, hence the protagonist in this remarkable bid for the Catholic Church." She felt it was a good move to refer to Tammy by her surname only. It suggested contempt.

"And the format will be a short opening speech by each party, followed by…" Ellsworthy took over and Sophie stopped listening. She had to work out some important things. How, for instance, would she leak the information about Barrow? She could not call a press conference for that would mean exposure. There must be ways of leaking things to the press quietly.

And when was she to do it? What would be the best timing? But how could she decide timing when she did not know when she would get access to the reports? She would have to play it by ear.

"Sophie, have you been listening?" Father Ellsworthy broke into her wanderings. "We just asked you for a summary of the key points for debate, then we will do a dry run over the remainder of the flight."

"Yes, Father, I'm sorry. I was running through some important things in my head. I have a printout of the arguments. Let me just get it from my bag."

The aeroplane wound its way to London with a host of priests acting as both defender and aggressor of the faith inside, voices raised but lost to the world below where they settled down for another ordinary night.

The moment the plane came down and bumped against the runway, Sophie had her phone out. The pilot had just informed them that the local time was 10:42 p.m. She saw that her phone had adopted British time as the luminous glow came alive. She clicked on the screen, entered her password:

SisterMaryJohn2025, waited until she saw the word 'Access' on the screen and sighed. She would have to wait, probably until morning.

But something was different. She looked again. It now said 'Access Permitted'. She had got into the reports area and could now complete her assignment to gain revenge for poor Sister Mary John.

She fiddled with her phone, wishing she had a laptop she could open up. She clicked and clicked, screen after screen, hoping and expecting to see the reports in a neat list at any moment. More clicks and more options, like progress through a maze; dead ends everywhere.

Finally, she came to her old friend 'Access pending', buried deep in the options. She had only got halfway and time was running out.

"It seems like I'm going to have to look after you!" Sophie looked up from a trance into the amused face of Father LaPetite. "You were miles away with that phone of yours, my child. I have located your suitcase and retrieved it from the conveyor. Follow me, my dear, and you won't go wrong." Father LaPetite turned and headed towards customs, holding his head high, as would any self-respecting Frenchman on entering enemy territory.

The Scramble

Fi slammed the door of the car and made for the front door. "Calm down," urged Bill, scrambling to get out, lock the car and catch up with her. "This temper won't do any good at all."

"I'll be any damn way I choose," she shouted, causing two lights to flick on in neighbouring properties, as if voice controlled.

It was 4:00 a.m. in Mayfair, not the best of times and places for an argument. Bill got Fi inside where the staff were waiting, despite the late hour.

"Hot milk, please," said Bill, thinking no more caffeine.

"And for you, madam?"

"Same." She longed for alcohol but owed something to Bill.

The house had five floors. Top and bottom were allocated to the staff, leaving three; one for entertaining, one for the bedrooms and one, second from top, with a cinema, an anteroom with a bar, and a small study at the back they had never used before. For some reason they went to the study, perhaps it had a sense of campaign headquarters about it, a place they could bunker down in. A maid brought in a large pot of hot milk and left them, on Bill's instructions, to pour for themselves.

"Is there anything else?"

"No, Elsie," Bill replied, "go to bed, nothing more until morning."

"What on earth are we going to do?" Fi asked as soon as Elsie closed the door.

"You're going to finish your milk and go to bed."

"Bill, we've got interviews lined up for tomorrow morning and nobody for them to interview!" Fi looked at Bill, large imploring eyes, suddenly seeming so fragile.

"All the more reason for you to get some sleep before tomorrow. I'll wake you nice and early."

"But…"

"But nothing, Fi dear. I'm taking charge right now, at least for the next few hours. You need to sleep because we'll be expecting wonders from you tomorrow." That argument appealed to Fi's vanity and it worked. Bill saw his advantage and pressed on. "Leave the early arrangements to me. I'll work on them quietly up here and catch forty winks when I'm done."

Fi nodded, sipped her drink a few more moments, stood and yawned.

"Right, off you go."

"Goodnight, lover boy," she joked. "Oh, you'll need this." She pulled a slim folder out of her briefcase. "It's the schedule for tomorrow." They were exhausted, but kissed again warmly, then Fi left the room.

Bill finished his hot milk, the folder open on his lap. There were only a few pages in it. The first was a schedule. He saw that Tammy was due for a breakfast television interview at 6:15 a.m. The next page gave two paragraphs on instructions, specifically that she had to be there for makeup at 5.40 a.m. That was an hour and 20 minutes from now. What was he to do? It was one thing to send Fi off to bed with quiet words of confidence, another thing altogether to work out what to do.

He flicked back to the day's schedule. After the breakfast television interview were three in rapid succession with radio stations in studios dotted around central London. As a taxi driver, he knew they would be darting here and there in a crazy race against time. Then they were due to head out to Wapping for the same with several newspapers, then finally to lunch with Christian Television Magazine, or ChristTV as it was called. It had a huge following since it had started a dozen years earlier as a determined response to the decline in Christianity in the western world. In many ways, everything else was a dry run for the lunchtime interview, for that was the one that really counted.

He rang the service bell without thinking of his previous instruction for Elsie to go to bed. She entered in bizarre fashion in a dressing gown with her black court shoes hastily shoved on over bare legs and her long hair down her back like a waterfall.

"Sir?" she said, standing in the doorway.

"Oh, I'm sorry. I forgot I sent you to bed. Please go back. I'm sorry."

"You must have wanted something, sir?"

"I was just hungry. I have a lot to think…"

"I'll get you some toast in a jiffy, sir." The door closed on Bill's remonstrances that she should do no such thing.

Elsie was back in a few minutes with a huge plate of hot buttered toast, a pot of coffee and two mugs.

"You've clearly got a lot on, sir," she said when Bill looked at the second cup, "so I thought I would help you."

"Are you sure? It's so late." But Bill was not fighting hard and welcomed the help for he knew he could not do it alone. He quickly explained the problem: Tammy was missing and they had a busy schedule starting in just over an hour.

"Well," said Elsie, making Bill think for a moment that she regretted her offer to help and might now agree that it was late and she needed to go, "it's clear that we need to tackle this from both sides."

"What do you mean?" Bill asked, seeing only one side to this enormous problem.

"Have you got contact numbers for the interviews?" They were in the folder. "And you say the really important one is at 1:30 p.m. with ChristTV? Okay, one more question, do you have any idea where Tammy might be?"

"No idea, just that she is with Miles because he texted Fi, I mean Miss D'Alianti, with the news they were disappearing. They could be in any one of a thousand hotels."

"Or they may be in the most obvious place."

"Where's that?"

"His fish and chip shop of course, silly. Sorry sir."

"No, my name might as well be Silly instead of Billy!" They laughed at the lame joke, duty from Elsie's perspective, relief that someone was taking on some of his responsibility from

Bill's. "I would never have thought of the shop," he added. "He has a flat above it."

"Where is it?"

"Somewhere in Kent."

"What's it called?"

"Some play on his name. I need to think a minute."

They came to a natural division of labour. Elsie rang the television studio, then the radio stations, arguing and pestering to get a re-scheduling by a few hours. Often, she had to call back in a mad attempt to fit everything in to a compressed timetable, chopping and changing slots of time that were forever getting thinner. She worked the phone nonstop for an hour, eating cold toast between calls, waving the half-eaten toast in demonstrative manner as she raged and cajoled the recipients of her calls.

Once she stopped and looked at Bill, said simply "My dad had a small building firm. We were forever rescheduling chippies and brickies and sparks. It's in my blood."

Bill's task during that frantic hour was to think. He had to remember the name of Miles' business so that they could locate it. All he knew is that it was a play on Miles' name. It was nothing fishy, nothing chippy, nothing that spoke of what trade he was in. It was something to do with his name.

"I've got it!" he cried, but Elsie waved him away, deep in a conversation with an irate radio controller who sounded half asleep when he should have been earning his bread at the radio station. When she eventually replaced the receiver, he said, "Miles Better, that's the name."

From there it was simple. They searched for 'Miles Better Fish and Chips' and there was only one in the whole country. "24, London Road, Bromley," Bill said. "Here's the phone number. Shall we call now?" He looked at his watch. It was 6.06 a.m.

"We've got to. I've pushed the interviews out as late as possible, but the first one is now 7.20 a.m. She's only got an hour."

Bill dialled the number.

Life Above a Fish and Chip Shop

Miles went to an off licence outside Charing Cross station and bought two bottles of red screw tops and a couple of cheap glasses that were on sale. They opened the first bottle on the packed train, standing in the corridor at the end of one carriage, jostling for position against a pack of young executives in off the peg suits and grubby ties.

"Here, this kind gent's got a bottle for us," the cheekiest spoke up.

"I'd love to share but I only have two glasses." This provoked comments like "That's okay, one for me and one for the rest" and "who needs a glass?" They made the witty scale, produced laughter all around, even from wide-eyed Tammy, but none registered as serious humour. Soon they returned to football, arguing over which player earned the most, leaving Tammy and Miles to drink in relative seclusion. Even with half glasses, however, it was tricky to prevent spills as the train stumbled and shunted down the track as if restrained from take-off only by large elastic bands.

"My flat is above the shop," Miles explained, as they passed through the ticket barrier. "We'll get there just before closing time."

Twenty minutes later they carried two paper-wrapped bundles up the stairs at the back of the shop. "My home," said Miles, wanting to carry her over the threshold. "It's hardly Bent Mountain but it is my place."

"It's real nice," said Tammy dutifully, searching for something to compliment.

"It's basic," said Miles in such a way that it took the need to find compliments away.

They sat together on the sofa, unwrapping their fish and chips on the seat between them, the second bottle standing on the coffee table like a guardian of good order. They munched but did not talk, unless the odd comment about the way the chips were cooked or what type of fish they were eating counted as conversation. Miles did not think so.

Tammy licked her fingers when she was finished.

"That was awesome," she said, "like real tasty."

"I try and please."

"Can you show me around?"

"The flat, you mean? You've pretty well seen it." He rose, held out his hand to assist her out of the low sofa. He was just about to make a joke about the sofa being ideal for improving leg muscles when he found her in his arms.

'Miles," she said and nothing more.

For there was nothing more to be said as he led her to the bedroom. They kissed just inside the door, tender raindrops that splashed against the skin and spread outwards. They made Tammy feel like she had never felt before, as if this was, after all, the reason to be alive. She did not know how to respond, so gave in to instinct. She leaned up and rubbed her slender hands through his thick hair.

"Do it more, I love it." This time the hands played leapfrog, jumping from head to neck and from neck to shoulders, feeling muscle, skin, hair; exploring the twists and turns as they went.

Miles fumbled with the heavy clasp of her bra, so she took her hands back, undid it with ease. They moved in an awkward adolescent dance across the floor to the bed. She gasped when he first held her breasts; she had never felt this way before, never known there were such feelings like a million pinpricks just below the skin, each pinprick an explosion of sensuality. She felt herself shiver as he undid each button slowly, deliberately, ritually, dropping her pale lemon shirt so that it hung just from her wrists like Moroccan baby-catcher trousers, ready to billow out when the wind came.

But there was no wind to wash and cleanse their passion, just two people making love, one for the first time. Tammy felt hot, burning sensations deep within her body. Could this be her body she was feeling? Could it be her body that was suddenly consumed with a longing she had never known before, like the discovery of a new continent?

He stepped back, undid his trousers and let them slide to the floor, turned her around with a deft movement so that she felt like a toy dancer on a string. Her long, November skirt fell beside his jeans. By unspoken agreement they removed their own underwear and stood naked, a foot apart. She thought it a foot because, looking down, she could count two floorboards between her feet and his. She noticed that he had hairs, fine ones, on each toe, also the left little toe poked inwards as if it knew a better route to wherever they were going.

Suddenly, she loved his feet. She went down on her knees, raised the left foot and kissed it all over. He responded with a single cry of delight, then bent down and picked her up, laid her on the bed.

When she came, she thought the rush was the waters of the River Jordan taking her to Heaven. She had never imagined such intense joy on earth. She turned to look at him, her loosened hair like a stage curtain over her face. Miles moved it to one side and they kissed again.

Early in the morning, long before the day, Tammy lay in bed, wondering about many things. She liked the way her body fitted next to his; cliff to cove and bay to headland. It felt right, but it was wrong. How could that be? He stirred, eyes fluttering open to smile at her. She decided then to put her conscience to one side, like an old-fashioned lady taking off her hat after church. Why did her thoughts always go back to church? Was her mind so constrained, so feeble, that it could only think inside an old wooden box with 'church items' painted in red on the lid? Dare she find a corner not quite tightened down, apply leverage and gain freedom? For freedom was the sunlight, the stars, the rocks and trees. It was humour and fear, exhaustion and exuberance.

Freedom was love like God was love.

Here she was with her mind back on God.

It was too much to think about so she pinched Miles delicately until he woke, then made love to him again.

It was after they lay spent and happy on damp sheets that the phone rang. At first neither of them moved. They could move but did not want to, resenting the intrusion into their spun cocoon. But it rang and rang like an insistent child calling for comfort.

"Miles Standish."

"Miles, this is Bill. I know it's early, but can you talk?"

Miles got out of bed, hooking the receiver in his neck as Tammy watched him cross the room and disappear into the sitting room and kitchen beyond. He was naked; still naked when he returned with two cups of tea in one hand and the phone, now dead and useless, in the other.

"We've only got a few minutes," he said. And Tammy knew exactly what he meant.

But she was ready for it now.

Access Permitted

Sophie lay awake in her pleasant hotel room. The silence was very occasionally broken by the call of a night porter or a late guest fumbling with the keys, perhaps too drunk to control them?

It was not noise that kept her awake. Nor was it light, for the curtains were heavy enough to block the watery streetlights outside. Nor was it the weather, for it was a light drizzle that folded upon the night-time world. It thoroughly soaked everything it descended on but did so without fury and without great victory cries.

And the bed was comfortable, excessively so, as it enveloped her in soft luxury.

It was none of these things that kept her awake; rather it was her crumbling plans for revenge on Father Barrow. How would she make it work if she could not get access to the reports? She twisted and turned in her soft nest, abandoning plan after plan as unworkable or laughable.

If only she had an accomplice, someone to share her burden with. This thought led her to making up grand phrases concerning the loneliness of her chosen trade as a double agent. She was a lone operator. She could only rely on herself, nobody else. That was the nature of her work.

But if she did not get some sleep, how was she supposed to operate tomorrow? She kicked off the bedclothes, pulled them back up her narrow body, only to throw them again. She tried to remain absolutely still, mind blank. But imaginary scenes of Sister Mary John in her untold misery came up whenever she successfully voided her mind. It was as if there was a projector up there, flashing images rapidly through her mind, preventing the blessed disregard of sleep.

The thought came to her precisely as the digital clock flicked from 3:42 a.m. to 3:43 a.m. Excited, she got out of bed, opened the curtains and window to feel the light spatter of misty-rain like a fine shower on her face. She thought it through again and again, running over it like a movie director, getting the scenes in order before the actors could start.

"Yes," she said, climbing back into bed, drawing the covers up against the cold air from the open window.

And she slept soundly then, only waking when Father Ellsworthy, seemingly destined to become the patron saint of late sleepers, knocked on her door at 6:40 a.m.

Sophie's English was proficient, giving her no problem in directing a taxi to the offices of the Daily Witness in Wapping. It was a little trickier to get past the receptionist, sat at a desk with two others that stretched across most of the spacious hall. In fact, she only made progress when the manager was called.

"You say you have some vital information concerning the Great Debate scheduled for this evening?"

"Yes, Mr Chimney…"

"Call me Smokie, everyone does." The joke was lost on Sophie; all jokes were at that moment, so intent was she on the task.

"Yes, Mr Smokie. I am the Director of Defence Strategy for the Roman Catholic Church. I have some important information I believe you will find very interesting."

"Save it for the journos, love. My job is to keep the nutters out and I'm letting you right in!" He had devised a three-pool approach to his job and it worked well. The obvious nutters were led back outside. Usually a kind word and a firm grip on the elbow were enough to get them out of the door. Sometimes, he would point them to the Daily Record across the square, knowing that a good proportion of the nutters he received had first been to the Record. When they failed the equivalent security there, they were carefully and reassuringly guided to the offices of the Daily Witness, back across the square. He knew his parallel security manager at the Record; they often joked about their practices over a pint after work. This pool they had jointly termed the 'no hopers'.

The smallest category was the obviously misclassified, or the 'lost souls' in their parlance. They should have been let straight in but, for some reason, a receptionist had referred them to security. He was keen to know if someone on the front desk was referring too many in this category because it told him of a need for remedial training. Once he had assessed someone as a genuine lost soul, they were welcomed with effusive apologies for the delay, plus mutterings about 'you never can be too secure these days sir/ madam'. It always worked.

But Sophie was clearly in the third and much harder to judge category. He could count on one or two a day like her. There were always two possible outcomes. They could be demoted to no-hoper status, recognising the attendant risk that vital information could go across the street to the Daily Record. Likewise, they could be promoted to the welcomed bunch; in this case, even more profuse apologies were called for, the intention being to embarrass the visitor so they would not want to complain. He always erred towards caution in making these assessments; what did it matter if he tied up the journalists for an hour or two? That is what they did, after all, dig around for gold.

"Thank you, Mr Smokie," Sophie said, not understanding what Smokie was talking about but sensing a need to display gratitude.

"Thank you, Miss, for considering the Daily Witness. If you would care to come this way, I will show you to a briefing room and tell the top bods that you are here."

Sophie followed the security manager, wondering what a top bod could possibly be.

Next, she experienced the triage system, very similar to that practiced in casualty departments the world over. She waited in the briefing room, actually a tiny cubicle with a metal desk and two plastic chairs. A moment later, a lady entered; enormous glasses and iron-grey hair with matching jacket and skirt, as if introduced into the canvas with left over battleship paint.

"Good morning, Miss LaNeve. My name is Caroline Jones." She took the other chair, the one wedged behind the desk, opened a folder and stared down at it, tapping out a waltz with a pencil on the page. There was only one page in the folder, but she turned it over as if expecting something more.

"Good morning, Signora," Sophie said in a slightly heavier than normal accent.

"Full name, nationality and date of birth please." Sophie complied with trembling voice, ready to leave at once, only Miss Jones' chair now blocked the exit. Sophie would have to spring up, topple Miss Jones in a heap, step over her crumpled body and jerk open the door; all before Miss Jones could right herself and gain control of the exit. The odds were against success, but that was the life of a secret agent. Sophie tensed; she would make her move in a moment, possibly as soon as Miss Jones stopped scribbling with her pencil on the page.

But then she was gone, closing the door quickly behind her before Sophie could react. She sat alone for seven minutes, wondering if this is what jail was like; never knowing what might happen next and when. She felt every bit a character in an adventure novel.

The door opened and a young man came in, not much older than Sophie. His white shirt, blue and yellow striped tie and blue blazer made Sophie think of a rugby team on tour. He introduced himself but was gone in four minutes, reassuring her after a dozen rapid questions that someone would be along very soon.

And they were. The next one asked Sophie if she would be kind enough to follow her. Or was it a man that led her out of the cubicle? Afterwards she could not recall. She did remember thinking this is how Kafka must have felt.

Or wanted others to feel.

Another closed door and another assurance that 'someone will be along really soon', but this was a proper conference room. Sophie settled back in a comfortable chair, feeling the promotion like a warm glow around her body.

"Would you like some coffee?" Sophie spun around in her chair to see a very thin woman of about forty; expensively dressed and with a smile that seemed to work upside down, curving downwards as she spoke. Sophie's gaze flicked from mouth to eyes; there was no doubt that this lady was smiling. "My name is Glenda." She did not give her surname.

"Hello, my name is Sophie. Yes, I would love an espresso." Glenda made espressos, offered Sophie sugar, declined it herself and then they sat and sipped. Glenda made great play of wiping her mouth on a paper napkin each time she took a drink; Sophie noted very few coffee stains but great smears of lipstick on the napkin that she spent time folding after each use.

"Sophie, please tell me what it is you came to see us about." When Sophie paused, Glenda added, "We are very interested in what you have to say."

Sophie started the story about Father Barrow and Sister Mary John.

"Slow down," Glenda called several times as Sophie poured it out, her English sometimes jumbling the words which were spattered with Italian. It did not matter to Sophie that she had not yet got full access to the reports. She knew what Barrow was like and she had read the first two. Everyone could see that Humphrey Barrow SJ was a bigoted, cruel man, certainly not someone who could be trusted with the future of the Roman Catholic Church.

Sophie had had the good sense to put her mobile phone on silent before entering the Daily Witness building. She was aware of it buzzing several times but was amazed on finally leaving the offices at the end of the morning to see 48 missed calls. It made her feel important, more so when she decided to ignore them all. But then, as she waited for a taxi the phone rang silently again. It was a London number.

"Sophie?"

"Hello, Glenda."

"I took your story to the assistant editor. He took it to the editor. We want to run with it. We'll have a draft ready for our website at 2:00 p.m. Can you come back to review it? There will be a cheque waiting for you as well."

Sophie had never thought about money and told Glenda this.

"Never mind, donate it to a favourite charity." The phone went dead. A journalist's time was precious as minutes ticked towards deadlines. Sophie checked the time. It was 11:38 a.m. She had enough time to get back to the hotel and then turn around again.

In the back of the cab, she tried accessing the reports again on her phone. She sailed through the first three gateways but failed this time at the fourth with the polite note that access was pending. She settled back and tried to think of a convincing excuse for her absence that morning, her smart shoes beating a complicated rhythm against the purr of the engine.

Sara felt that she was getting to know the first-class staff at British Airways as they welcomed her and Ernest at the lounge, en route from Rome to London again.

"We should get there in time for the debate," Ernest said, munching olive after olive.

"Did you contact the press?" Sara asked, a tone of authority in her voice.

"Yes, my dear. I contacted them all as you said." The same meaningless endearment, not evolved over 34 years of marriage, so that it was rubbed down to nothing much at all.

"Good," said in an approving tone. "Is anyone meeting us at the airport?"

"Yes, a lady called Glenda from the Daily Witness. She was real keen to meet with us."

"A lady? Then let me do the talking." Ernest did not disagree. Instead he settled back in his chair, closed his eyes and thought of when he would become the Life President of the Church of New Moderation. He would get some chains of office made for the inauguration.

With Ernest's legal training they were always early – time was billable, therefore to be respected. They had rushed for a flight that arrived at 4:45 p.m. in Heathrow, plenty of time before the debate started at 8:00 p.m. ,Glenda, now changed into a knee length black dress that folded over itself and spoke of quality, was waiting with a copy of the Daily Witness to identify her.

"Hello, Mr and Mrs Justice. We have a car waiting. If it's okay with you, we will go straight to the office while your luggage goes on to Claridge's. I'll deliver you to the hotel in plenty of time to change before the debate." Then she raised her hand to her curved down mouth to indicate something hush-hush. "I've got you tickets for the debate," she said. "They are like gold dust!"

The editor and assistant editor of the Daily Witness could have been brothers. They had the same wisps of hair straddled over similar bald patches, same deep green eyes that were too small for the surround of pink flesh. Fourteen years separated them in age, but that is possible with brothers, happens sometimes. The older one was taller, marginally more handsome, certainly more rugged with a scar running from right ear down to the neck. His wife won on looks too, altogether more charming than the younger one's partner.

But the younger one was the editor, the boss. And this made the older one consumed with jealousy.

They were, of course, not related by blood at all, only by mutual hatred, which they utilised to climb to new heights of ambition, making a very strange but successful team. The shareholder of the newspaper, a Saudi billionaire, disliked them intensely. In private he referred to them as 'that brace of filthy Englishmen'. He vowed a hundred times to get rid of them but never did, for the simple reason that they made a lot of money at a time when others in the newspaper business were losing equal amounts.

And now, quite by chance, they had the coup of all coups. They had, at their fingertips, the capability to destroy both candidates taking part in the Great Debate. Having deliberately gone against the tide by rubbishing the debate when it was announced, they had switched tactics a week ago and now backed it enthusiastically, somehow grabbing readership in the process.

"It will be a neat twist to expose the moral corruption behind both candidates," the editor said. A lesser assistant editor would have stopped the clock to argue that it had been his discovery, or at least his protégé who had run with both stories. But for all their hatred of each other there was also mutual respect. They were good on their own but unstoppable as a team. So rather than rise up, the assistant editor worked with the boss he despised for the greater glory.

"When shall we release the friggin' website articles?"

"When do you think?" The assistant editor was part of the decision process.

"7 p.m.," he said, "an hour before the debate." Then, anticipating the next question from his boss, he added that they had the resources to make a huge splash. "Even an hour before the bloody debate, everyone in the whole damn country is going to know about this bleedin' story." The swear words rolled out of him as if bare sentences could not make their way in the world without a cloak of profanity to bolster them.

"Cut the bleedin' swearing, matey," said the boss, not that he cared, more to put his sidekick down. But the assistant told him where he could stuff his instructions and left the room with a sneer thrown over his shoulder.

Sophie returned to the hotel to find angry priests in best black dress, demanding to know where she had been.

"Can't a girl go shopping?" she answered, careful not to actually state a lie. "Besides, I am not your secretary so I don't answer to you."

"But you do answer to me," Humphrey put in, seeming to regret it as soon as he spoke. Sophie got the impression Father Barrow saw straight through her as he watched her in the dining room of the hotel; hints of Jesus and Judas. She tossed her long blond hair and saw the impact it had on the priest. There are different ways to silence people, she mused, as she helped herself at the buffet.

The cheque took her breath away.
"Ten thousand?"
"More if the story takes off and we do a follow up," Glenda replied, secretly pleased at the reaction, such that her mouth moved down another quarter inch on each side. Almost a half moon, thought Sophie as she buried the cheque deep into her handbag.
She did not want to think of money.
But she earned her fee by making quite a few corrections to the draft. Some were factual, others reflected what she expected to be in the reports.
Then it was back to the hotel to change. She had a pale-yellow dress she had bought the previous week and was looking forward to wearing. It was an evening gown with a slash up the side so that she could reveal a little thigh, if she chose. She looked through her little jewellery box but there was scant competition. It had to be the sapphire necklace. She did it up in front and then twisted it around so that the dark stones lay on her chest, against her skin.
It had been her mother's necklace; the mother she had never known. But it made her think of her father, lying in bed and nearing the end of his life, tended by the housekeeper while Sophie was away. He was dark and small whereas Sophie was like her mother; tall, pale skin with a hint of an aristocratic past, all under brilliant blonde locks.
Then, when she felt quite sure she was ready, she sat on her bed and checked access to the reports again.

At that moment, Sara was also dressing, then helping her husband into the dinner jacket that Claridge's had rustled up. Somehow, they had an excellent fit, propelling Ernest Justice from a retired American lawyer into someone quite distinguished. She would have no qualms hanging onto his arm that evening as their joint plans played out on the stage before them.

Sara would have checked the story on the internet, only she did not have a phone. Never mind, she was impressed with Glenda and suspected the plan was in good female hands.

Tammy had long been ready and was sitting in a chair waiting for the makeup artist to get her ready for the cameras. She was not short of companions and suspected that Miles, Bill and Fi were all there in case she did a runner again. They were her best friends but also her jailors.

She had been dressed by Fi and so was elegant in a cream skirt and jacket with a black blouse. Her shoes were cream and high-heeled, giving her a look of the young executive.

She would have dressed in a plain skirt, probably dark brown, with a cardigan over a white shirt. Plain study shoes would have given her a firm footing on the stage.

But everyone, Fi especially, knew better. "This is your chance to make an impression, Tam dear."

As she sat in the swivel chair, looking at the young executive image staring back at her from the mirror, she reflected on her day. It had started when Miles took the call at 6:40 a.m. that morning. She had then done six telephone interviews in short order, all from the flat above the fish and chip shop. Then Bill and Fi had turned up in the Aston Martin. The four of them had charged around London, parking where they should not park, as interview after interview merged into one big interview; one large, middle-aged man asking her repeatedly what she hoped to achieve through this bid.

And, as happens when the same question is asked time and again, the responder starts to doubt their replies. Could the interviewer be asking the same question in slightly different ways and totally different voices because he did not believe her? Should she try and vary her reply, give more reasoning behind her words? Fi was in no doubt that she should not; "stick to your guns, girl," she had said each time the Aston Martin made its dash to the next studio, hoping to shave a second or two off their lateness. But then Fi's advice merged into a caricature, like a puppet that had just one catchphrase "stick to your guns girl, stick to your guns".

Physically, she was alright, wanted to stretch and loosen her muscles, feel the flow of lifeblood in her toes and fingers. But mentally she was in a daze.

And in 40 minutes she had to stand up and debate with some priest to determine the future of the Catholic Church. She felt a small cog right then, even as the others fussed over her. There was a great weight of wheels and sprockets, valves and dials above her, pressing down to squeeze the very breath from her.

Humphrey Barrow seemed at ease, milling with the two-dozen priests in their party as if he were just one of them.

Sophie watched him from across the room, as Father LaPetite went over the 'order of service' once again. She noted the fingers up at his neck, squeezing into his white collar as if he longed to break free and fly above the hustle, spread wings and go up and up and up. He looked at her, a faintly quizzical expression, as if asking why she looked at him.

I'm looking at you because I am about to bring you down, Father High and Mighty. She thought it but did not say it. Instead she blew a kiss which sped across the crowded room, blasting a way through the mass of black-robed individuals, with their white collars and pale, indoor faces, making them like a host of magpies looking for scraps on the road.

Humphrey looked shocked, suspected she was mocking him but not quite sure. Then he was called away for makeup and Sophie was alone, other than the rest of the magpies who, by and large, did not count.

To pass the time, 25 minutes to go, she looked down at her phone, checked access as was her habit now. She clicked and entered the password with a growing premonition that this time it was going to be different.

She was through! Every level of access was now permitted. She fumbled the selection of reports, had to go back to the main menu and start again. Finally, she got to the section on Father Barrow's trip nine years earlier to investigate and resolve the situation arising at the Sisters of the Holy Cross Convent in Vigilance, Virginia.

She saw the reports were in a section entitled 'Operation Deliverance'. There were three reports. She downloaded the second and third, disregarding the initial report he had written on the aeroplane.

She paused, placed a hand on her thumping heart, took a deep breath, then read about Operation Deliverance with total absorption.

She did not hear the call to come and sit in the front row of the audience, did not see Humphrey stride resolutely out towards the stage, nor the exasperation of Father LaPetite who could not get her attention and so gave up with a word he should not have used.

Operation Deliverance

September 28 2025, written in the guest suite of the Convent of the Holy Cross, Vigilance, Virginia.

It has been a hectic three days since my interim report on 25th. I have now concluded matters and trust that the arrangements I have made will be satisfactory to all concerned. I have several regrets and cannot rest assured that all parties are totally happy. This morning, in order to break the deadlock between certain of those parties, I took the initiative. I have described this and the general circumstances and reactions below and trust it meets with your approval.

Too right, thought Sophie. You have sold out that poor nun. But now you are being sold out in turn! I can't wait to see your face as the boat sinks around you!

I think it best to start with a reminder of the objectives of Operation Deliverance.

Sophie was aghast. There was a word to describe his attitude, but she could not bring it to mind. He seemed like a young prince playing with the lives of underlings. It was a type of arrogance that also sounded pompous and…that was it, obsequious. Fancy calling his sordid mission Operation Deliverance: what was he thinking of? The name suggested something good coming of this awful series of events.

The key objective, allowing some rephrasing, is to determine a resolution to this situation such that no party is unduly upset and tempted to go to the press or other authorities. Secrecy is an important requirement for the church.

Well, just think of the publicity you are going to get this evening, Father Barrow! It will blow all your clever words and horrible actions straight up the chimney. She thought of Mr Smokie, the security manager at the Daily Witness, imagined his bulk and rough ways sorting out Father Barrow.

This would seem to necessitate a huge compromise as, despite numerous interviews since my arrival six days ago, I had not been able to get assurances as to what truly happened, hence any sense of progress had been totally frustrated.

I mention this because very recent events have constituted a breakthrough and I want the review of this report into my actions to fully understand these conditions prior to making a judgment as to my performance.

Me, me, me, thought Sophie, turning over the page, shifting her chair to get better light. She looked up momentarily; saw the room empty. She remembered people calling to her now to join the audience but hang that; this was the real truth. She heard voices from the studio next door. They were angry voices, arguing, rising in volume and pitch. She thought she heard Barrow's voice in vigorous denial, certainly more strained than normal. That would make sense. The truth was coming out now.

But next door it was a different truth breaking out; not one that Sophie could have imagined if she lived to be a hundred. And Sophie was wrong about something else. It was not anger she heard at all but another emotion; an emotion that fits under the general umbrella of wonder, in every aspect of that word.

For Tammy, on entering the studio, saw first rank upon rank of faces on seats, looking at her and waiting. She hesitated a moment, was edged on by Fi who whispered, "Don't let them bother you, pretend they're not there".

She rolled up her courage into a great big ball and climbed the steps to the stage. She was guided to her seat. There were two chairs on the right-hand side, behind an oblong table. Two glasses and a jug of water, plus two pads and two pens made the setting complete.

"Your opponents are on the left," said the producer. Tammy looked across the stage. At first, she saw only the bulk of Father LaPetite, standing in front of the table, pouring two glasses of water, spilling a little and wiping it with his sleeve. He looked up and smiled a respectful smile. Then he sat and Tammy saw her debating opponent for the first time.

And she fainted, flopping down on the table, head slamming, empty glasses jumping.

Fi reacted but too slowly. She was beaten by Father Barrow who jumped across the divide and came the other way around the table to stand by Tammy's side.

"She's fainted," Fi said the obvious.

"Help her into the chair." Humphrey was far more practical. "It must be too warm in here." He turned to the producer and asked for fans. "I was feeling it myself," he added, fingers back under his stiff collar to let a little damp air in.

Next, Miles was on the stage, jumping up between the footlights from the audience. "She's coming round," he said, taking a protective position over his girl.

But it was not the heat at all. It was her past coming back to be the present again, as it did with marvellous irregularity.

"Is it you, Father Burrow?" she said, her skin whiter than his collar.

"Barrow, not Burrow. Do we know each other?" Her voice had a tone, a quality he had heard before, but he could not place it. All the Americans he had met rushed through his mind.

"Yes, we do, Father." She hesitated, then drew down within herself and brought up her ball of courage, placing it on the table between them, next to the glass and the paper pad. "Do you not remember me? I expect my appearance has changed a great deal in nine years."

"Nine years," he repeated as if reeling in a particularly tricky fish. "Nine years." He had an image then of a truck disappearing into the night, a girl in a summer dress in the passenger seat.

"Vigilance, Virginia," she said. And it all came back.

"You're Sister Mary John?"

"I was Father. Now I am Tammy Shroton."

"If Miss Shroton is recovered, can we please take our places? We are scheduled to start in less than five."

Father Barrow re-crossed the stage, thinking suddenly of the First World War armies that had crossed No Man's Land on Christmas Day to play football and share chocolate and cigarettes. He did not want to debate with Sister Mary John or whatever she was called now.

We have four minutes now until the debate starts. Let's use that time to cross the stage ourselves and enter the green room where Sophie sat alone against the far wall, staring fixedly at her phone. She had missed the drama on stage, for her world was also turning upside down.

The breakthrough started with a sad occurrence. Yesterday morning I was sitting moodily in my room, wondering what to try next. There was a knock on my door. It was Sister Mary Paul, the mentor of Sister Mary John, in some state of agitation.

"Father, please come quickly. It is Mother Superior. She is unwell and I think she may be on her way..." She did not complete her sentence but I knew she meant her way to Heaven. I followed her immediately down the stairs, across the quadrangle and to Mother Mary Francis' austere apartment. From the large study she used for occasional entertaining, I was led to a cell-like room where she lay on a narrow bed. It seems she had the exact same sleeping accommodation as the nuns in her charge.

Hurry up, hurry up. I don't need a rundown of every little detail.

Mother Superior was dying, that much was clear. I administered the last rites, then sat and prayed with her as her soul tried to leave her body.

"Father," she said, "I have done a great wrong." She did not ask for confession so I am at liberty to tell it to you. But it was to all

intents a confession. She told me what troubled her; that she had lied about Sister Mary John. Father Davies had abused several of the nuns over the years, picking on the younger ones. She had no proof, but a high level of suspicion, that Father Davies had done exactly what he was accused of. "I hid it from you because it worried me that the convent would get a bad name." I could not condemn her, for immediately I saw that her actions were ours on a smaller scale. She was concerned for the reputation of the convent, while we had the whole Catholic Church on our minds.

I turned to Sister Mary Paul. Evidently my face asked the question my mind was working on.

"It's true," she told me in a hushed, bedside voice, "Father Davies has a terrible reputation, but Mother Superior told us to keep it from you for the sake of the convent… and the church." After a few minutes of ragged breathing from the Mother Superior, Sister Mary Paul spoke again. "I know it was wrong, but she convinced us all that our first loyalty was to the convent." The silences became longer as Mother Superior worked her way towards the next life and Sister Mary Paul tended to her bodily comfort.

Finally, Mother Superior spoke again. "He had a reputation for going after the innocent."

"The innocent?" I asked, stupidly.

"The young ones," Sister Mary Paul explained, for Mother Superior could only talk now in faltering words, as if all her energy was focused on the path ahead.

But her telling, her 'confession' if you like, did lift a weight from her. It was as if her soul was trapped until the weight was removed, then it could rise and join the angels. I said many kind words to her, telling the truth that I, and many others, would have done the same thing. I kept talking, dispensing my cheap kindness like confetti as her body sank and her soul rose.

"She is departed now," Sister Mary Paul spoke from my right shoulder, then leaned over me and pulled the sheet up over Mother Superior's face. "Rest in peace," she said.

I knew then what I must do. I left Mother Superior's apartment and went straight to Sister Mary John. I begged forgiveness for doubting her. She was gracious and I was humbled by that grace.

In the morning I went to find Davies. I found him eating in the kitchen of his house. He had a hamburger that looked like the Tower of Babel and enough Coca-Cola to float the ark. "A hearty breakfast," he joked, but he picked his teeth while we spoke, showing his disdain for me and the authority I represented.

I told him he was finished as a priest. He was in denial all the rest of the day, arguing that Sister Mary John was a vixen out to cause trouble, that Mother Superior was confused, bitter, twisted by bad influences; a different adjective for each hour I spent with him.

"Davies, let me make it absolutely clear," I said, bluffing I know, "if you do not resign from the priesthood today, I will have no qualms in exposing you and letting the law take its course. I doubt very much any Virginia judge is going to look kindly on you with several rape convictions in tow." I know this was the exact opposite of my brief, but I was compelled to act by the disgust I held the man in. We are all sinners etc. etc. but I knew that I had to get this man out of the church before he abused someone else's innocence.

He left with two suitcases later that day, looking less like an ogre in civilian clothes. I gave him $1,000 from the settlement money and asked if he wanted to pray for his future. His answer should not be written down.

In the early evening I arranged to see Sister Mary John with her brother, the lawyer, who drove up from Johnson City. We knelt and prayed. Then I gave the money to her brother for her and suggested she leave with him. I said there would be more money to ensure an education and a home for her. She asked after the child's future. I told her the church would pay for the birth and then find a good home for it where it could grow up safe with the Lord. From her, I required a signature on an agreement guaranteeing the secrecy of the whole affair forever. In my brashness, seeing the finishing tape ahead, I pulled the agreement out of my briefcase and slapped it down in front of the lawyer, much as I expect lawyers to act with lawyers. This was only a few hours ago but already compared to the grace of Sister Mary John, I feel like a churl with my silly pretentious behaviour.

I did not expect her to accept these arrangements. In her position I don't think I would go along with it. I felt I knew her now. Although I had never seen a square inch of exposed skin other than her slender left hand, the cumbersome brace on her right and the hint of face visible through her heavy habit, I felt as if we could have been friends in another world. At first, I thought her a mouse, but as our conversations went on I realised what a mistake I had made. She is quiet like a mouse, but there is a steely confidence within her. I think this is her faith, shining out of her like the beacon on a lighthouse. I have come to admire greatly the person beneath the heavy and restrictive habit.

Faith takes such different forms; as many forms as people in God's world.

Deep within that habit, I could sense her fighting to control the tears. Her brother explained that all she had ever wanted to be was a nun and now the very people she had turned to for her life of prayer were turning her away. I left them to talk. I had nothing else to contribute, nothing to give this noble girl of God.

An hour later her brother came to see me. He said his sister had left the convent, changed out of her habit and was waiting in his car. They would leave forever. Did I want to see her again to say goodbye?

"I can't my friend," thinking how dare I call this fine man a friend? Then I told the truth. "I have not behaved well and do not feel I could face her. To see her face and the hurt I have put there would be too much."

He handed me the agreement, signed in her real name, Rosie Pascal. I signed it for the church and handed over a cheque for the money. I felt cheap, buying a solution for the sake of our church's reputation.

We spoke of practical matters – the arrangements for the birth, adoption, a new life. I told him these matters would be managed by an agency and he said he would follow up in the morning.

I saw his car leaving the convent. It was a big pickup truck, red and black. The rear brake light on the left-hand side did not work. I saw a glimpse through the night of a girl in a striped summer dress and her long brown hair tied in a bunch. She looked back once at her past, then turned towards the future.

That was an hour ago. I spent the next thirty minutes feeling miserable and pitying myself dreadfully. Then I got hold of myself, said a long prayer and turned to this final report.

What is done is done. There is no going back. I am not proud of my role in bringing about this solution. But I am a little proud that I started this project as if I was moving chess pieces on a board, saw that I was dealing with real people with raw emotions; people who had placed their trust in our church only to have it abused by some in authority. I thank God that I have seen the light and that, mercifully, the abusers are a tiny minority in a vast and spreading force for good. I also believe that, although more expensive in settlement, it is money well spent because Davies is out of the priesthood and will never again be able to take advantage of his position to satisfy his own desires. Perhaps he will be better off finding a woman who will put up with him on the outside. I attach to this report the agreement we concluded and full details of the arrangements made.

I hope this report is received well. I have sinned, particularly pride, conceit and bigotry, but learned something incredible while bringing about a settlement that is at least bearable for all concerned. I commend my actions to you and await your judgement.

Sophie stared at the last paragraph, tears spilling down and threatening her phone. She sat until a roar from the studio next door brought her back nine years to the present.

She had done a terrible thing in besmirching this fine young priest who, most importantly, knew he had done wrong and corrected it to the best of his ability. Now she had seconds to right the wrong she had done him.

Without thinking, she rushed from the green room into the studio next door, right onto the stage, shouting "No, it's not true, none of it is true!"

Five on Stage for the Great Debate

"**L**adies and Gentlemen," began the host for the debate, "thank you for coming tonight to take part in the Great Debate, as it has come to be termed. I look forward to an hour and a half of lively discussion on the subject of the takeover bid by the Church of New Moderation for the Roman Catholic Church.

First the introductions. On the left we have Father Humphrey Barrow SJ. Father Barrow is a young man with a great intellect that he has dedicated wholeheartedly to religious life. He has accumulated a total of four degrees and is currently an educator of seminarians in Rome. He is aided by Father LaPetite, a priest of many years' experience in policy and administration at the heart of the Catholic Church. These two make up the defence team. It goes without saying that the Catholic Church is one of the oldest religions in the world, having survived many crises over the centuries.

On the opposing bench, as it were, we have the bidders. They are led by Miss Tammy Shroton, the Life President of the relatively new Church of the New Moderation. This church started in Roanoke, Virginia around the turn of the century and has spread rapidly so that it now numbers some 12 million members. I do not know of any other church that has grown so quickly in the first generation of its existence. She is assisted today by Fi D'Alianti of D'Alianti Investments. She is a leading financier and, some would say, an unlikely candidate for the podium tonight. However, Miss D'Alianti is a renowned supporter of religion and, I am reliably informed, was expelled from her Catholic high school for pinching the communion wine and getting drunk in the sacristy – if that does not qualify one for this debate, I hesitate to know what does!"

The question master took the chuckles and applause he expected, then continued. "But ladies and gentlemen, this is the people's debate and it behoves me not to keep babbling on. We will now have a sixty-second introduction from each team, followed by questions from the floor. I add that not one of these questions has been vetted by us. The two sides and the production team simply do not know what you, the people, will ask."

Two minutes and 32 seconds later, allowing for the obligatory clearing of the throat before and the polite applause after, a balding man in his thirties shot to his feet.

"Yes, sir, your question please." The microphone on a long pole swung to the press gallery on the left-hand side.

"Marcus Brandywine, editor of the Daily Witness. My question is to both teams and is simply this: how do you dare sit up there on the stage as authorities and leaders in your respective churches when we all know you both to be absolute frauds? Miss Shroton, you have a very mysterious past, so mysterious that nobody can find out anything about you, other than you are most definitely not who you say you are." Tammy, visibly battered by his words, opened her mouth but no sound came out. Fi started to rise from her seat, angry expression on her face, but she was silenced by the editor continuing smoothly into the microphone.

"And Father Barrow, as for you," said with a sneer that struck the audience more than the actual words, "perhaps you can explain your despicable behaviour with a young nun nine years ago. Perhaps I can refresh your memory and take you to Vigilance, a small 'one-horse' town in rural Virginia. Perhaps you thought it was so out of the way that word would never leak out. Well, Barrow, I've got news for…"

"No, it's not true, not a word of it. Father Barrow is a good man, a really kind and loving man and someone everybody should like and…love." Sophie's voice found volume without a microphone to aid it. She was on the stage, standing at the end of Humphrey's table, a host of eyes on her tear-stricken face.

The question master scratched his grey beard, sensing opportunity but not quite seeing it. Then the producer's voice came through his earpiece. "Ask her to bloody well explain herself."

"Miss, who are you? I say, Miss, can you give us your name?"

Sophie heard nothing. All she saw were the footlights like headlights screaming towards her. She stepped back, expecting an impact, tripped on Father LaPetite's chair and the two of them fell in an untidy, sprawling heap. Phone flashes from the audience added to the confusion, as if each flash was a strident, had-to-be-answered, question fired at both teams.

Through the flashing lights, Humphrey saw his friend and Sophie on the floor, a mess of flesh and limbs struggling for order. He jumped up, helped them both to their feet; Father LaPetite was an effort to pull upright. They sat, taking both available chairs. Nowhere to sit himself, Humphrey grabbed a microphone, swung it over in front of him like a rock star.

"May I introduce Signorina Sophie LaNeve. She is our Director of Defence Strategy."

"With her in charge, the other side only have to turn up!" came a cheeky cry from the audience. Humour had entered the studio uninvited, driving shock and horror out of the illuminated exit doors as if they were failed audition candidates. Laughter spread across and down and up the rows until it reached the stage and rippled across the bare boards at the front, climbed the table legs and infected the debaters with its virulent germs. Everyone was laughing and nothing could stop them. As soon as one chorus died away, someone came in with another joke, or repeated the last one with a 'my word' or 'well, I never' and the laughter was off again, lapping the studio time and time again.

"Enough!" cried Humphrey after what seemed like most of the programme had been given over to laughter, in fact it was only a few minutes but such is the trickery of time.

He had a motive for wanting it to end for he had suddenly realised why Sophie had been so angry with him.

And why she was no longer angry.

And at that moment, all he wanted to be was alone with her.

But that was not going to happen any time soon. The question master spoke to the now quiet audience, as if breathless from a sprinting race just done, occasional guffaws like runners gasping for new air.

"Ladies and gentlemen and members of the press," he started, causing a new, but more subdued, ripple of laughter across the ranks with his reference to the press being neither ladies nor gentlemen. "Did I not say that this was the people's debate and that the questions were not known to the debaters or the studio staff? I think the first question is adequate proof of our integrity!" This time the laughter was politely minimal, as if laughter was kept in a tank and was drained now, awaiting refill.

Realising that the mood had changed, that you cannot build mirth on mirth unless you have a very special talent, the question master changed his tack, taking on full sail to regain control of the proceedings. It did not help to have the producer shouting in his ear so, on impulse, he removed the earpiece and placed it in his jacket pocket.

"I will now invite each team to give a reply to the accusations made tonight." He looked at the two teams, the journalist in him taking over, noticing that Tammy seemed the weaker of the two, the less in control. "Starting with the leader of the Church of New Moderation. Over to you, Miss Shroton."

There was a long delay; seconds ticked away, quite a few of them, Tammy remaining in her seat. Fi made to rise, finally prompting a reaction from Tammy.

"Good people," she began, then thought it too pompous, "I mean ladies and gentlemen…"

"Come on! We've not got all night." Humphrey was certain that call came from the man sitting next to the Daily Witness editor. From a distance, the two looked like brothers but some years apart in age.

But his heckle elicited no laughter, his narrow voice bumping against the walls and sliding down to the depths below the seating. The editor's deputy had been left behind by the audience, the light mood of earlier turning, like a yacht tacking on the open sea, to head on a serious, considerate course.

"Ladies and gentlemen," Tammy tried again, clearing her throat and sipping too much water, "I understand there are questions about my past." Her eyes were fixed on a painted red line on the floor, mid-way between her and the first row of seats, meant to mark a track the cameras could run around.

"Could you speak a little louder please, Miss Shroton." The question master had picked on her but now wished he had not.

"I'm sorry. Ladies and gentlemen," louder now, but could she make progress in her speech? "I do not deny that I have a mysterious past. It is a history that has its share of sadness and I had hoped to leave it behind. But seeing my debating colleague here today as Father Barrow has been a shock to me, one I am struggling to get over. I knew Father Barrow nine years ago, when my life was just starting to turn upside down. I thought my opponent would be a different man. I thought the man I met nine years ago was Father Burrow and I made no connection with the man leading the defence against our bid for the Roman Catholic Church. I never imagined that someone so young would be selected to lead the defence. In retrospect, I should have made the leap between Barrow and Burrow, imagined someone as intelligent and honest and open as Father Barrow could easily be selected to counter our bid."

"Hear, hear!" Sophie shouted into the pause. "He is a good man indeed!" She vacated her chair and sat on the edge of Humphrey's table, as if saying, 'my resources are at your command'.

"Stop pussy-footing around and tell us the sordid details." The editor of the Daily Witness saw his grand coup slipping through his fingers, but his coarseness was a step too far, a misjudgement from a man who made very few. The question master beckoned to two security guards standing at the back.

"Please remove those two from the room," he instructed. Then, when they had fought the heavy hands on their collars, scrambled against the forced march to the exit and been shoved rudely into the empty outside, he turned to Tammy. "Miss Shroton, I apologise for the behaviour of those men. However, we would very much appreciate a full disclosure of what went on nine years ago, if you feel able to tell us. If not, we will move on to Father Barrow's 'defence'." It was a masterpiece of gentle manipulation; just enough pressure.

Tammy told him and, because she told him, she told the listening world. And Sophie nodded and clapped at key points, turning on the table top to face Humphrey, her face saying, 'he's the one, right here. This is the man I doubted but now know I was wrong to do so.'

Tammy's tale took only a few minutes. It came to Sophie, and to Humphrey for that matter, as a mirror image of Humphrey's trio of reports. And this was in more ways than one, for whereas Humphrey started with doubt, Tammy could only commence with certainty.

"On July 12 2025, I was raped by a priest." Her voice was reedy thin, as if the fear was still with her. It drained her accent, taking the warm, homely long tones of the southern states and replacing them with clipped, nasal sounds that were of some other distant place. The whole studio and all the houses beyond where they had tuned in to watch, went silent. "I was raped not once, but six times. I was ashamed at first, ashamed that my body was the cause of lust to someone who had vowed against lust. I was twenty-one years old at that time. I had known only two homes my entire life. My first home was in Johnson City, Tennessee, where everybody is a Baptist. My second home was the Convent of the Sisters of the Holy Cross in Vigilance, Virginia. I joined the convent the day after I left high school. It is all I ever wanted to do. I had a calling and I answered.

I was a novice, nearing the end of my time, getting ready to take my vows. I was content. It was the life I was made for. The priest who raped me had no name, at least no name that I choose to speak and he is a priest no longer. He took me one day to his house. He said it was for instruction for the 'big day'. In my total innocence I followed him to his car. Even when his right hand went to my knee as he drove, I thought it an accident. No man of God would hurt a young nun. It was not that I considered and dismissed the threat. It was that I saw no threat, I imagined no threat and I felt no threat.

He forced himself on me in the sitting room of his house. He raped me on the rug on the floor. He was heavy and fat, smelt of liquor and grease. He was not careful with me.

Afterwards, he explained that it was my fault. I was guilty of the grave sin of temptation, of wearing my lustful body on the outside of my habit. I cried and he said he did not like blubbing girls so he raped me again and lay on top of me, crushing my resolve.

After the sixth time, and with six grave sins for me to answer for, he heard my confession. I knelt in the corner for a long time. The pebbles he fetched from the drive to his house cut my knees painfully. This was my penance. After this he took me back to the convent in his car and told me he never wanted to see me again."

This was the end of chapter one. Tammy paused, looked at the audience through a mist of tears, looked sideways to focus on Father Barrow. He was white, frozen immobile, fixed in anger. She had not gone into anything like such detail when Father Barrow had interviewed her at the time. Moreover, it was like hearing someone else with a terrible story – she thought she had put this away a long time ago, gone on to better things with the Church of New Moderation. But now her rage was surfacing for all to see.

"I first realised I was pregnant in late August. I went straight to my mentor, Sister Mary Paul. We prayed together. Then she took me to Mother Superior. Mother Superior reminded me of my promise of obedience to her as the superior of the convent. She said she would think and pray on it, but I was to tell no one of my situation. Whatever happened, I was to keep silent.

I heard nothing more for three weeks. I wondered whether it was really all my fault. I was being punished for wearing my desirability, or beauty or whatever it was, on the outside. But then I thought that God was a God of love and would never use a baby to punish an adult. I did my duties each day, I prayed doubly hard and I waited.

Then one day in September, I was called to the Mother Superior's study and left there with a young priest who I thought was called Father Burrow, but I misheard his name. It was in fact Father Barrow who is on the table opposite me tonight, my competitor in this debate. At first, I thought that I was to be raped again, this time by a young and lean priest rather than an old and fat one. But immediately Father Barrow exhibited good and trustful qualities. I felt safe with him. I felt his goodness penetrating through the layers of my habit.

Father Barrow asked me a lot of questions. Sometimes it felt like he was asking me the same question in lots of different ways. I am afraid I answered each one as shortly as I possibly could. I am sorry, Father Barrow, that I was not more helpful and forthcoming."

He nodded grimly in acknowledgement. At the time, he had pieced together some of the facts from her short answers and the multiple denials of others, but now every act, every scene was being played out before him.

"Well done, keep going," he mouthed across the gap between them. And she did, telling of the Mother Superior's harsh distortion of the truth and the likelihood, seemingly endorsed by her inquisitor, that she would be held to account; one more rape victim being blamed for a convenience.

But then Father Barrow had come to her one day and it was obvious that he knew the truth. He begged her forgiveness, which she readily gave for she understood he held her future in his hands. And that future was to be very different. Not that it ever shook her faith. She felt nothing could ever break the bond she had with God. But it changed her so much. Maybe it gave her purpose as she took off the habit and put on a summer dress with a tangle of roses printed in red and green. Maybe the thorns pricked her gently, but the overwhelming sensation was the sweet smell of dying summer.

She noticed the question master looking at his watch, read the need to wrap things up.

"So, I left the convent, escorted by my brother. I let the Lord guide me and, after several years in the 'wilderness', He led me to the Church of New Moderation. I thought the name so sweet. Prior to hearing of them I had made my own church.

I was my own pastor and congregation. I prayed every day to learn what He intended of me and, suddenly, my path was clear. The task He set me was to cleanse His church of the evil of lust. Not to do it by prohibitions and laws, but by removing the temptation, relaxing the law, taking the sin out of the act. For many years I was angry, so angry that my vocation as a nun had been wrecked by the great big demolition ball of rape. It took a long time and much prayer and reflection to understand that it was as much the system as the man that was at fault. If priests could marry, if women could be priests, at a stroke the frustration is gone. Problem solved.

That is my story. Like it or hate it, it is what my new vocation is. I hope very much I have explained myself adequately."

She sat down to a barrage of applause, echoing and building into a crescendo. There were few dry eyes in the room and Sophie led the way with large tears rolling.

Tammy looked down at her empty notepad, picked up the pen and doodled, drawing a nun's habit with the familiar restrictive cross giving access to nose and eyes only, deep shade covering the rest.

The debate went on but everything else seemed pale after the tumultuous revelations by Tammy; even Humphrey's considered and thoughtful reply went virtually unnoticed.

And nobody saw two empty chairs in the audience where Ernest and Sara Justice had sat before quietly slipping out, almost as if they had come to the wrong meeting altogether and now needed to exit with minimum disruption.

Tammy's words had been gentle and honest. They gave hope to many, Humphrey included, but destroyed an old man's ambition. He and Sara left the next day on as early as flight as they could; Heathrow to Dulles and Dulles to Roanoke, they were back on home territory before the Great Debate was 24 hours old.

News from Rome

In the excitement of the Great Debate, nobody noticed the absence of one man, although his reserved seat was in the front row, directly below the stage. Cardinal Forrundiker, hotel bound, took another glug of Scotch from the flask he carried on journeys. It was Johnny Walker Red Label, his favourite blended whisky.

But it did not help. Rather it closed his world in, causing his emotions to shake and totter like bombed out ruins in a war zone. He knew he should be showing the flag at the debate but could not summon the energy to attend.

He did not think he could take much more but then it was not about him.

It was about Sophie LaNeve.

The cardinal had received some very bad news early that morning. He had prayed long and hard, but it seemed no amount of prayer could summon the courage he now needed. Signor LaNeve, Sophie's father, was no more of this world. Had he waited for Sophie to be out of the house before making his last journey to the Kingdom of Heaven? Or was her departure from Rome and his from life just a bitter coincidence?

There was no doubt in the cardinal's mind that LaNeve Senior was now in Heaven. But he hoped that the dead man was not reunited with the wife he had barely known, dead just weeks after the birth of young Sophie. He had another reunification in mind for her. And that could not be too long away.

LaNeve's death gave the old cardinal two tasks, neither one the slightest bit pleasant. First, he had to tell Sophie. That would be hard enough. But the second matter was even more difficult, for he had to tell the truth after all these years. It was the promise he had made as Sophie lay as a new-born in a tiny cot below the window. Even at that moment he had known that she would look just like her mother.

He put away the hipflask, now only a third full of Scotch, and took out his rosary. He was unsure, doubting himself. This was a painful subject displaying what the years had confirmed to him: he had acted without honour or integrity. It was one thing to own up to oneself, quite another to air it before others, which is what he now had to do with the ultimate confession.

As always, when faith failed him, he turned to his creator and prayed for its restoration.

But this time he did not get far through the rosary, for at the first Hail Mary he came across words he had muttered, said and sung countless times before.

"Blessed is the fruit of thy womb," he mumbled it first, as was his normal rosary practice, then said it aloud several times, each word distinctly, its import allowed to settle. It made him think of the womb of Sophie's mother, then of Sophie's mother herself; the woman he had loved beyond love, held in his arms as his vow of celibacy had crashed about him, gorging channels in his heart, his stomach, his soul.

The cardinal felt very old as he lowered his body from kneeling position to a sprawl on the floor, much as someone would sit, half lying, on a rug at a picnic. He had been quite old when Sophie's mother came into his life, but now he was 35 years older. He saw his grave now as an opening to a new world and often welcomed the thought of laying down his troubles, his weaknesses, his sins before the Lord and being not a senior church official but a child of God.

But that did not fit with the ambition God had given him.

He knew about love, this old man. He knew also about hate. He knew how close they were. He had hated Sophie's mother at first as he fought temptation. But he had not appreciated at the time that temptation, like a bottle to an alcoholic, never goes away. Thus, this man of flesh and blood yielded, gave in to her beauty.

And for a dozen years at the turn of the century, they had indulged themselves and their love had become central in his life. He woke and thought of her. When he closed his eyes at night, she was there, even if not physically.

He had remained a man of God; had done great things in the name of the Lord. He had become a bishop, then an archbishop. He had concentrated on Catholic education; specifically, as he saw it, bringing it into alignment with the modern world without compromising the principles he held dearly. He had come too far to fall now. In fact, there was only one more promotion to come, one remaining slope to clamber up.

He remembered when she had told him she was pregnant. His first thought was his career, continuing to do good for others. His second was his reputation. He was quickly ashamed at his thinking and rushed to make arrangements for Sophie's mother.

They found Signor LaNeve, a gentle soul and unmarried. He was a devout Catholic and had a religious bookshop, specialising in old Latin, Greek and Hebrew texts. He spoke all three languages, as well as Italian, English and French and lived in a tiny apartment above his shop.

Archbishop Forrundiker approached him first through an intermediary, a young French priest on his staff called Father LaPetite. He was then stick thin and very tall, like a man on stilts above the heads in a crowd. He had a gruff aura, like an Italian rugby professional he had prepared for marriage years ago: tough, devoted and with a seriously good sense of humour.

He recalled the expression on LaPetite's face when he first took him into his confidence. "Twelve years?" the young priest had mirrored, seeing his superior as someone he had not known until then.

But he had reported back after the first meeting with LaNeve that the chosen man was conducive to an arrangement. Thereafter, LaPetite had taken control, even convincing Sophie's mother it was for the best to make a clean start, break off relations with her lover for the good of the church.

They were married quietly when Sophie's mother was five months pregnant. She had a dress made that disguised the baby well. But there were few in the congregation as they exchanged their vows. There was a modest financial settlement, efficiently arranged by LaPetite. It allowed LaNeve to buy a house in a tiny square with four narrow floors and a central staircase going up and up.

It was nobody's fault that Sophie's mother died from complications shortly after giving birth. But, before she died, she made the archbishop promise to look after their child throughout his life. She knew that she had a girl. She named her Sophie, the same name as she had. Perhaps she knew instinctively about the infection that caught hold of her as she held her baby on the third floor of their little house. That infection drove life out of her like an invading army. Perhaps she called the baby Sophie to remind her ex-lover of his responsibility towards her. He recalled the dog-eared way she had gone after the two promises:

1. *I shall look after our child, although staying in the background, until the end of my days.*
2. *When it can do Signor LaNeve no harm, I will take Sophie in my arms and tell her the complete and absolute truth, whatever her age.*

Archbishop Forrundiker was there when she died, minutes after she had extracted these promises and demanded he recite them three times: military orders in triplicate.

"I have carved them on your soul, my love," she had joked, placing her weary hand in his, looking at him with the power of love.

He gave the last rites, sat a long time alone in the room as the sun moved shadows across the floor until the gloom in the room matched the gloom in the man.

Forrundiker lived frugally and could manage a small stipend out of his allowance for Sophie's schooling. He tried to visit the young girl. At first it worked, but as she grew she resembled her mother more and more and the visits became fewer until a whole year had gone with no visits at all. He had gone towards the LaNeve house several times over the years when Sophie was a teenager, but each time there was no courage left when he hit the little cobbled square that told him he was almost there.

He still sent the money and increased it a little every time his conscience told him to.

Then Signor LaNeve came to him one day. Sophie was leaving school and needed a job. He would bring her to meet with Forrundiker the next evening after school.

"She's a lovely girl but a bit strange," LaNeve told the cardinal.

"How so?" but he already knew. She would be direct, bubbling over with energy and blithely unaware of normal behaviour; a magical child in a young woman's body.

She would be like her mother, the woman Forrundiker had loved to the end.

"I can't promise anything," Forrundiker added to LaNeve, hoping somehow to gain the upper hand.

But there was no upper hand to be got with Sophie as he discovered the next evening. She was everything rolled into one, like a recipe put together with complete abandon, but somehow tasting perfect. He saw arrogance, intelligence, good and bad, kindness, dignity and wilfulness. But most of all he saw her mother come again and he could not bear it.

Some years earlier the archbishop had been promoted to cardinal. As one of the most senior church officials, he could not afford any scandal, especially not with his final ambition as yet unfulfilled.

So, when Sophie stood before him, like her mother all over again in all her beautiful glory, he could not concentrate on what they discussed. He took part in the conversation, heard his own voice making sensible remarks, but the import of that discussion might as well have been the roar of aeroplanes coming in to land.

"Thank you, Your Eminence," said Signor LaNeve, guiding Sophie out of the room with his arm. "It is very kind of you to take my daughter on to your staff. I'm sure she is very grateful and will work hard. She will start, if it is agreeable to you, in two weeks when her school finishes."

"Yes, yes, of course."

But he was encapsulated 20 years in the past. Every time he saw Sophie over the next three years, he felt a great flood of sorrow for what he had and then had lost. Was it any wonder that he reacted harshly to the young girl, desperate to keep her at arm's length? His hostility was the armour he put on each morning to guard against his soulful memories.

But then one day recently, he had come to her in his distress, bumbling along the corridor and into her office, just as countless times before he had gone to her mother for solace.

And he had found it again with his daughter.

But now it was his turn to give solace and he did not know if he had the strength to do it.

It was a mighty trial he faced, for the more he thought of the past, the less he liked himself.

But then, the more he honestly disliked himself, the more open he became to solutions. Such is the nature of time as a healer; a wonderful concept that, in most instances, slips into place as the original sin fades with time, like curling wallpaper or tatty favourite novels with crinkled covers and yellowed pages.

And the first move is always the hardest. After that first move, it is downhill all the way. Or so the elderly cardinal repeated to himself, muttering truths as if saying the rosary.

Thus, the hardest part, in theory, was already behind him when he had Sophie alone in his hotel suite.

But Sophie had first to spill out everything about Tammy and Father Barrow, open questions mixing with awkward answers like juggernauts merging on the wide-open road, shunting and shoving for space and then fitting in to one coherent convoy of thought.

Sophie was full of it, like a child gone to see a favourite film. But all the old man needed was patience, something he had a large reservoir of, as he waited for the opportunity to insert an opening fact.

"What did you say about my father?"

This was the opportunity. But, just as he needed it, his courage went away.

"My dear," he said, lying though he spoke the truth, "this morning your father breathed his last."

He went no further with his story, telling himself how could he when this lovely girl, his daughter, cracked her face open and flooded the room with tears for the loss of the father who was not?

He spent the hours after her departure trying to tell himself he had done what was best. It was not the right time to divulge everything. There would be time enough for the whole story. Better not to hit the poor girl with everything at once.

But then, just as the day came around again and Sophie was gone to the airport, back to Rome, he admitted it to himself; the weak sunshine after several days of rain was just sufficient to light up the truth in the cardinal's heart.

He would have to do a lot better next time. He spoke in his heart to Sophie's mother, promising a better performance, promising to keep his promise to her. Then he lay down his weary head, two days without sleep, just the bare walls of his hotel room, so that the soft hotel pillows encased him in the luxury of oblivion.

And he slept with the Lord, his God, watching over him.

Mostly About Men Struggling

Ernest Justice was back in Roanoke, humbled by Tammy's revelations, shorn of ambition like a clean new haircut, but strangely re-growing that ambition in twisted, stunted form as the familiar trees and streets of his hometown settled his mind. In normal circumstances, he might seek the company of Chesington Bloakes III, perhaps confiding in Tammy's friend that he had worked against her, then falsely adding that he now had seen the light. Only Ches was no longer in Roanoke. He had watched the debate on television and, seeing Tammy bare her soul to the world, had made plans to get to London as soon as possible. He had to be there for Tammy and nothing would hold him back.

Miles, however, was not so inclined to rush to anyone's aid. He did what was required, of course, taking Tammy back to the flat above the fish and chip shop, providing emotional support, arranging for Bill to pick them up in the morning for the inevitable round of interviews and press conferences as they frantically worked out what to do. But there was a great big yawning gap in their relationship that a space ship could happily pass through. Neither Miles nor Tammy knew how to cross that gap.

And remember that Miles is British and male, so Miles did what British men do and carefully stepped around the problem; politeness substituting for emotion. Ultimately, he would be there for Tammy. She knew that and he knew that. But there was an unspoken breach that no bridge could span.

She had confided in the public at large before she had confided in him and that was the threatened ruin of their relationship.

On the night of the Great Debate, back eventually in the flat above the fish and chip shop, they went through tender motions but only the motions. They did not make love. They shared the only bed, were gentle in a respectful way, but the passion was removed, lost in her recent dishonesty.

Tammy might have wondered at the impossibility of a dishonest state arising from the most honest declaration of her life. Only she did not marvel at the irony because there was another dominant force that pushed all others aside. As Tammy closed her eyes, jammed against the wall at the far edge of the bed, she was thinking not of her boyfriend, not of the passions of this life but of another life altogether.

The one that had been taken from her nine years before.

And so Miles Standish, kind frustrated soul, bit down on his lip to control his feelings and be there in some form for Tammy. At first, he lay awake and watched her sleep in his bed, seeing her solid beauty slip from his grasp. How can one day of 24 short hours make the difference between love in abundance and love lost? How can the earth in one revolution, tipping this way and that as it rushes through the nothing of space, bring about such change? It was not just peak to trough; there was an element of that. But it was also evaporation; gloriously thick fog at the start of a cold winter's day turning to hard brittle sunshine that bounced off the ground without dispelling any heat; both fog and sun leaving nothing behind to hold on to.

Then, when he slept eventually, it was her turn to wake and look at him in the glow of the street light outside.

"Dear Lord," she whispered, "let this man be happy as he deserves. For me, I ask that You reveal Your plan so that I may follow Your will." She was losing the battle to love another like she loved Him.

But when Miles opened his eyes the next morning, something had changed with him. He woke to the grey late November day, marred further by the street grime on the windows to his flat, feeling much like he imagined the redcoats felt at Roarke's Drift, Zulu chants pressing from every side. He faced a hopeless task but would carry on regardless. He would be there for Tammy, no matter the cost to him. Thus, he became a church of one, a congregation of one, standing alone as a quiet hero in a noisy world. He would not have owned up to a relationship with any god right then, but relationships happen when they do, not when we want them to.

And in a twisted way, he had found his god, although it took some time to recognise it.

Father Humphrey Barrow SJ faced another struggle between God and man, so similar yet so different. He sat alone that night, long after the last journalist had rushed to a deadline, long after Sophie had kissed him warmly on both cheeks, issuing an unspoken invitation he did not know how to respond to. He sat there, reasonably comfortably, coffee going cold at his side, clock ticking merrily towards another November morning. He sat in the lobby of the hotel where great big double height windows spoke of the dark world beyond. He wondered how the new day would come. Would the light follow the streets, twisting around the buildings to brighten his view? Or would it play games and dance and jump about, gradually filing the pixels of his vision with colour until all darkness was banished?

How, he wondered, could he tell the future? What actions should he take now that might govern that future? More to the point, why, suddenly, was the future so important? His future had always been given to Another, yet now he claimed it as if givers could be takers-back. He was entering new territory like a virgin explorer, no maps to guide and no certain destination to seek.

Why could he not pull himself, the individual, the human being, out of the picture as he had always done? Then he could look down at the humans with appropriate and balanced measures of compassion, tolerance and wisdom. Why, instead, was he stuck now in the very scenes he should be observing?

The answer was simple. For the first time in his 35-year life, this man was faced with hope. And hope is a wonderful thing.

Only he could not see it.

Instead he wondered why his thoughts always went back to Sophie. Why, for instance, when he closed his eyes he saw not dark, the night outside leaking into his mind? Instead, he saw those beautiful blonde locks as they flicked around and caught the sun that should be banished from night. He opened his eyes to the dark, then closed them again and the light returned, bringing with it the curve of her body, next time the look of laughter on her face.

It was a world turned upside down, so he sat motionless, only the mind-wasting energy in perpetual motion, coffee turning even colder. Four spectacular degrees from the best universities could not insulate one from falling in love, just as even a hundred thousand vows of celibacy would fail. Love happens whether you seek it or not.

And every time he turned to the dark, her face entered in and danced and jostled its way to centre stage.

It was so unfair to fall in love.

But then, what has love got to do with fairness?

And the night wound on, springs tensioning so that the new day could be leveraged in, as the clock worked around to the correct position. Yet it seemed the clock would never get there so that the welcoming routine of day would supplant his night-time torment. By half past three, Humphrey had become restless enough to rise from his chair and seek solace or advice or anything that was human and outside his own tortured mind. His path, unplanned, led in the direction of experience so at twenty to four, his fingers tapped quietly on the door of Cardinal Forrundiker's room.

The slightest knock was sufficient, for the cardinal was on his knees again, reports of the evening's debate echoing through his mind as he tried to pray, tried to be a force for good in this rapidly changing world.

"Come in," he called, bones creaking as he got off his knees.

"Your Eminence, I'm sorry…"

"That's quite alright," replied the cardinal, all abrasiveness evaporated. Gone for good to another place or merely in hiding and awaiting its turn? Who could tell? Then the cardinal added that he had hoped, no, expected, Humphrey to call on him.

The use of Humphrey's first name was like a young girl presenting flowers to an aged monarch on a royal visit. It bridged both rank and generations in an impossible way. Humphrey sat on the only chair in the hotel room and felt able, despite being British, to bare his soul to the old Italian.

Even so, it was not easy. How does a vocation-bound speak to another of things that threaten the very establishment they are part and parcel of? And to the one so senior, so much older and so much wiser?

Yet he did it. He did it clumsily and hesitantly, stumbling over words, including great pauses as if they imparted as much as the words that peppered the silences.

And as Humphrey spoke, he saw the great impassive face of authority. He panicked at that impassiveness, thinking his instinct had led him badly.

But he was wrong in this assumption. Honest and true instinct is never faulty. It is the backbone of humanity, the building block of our history and who we are.

As his sin-riddled tale neared its end, his cardinal, a leader of the church, broke his impassivity, his face crinkling into understanding.

And then the cardinal switched from English to Italian and told his tale, much more eloquently than Humphrey's spluttering. It flowed with Latin passion; the tale of his middle years and the joy that had been Sophie's mother.

And this time he told it all.

The Funeral

Sophie's square, on which the narrow LaNeve house stood had everything required for daily life. Three doors down from Sophie's house lived a doctor who years before had married a midwife. As a young girl, before school had featured in her life, Sophie had gone to the midwife's house during the day while her father was in his shop. She had gone out on calls with her, sitting in the corner with a book but picking up much of the midwife's trade in the effortless way that only children can. Next door to the midwife was the delicatessen where Sophie sometimes stopped after work for a glass of wine in the cool of the stone-pillared overhang that overlooked the square.

The next length of that square, going clockwise, contained a hairdresser and a greengrocer plus space where an old man with a large barrow sold fish and seafood each morning except Sunday.

On Sundays, of course, they went to the far side of the square where the Church of San Cristoforo lay like the tomb of a forgotten soldier. You could easily miss the tiny door. Even if you found it, that door led to a plain octagonal, stone-flagged chamber with a low table and another small door on the righthand side. Only through that door did you enter the church of San Cristoforo running along the whole side of the square. High small windows and heavy stained glass kept a dimness about the place, punctuated with strands of different colours as the glass translated sunlight outside into holy light within. Above the altar was a woodcarving of St Christopher crossing the river with Christ on his back. It was old, worn and dark, showing a man with a great burden struggling across the water. Sophie had thought him a hunchback when she was a child. She had talked to him when the Mass went on too long, explaining her hopes and fears and why she did the things that she did.

Someone in the square had wanted to change the name of the church, claiming St Christopher to be de-canonised. They had started a committee when Sophie had been thirteen and she had led the defence against that change, much as she did now as Director of Defence Strategy, defending her church against the unwelcome bidders. The committee had petered out and the name had remained, St Christopher surviving for another generation.

Now Sophie stood in the dark church once more, noting the familiar dust specs that made a shower around them.

They had carried the coffin in through the far side entrance. This newer and wider door led on to a sweet graveyard, now damp and forlorn, then the priest's house on the other side. The original door was too small for a coffin plus its carriers; built, perhaps, without thought to the needs of those in transit to the next world. Maybe the architects had thought that St Christopher would carry them there on his back.

Sophie stood by her father's coffin, her lovely long blonde hair severely restrained, as if an enemy of true mourning, its intentions given away by its bright yellowness. Her head was covered in a long black veil anyway, to void the world of all colour.

Sophie wept for her loss. Mia, by her side, stood grim and upright, arm around her friend, folding her back into Mia's body; a form of comfort. The church was full. Signor LaNeve would never have predicted it. All his regular customers were there, as were the entire inhabitants of the little square they had moved into just before Sophie's birth.

The organ started. It was not a very good one, wheezing like an old nag at the races. The organist had been Signor LaNeve's best friend, sharing their love of antiquity. Tears slid down his face, blurring the music sheet so he stopped and started as if just learning to play.

Into one such pause came the heavy sound of multiple footsteps, then the door banged open and a voice sang out "Good Lord! Whoever would put such a tiny door in a church?" Sophie turned to see Father LaPetite's great bulk as he shouted, "Coming through, make way, make way. More to follow!"

They streamed through; half the office led by the huge French priest. Sophie, looking back over her shoulder, saw familiar face after familiar face. Father Ellsworthy was next; then the entire contingent of her own team. The cardinal came through the door as if a character in a play entering the stage as the central part of a grand procession. She watched each person come through the doorway like they were popping from one world to another. She waited patiently for the one she hoped to see.

He was last through. Humphrey Barrow led the rear, closing the door deliberately, as if pulling up the drawbridge. People shuffled along the seats, trying to fit three-dozen more into a crowded church. The cardinal was led to the front row where everybody squeezed along the bench. Sophie signalled for Humphrey to join her at the front, but her signs were misread and Father Ellsworthy pointed at himself with a quizzical expression, then came to sit next to Sophie, blocking out any possibility for Humphrey to join her.

She looked back one more time and saw him standing in the extreme back right corner. He wore his arms before him, hands clasped, as expected of a religious fellow in church.

But the consolation was that he saw her looking and smiled. That smile was only for her. Sophie doubted that anyone else could even see it. It was a targeted smile; a private smile. It was a smile just for her.

She turned back to the front and turned her mind to her dead father.

She had not seen Humphrey since the evening of the debate. She had left him when summoned to the cardinal's room to hear of her father's death; told tenderly by a man she never thought could be tender. From there, someone else had taken over, an efficient secretary she did not know. Early the next morning she was on a flight back to Rome. By midday she had seen her father lying in their sitting room on the first floor. He looked to her like he was already in another place, the place he had always hoped to go after this world. It was where Sophie hoped to go too one day in the distant future.

All that was left was a shell, wizened, shrunken, life gone out. But calm, so very sweet and calm, as if he held a ticket to Heaven in his right hand.

Mia had taken the week off work. It was Mia who accompanied her to the lawyers, who made the arrangements for the funeral and the party afterwards. Mia reminded her to get her hair done the day before, helped her dress that morning, chose her jewellery and held her hand as they crossed the square to the Church of San Cristoforo.

The Mass was not long, but it was tender like an open wound. The priest gave a short eulogy, speaking in glowing terms of the quiet man who had lived for 21 years in their midst; generous with both time and money, devout, fun, a good man to have in your life. Then the cardinal stood and said a few words, as was expected of cardinals. He spoke mysteriously of Christ coming into people and making good from evil, hope from fear, love from something, but Sophie had stopped listening, thinking instead of the gentle man who had always been there for her.

Afterwards they filed out through the side door into relentless rain. Mia had not thought to bring an umbrella and Sophie most certainly had not. They hesitated at the door, then stepped out, holding hands. The sharp wind picked up the sodden leaves, blowing them against the mourners as if trying valiantly to keep interlopers out of their graveyard.

Then Father LaPetite appeared behind Mia with an umbrella. Sophie turned to say hello to him but bumped instead into Humphrey. He stumbled and used the opened umbrella he was offering to Sophie to break his fall. The spokes hit the wall of the church, bending sharply outwards, turning the umbrella inside out. Sophie grabbed his arm, steadied him before he slid into the mud.

It was with broken umbrella, one side hanging down like a badly erected tent, that the two went out to stand by the grave. Sophie felt the tears again as the body was lowered on ropes. Humphrey gripped her arm instinctively, feeling the pulsating warmth that was Sophie.

They said a silent prayer together. They did not know what the other said but understood the intent, the message.

"We should go now," Sophie said.

"Yes," was all Humphrey said.

"You will come back to the house?"

"If you want me to."

"I do."

"What news of the takeover bid?" Sophie asked a group of priests, mirroring her own black dress.

"Have you not heard?" Father Ellsworthy replied. "There is to be a conference here in Rome."

"A conference?"

"Yes, to try and find a solution. It was their idea." This last statement was without malice altogether. In fact, Sophie detected a note of admiration.

"You approve?"

"We all do."

"But talking means compromise. We have sworn ourselves not to compromise." Sophie's voice was rising as her face reddened. The room was stuffy. She left the room suddenly, got some air on the balcony that looked over the square below. This was her square encompassing her little world. She went out each day to the Vatican, but this is where she belonged. This was where there was order and right in every stone, every cobble, every street sign and shop awning. This is where she greeted everyone by name, had grown up with them, asked them of their illnesses and wished them speedy recovery. Sometimes she thought that she should have trained to be the next midwife in the square, taking over when her friend finally retired. Then she would bring new life into this little world of hers, oblivious to the world outside, concentrating just on her square.

But then she shook herself. She did not have the patience to study midwifery, nor much else for that matter. She was all about the present. And the present was now without her father, the beloved Signor LaNeve.

With a shock she realised that she was the only LaNeve now. She was the sole survivor of the great snow lords she imagined her family descended from. Why else would they have that family name? It was her task to carry on the traditions to her dying day.

She had no family.

"It must be awful for you." It was the voice of Father Barrow, also on the little balcony overlooking the wet twilight in the square. "You know, I never knew my father."

"Really?" That was just like the mother she had never known.

"And my mother died earlier this year, just a few months before I came to Rome."

"Father," Sophie reverted to the requested address, "Father…"

"Don't call me that. My name is Humphrey."

But when Sophie said his name it came out with an extra syllable and a Latin tail that rose at the end as if wagging to the world. That made them giggle uncontrollably each time she repeated it.

But laughter wears out eventually like bones and eyesight. They could not laugh all night because there was something serious lurking in that humour. It waited patiently for the laughter to fall away, for the comedians to exit so the tragic actors could take centre stage.

"I love you, Humphrey," she said, same Latin tail to his name but all humour gone. He was just about to reply when there was a cry from behind them.

"Ah, there you are, Barrow." The cardinal walked onto the balcony, making it a squeeze. "And dear Sophie as well." Sophie jerked to attention, body reacting to mind. The old man had lost much of his ferociousness recently, but a term of endearment? "I'm a little tired, Barrow, could you possibly tear yourself away from this delectable creature and take me home?"

"We were just talking about the latest developments following the debate," Humphrey lied. Sophie nodded her agreement, but she was okay with the sin as both sets of fingers were double-crossed behind her back. "But, of course, I will take you home, Your Eminence," Humphrey continued.

Sophie tried for a glance from Humphrey as he left the balcony and made for the stairs, collecting his ridiculously damaged umbrella on the way. At the last moment, as he followed the cardinal out of the door, she was rewarded when he looked back and up at her, now on the staircase landing. He did not wave or speak, nor did he smile, but his eyes said everything and that was enough for Sophie.

In the car on the way back to the cardinal's lodgings, there was only one topic of conversation, for the old man was truly tired.

"You have not mentioned anything about Sophie's parentage?" It was easier to refer to the plural of 'parents' than to be specific that it was the father. Using the singular would be just a little bit too honest.

"No, Your Eminence, I am sworn to secrecy by you."

They drove on in silence; if silence can describe the wind and rain beating against their car, while the windscreen wipers scraped against the glass leaving smears so that Humphrey had to adjust his position to see the road.

"She is a delectable creature," the cardinal repeated his earlier observation, as if saying it again proved the point.

Humphrey considered feigning ignorance, but there was too much truth in the air; an untruth now would register on all the screens, sending warning signals back to HQ. He reflected how relative truth was. They were at that moment around 75: high on the scale but short of a century. There were some small but significant lies mixed in with the truth, bringing the overall score down. But those lies were not from his tongue.

"Yes, she certainly is," he said, the sigh escaping from his lips as he spoke.

Cardinal Forrundiker was about to say something, thought better of it and went back to silent mode for the rest of the short journey through rain-battered streets.

And Humphrey drove on through his agony.

No-one left the funeral party until the cardinal went. Then there was a steady trickle so that two hundred guests were reduced two hours later to half that number. The clock of San Cristoforo struck six, prompting a fresh batch to depart. By 7:15 p.m., it was down to a hard core of priests encircling Sophie and Mia, Fathers LaPetite and Ellsworthy among them. Sophie had lifted her veil but otherwise was clothed all in black from head to foot; just her pale face and yellow tied-back hair staring out on the world. As she looked around, she believed she looked just like the priests. The only contrast they had to their black garb was their stiff white collars. We're all like magpies, like people from the black and white movie era, she thought as she listened to the conversations limping along.

Then she realised that she and Mia, also completely in black, were the only girls in the room. She felt momentarily like an honourary priest, invited into their circle so that her friends could parcel out her sadness, spread it more evenly, make it more bearable.

It was a false feeling. Her sadness was heavy, that much was true. But she did not want to share it, even resenting others muscling in on her sorrow. She felt like a female figurehead on a fast sailing ship, streaming black robes flowing as they roared through sea and wind. It was her loss, not theirs. She wished they would all go, even Mia, but maybe just to the square outside so they could look in and witness her in mourning.

There was a second reason why she was not an honourary priest that day.

She was female and priests were male.

"Father LaPetite, what do you think of the Church of New Moderation's proposal to allow women to become priests?"

"Preposterous idea, Sophie." But shortly afterwards, the fat priest led her by the arm back to Humphrey's balcony as she thought of it now. "Actually, I think it is a good idea," he said quietly, looking back over his shoulder as if he expected spies behind the curtains.

"What's a good idea?"

"Female priests."

"But you said…"

"I know what I said, my dear, but the truth is I can't risk my views being discovered by the cardinal. He would have me out on my ear in a twinkling if he even suspected. I've long thought it wise for a number of reasons. I'll list them if you like."

Sophie nodded, looking up at the big man.

So, he listed his reasons, stating they were in no particular order. First was a practical one. "The church is woefully short of priests," he said, "yet we are ignoring half the population of the world."

His second reason was more concerned with fairness: why deny and disenfranchise half the population of the world? Talk of disenfranchisement made Sophie think of the bid for the church; it was based on one person one vote, leaving no-one disenfranchised.

"Then there's the question of sexual abuse. Quite possibly this is the most important reason of all. I actually believe the New Moderation movement is right in this regard. By denying priests sexual relations we are creating a manic seething pot of frustration. It often leads to abuse in some form or other. If priests could marry and women could be priests, that whole incredible mess of frustration would be gone in an instant. That can only be a good thing."

They talked on a few minutes, Sophie soaking up the thoughts and words of Father LaPetite. Back in the sitting room the party numbers dwindled again, until there was barely a handful clustered around Mia.

"So, Sophie, it must be time to go now. But tell me first, why you think it important to have female priests."

That was easy, so easy the answer trotted out before the brain instructed it.

"Because I would like to become a priest."

This sentence hit LaPetite hard in the stomach. He never would have expected it.

"You could be a nun," he replied, struggling to process what she had told him.

"No way!" Her thoughts went straight to Sister Mary John. She shivered at the idea of subservience. It could never be her way. "I need to be in the first order of things, making the decisions," she tried to explain, "I mean also I want to get married and have children and live a normal life here but also be a priest. What is wrong with that?"

Her pale face had gone red. Her hair was working its way loose as if emotional restraint had kept the locks in place rather than the black metal clips Mia had found. She trembled as she looked at this big man, this mound of flesh, this good but sharp-tongued priest in front of her. "You are one of my best friends, Father, so I tell the truth to you always."

'I know Sophie, my dear. And you are one of my best friends too!" He kissed her as friends would kiss, as if to make his case. Then he held both her hands and looked into her eyes. He knew the truth of her parentage and itched to tell her but was sworn to secrecy. So what sort of friend was he? Secrets were often such hateful things, especially with someone like Sophie who shone with an honesty born of good and bad in equal measure. "I seem to be the last person here, must not outstay my welcome!" He made a jest of his awkwardness, turning embarrassment into something easy in one fluid sentence as some can do. And mainly because his companion wanted him to be easy again, had never wanted to cause difficulty for this generous man.

"Of course, Father," she replied, pecking him on the cheek as if he were a favourite uncle and she a lovably errant child. But the import of what they had discussed would remain with Father LaPetite long after the memories of the day had faded.

Bill's Idea

It had been Bill's idea. Fi later said he had created the problem and then he had solved it.

She would go on to explain that it was Bill who had first voiced the idea of a Great Debate, thus raising the temperature between bidder and defender to fever-pitch; or at least raised it amongst the press who would not leave either party alone.

But just as this increased the heat to scald-level, so his idea of a conference to resolve matters spread a soothing ointment on the raw, open burns.

Afterwards, allowing an ounce more perspective than evident at the time, Bill would expound that sometimes these ideas work together in unison.

"First, you create antagonism as this isolates the ideas and sets out the opposing views perfectly. Then you work to bring the parties together, find common ground."

But, in quieter moments, he would readily admit that it was just another idea he had come upon.

He first suggested it to Fi in bed early one morning as her restlessness had woken him again.

"Are you okay?" he asked as she returned to bed.

"Just feeling a little off-colour," she replied. "Plus trying to think of a way through this mess."

"I'm sorry, my love. It seems like my debate idea has caused you all sorts of problems. I guess we need no more public debate now, just the key people sitting around a table to sort out their differences. Then you can get back to what you're good at – making obscene amounts of money every day of the week!"

But the joke fell flat, for Fi was transfixed by the first part of Bill's comment.

"By all that is holy," she cried, "I think you've got it, Bill!" She kicked off her bedclothes, launched herself up out of bed, feeling lighter than she had for a while; danced then, nightie only, on the bedroom floor.

"What is it? What did I say?" Bill spluttered through his laughter. "Why the rain dance?"

"It's not a rain dance, silly!" She came over and kissed him on the lips, the cheeks, the forehead, the eyelids; any place she could find. "How can it be a rain dance when it has not stopped raining for a month?" she laughed, then solemnly explained that it was a victory dance she had been doing.

Even in seeking compromise, Fi could discover a victory.

Tammy loved the idea. All fight had gone out of her since the debate, so that Fi had worried endlessly how to progress matters. The life president of the Church of New Moderation had attended interviews and meetings throughout the weeks that followed the debate, as Christmas came into view as sparkling matter on the horizon.

But she went from interview to interview in desultory mode; the real Tammy had been exposed, not as a radical reformer but as a demure, obedient woman of God. She could no longer play 'let's pretend'. She had to face up to being a grown-up now. Even her dress moved by stages, from the smart business suits Fi had ordered to drab blacks, greys and whites; dowdy affairs growing daily more like convent garb.

"It's like she's in sackcloth and ashes," someone had said, sadly within Miles' earshot.

Everyone in the team was delighted when Bill's idea brought back a tiny part of Tammy Shroton's energy. Perversely, everyone other than Miles, that is, for Miles was angry with whoever the god was that he thought he had come to know since meeting Tammy. The god his girlfriend was so keen on seemed like a chemist, mixing slight differences in chemical composition each day and noting the resultant changes in behaviour. Was god really so bored that he had to play with lives to add a little spice into his tedious forever-ness, world without end? Would god not prefer to be mortal, thus valuing the passing of time, rather than spending days that did not exist, aging without growing old, tinkering endlessly with the lives of people? He particularly hated the rosary that Tammy had now started to use, for it was a never-ending circle. The end of the chain brought you not the exhausted satisfaction of a task done but right back to the beginning again; just as this god made a new experiment with every single division of time; never changing, never growing, always back around the loop one more time.

He had tried to dissuade her from the rosary. It did not work, at least to start with. He had tried to reason that it was a tool of the other party in the bid, thus weakening the case Tammy and her team made. Then he had argued more stridently that it was a weapon for the devil to utilise, designed to enslave people into repeated mutterings; developing a trance-like status that denied reason, denied humanity. Tammy did not buy Miles' arguments. She was prepared to discuss it but would not give it up.

Finally, one night he asked her again. They had just made love. It had become something they had done without thinking or talking. It just happened. And afterwards she had clung to him long into the night, as if clinging to a cliff edge, frightened to fall into the world below.

He had spoken into the dark, not thinking she was awake. He had said simply that he loved her and felt the rosary had come between them. He felt her body tense, wondered if she was in fact awake, then weariness took him to sleep.

But he never saw the rosary slide through her fingers again.

One person fully behind the conference was Chesington Bloakes III. Recently over from Roanoke, he represented fresh troops from the homeland and was very much a leader in that time of need. He had an energy that belied his 69 years. He seemed bigger out of his native land, as if he had fitted into the landscape at home as one more American, but in London his big body and loud voice found a purpose and an audience.

"Hi, I wanna talk with Father Humphrey." He was one of those types who handled a phone by putting volume in to get volume out. "This is Chesington Bloakes III of the New Moderation outfit." He sounded like a cowboy, branding iron in hand.

"I'll see if he is available, sir," replied one of the young priests on phone duty.

"Dear Mr Bloakes, this is Signorina Sophie LaNeve. I'm sorry but Father Barrow is tied…"

"Soph! Well, this is a treat. Listen Soph, I've been asked to come over to Rome and sort out the arrangements for the conference: venue, agenda and so forth." He assumed her English was up to understanding his easy-going way with words.

"Then you need a speak with me as I am the Director of Defence Strategy. When do you come to Rome?"

"Hey, I'm here right now, at the airport, but flying solo for a few days; my wife is staying with friends in London, England. Say, how do I get to your place?" Sophie thought of the cramped offices, overflowing with seconded priests writing reports, answering phones, making press appointments. It was no place to invite the enemy. She thought hard for a venue.

"Ask the taxi to take you to Via Romulus, it's in the old quarter. I'll meet you at number 14. It's the big red house, you can't miss it." She replaced the receiver and immediately called Old Ma Silver, asking for use of her house for a meeting that morning.

"Of course, dear Sophie. I'll come right over and let you in."

"Can you be quick? This American with a big voice is going to be there in thirty minutes."

Twenty-five minutes later an unused salon on the first floor had been hastily dusted, the musty smell disguised under fresh coffee in a large pot.

"Great, you've got coffee over here too!" Ches said, "I'm beginning to like this town." Without being asked, he crossed the room and poured a cup for himself. "Delicioso, or whatever you say over here. This coffee fills a need." He poured himself a second cup, drank it, refilled and poured two others for his hosts. "Drink up guys, we've got a lot to cover today."

Whether it was coffee during the meetings or beer for lunch, Ches consumed vast quantities. Old Ma Silver went out at midday and brought back fresh, piping-hot pizza from the shop on the corner.

"You didn't need to buy American," Ches said, then refused to believe that pizza was Italian.

"Don't you think you got pizza from somewhere?" Old Ma Silver asked.

"Sure," he replied, "it came from New York."

They all laughed. In fact, they laughed often and long. Sophie felt it was the first time she had laughed since the cardinal had taken her into his London hotel room and told her that her father had gone on his last and greatest journey. She fought the laughter, the joy, at first. Guilt at mirth so soon after her father had died mixed with guilt that she was laying with the enemy. But Chesington Bloakes III was nobody's enemy. You could not help but warm to the big, square frame that housed his winning personality.

Old Ma Silver was caught in his charm net as well, especially when, after failing to find a venue for the conference, he suddenly said her house would work perfectly.

"It's a real fine old pile," he said, "perfect for our needs. We can tidy it up a might, set some big tables in this room. I can't think of a better place."

And that's how 14, Via Romulus came to be the venue for Bill's conference.

Perfidy amidst Preparation

There was a neat circle to their claims.

The editor blamed the assistant editor who, in turn, blamed the editor.

They both also blamed their source, but that did not wash at all.

"I want you both out in fifteen minutes. Clear your desks and get out." The Saudi billionaire had watched the Great Debate, found it shameful that his newspaper had played the part it did.

"You'll lose money if you let me go," the editor tried his usual approach.

"Is that right?"

"It most certainly is," the assistant editor spoke up, muscling in on the argument. "You know we're the only team to make money on Fleet Street."

"You're right, gentlemen. I would hazard a guess that you make more money than all the other newspapers combined." He was going to enjoy this. He saw their shoulders jerk up, postures back to arrogance on the dial. Time to pounce. "Gentlemen, as you know I am wealthy, fabulously wealthy I can boast." He watched his prey with professional interest. "So wealthy I can happily lose a pile of cash by doing what I should have done years ago." The owner lent forward, causing the editor to shrink back in alarm. But it was just a move to locate the phone, press the speaker button. "Security, please send all available staff to my office immediately. I need you to escort two ex-employees out of the building." He replaced the receiver, giving a thin smile to those ex-employees. "Don't worry about clearing your desks. Everything personal will be forwarded to you."

As they were shunted down the passageway, the billionaire could hear them stubbornly blaming each other. He settled back, poured a large Scotch that his religion forbade, and thought about replacements. The sacking needed to be presented positively. That way circulation would shake off the downward spiral of the last three weeks since the debate. Who knows, played correctly it might even start to rise again. That was key for advertising confidence, the real money earner.

He swilled the single malt around his mouth, drawing it through his teeth in a way that infuriated his mistress. He felt sure that enough of the newspaper business had rubbed off on him over the years of ownership. He would head the paper himself, at least for the short term. But who would his assistant editor be? He reached for his phone again.

"Tell Glenda I'd like to see her immediately."

Marcus Brandywine, ex-editor of the Daily Witness, saw life in black and white and his ego was an egg on which nothing would balance. Either people fawned over him or they affronted him. He shook off Eddie Bathurst, his odious ex-assistant with a "meet me tomorrow, 11 a.m., Red Lion. Don't be late."

"What are you going to do?"

"Phone calls to make, plans to put in place, now bleedin' well scarper."

Yet for all his hatred wrapped in bluster, it was Bathurst who came up with the best idea over a pint the next day.

"I think we should get together with that American guy Glenda brought in. What was his name?" He looked through his phone. "Ah, Ernest Justice. We'll use him to get some justice!"

But first Brandywine had to be convinced that it had been his idea to contact Ernest. Eddie did some deft word-work over the next few minutes.

"Got his phone number?" the ex-editor asked.

"Yes, boss." It had worked. Eddie knew that his idea would now take root.

"Well, what the hell are you waiting for, bleedin' Christmas?"

The time difference, five hours ahead, worked in their favour. They got Ernest at breakfast, wondering despondently what this tedious day would bring him, along with all the other tedious days to follow.

"Ern," Brandywine knew how to relate to Americans, "it's your buddies from the Daily Witness. We need your help, amigo."

They quickly arranged, on scanty explanation, for Ernest to come back to London immediately.

"Piece of cake," Brandywine said on clicking to end the call.

They drank a few more, got a bottle of Scotch at an off-licence so they could strategise that afternoon; Bathurst woke on the sofa in Brandywine's flat with a raging headache and an urgent need to get to Heathrow to welcome Ernest.

Sophie let Ches make all the arrangements. He seemed born to it.

Besides, she rather liked working with this good-natured American.

"I work from the top down," he explained to Sophie as they sat around the table in Via Romulus. "First, I work out how many people will be coming."

"That's easy," she said, counting on her fingers. "There's the cardinal and Father Barrow and myself and…"

"I got the numbers direct from the cardinal's office. Here's the list." He handed her a printed piece of heavy paper. Six weeks ago, it would have been Sophie doing the admin; now some unknown secretary did the thankless tasks. She looked it over with an air of self-importance, as if she had to approve the inclusion of more junior members.

"Just a minute, where's my name?" She read the list again, turned over the page, handed it back to Ches. "There's a mistake here. I should be on the list. I should be near the top. It should go first the cardinal, followed by Father Barrow, Father LaPetite and then me. I should be before Father Ellsworthy. I'll need to get it retyped." She set it aside, face flushed with embarrassment at the omission. "Let's move on. What do you do second?"

"Second, I look at space."

"That's obvious." She could feel her skin like the burners on an electric stovetop, despite the crisp late November weather.

"Not so obvious as you might think. It's not just a meeting room. We have that right here." He looked around, a moment of appreciation for the splendid surroundings given for the duration of the conference. "But we have to think of separate meeting rooms for sub-committees, private rooms where each party can discuss matters. Then there's bathrooms, catering and so on. Also, Old Ma Silver has offered to put up the visiting delegation so I need to give her numbers of bedrooms."

They discussed the visiting delegation. There would be Tammy, Fi, Miles and Bill, Al and Sid and Ches, so a total of seven.

"Oh, and also one other board member so we have a quorum. That will be Ernest Justice as I heard this morning that he has made himself available and is now in London. So, eight in total. It's real generous of Old Ma Silver to give over the top floor for us."

"I think she loves the house being used and I'm happy to help by taking over the top floor arrangements," Sophie replied, thinking why was she not on the list? Was it just an error?

It was not, as she found out an hour later, from the cardinal. She had caught him between meetings occupying a chair in the busy campaign office; his tired frame sagging like a tent with broken fly ropes.

"Sophie, my dear, let me explain." It all seemed so much effort for the cardinal. "You are the organiser and you've done a great job of that. But for the delegation we need scholars in religion. We're going to be talking about doctrine. They have eight delegates and that limits us, by agreement, to eight also. I'm sorry, my dear, but this is how it is."

"No," said far too loudly in a public place. "No, no, no. This is everything I've wanted and worked for. I am an important person! It's not...not fair."

The sound of outrage brought Father LaPetite into the room. And he had an idea as soon as he had been briefed on the problem.

"Simple, Your Eminence. If we want nine attendees at the conference we simply have to open it up to allow one more on the other side. The agreement was for an equal number of delegates from each side, not necessarily limited to eight each."

"Quite so, I forget the details." The cardinal sounded distracted as he stared at Sophie, as if querying who on earth she was. His mind was working overtime, going through hundreds of outcomes like a computer whirring away. He could not yet be certain, but the conference seemed a fantastic opportunity to the cardinal. He just had to play it right.

"I suggest we should take the initiative and propose Mrs Justice as she is known to us and seems pretty reasonable. I'll put it to Mr Bloakes right away." Father LaPetite turned to leave, then thought better of it, adding, "After all, we would be shooting ourselves in the foot to exclude Sophie if we had half a chance of having her on our team!" This got a nod and an odd smile from the cardinal, as if he was only sometimes visiting this world but rather liked what he saw when he did.

And so, unknown to Ernest arriving in London, Ches had a call with Sara later that day. The gist of that conversation was that they needed her badly. And they did, for Ches had jumped at the suggestion made by Father LaPetite. Ches needed to keep Ernest in his box and his wife seemed the best way to achieve that.

He knew trouble; had faced it head on countless times.

They made a good act, editor and assistant-editor, standing at arrivals at Heathrow, greeting Ernest as he walked through, bag in hand.

"Where's Glenda?"

"She's on another assignment." Lies came easily to both of them, in this case it was Eddie, the assistant-editor. "We're going to look after you this time. And believe me, we know how to look after our important guests." Ernest broadened his smile from formal to cheeky grin, buoyed by the flattery and floating on the platitudes that tripped off their editorial tongues.

If Ernest liked his greeting at the airport, he loved his treatment that morning. A sleek black and elongated car took them effortlessly to a hotel in central London. This hotel prided itself on awareness and lack of procedure. Thus, a text from Eddie had Ernest checked in to the King's View Suite on the top floor before the car pulled up at the broad entrance. The same text ensured the general manager was waiting just inside the door to welcome Mr Justice to his humble concern. The champagne was perfect temperature and, as Marcus explained, the "perfect antidote for jetlag."

Marcus and Eddie disliked champagne, Marcus, in particular, found the bubbles irritated his sinuses. But, in the interests of sweet revenge, they found a way through two bottles. There is, after all, nothing like champagne to make a fellow feel important, and they certainly achieved that with their American guest.

But sooner or later they needed to move on to the serious stuff. Eddie timed the unveiling of the single malt perfectly, introduced with an inane comment about preferring the peat content of this particular brand. In truth, he drank anything on offer and taste did not come much into it.

They were not experts on whisky. But they were masters at manipulating others in their cause.

"Ern, old chap," Marcus started, "you know we're all the way behind you and what you're trying to do."

Ernest had enough about him, too many years as a lawyer, to make him a little suspicious at their approach. He asked what they damn well meant.

"Buddy, we just admire what you're about and want to help."

There are all sorts of lies in this world. With the truth set at zero, the sincerer denials kick in at 50 but our ex-editorial team worked firmly in the upper regions of the scale. They specialised in the most subtle and devious twists, starting at the 75 mark and, from time to time, bumping against the top of the scale. Lies also fall into sub-categories and the ones they employed fitted into the 'omission range'. In all their half-drunken discussions that morning they never once mentioned that they were ex-employees of the Daily Witness. On the contrary, every statement that eased out of their mouths, whether from the front through their teeth or sliding out the side, stated boldly or murmured quickly, implied that there had been no change on the employment front. They were acting for the newspaper and had the full weight of the paper behind them in every regard.

"Let's go over this again." Marcus poured fresh whiskies, doubles for Ernest, scanty singles for himself and his colleague. "We have an apparent crime against the body of a lady who we know as Tammy Shroton, whatever her real name might be." Of course, this was another type of lie, for Marcus knew very well that Tammy's birth name had been Rosie Pascal, but it served his purpose to seem confused by her various names. "Shroton disappears after some peculiar arrangements are set up by none other than our dear Father Barrow who was assigned to hush up the whole incident on behalf of the Catholic Church. The next time we hear of Shroton, she is suddenly head of a new church, membership growing rapidly. She jumps, perhaps literally, into bed with some financier and together they make this preposterous bid for the Catholic Church." He paused to pour more Scotch. "What we have to do is find a way to put the brakes on this takeover bid and get Shroton replaced as life president of the Church of New Moderation by a more suitable candidate." Heavy looks from both conspirators towards Ernest, who knew exactly what they meant despite the drink.

"Has anyone looked into the original police report on the rape?" Eddie asked.

"Don't be stupid. It was hushed up. There will be no police report."

"Not so stupid," Ernest was finding it hard to think and talk, but there was something urgent to say. He took a deep breath, tried again. "Ever heard of the Bates Bill?" They had not. "It's a law, went through Congress in maybe 2025. It made it a federal offence to fail to report a rape to the authorities." It took Ernest a long time to get the word "authorities" out of a mouth that slid sideways instead of opening up and down.

"2025 you say? When in 2025?"

"I dunno. Look it up."

Eddie was first out with his phone. Marcus was tempted to try his own, but knew Eddie was faster.

"Bates Bill," Eddie said. "Here it is. Sponsored by a congresswoman called Sally Bates whose daughter was raped in 2019."

"But when did it come into effect?"

"I'm getting there, don't rush me. Ah, 1 July 2025."

"And the rape was, let me see," Marcus pulled out his notebook, flicked through the pages. "Yes, yes, yes!" He punched the air. "12 July, so both Shroton and Barrow broke the law. Good god, they were probably the very first offenders under this new act and yet were not brought to book for it. Well, we can certainly do something about that. Ern, how do we go about it?"

"Guys, I was a corporate lawyer but leave it with me. I'll get onto it pronto." He looked at his two new friends; saw the warmth in their expressions and felt the glow of approval hit his body and spread within him. Tammy would get her comeuppance at last.

And it would be coming from him.

As soon as he got rid of his headache.

"Then you get down to the details," Ches said, loving the way Sophie took him so seriously. "Best way to do that is to picture yourself going through the event. What are you going to do first on arrival?"

"Meet everyone of course," Sophie replied, thinking the question a little simple.

"Before that?"

"Before you arrive, you are just about to arrive. After you arrive, you have arrived and you greet people." Sophie's voice was that of a frustrated teacher, irritated by a level of ignorance more than expected.

"No Soph, after you've finished arriving and before you start greeting people. You've got to close your eyes and picture yourself in the scene. Close your eyes now."

She complied, seeming to screw them tightly closed. Ches used the opportunity to lean forwards and pinch her chocolate biscuit from her coffee saucer.

"I saw that!" she cried. "You're a thief Mr Chesington Bloakes the thirty-third!"

"And you're a cheat," he laughed, handing the biscuit back. "You didn't close your eyes."

"That's because I'm getting to know you. But I did work it out, what you do, I mean."

"Go on."

"You go to the little girls' room or the little boys' room, of course."

"Perfect answer, although I won't retract my accusation that you cheated, because you did. So, we need bathrooms on the ground floor. Then we need a sign up to the main meeting room here on the first floor. Then we need…" Ches and Sophie made the arrangements for the conference that was due to start the following week; his planning interspersed with bouts of frenetic teasing, as was his way.

Perhaps there is an equal amount of each emotion in the world at any one time, it is just the distribution across the face of the earth that differs. And maybe one role of God is to parcel the packages of emotion out, here and there, making sure each is in overall balance. Not that it is for us to decide what the role of God might be, but we are allowed to surmise and suppose.

Following this theory, if we allow for a certain light-heartedness in Rome, silly banter as they make preparations for the conference, we have to recognise a shortage of humour elsewhere in the world. This we find, quite easily, in London, more specifically in the King's View Suite where Ernest Justice reawakened his lawyerly instincts and sought new contacts in the areas of criminal law and federal extradition treaties.

But then success in a miserable occupation brings reward. Not good humour, for Ernest, over the initial flattery of attention, had sensed his new friends were not about laughter, rather grim satisfaction from a job well done.

Thus, the smiles on the faces of Marcus and Eddie when the judge signed the US extradition orders four days later were nothing to do with goodwill or companionship forged by teamwork and togetherness. If that was the case, there would have been rough and ready slap-on-the-backs with friends slightly embarrassed by friendship crossing official lines.

Instead, there were the sweetest of human smiles, for they dealt with two of the juiciest emotions: anticipation and revenge.

The only problem with the whole exercise was that they were a day late. Tammy had left the previous day to get ready for the conference in Rome. Humphrey had left quietly two weeks earlier for the funeral of Signor LaNeve. There was no-one left in London to brandish their triumph in front of. London thus phases out of our story.

Now the trio of conspirators would have to follow to Rome and go through the whole exercise again.

But nothing is ever achieved without effort.

Marcus used his remaining air miles to buy two economy class tickets to Rome. He explained to Ernest that it would be best if he bought his own ticket to maintain independence from the newspaper. Ernest went a step further and upgraded their tickets to first class so they could sit together, all courtesy of the New Moderation charge card he carried in his wallet.

Perfidy Wins the Battle

Fi had never seen a takeover bid so lacking in rancour. It troubled her, like a wild animal sensing something not quite right on the savannah.

"I'm keeping my eyes wide open," she told Bill as they worked their way through baggage reclaim and immigration in Rome. "Tammy, you're at the wrong conveyor belt. It says belt four for the London Heathrow flight." Tammy went on looking for her luggage amongst the bags in from Istanbul until Miles led her by the arm, gently, back to belt four.

"I've found your bag," he said.

"Thanks Miles." She splashed a beautiful smile across her face, then returned to pensiveness, lost to the world around her. Airports, schedules and destinations were not of her concern.

Miles was used to it but it hurt each time. In fact, it got worse each time. Every repetition of her other worldliness settled the trend like motorcycle tracks in the dirt. "Come on, Tammy." He held her hand, feeling like he had almost become a parent in a few short weeks.

Earlier that day there had been a row. Tammy and Miles had travelled from Bromley to the Mayfair house for a meeting on progress prior to their flight to Rome. But the row was not between Tammy and Miles; there was a strange tranquillity between them, as if they moved together but in separate bubbles.

It had been Fi that started it.

"Let me see your clothes," she had said to Tammy, grabbing Tammy's bag and pulling out a bundle of untidy clothes in the darkest colours. "What do you need these for?" She held up a long black skirt, pulled from the wreckage.

They had fought, Tammy claiming she could wear what she wanted. Fi kept reminding her of the responsibility she bore to her followers "all 12 million plus of them".

"You look like you don't care about anything in this world."

"I do!" Tammy sounded like a child with hurt feelings. "I do so care."

"Then show it."

Fi won, as she expected to do. She went to the wardrobe in the room Tammy had used, selected a smart turquoise suit that Fi had chosen but Tammy had never worn. Fi then fussed over her, fetching earrings and a necklace and trying several different colours of nail varnish.

"We'll be late for the flight," Bill warned.

They made it but only just. Miles had expected Tammy to be in a sulk over her enforced change of clothes, but she seemed oblivious to it after the initial complaint.

"You look the part now, Tammy," Fi said as they waited for a cab to take them to Via Romulus.

"Thanks," she replied, as if it had been at her request. Fi, disconcerted by her perverse response, concentrated on providing a commentary on the architecture, reading from a guide book she had picked up at Heathrow.

Bill pulled the bell cord and heard a distant chime that seemed to echo through the house, falling away as it channelled into backrooms. The door opened and Sophie stood there, jeans and a crop top replacing the evening dress she had worn on the night of the debate, the last time they had seen her.

"You're very welcome to Signora Silversitrinnii's house," she declared, explaining that their host was doing some final preparations in the meeting rooms. "You have the whole of the top floor for your sleeping arrangements. Ches is already…I mean Mr Bloakes is already here and with you six, that leaves just Mr and Mrs Justice to come."

"They're still in London?" Tammy asked. "But why are they coming to the conference?" She remembered the friendliness of Sara compared to the abruptness of Ernest. She did not want to see him again.

"Ches and I discussed this," Fi answered. "We needed one more for a quorum of board members. Then there was a request from the other side for a ninth member so we had to add one more and Ches suggested Sara as her husband would be here anyway. Signorina LaNeve…"

"Pleased to call me Sophie." Sophie got her English in a slight twist, seemed suddenly flushed.

"Sophie, do you know who the ninth member on your side is going to be? Ches didn't let me know."

"I simply do not know," Sophie lied, justifying it as a requirement to keep her status in front of the enemy, then remembering to cross her fingers.

"Oh, you do that too," Tammy said, suddenly in this world.

"Do what?" She hurriedly uncrossed her fingers, trying to fit her hands into the tiny pockets of her dress.

"Cross your fingers when you're nervous!"

"Oh, yes, of course I do, every time," she said, crossing them again.

There were five bedrooms on the top floor, but only two bathrooms. Sophie explained the arrangements she had made.

"There aren't enough bedrooms for each person to have their own room. So, I've put the Justices in the double room at the front. Then this big room over here is set up to be the boys' dormitory. That's for you four. Ches, I mean Mr Bloakes, has this little room where he's been since he moved out of the hotel. That leaves the two pretty rooms overlooking the garden for each of the two girls. There are two bathrooms. This one is for the girls and the one down that long corridor by the water heater is for the boys. Meals will mainly be in the small dining room on the ground floor. Later on, I'll show you around the whole house but right now I expect you'll want to get settled in. You also have a sitting room for your own use on the first floor. It's right next to the main conference room."

She turned to leave, then turned back. "Silly me, I forgot. Supper is at 8 p.m. It's something I've prepared so I hope you like it! And if you want to come down half an hour early, there will be drinks on the terrace at the back. There are some lamps out there to light up the place in the dark." This time she did leave, closing the little door behind her that sealed off the top floor, the area given over to the New Moderation delegation.

"I guess we better unpack and get changed for supper," Fi said, taking charge as she did. Nobody mentioned that Sophie had split the two unmarried couples. Did she not know they were together or was it a Catholic thing?

"Give me some of that sparkling water," Fi said in response to the offer of a martini on the terrace.

"I think it is one of the last days of the year for drinks on the terrace," Old Ma Silver said genially. "It's steadily turning colder."

"And wetter too," someone added.

There were eleven people to greet them when they came downstairs and outside. The cardinal stepped forward, leaning on the stick he had acquired recently 'for beating the seminarians,' he joked. Usually the joke had referred to beating the new moderators, but civility demanded the alteration.

"We've got the nine members of our delegation." He introduced each of the other eight in turn, then turned to Ches. "You know young Ches, of course." It is a delight of the very old to refer to the merely old as 'young'; one of the solaces of increasing age. "We are overjoyed that you sent Ches over to help with all the arrangements. He has been a great help"

"Well done, Ches," Sophie rammed the air with her first.

"And then, leaving the finest wine to the end, we have our gracious host, Signora Silversitrinni," the cardinal continued.

"You're all very welcome to my home." Old Ma Silver sounded more English than ever, belying half a century in her adopted country.

"So, we're all together barring the Justices. Does anybody know when they are arriving?"

Ches answered that Sara was flying over from America that night, so would be arriving in Rome in the morning.

"Did she go back to Roanoke then?" Tammy asked. "I saw her in London not so long ago and someone told me Ernest was still in London."

"It seems he went home and turned around again, this time on his own."

"Strange indeed," Tammy replied, thinking of his aggressive behaviour in London.

The first course was simple in the extreme. Tiny squares of Parma ham sat on lightly toasted bread cut to size, sprinkled with pepper, lime and herbs that Sophie would not divulge.

"Every cook needs her secrets," she claimed, wondering if anyone would guess what her particular secret was.

"Delicious," said Tammy, warming to the vibrancy in Sophie, drawn to her.

"Wait for the main course!" Sophie and Old Ma Silver cleared away the plates, aided by Tammy who sprang out of her chair as if electrically driven.

"What are we about to receive?" asked the cardinal, making it sound like grace again, for he had already said grace formally as they sat at the table.

"Wait and see," Sophie teased.

Her theatricals were aided by the large metal dome that covered the dish she brought in. "Tra-la-la!" she cried as she lifted the lid to reveal slabs of pure white cod, decorated with sprigs of rosemary and surrounded by little round balls that could be new potatoes but were not. "Cod and gnocchi," she said. "And salad that Old Ma Silver made." She stretched across the table, knocking over Father Ellsworthy's wine in the process, and took the lid of a huge wooden bowl to reveal a salad of tomatoes and oranges, lettuce and peppers of all colours.

Sophie's secret came out while they cut into the cheese, spreading it on delicate biscuits to give mouthfuls of flavour.

"You're such a good cook, Sophie," said Fi, talking with her mouth full.

It was then that she owned up, her courage a little buoyed by the wine she had been drinking. "The food came from the delicatessen on the corner of my square," she said into sudden silence, then adding in a small voice "but I did heat it all up on the stove."

"Bravo," said the cardinal.

"Bravo," said Humphrey, thinking how beautiful Sophie was when the colour rose in her cheeks; like a sunrise, full of promise. Even more so in the evening when her sunrise seemed in defiance of the natural cycle of day and night.

"Bravo," echoed Fi, then Tammy and Miles and all the rest. Wine and goodness mixed to produce laughter and fellowship, one working on the other in a never-ending circle of hope.

Thus went the evening until the ding and the dong from the front door broke into their bonhomie like the bell calling the boxers to a new round in the ring.

Old Ma Silver went to the door, returned with ashen face at the head of a small troop of uniforms.

"I, Lieutenant Sitrokoski," their leader announced in bad English. "I comes for," he read from his notes "for Signorina Rosie Pascal and Father Barrow. "Are these peoples here tonight? I think yes."

"What do you want?" Fi was on her feet, the only one completely sober.

"Please sit down," the lieutenant asked. It was a request but something made Fi sit down immediately. "I have arrest warrants for these peoples. They are to come with me."

"Do you know who I am?" the cardinal asked in quavering voice.

"Everyone knows who you are, Your Eminence."

"Then perhaps you will take my word that nobody will leave the room while you and I go next door and you tell me what on earth this is about."

There was a rush to steady the cardinal as he rose shakily. But it was the lieutenant who guided him across the dining room and into the drawing room.

"You married my parents, Your Eminence. It was back in '96, when you were the parish priest at San Lucerno."

"I don't remember a Sitrokoski family I'm afraid."

"Of course not, but when you were a bishop you came to my school. You gave a talk about being saintly in the modern world."

"I don't recall that either, Lieutenant. I have observed that age plays terrible tricks with memory. It invents new things and obliterates the truth quite randomly, or at least it seems to be random." He sat in a large armchair, waved the lieutenant to sit also. "Thank you for helping me across the room. I'm not the man I used to be." He reflected that it sometimes seemed helpful to appear a little feebler than actuality. "Now, what is the problem with my fine friends?"

It was a grey old man, leaning on his stick, that came back into the room ten minutes later. The subdued chatter died as the door swung open, remained like the graveyard throughout the shaky walk on the arm of the young lieutenant, stick tapping on the tiled floor like a blind man walking.

But the brain was working furiously. No leaking valves or worn gaskets in that fine engine.

"Tammy, I have not known you long but have enjoyed every minute of our time together. Humphrey, you have become dear to me over the last few months. Both of you now need to go with the lieutenant." He explained about the arrest warrant driven by an extradition request rushed through the Italian courts. "It seems there was a transgression, or I should say, possible transgression in Vigilance, Virginia nine years ago. A rape was alleged."

"But why?" Miles was on his feet. "If some punk raped Tammy, why is she in trouble?"

"It appears the crime was not the rape itself but the failure to report it to the authorities." The cardinal spoke with his head in his hands, muffled voice seeping through his fingers, cracked sounds from a very old man.

A rather fine actor also.

The door closed behind the lieutenant. Tammy and Humphrey were gone; gone to face the authorities. They left behind a desert of emotion, for shock often has that effect.

It was Sophie who recovered first.

"We've got to help."

"Yes," said Miles, second out of surgery. "But what do we do?"

"I'll get the church lawyers onto it first thing in the morning," the cardinal offered. And it seemed the only answer. They discussed it long into the night, trying out all sorts of ideas, but none were sustained. Finally, as the clock in the hall chimed three, the cardinal left Via Romulus with a promise to call the lawyers as early as possible the next day.

"I'm staying here tonight," Sophie replied. "Father Ellsworthy will take you back, Your Eminence. I just need Father LaPetite for one more moment."

"Then he should stay here also, as we only came in one car. Is that alright, Old Ma?"

"Yes, of course. Sophie can sleep in my dressing room. Father LaPetite, we will find a bed for you, don't worry."

Sophie pictured the huge man crammed onto a put-up bed or jammed into an armchair.

Sophie huddled with Father LaPetite for 20 minutes, then called Miles over. Eventually, everyone went wearily to bed, leaving the three in deep conversation.

"Goodnight, you three," Fi said, with Bill by her side. "We'll make it work in the morning."

But in the morning, as intermittent sleep brought them down in a straggle to the dining room, there were three less in their party. Father LaPetite, Sophie and Miles were nowhere to be seen, although it took the others a few moments to recognise their absence.

The cardinal was as good as his word. He called Via Romulus at 7:54 a.m. asking for Father LaPetite who could not be found. He talked to Fi instead.

"I've briefed the lawyers. They've contacted the police and the courts and are obtaining copies of the arrest warrants. They are hopeful of getting the warrants dismissed."

The second call was at 8:23 a.m. Again, the cardinal asked for Father LaPetite, prompting the discovery that he was missing along with Sophie and Miles. Fi thought she heard a sharp swear word when the cardinal heard that Sophie was not there; perhaps he was worried about the young girl.

The cardinal passed on the news to Fi that the lawyers were scheduled in court that morning. "I think it best we delay the start of the conference until next week." Fi agreed and suggested they form a committee to handle the press. "Yes, of course, Fi," the laboured voice grew more distant down the phone, as if he was shuffling away as he spoke. "I'll send over Father Ellsworthy to assist." It was an unspoken decision that Old Ma Silver's house on Via Romulus would be the centre of operations.

This second phone call was followed by a third, fourth and fifth during the morning, and several more on into the afternoon, each time asking for Father LaPetite but talking to Fi in his place. Each time there was an ounce too much concern for Sophie, an ounce less for the others.

Father Ellsworthy arrived between phone calls three and four and Fi led a small delegation up to the conference room to set up a press co-ordination committee. Lieutenant Sitrokoski returned with an identical looking troop of policemen as the previous night. People withdrew mentally, wondering who was to be summoned this time. But there were no more arrests, or at least not amongst Old Ma Silver's guests. They stationed themselves around the building to keep the press at bay, leading away several overzealous reporters and photographers, manufacturing a strange calm in the interior. Several times a reporter got through the cordon and pulled the front door bell to send the chimes ringing through to the back of the house where the dining room and drawing room looked over the walled garden. Nobody answered. Instead they listened for the shuffling of feet and the angry cries as the police led them gently away.

Just before midday, Sara Justice arrived. Lieutenant Sitrokoski came to find Fi.

"There's a lady in a taxi who says she is a member of your church and needs to see you. She is an American," added as an afterthought, as if it explained something.

"That must be Sara," Fi replied, turning her head up from a draft press release they had been working on. "Please show her in."

Sara had just one small bag, slung over her shoulder like a student on her travels. Fi welcomed her with a hug even though they barely knew each other.

"I heard the news," Sara said. She drew back from Fi, not too far, leaving their arms remained linked in a loose embrace. "I have a confession to make."

"A confession?" All heads were raised now. Others, drifting in to greet her, stopped as they heard Fi's question, then moved into the room with expectation inked on their faces.

And it was a justified expression, for Sara had put two and two together and come up with the obvious explanation.

"I think my husband is behind this," she said. Her dyed-blonde hair hung over her face as she struggled to raise her eyes to meet those focused on her. "I had a text message on my cell phone this morning when I got off the flight. I'll read it to you if you like."

"Please do," Ellsworthy replied, motioning the last of their group into the conference room.

"It just says 'Expect justice to be served. Life presidency looming.'"

"What the hell?" Fi shook herself free of Sara, stepped back, reversing into the conference table. "You mean…?"

"I mean that my husband appears to be the architect of Tammy's misfortune, also of Father Barrow's. I am very sorry for his actions"

"You're not responsible for your husband's behaviour," Father Ellsworthy replied, trying to eliminate any antagonism before it swelled. "It is worthy of you to state your suspicions frankly and we thank you for that."

"The important thing now is to counter his efforts," Sidney said.

"Quite right," Sara replied, relieved to have got over the first hurdle. "And I have an idea about that. The one thing my husband wants is the life presidency of the Church of New Moderation."

"He's the one person least qualified for it!" That was Bill, receiving several nods and murmurs of approval.

"Clearly that is the case," Sara replied quickly, feeling the anger now firing the room as if she had to cross a burning pit to prove something. Courage perhaps? Or endurance? "But sometimes giving someone what they want is the best way to undo them."

"You want to undo your husband?"

"I want to correct a wrong. If that involves bringing him down then so be it."

There were a dozen people and a dozen views. Discussion raged like volleys across a battlefield. Fi slipped away when the phone rang again. Old Ma Silver had answered it and handed the receiver to Fi. "It's Sophie," she whispered.

"Sophie, where are you?"

"I'm in America," she replied, excitement percolating through her voice. "I'm with Miles and Father LaPetite. We're going to sort everything out." She did not explain how, but Miles came on the phone next.

"Fi, is all okay your end?"

"Yes, Sara Justice has arrived and she thinks her husband is behind this."

"That's exactly what I thought. That's why we came over here."

"I don't understand," Fi said, thinking hard. She must have missed something. Was she losing her touch? She flushed hot, then cold, like someone sickening. Yet she had not been sick for 20 years.

"Listen, we don't have much time. We need the phone number for that private investigator you used. Can you text it to me right now?"

"Sure, I'll get Al to send it. He'll have it on his phone. But Miles, what are you trying to do? I don't understand why you've gone to America. I've got hotshot lawyers in New York working on this. The cardinal's got the Vatican legal team on it too.

What can you add by flitting over to the States when we need you here?" But she was talking to a dead phone; connection was lost for some reason. She replaced the receiver, sat in the stiff, high backed chair a few minutes to think, realising a desperate need to think and plan. Then she rose and returned upstairs to the conference room where voices were raised.

"Silence, everybody. I said quiet please!" The volume and movement around the room ratcheted down; people found places and settled. Fi waited for absolute silence within; outside she could never hope to achieve the same for there was a clamour of journalists clogging up the Via Romulus below their window. That noise was going nowhere, sitting in the street like neighbours perpetually partying. But the heavy blinds were closed now, for the short day had ended even earlier than its allotted time, cut short by a curtain of rain. Those blinds muted the sounds somewhat, making them seem a football crowd but three or four pitches away.

"Friends," she started to say into waiting faces. "Friends," she said again, reflecting that they were her friends. Even the new acquaintances like Father Ellsworthy registered high on the friendship scale. She thought of clouds with silver linings and ill winds, then a polite cough from Bill brought her back to the conference room and the problem at hand.

"Friends, we're getting nowhere sitting around the table in endless discussion. I want us to split into groups. Al, please lead a practical group. I want your team to handle external relations, incoming phone calls and plans to delay the conference start date. You can also co-ordinate the results of the two sets of lawyers we have working on this, those from the Vatican and ours in NYC. Set this room up as an incident room. The first thing you can do is text Mercer's number to Miles. Yes, I've heard from Miles and Sophie. They are in DC and have some plan, but we got cut off after I said I would text them the phone number. They are with Father LaPetite. I'll pass on more news through the co-ordination team as I get it. Now, I want the rest of us to split into three groups, whichever way you want, it matters not. Go to three different rooms, elect a leader and go over all the ideas you can think of as to how to solve this situation. Report back to the co-ordination room in two hours. Sara, you stay with me. I want a complete briefing of what you think has happened. Any questions? Good, let's go. Remember, if anyone can make this right it's us and our lawyers. So, let's make it happen."

Thirty-Six Hours in America

The offices of Huntington Mercer and Goad were pretentious in the extreme. A large marble floored and walled foyer was the first sight, with a receptionist's desk that was matching marble, sweeping up from the floor, then sweeping down again in one continuous curve. Anyone walking in from the street without knowledge of their occupation would assume they were modern architects, run by a senior partner who thought more of fashion than substance.

Mercer's office was little better. Heavy mahogany panelling on three walls gave it a laboured Victorian study air, yet the fourth side contrasted sharply with a full-size plain window.

"When it's daylight you can see the White House from here," he said before any introductions were done, as if there was some spider's web of wires that connected his office with the central executive of the most powerful nation in the world; perhaps in Mercer's world vital information flowed, both ways, down those wires.

"What can I do for you?" Mercer asked, when the office assistant had poured coffee into four gold-rimmed white cups.

"We need you to find someone," Father LaPetite replied.

"Okay." He reached into a drawer and pulled out a monogramed sheet of paper. "Standard rates," he said, pushing the paper across to Father LaPetite.

Father LaPetite related everything he knew of Peter Davies, the priest who had raped Tammy six times during the night of 12 July 2025. "He was forced out of the priesthood and has not been seen since September 2025 when Father Barrow ensured he left his home, never to return. Now we need to find him as soon as possible. There is a lot riding on this."

Mercer winced at the connection with Tammy, but there were dollar signs floating in his vision, clouding his judgment. He took down a few more details then dismissed his clients with a promise to get on it immediately.

Finding Peter Davies was easier than he expected. Thinking rape, he went through the federal conviction records and found nothing. Then he thought Vigilance, Virginia so searched the state records. "Gotcha," he cried, drumming both fists on his desk. "Davies Peter Edward, conviction for rape, March 21 2029, sentenced to seven years." A quick reference to the Virginia penal code and he was ready to go.

Being unmarried, no children, no current girlfriend, Mercer could do as he liked. And he knew how to wing his way into prison visiting rooms. He remembered at times like this the first piece of advice he had received on entering the private detection industry as a new graduate at the turn of the century; flexibility is key, always be ready to travel. After his first assignment, in which he had been charged with watching a matrimonial breakup for five tedious days in the same suit, he had always kept an overnight bag in his car. He left his office that evening, driving his sleek Mercedes out of DC and not stopping until he hit Vigilance, set hard on the border with Tennessee. He drove past the Convent of the Sisters of the Holy Cross as he entered the town. But he did not stop. His destination was not the convent and he failed to notice the worn sign and weed-strewn drive. He had selected the only half-decent hotel in the town. He arrived at 1 a.m., drank three bourbons from the minibar and set his alarm for 6 a.m.

The simplest way to get into prison is to commit a crime. But it is not always the quickest and can present problems in getting out again. The next easiest, and often instant way, is to be a visiting attorney. Before leaving the office, Mercer had checked the attorney representing Davies at his trial and his assistant had printed a dozen business cards in the name of the legal firm, keeping his own name so that his driving licence matched the business card.

By 7 a.m., a bewildered Davies had been called away from his breakfast to meet with his attorney. He had never expected them to be in contact again and there was the question of the unpaid bill for his appeal five years earlier. He was two weeks away from release on parole and wondered whether this was bad news.

"I'm not a lawyer. My name is Mercer and I am a private detective." The room they sat in was uniform in the extreme. It was rectangular, no windows, a door at each end; one led to reception and freedom, the other to the innards of the prison. The table was rectangular also, so that it could be placed exactly in the middle of the room. Furniture was rudimentary and fixed to the floor. Just as with the doors there was one chair for the lawyer, facing the prison, one for the prisoner, facing freedom, taunting him with what he could not have. The walls were cinder block and dirty grey, the floor was darker grey and the ceiling a lighter variation.

But at least for lawyer visits one had total privacy. The guard who led Mercer in showed him the panic button under the table. "I'll be right outside if you need me. I can't hear a word so press the button when you've finished."

"Yes, sir," said Mercer. Like with policemen, there was always a little fear that he would be hauled away. A respectful response cost him nothing, at least not something that was tax-deductible.

"What do you want?" Davies provided contrast against the greyness of the room. It was not only the bright orange overalls but also the abundant hair, whiter than white. Davies had been described in the brief newspaper reports at the time of his trial as corpulent, yet the man in front of him was stick thin with papery pale skin and a network of veins like a map of a subway system.

He supposed that is what prison did to a man, shuddered involuntarily, moved on.

"You used to be a Catholic priest?" Mercer ignored the old man's question.

"Yes, but you know that, I mean as my 'attorney'."

"Just checking," Mercer replied, impressed at his mental sharpness. So many of the cons he had met over the years were dumbed down by drugs or the mind-numbing tedium of their lives. "When do you get out?"

"December 8."

"The Immaculate Conception?"

"Too right. Why are you here?"

"Do you remember a young nun called Sister Mary John?"

"I do." His body and mind withdrew, closing up. Could this be the beginning of another long sentence? Just as the hell of the last seven years promised to end?

"Some friends of hers want to meet you."

"I'll be out shortly."

"They want to meet you later today. I need you to fill out a visitor request form. Look, Davies, there's no need to be concerned. I believe they want to ask you a few questions, that's all." He took out a folded piece of paper from his jacket pocket. "You'll see from this signed statement that they mean you no harm."

"How am I going to get approval for new visitors in just a few hours?"

"Ah, that's where my expertise comes in," Mercer replied with a smile that was too brittle and struck harmlessly against Fortress Davies. "There's a little-known law that every Virginia state prisoner cannot be denied immediate access to visitors of good standing during the last fourteen days of incarceration. Moreover, the authorities are required to allow you to make visits outside the prison provided you are accompanied by a designated responsible person. Your lawyer is automatically a designated responsible person. The law was designed to allow prisoners some freedom in their last few days inside so they can meet potential employers, arrange accommodation and so on. Your release date is 12 days away. That's why I checked earlier."

"You give me your word this won't turn out badly for me? I'm too old to spend more time in here."

"I give you my word, Mr Davies." He reflected briefly on what his word was worth but only briefly.

"Am I to meet Sister Mary John?"

"She was not part of the group I met yesterday. Frankly, I think it unlikely. She was arrested in Rome recently for an alleged breach of the Bates Act."

"Bates Act?" So, Mercer explained the law that had come in just a few days before Davies had raped Sister Mary John. And for the first time in seven long years, Davies' sharp mind saw the tiny prospect of hope. These people wanted something from him and, therefore, he could expect something in return.

What he most wanted was relief from the urges that drove him wild every time he saw a vulnerable young woman.

What he second most wanted was an ice-cold beer and a real conversation with his God who had seemed to desert him in his time of need.

They talked on for 40 minutes, Mercer steadily working away at the old man's suspicions.

"I'll do it then." Mercer slid the visitor forms over and Davies started filling them out with Mercer's pen.

"Put down LaPetite, LaNeve and Standish as the visitors. Here, I've written their full names."

On his way out, his cell phone restored to him, Mercer called Father LaPetite. "I've found him. He's in the State Penitentiary near Vigilance, Virginia. It's about a seven-hour drive from DC. You'll need to rent a car and get a move on. I've arranged a visit any time before 5 p.m., that's eight hours from now."

But Father LaPetite had other ideas. "Where's the nearest airport?"

"Probably TriCities near Johnson City, Tennessee. That's for a commercial airport. I think there is a grass strip near Abingdon."

"How far from Abingdon to Vigilance?"

"Two hours maximum, could probably do it in one hour 40."

"Can you meet us there at 2 p.m.? We'll charter a Cessna or something."

"Sure." Those dollar signs wavered up and down across his vision, growing bigger by the minute, like the psychedelic scenes of a 1970s film. "The drive from Abingdon will give me some time to brief you."

Father LaPetite replaced the receiver and called the hotel concierge to make arrangements. Then he called the other two in their rooms. "He's found him already. We've got a flight to catch so we leave in 20 minutes."

The plan had been eight hours in the making. They had spent exactly eight hours in the plane the day before. Asking to sit together had meant they were allocated the last row against the bulkhead so no room to put their seats back. Father LaPetite did not fit in an economy seat, the only ones available at short notice, and folds of flesh spilled over onto Miles and Sophie on either side.

"Discomfort concentrates the mind," the priest had said, before taking the initiative in terms of planning.

All they had known as they boarded the flight in Rome was that they needed to find Peter Davies. They had booked their flights on instinct, now, as Miles pointed out, they needed to get logical and practical.

It was amongst the most uncomfortable eight hours Sophie had spent but also some of the most interesting. If it was not that Humphrey was in jail awaiting extradition to some dreadful courtroom, she would have actually enjoyed it because she was in the thick of things.

"Let's recap. The crime occurred on 12 July 2025 in Vigilance, Virginia. It was never reported and no accusations were ever made, still less proven…"

"That's the crux of the problem," Miles interrupted. "If the crime had been reported, the Bates Act would not apply. This new law was intended to ensure acts like rape were reported."

"By making it a crime to know yet do nothing."

"Hac igitur data sua lege in manus vestras," Father LaPetite said.

"What on earth was that?" Sophie asked, having never concentrated in Latin classes.

"It means taking the law into your own hands. Only normally that implies action and not inaction."

"I see," said Miles. "The crime is essentially the decision to do nothing when you should be reporting it to the police. In that way Father LaPetite is spot on. But it was the church that decided to do nothing in order to cover it up. Humphrey is guilty only of obeying orders and even an eight-hour flight is not enough time to debate the issue of culpability when obeying orders."

They returned to practical matters as the plane followed its great circle track across the Atlantic.

"What evidence is there of the original crime?"

"A child," piped in Sophie, remembering the confidential reports she had got hold of. "Tammy gave birth to a child. They will be able to determine the parents if they trace the child."

"Ah yes," replied Father LaPetite, "but think about it a moment. That proves parentage, but it does not prove rape."

Over Greenland they determined that there was no definite proof of rape. There was the confession signed by Davies and there were the reports buried deep in the Vatican computer systems. Both were evidence but not proof beyond reasonable doubt.

Their plan was beginning to take shape.

Just as the plan back in Rome was falling apart. They had waited all day for news from either set of lawyers. Fi fired hers, moving to another set of expensive attorneys. The cardinal exhibited more patience, but seemed to be distracted, thinking more of Sophie than those arrested. He asked for updates several times after being fed the initial briefing that Sophie and the other two were in Washington and were seeking a private investigator.

"What can she be up to?" he kept asking himself or anyone who was within earshot. Father Ellsworthy became suspicious when the cardinal arrived at Via Romulus the following day asking about Sophie again as if no- one had been arrested and now faced extradition.

Then, in the evening in Rome, came an excited call from Sophie. Old Ma Silver pressed a button on the phone and her voice boomed out on the speaker.

"Slow down, Sophie dear," the cardinal said. "Are you sure you are alright? I think you should get the next flight home. Go now to the airport. I'll have my secretary check flights to Rome."

"Your Eminence, we've found Peter Davies, the rotten priest who hurt Tammy. He's in prison. I've got to go now. We're travelling to the airport…"

"Good!" The cardinal assumed she was coming home. "What time will you get home? I'll meet you at the airport."

"No, silly, we're getting a private flight to go and see the rotten priest in prison!"

It was only after the phone call that both Sophie and the cardinal reflected that she had used her most favoured endearment on him, 'silly' being reserved for those she was fondest of.

The only plane they could get that morning was a swanky private Learjet with huge bucket seats that made each of the three passengers feel like they were the captain of the flight.

"Yes, I know," said Father LaPetite, "the seats are even big enough for me!"

Father LaPetite had several brandies with the lunch served by a stewardess out of the 1950s. Miles had a beer while Sophie drank three bottles of sparkling water, declaring that she was already drunk with excitement.

"That was a passable meal," Father LaPetite declared, wiping his mouth on a linen napkin. "Now to business! Mercer texted me just before we boarded. We're being picked up by him and taken to somewhere in Vigilance, maybe a coffee bar or something. Then Mercer is going to go and collect Davies on a temporary three-hour pass."

This gave them plenty to discuss for the remainder of their short flight.

"This rotten priest is the cause of all our problems," Sophie said, hating him already.

However, Sophie found it impossible to hate Peter Davies. On first sight she thought he looked like the cardinal. Not the same but with similarities. He was younger, less crooked with age, but his pockmarked face and white hair reminded her of her ultimate boss. He was thinner with hollowed cheeks that seemed drawn in by internal threads. In a young girl they would be called dimples, but this was not appropriate for someone who looked to be approaching 80 years old.

"How old are you…Father?" It was the wrong address but it seemed right to Sophie.

"Fifty-nine."

"My God!" she cried, unable to hide her astonishment. "You look so much older."

"That's prison for you, my dear," Father LaPetite patted her hand as he spoke.

"And a life of debauchery before that," Davies said, indicating what Sophie had sensed. There was a type of honesty about this man that made him likeable. It was as if he knew himself so well. Perhaps seven years in jail was enough time to achieve self-knowledge to perfection.

"You accept your guilt?" Miles asked, not knowing what else to say into this awkward meeting.

"I do, Mr Standish. All my adult life I've had a weakness for young girls and this is where it has led me. I don't deny it. I don't explain it. I am what I am, only wish I could be different."

"That brings us to the point neatly, Mr Davies," Father LaPetite took over. "Would you say you are a dishonest man?"

"Totally." Yet there was something so washed-out honest about this convict sitting across the table, nursing a hot cup of coffee, nibbling at the large round cookie he had been given with his cup, as if he accepted everything handed to him in true prison fashion. Miles wanted to say something, but the words eluded him. He lined them all up in his head but knew they were wrong. There was something there to be said but he could not drag it out.

"Good," Sophie said, playing her part while Miles sat frowning with concentration.

"It's not good, Signorina LaNeve. I am a bad man who deserves what I got."

"No, silly," there it was out again, her favourite endearment, "I don't mean it is good to be dishonest. I mean it is good that you…well, that you know you are dishonest." She flushed red, thoughts ahead of words, changed to silence and examined her cappuccino.

With Miles scraping his brain for the thought he wanted and Sophie's thoughts jumbling out all over the place, it was down to Father LaPetite to explain what they wanted of this broken man. And he was doing it against the clock because Mercer kept looking at his watch, muttering about not being late back at the prison.

But Father LaPetite knew that he had to be honest about this too. He could be clever and twist Davies in neat circles, but far better to meet him head on, man to man with truth instead of wiliness.

"How would you plead if you were accused of the rape of Sister Mary John?"

That warranted a glance up for direct eye contact. Father LaPetite had scored early for he discerned a flicker of calculation in the new man that sat before him, washed of sin and vice like a shirt through a mangle. Yet here he was, pausing to consider his answer.

But then Davies hit back without cleverness or artificiality. "I would plead guilty for I raped that girl several times." There was no attempt to build support or elicit sympathy; Tammy was 'that girl' not 'that poor girl'. Factual narrative speaks louder than emotion.

"Six times actually, but I'm not here to condemn you."

"Then why are you here?"

"To ask you to do something dishonest."

"No." Davies rose from his chair, kicking the table leg in his rush, spilling coffee over the top of his cup. "If there's nothing else, I need to get back to you-know-where."

Again, Davies scored because he left nothing for Father LaPetite to latch on to.

"Can you do me the courtesy of hearing me out before declining to help?" It was the only response, given that Davies had backed Father LaPetite into a corner.

"I'll listen, yes." Davies sat back down again. Miles noted his eyes fixing on his coffee and cookie. He doubted the man had drunk a decent cup of coffee for close to seven years.

"I believe Mr Mercer informed you that Sister Mary John is now known as Tammy Shroton. She is the president of the Church of New Moderation."

"You mean the outfit that has made a bid for the church, the Catholic Church I mean?"

"Precisely." Now Father LaPetite had Davies' full attention. Was there a little part of this man that remained attached to the church that had dismissed him.? Whether right or wrong to do so, the church could certainly be accused of taking the law into its own hands with an astounding level of arrogance. Father LaPetite had a momentary crisis of confidence: could all his efforts be distilled down to the same wilful approach, acting to save the church rather than the souls that were its constituency?

But it was momentary, for Father LaPetite had lived too long as a Catholic priest, too long defending the faith – his faith.

"Precisely," he repeated. "But we have a problem and you can help with that problem."

"I know that she was arrested for contravention of the Bates Act. Mr Mercer told me this morning."

"Exactly, and that is where you can help."

It did not take long to explain to Davies. He would be questioned by the police any day now. "If there has been no original crime, there is no reason to hold her. She will have to be released. But your cup is empty. Would you like another coffee?"

"It won't influence my decision."

"What do you take me for?" Father LaPetite fired back, a little bit of the old self.

"Just stating the obvious," Davies replied. "Sometimes it needs saying."

"Amen to that." Their eyes met, then Davies deliberately and slowly moved to make visual contact with Sophie, then Miles.

He's weighing us up, thought Miles. In return, he locked into Davies' grey eyes and did not waver.

"We mean you no harm, Signor Davies," Sophie said into the silence between Davies and Miles. Her voice sounded like a referee trying to make her decision known.

And it broke the mood, for Davies was suddenly certain.

"It's less deceitful than I've been my whole life," he said, this dishonest come honest man. "I'll do it, just for Sister Mary John. But I would like another cup of coffee!" They laughed long and loud, turning most of the few heads in that little coffee shop on Main St, Vigilance.

The Scene of the Crime

Second cup of coffee downed, time was moving on.

"I'd really like to pray with you," Davies said, "if you don't mind, that is."

"Of course not, Father," Sophie replied immediately. "I know, let's find a church."

"There isn't one here," Davies replied. "At least not a Catholic one. This is Baptist territory. Catholics are in short supply." He seemed to stop and consider something, then continued. "I was the last priest in Vigilance. When I resigned, the bishop deemed it unnecessary to replace me. There is too little demand around here and supply has to meet demand, of course."

It wasn't too bad a joke for someone coming through a seven-year prison sentence.

"There's always the convent," Miles said. Everybody looked at Peter Davies, expecting him to shrink back. But he did not, simply got to his feet, said to lead on. He was ready; they had made him ready.

The convent church was deserted. It was also gloomy and dusty, reminding Miles of a set in a corny horror movie, something like 'Death in the Graveyard' or 'Ghosts at Prayer'. They entered and followed Davies to a pew about halfway down. Miles, last in, found a bank of light switches and tried each one in turn. One, three and four did nothing, number two flickered with promise but then failed to deliver, other than buzz like a bee lost amongst the rafters. He abandoned his lighting plans, leaving the church in its natural gloom. The three Catholics genuflected in the aisle, but Mercer and Miles slipped into a seat without bending a knee.

They prayed individually for a long while. Sophie's mind wandered first. She started speculating as to what her colleagues were praying about. She imagined Miles was praying for Tammy. She was spot on. She believed Father LaPetite was praying for the Catholic Church; again, she was accurate. It was easy to guess Mercer's prayer; probably a fat cheque as a reward for finding Father Davies.

But here she was wrong. For Mercer was praying not for financial reward, nor for recognition. His objective was seemingly far higher, although still concerned with himself; proving that the human race was set apart from other forms of life. Humans twist and turn throughout their lives, never following the same trails. Some turn all the way around in a great big sweeping arc of reform, improvement, remorse – call it what you like. Others stay centred on themselves, wavering towards kindness but never quite making it.

Mercer, in fact, prayed fervently for grace like he had witnessed, never thinking he would envy a prisoner. But he wished for grace so that good things would happen to him and he would find happiness in the form of a long-legged girl with a pretty face.

Sophie then turned to the last in their little party. She puzzled over his expression as he knelt, looking up at the cross fixed above the altar. There was no doubt about his sincerity and she liked the 'rotten priest', as she had nicknamed him back in Rome. Sometimes, in the coffee shop, he had seemed to have more goodness in his little finger than the whole body of anyone else, even the vast bulk of Father LaPetite. But now, kneeling at the end of the pew, he looked like any other bag of skin and bones, drawing in and pumping out air with his own particular rhythm. Yet the man was a multiple rapist. Was he praying for his victims, that they would eventually recover from the terrors he had inflicted on them? How is remorse worked out on an everyday level? How do you be sorry, day in, day out, for what you've done to others?

As she watched the white-haired old man of 59, she imagined she perhaps knew what he prayed for. She was wrong again, for a total score of two right out of four.

For Davies was praying for nothing but peace with his God, the God who had stopped listening to him long ago but now seemed to have come back in some small way.

"We need to get going," Mercer said, standing up, bored. His praying was over.

At that moment, the door opened at the other end of the church. A nun walked through from the convent, pushing a trolley of hymn books and half-used candles.

Sophie saw, for the first time, the habit Humphrey had described as old-fashioned in his reports. There was no face to see, just a cross cut into the white cloth, giving deep shadow contrasting with the white of the habit. There was no skin visible, nothing to mark her as human, other than two hands upon the trolley.

"Hello," she said, "we don't get many visitors."

Sophie thought 'well clean your church a bit and you might get more'. She was considering how to make her observation a little less pointedly when the nun stopped in her tracks suddenly. She stared at Davies; while the trolley continued rolling a short distance, stopping in front of the altar like an offering to the Almighty.

"Father Davies?" she asked. "No, it can't be."

Davies looked up, looked blank.

"It's…"

"Sister Mary Paul."

"Actually, I'm Mother Superior now."

They all had coffee together in Mother Superior's study. She had to call another nun in to find the coffee, explaining to her guests that she normally only drank water.

But it made cup numbers three and four for Davies who drank it greedily.

"I have some cookies somewhere, let me have a search." But the cookies were stale so they made do with some withered apples from the convent orchard.

Then Peter Davies, one-time priest seconded to the convent, told the Mother Superior of the last nine years. He spoke of his life between the sheets, his increasingly frantic search for pleasure, leading inevitably to a court date and a long sentence. Then he told of the periods of fear, anguish, self-harm. For almost five years he had been in a form of detox, burning hot then burning cold, soaked in sweat, not rational nor reasonable.

"I hated myself violently. I hated what I was, what I had become and what I had done to my victims. I reached a low point late one night. My cellmate had just been released and no new one had been allocated to my cell. I was alone. I took off my shirt and tied it to make a noose. I remember congratulating myself on the ingenuity with which I fixed the shirt-noose to the vertical window bars so there was enough height to do the job."

"What happened?" Sophie had to ask, looking intently at Davies' neck, expecting to see great red welts surrounding it.

"I forgot my physics," he said, with the faintest of grins, his mouth like the suggestion of a painter experimenting with new styles. "I must have weighed 180 pounds then, down from 300 pounds at my peak, but it was enough to tear the shirt at the seams." His hands went up to each shoulder to indicate where the sleeves had ripped off.

"Thank God," said Sophie, so ready with her thoughts, held just below the surface. The others were silent, soaking in contemplation. Davies returned Sophie's exclamation with a grim smile in her direction, a mark of appreciation.

Suicide was a mortal sin, yet even Father LaPetite could understand the despair Davies had felt, was sobered below zero-alcohol by the thought, like negative drunkenness.

"That was rock bottom for me. Despair was my cellmate from that day on, self-pity my constant companion. But I'm getting over-dramatic, even poetical!" For the second time in Mother Superior's office, Davies smiled. This time it was bolder, heavy charcoal lines showing how he must have grinned as a carefree boy; before he had grown into an adulthood of vice. He cleared his throat and ended his history with two final sentences. "Then one day eighteen months ago, I magically woke up calm. It was like I had died and, despite the harshest of surroundings, was actually in Heaven."

"I wish I had known of your torment," Mother Superior replied. "I would have liked to help you."

Mercer was tired of all this. It had been a long day and he still had to prepare his invoice. Plus he needed to get these people back to the Abingdon airfield.

"We really must be getting Davies back," he said again, justifying to himself that they might have roadworks or other holdups and they could not afford to be late.

"Just a minute, Mr Mercer." Davies was deep in discussion with Mother Superior, huddled like the gunpowder plotters must have huddled.

Plan B

Plan B was down to Sara, with Fi providing the expertise. The Catholic contingent was told to make themselves scarce. Before the cardinal led the black-robed chain out of the house, he had several long meetings with Fi, heads bent in a corner of the hall or over the dining room table.

Fi's role, she realised as she pondered the variables, was to make certain of Plan B, a job made harder and yet easier by the fact that she was working with the enemy. But who exactly was the enemy in this topsy-turvy world where foes became friends and friends were secret foes? She sat for a moment after the cardinal left, gathering her mental notes like a pilot on a mission, then strode into her preparations.

The bedrooms at Via Romulus were quickly rearranged so that the Justices had their principal guest suite on the first floor back again. Old Ma Silver placed fresh flowers on the table and dried flowers in the old hearth, straightened the bedcovers while Sara moved her suitcase in and unpacked.

Ernest caught a flight from Heathrow to Rome and was welcomed at Via Romulus.

Plan B depended on egos, in particular stroking an oversized one.

But that was what Fi dealt with time and time again. In essence, oversized egos had made her fabulously wealthy.

"I am so pleased you could make it, darling," Sara started as she met Ernest on the steps. They kissed like familiar strangers, Ernest slightly lingering on the embrace when he saw other people watching them.

"Let me take your bag for you," Bill said, thrusting out his hand. "You're in your usual room." That was a nice touch, suggesting privilege and long-established hospitality within a single sentence.

Ernest beamed a patrician smile.

Fi started work the moment Ernest had a bourbon and ice in his hand. It was too wet and cold for the terrace so they were in the grand drawing room.

"We really need you," she laid it on thick from the start. "You've no doubt heard about Tammy's predicament?" Fi knew it was important to disassociate herself from Tammy early on. "It's put us in a jam at a critical time. Frankly, I'm not surprised."

"What do you mean, Fi?"

"Can I be frank, Ern?" Fi sounded sincere.

"Sure."

"Well, I've been worried about her leadership ever since the debate." The words were true but the implication was not. "Ern, we need someone strong and dependable."

"Did you have anyone in mind?" It was a line straight out of a movie script, but that was how Ernest led his life. It was how he had balanced the boredom of his profession over many years, the dull reaction in parties when asked what he did for a living.

"Yes, as a matter of fact I do." Fi played her role to perfection. She even came over to the armchair he was in and sat upon the arm, her skirt rising up to reveal a perfect knee of forty-something summers. "I think you should take over as life president of the Church of New Moderation."

He saw her knee, read the meaning and was sold before the words rammed into his head with their reinforcing message.

"Is this just your opinion?" he retained enough lawyerly caution to ask.

"Lord, no!" Fi stood up and turned to face him, then squatted in front of him so she could look up into his face. "I'm nobody, not even a board member. I'm just the messenger, sir." The ounce or two of deference she threw at that 'sir' worked wonders, like a secretary congratulating her boss on his promotion to the higher echelons. For it meant the moment passed successfully. Fi had been concerned that Ernest would ask for names of those board members that supported him, thus requiring her to lie, which she would not do. Instead, her deference caught his vanity unguarded and encircled it with platitudes, undermining the very structure that made him.

"Well, if you're sure…"

"We are sure."

"But how will we secure the life presidency for me? Doesn't Tammy or Rosie, or whatever her damn name is, have to be fired first?"

"No, not at all." Fi pulled out a small booklet, opened it at a pre-marked page. "Read the relevant rule. It says if a life president is arrested they automatically open themselves for challenge. Any board member can stand against them. See, it says so in black and white." Her deference was still there, but with an overlay of stridency now that she had him.

Had him exactly where Plan B needed him.

Ernest Justice was elected that evening. There were no dissenters; the board voting almost unanimously. Tammy resigned, then abstained in the vote for her replacement, persuaded on both counts by Fi on a rushed visit arranged by Lieutenant Sitrokoski. Fi concentrated on squaring Tammy away while Sara and Bill, both new to the job, worked quietly on the other members.

It worked; every board member except Tammy voted for Ernest.

Sara watched her husband's chest fill out just like a mainsail hoisted to catch the wind.

One of his first acts as the new life president was to find Old Ma Silver and demand an office of his own, "just while we're staying your place". Old Ma Silver smiled, looked at her rooms and shunted some of the others around to provide a smart corner suite with high ceilings so his ego would have somewhere to rise to. Everybody played their part, congratulating President Justice, welcoming him to high office. Some hinted that things must surely get better now.

They hinted with slightly exaggerated sighs and expressions like hammy actors, but nobody actually said it.

"How are they?" everybody wanted to know of Fi. They had prayed, collectively and individually, for Tammy and Humphrey since their surprise arrest three evenings ago.

"They're fine," Fi stressed to each enquiry. "They're holding up well."

And it was true; both Tammy and Humphrey were being kept in relative comfort, but that morning had brought an ominous arrival. A US marshal had landed: crew cut, black suit and tie, white shirt below a face that did not smile, did not know humour. In fact, as they discovered over the next few days, very little emotion ever escaped through his mask-like face. Bill and Father Ellsworthy took him on a whirlwind tour of Rome. Everything was taken on board by this impassive man, as if the tour was actually a mission briefing and his life and others depended on precise recall.

But the tour and all other niceties were mere distractions to be endured for the marshal's job was to take the prisoners back for justice and he took his job, like his life, seriously.

However, the Vatican lawyers had different ideas. They managed to organise a review for the next morning in front of an Italian judge. They pushed paper, filing arguments and rebuttals by the cartload; each avenue living and dying in an attempt to win the crucial argument.

"We need something bigger," Father Ellsworthy summarised, having been delegated responsibility for co-ordination with the lawyers. The cardinal had complained that normally Father LaPetite would have this task, but he had shot off to America on some jolly.

But the cardinal knew it was not a jolly as he had just heard back from a jubilant Sophie, which was then confirmed in more reasonable tones by Father LaPetite. That meant they had something bigger. They had Davies' detailed statement, denying any incidence of rape. The cardinal's quick mind worked double speed to assimilate all developments and amend his plan accordingly.

For his was Plan A and a huge amount was at stake.

The tall stooped man, as senior lawyer, did the talking after the cardinal explained the achievements of the team in America.

"Well done, Your Eminence. That is excellent news. Now, as with every solution in the law world, it presents further problems. We have a written statement from Peter Davis. That is a problem solved but it presents other problems."

"Those being?" Father Ellsworthy had little patience for anyone paid by the hour. Taking forever to state the obvious was a form of theft wrapped in professional gift paper where nothing was a true gift.

"We have a problem of procedure and one of timing. I'll deal with the procedural question first." The tall stooped lawyer waited for his audience to still, coughed once or twice to ensure he remained the centre of attention. "The procedural problem is that it takes two parties in unison to destroy a prosecution."

This is where Father LaPetite would have said "explain" with such suitable disdain to his voice that the speaker would have rushed over the words to get his argument out. Instead, his audience, cardinal included, sat still, minimal fidgeting, waiting on the lawyer to push his limelight to the extreme.

"What do you mean, I hear you say. In any crime you have a perpetrator or suspect on the one hand and a victim on the other. Let's take some scenarios…"

"You need to get to the point." Father Ellsworthy's outburst was quite out of character but wholly deserved.

"I was just coming to it," the lawyer replied. But Ellsworthy's interruption worked as the lawyer then rattled through his explanation. "If the victim says a crime has been committed and the prosecutors agree, then the suspect has a case to answer. If, however, neither party allege the crime and there is no external evidence for the police or prosecution to latch on to, then there is patently no case to answer." He stopped talking, expected applause or other recognition but was disappointed.

"So," the cardinal caught on immediately, "we have to persuade Tammy to state that no crime was committed."

"Precisely."

"But how on earth are we to do that?" someone asked.

"Leave that to me," the cardinal answered, his ideas suddenly forming and fermenting. "Leave that to me."

The meeting began to break up, but the lawyer was not yet finished.

"Hey," he cried, "don't you want to hear about the timing problem?"

"That's easy," Father Ellsworthy replied. "We have until 9 a.m. this morning when the judge hears this case. If he goes with us, we get, at worst, a stay on their extradition to America, at best a dismissal of the entire case. If it goes the other way they are on the next flight to the States. Am I correct?"

"Exactly, moreover…"

"And that gives us just under four hours to get everything in place so we better get moving – all of us."

Nobody knows for sure who wrote the 'Universal Rules of Life'. Some say, rather fancifully, that it was passed down to Moses or Abraham by God the Father, upon a mountain somewhere where it is dry and stony and close to the origins of life. But most educated people believe it was written by a minor Roman nobleman called Rotundo. Rotundo lived and passed his life with no other claim on history and nothing much is known of him. He appears to have lived at the height of the Roman Empire. He appears to have inherited enough wealth to never have to worry, but not enough to be remembered. He may have loved and wed, had children and known the joys and sorrows we have. But we do not know if he did.

All we know is that the 'Universal Rules of Life' is a masterpiece of insight into human nature. And he must have led an extraordinary life to gain that insight.

Or else, it really was passed down from God and all Rotondo had to do was write it in his neat hand.

The book contains a chapter on expectations achieved. That chapter contains three sections, one for each classification of the human race.

The first section covers those few who achieve their expectations and things continue to work out. It terms them 'The Lucky Few'. But these lucky few are not our concern.

Neither are the 'Bumblers' of section two, who are so used to making do, getting by somehow, that they don't really notice much difference. They are genetically designed for a struggle and happy to carry on so. This is by far the largest group in our population. Rotondo gives excellent examples of the bumblers he knew in his everyday life, but, infuriatingly, he changed all the names, so we have to speculate as to who he satirised and why.

It is the third category that Ernest Justice fits so neatly into. Officially termed the 'Lamentables', they are more commonly known as the 'Evaporated', for at the very pinnacle of their achievement their happiness evaporates in a mire of frustration. It seems that, once achieved, their targets were simply not worth the struggle.

For 24 hours, Ernest Justice was drunk on a wash of power. Then the rot set in. He gave what he thought were simple instructions but spent hours correcting misunderstandings, redirecting people back on to task and coping with a dozen diversions every hour of each day.

Some people cope well with such endeavours and pass easily for Bumblers or even, occasionally, as a member of the Lucky Few. But not Ernest. For him, being in ultimate charge was a nightmare of contradictions, counter-arguments and plain disobedience. All his working life he had been supporting someone else who took the decisions.

Not now.

His aloneness with responsibility was terrifying.

He tried, of course, to talk to Sara about it. But Sara was the architect of his trials and, accordingly, confounded rather than assisted him.

"You've got to try harder," she said when he complained. "Don't let them grind you down. You need to get the better of them," she continued, but spectacularly failing to guide him as to how.

Ernest should have known the deck was stacked against him. When even your wife seems at odds to your goals, what hope is there? Should he risk all and remind her of her lifelong contract to support him through thick and thin? Or should he stay quiet, try and dampen the new fervour she had in her now?

And then there was the matter of his ego; the voice that kept reminding him that he was now the life president of the Church of New Moderation. All he had to do was push harder, so the treadmill continued to turn with Ernest Justice tramping hopelessly around its circumference.

Vows are Made to be…

Tammy and Humphrey were released from their gentle custody before lunch. Lieutenant Sitrokoski drove them back to Via Romulus in an unmarked police car, having called ahead to announce his intentions. The weather joined in the celebration, donating a pale but warm sunshine to the December day. It seemed to Sophie, as she stood on the steps outside the front door, to be the last echo of the fierce summer sun, sent to cheer their souls.

Or perhaps the sun was more like an old man, papery thin skin, spending his last days on earth.

But perhaps that old man had reserves of strength that would keep him in his last days for a long time to come.

'The Triumphant Trio', as Fi had named them, had been welcomed back as heroes from their short American adventure. Sophie loved the glow, the aura, the heat of the spotlight like the heat of the day. She flung her yellow hair like a movie star but kept yawning, with Father LaPetite and Miles joining in from left and right. Now they waited on the steps for the final two missing from their company. Sophie started a game, guessing how many cars would pull down Via Romulus until the lieutenant's car drew up at No 14. She got into a squabble with Father LaPetite because he counted cars in both directions.

"But they'll come from the left," she cried indignantly. "It's not fair to count cars coming from the other end."

"Hush, children," said Fi, "or you'll be sent to your bedrooms."

The lieutenant's arrival with his cargo of two was delayed; perhaps the traffic was bad? Father Ellsworthy went back into the house after whispering something to Old Ma Silver. He returned with a large chair from the dining room. "For the cardinal," he grunted as it bashed against the frame of the door.

Miles took one side and guided it out, placing it down on the top step like a throne.

But the cardinal did not think of it as a throne as Bill and Sid guided him over and eased him down. His throne was not yet earned but come the day for glory and it would soon be his.

The lieutenant's car finally drew up, turning into Via Romulus and approached the house from the right, much to Sophie's annoyance. The cardinal sat on his throne, still leaning on his stick, others flanking him down the steps. Humphrey's first thought as he stepped out of the car was why the Catholics had grouped on the left and the New Moderators on the right, like wings of opposing armies. Yet the comparison only went so far, for there was no aggression amongst them, no competing rivalries. It was more a natural order of things, as if some unseen hand had carefully guided each soul to its rightful place in order to meet unspoken rules of decorum. Tammy, climbing out after him, went left and first took the hugs of the Catholics, so Humphrey went right and was welcomed by the New Moderators.

They came together in front of the cardinal, who let his stick slide to the ground, took a hand from each of them and mouthed "my children".

Humphrey, being English, looked slightly embarrassed. Tammy, the American, dropped to her knees and kissed the cardinal's hand.

As any good Catholic would do.

And behind the throne, Sophie grinned and tossed her long yellow hair so it caught the breeze and broke ranks.

"Father Humphrey," she said, her heart breaking out of her body. It was the last time she ever called him 'Father'. And the first time, in public, she had used his given name.

Meanwhile, Tammy turned back and was making her way down to Miles at the foot of the stairs, right-hand side. She noticed Sara, standing behind the others, diverted to greet her but suddenly Ernest was in her way, stepping forward and obliging Sara to move sideways.

"I'm glad you got out of jail," he said, thrusting his cheek forward for a welcome kiss. "But you've heard that I am the new life president now, haven't you?"

"Yes, Mr Justice." She avoided the kiss with a neat step downwards so that Ernest, coming to meet her, lost his foot and stumbled on the stone steps. "You'll be leading the talks in the conference now. I wish you luck."

Ernest regained his footing, started to say something, then thought better of it. He had an ace up his sleeve and there was precious little point in declaring it now. Instead, he stood back, smug grin, congratulating himself on his restraint. All things in their own time.

And his time was coming. He could feel it in his bones. He looked around and saw Fi looking up in his direction. Soon everyone would look up to him.

Admiration or envy or whatever. He had something Fi and others wanted and that was what counted in this world.

Just wait, Financier D'Alianti, for when I play my ace that expression will magnify many times over.

After a celebratory but quiet lunch, the cardinal took charge and sent Humphrey, Tammy and the Triumphant Trio to rest. "We'll reconvene before supper and start the conference proper in the morning." He needed time to go over the changes, step by tiny step. Thinking of steps, he had one more to achieve on this earth and with the Holy Father so close to death, these circumstances had to give him his chance.

But he had to get it right.

Hence the need for time. Time and careful planning made even the ultimate goal achievable.

Old Ma Silver was running out of bedrooms but remembered an old servant's room in the attic. "It'll do for Father Barrow," she said. "I'll just pop up and make it ready."

"I'll help you." Sophie jumped up from the table, knocking her coffee so a deep brown stain spread across the white tablecloth, drowning the roses that lay in borders around the edge of the linen.

"Typical Sophie," laughed Father LaPetite, but Sophie was already out of the door.

Later, there was a knock on the door, waking Humphrey as he dozed. Humphrey made to ask who was there, but Sophie was through the door before the words could cross the bare floorboards.

"Hello, Humphrey."

"Hello, Sophie."

They circled, eyes fixed on each other, one-hundred-and-eighty degrees so that Humphrey had his back to the door and Sophie's knees were level with the low bed under the window. Their gaze never left each other. Sophie felt particles of something good shooting out of their eyes, merging in a mid-air dance. Her heart was thumping and in the otherwise stillness, she swore she could hear his heart beating in reply, like a jazz singer and saxophonist in a game of echoing copycat on the melody.

"I was worried about you," Sophie said, thinking she had to say something. But her voice sounded like an actress playing the role of Sophie. It came from her mouth, was channelled up her throat, the words formed by her tongue. Yet it seemed like another talking in her body.

Her body, the one with the strange voice, was hot and sweaty.

"I know," Humphrey replied. "Sophie, you did so well. I would be rotting in jail if it hadn't been for you. No, worse than that, I'd be on my way to an appointment with the American justice system." It was his last defence. He employed a sickening amount of gratitude, giving a syrup-sweet tone to his words. He made to clear his throat, to evict the sweetness before he talked again.

But before he could speak, she had crossed the room and was standing right before him.

"I want you, Humphrey." The same tail to his name, the same uplift, as before. But instead of finding it funny they were both deadly serious. Humphrey found himself holding her in his arms, getting as close to her as possible. He felt the urge for skin to touch skin, to feel her body next to his; two bodies in communion.

"No." That one word cut across their contact, reverberating against the walls and bouncing back to penetrate both bodies from all sides. For a moment Humphrey was not sure who had spoken. Was it he or Sophie? Both voices had sounded unnatural during their encounter, as if put through a child's toy that distorted speech, turning it into a parody of the actual tones employed.

But he was in doubt for only a second; until Sophie stepped back, breaking physical contact.

"No," she said again, this time her voice was her own. "It's not right. Your vow."

Sophie left Humphrey's room three minutes later. It was the longest three minutes they had ever experienced. They both changed their minds several times, grasping on to each other, then stepping back in confusion.

There were very few words spoken. All communication was through their bodies until Sophie had her left hand on the doorknob, making a commitment she did not want to make.

"It would have been so beautiful," she said.

"Yes," was all that Humphrey could think to say.

"But your vow is so important. You wouldn't be you if you broke it."

"Yes, you are right."

Then she gripped the door handle properly and swung the door open, watching where the old carpet was worn badly by the entrance, then examining the simple skirting board that did not warrant serious inspection.

"I should go."

"Yes, that might be for the best."

"I love you, Humphrey."

"I love you too, Sophie."

The door closed and, for the longest time, Humphrey stared at it. He listened hard for returning footsteps but there were none.

She was gone.

Humphrey eventually moved, falling onto his knees in the middle of the attic room, hitting the floorboards hard through the thin carpet. The pain brought him out of his trance. He started to pray, but words did not come. And when they did finally arrive, they seemed blunt arrows, clattering off the walls and ceiling instead of piercing through to the world outside.

He was in another kind of prison, bound not by walls but by the vow of celibacy he had made all those years ago.

"My God, why do you put me in this position?" he asked, but the words fell harmlessly to his feet, pooling like the red wine stains in Sophie's secret cubby hole.

It took a long time and many wasted efforts for this intelligent man to stumble across the right question of God.

"How should I love Sophie LaNeve, my Lord?" And these words, newly sharpened with honesty, pierced the roof and shot through to Heaven. And God responded instantly, before he even heard the words, for, of course, he knew they would come in time.

"With all thy heart, my child, with all thy heart."

Then Humphrey Barrow SJ rose from the floor, lay on his bed and closed his eyes to a sleep that only the most honest ever know.

Sophie was brim-full with tears as she helped Old Ma Silver prepare for supper, several drops slipping down her face and plopping into the soup she had responsibility for.

"There will be nineteen of us," Old Ma Silver said. "Nine from each contingent and me as well. Unless you think I should not attend so you can talk business? Sophie, I was saying…"

"Yes, of course, whatever you think is best, Old Ma."

"You weren't listening to a word I was saying!" Old Ma Silver stopped cutting up vegetables for the salad and looked closely at Sophie. "Whatever is the matter?" she cried, rushing over to her friend. "It's okay, Sophie darling. Nothing can possibly be that bad. Tell me all about it and then we can work out what to do. Let the salad wait!" Old Ma Silver tossed her knife into the sink and led Sophie to two worn armchairs in the corner, usually used by the dogs.

Old Ma Silver had a genuine interest in people and was one of those rare species who places the happiness of others above her own. She listened in absolute silence, just squeezing Sophie's hand at the pauses. But her mind was racing on the problem.

"My dearest Sophie," she said at the end of the sorry tale, "it was so brave of you to step back and resist temptation. In fact, you have both behaved remarkably and should be very proud of yourselves."

"Yes, but I just feel miserable," Sophie cried. "I love him so much!"

"I know, my dear." She hugged her friend, stroking her lovely and lively straw-coloured hair. Then Old Ma Silver went on to explain that some things were so important in this world that they came before the joining of two bodies. Over time she got a first smile from Sophie; boosting her sense of self-worth by telling her how magnificently she had behaved and how proud she was of her. "What you have done is operate on a totally different plane to everyone else. You have recognised a higher moral ethic and been the principal party in enforcing that ethic."

Sophie was smiling through her pain now. She even made a joke about the soup burning.

But it was no joke, for when she jumped up to check on it, she lifted a pan that had burnt dry.

"For lunch today we are going to have some rock-hard chicken soup," she said, banging the solid mess at the bottom of the pan with the wooden spoon. "Ah, delicious," she added as she raised the spoon to her mouth, pretending to taste it.

It is strange how close laughter is to tears. When we feel our most miserable, most let down and dejected, we, as a race, seek laughter as if it were the wind to sweep away the storms.

Laughter is the breeze we feel on our faces, just as it is the warm sun, not too hot and not too cold.

Laughter is our saviour. The greater the fall, the further down laughter stoops to pick us up and dust us down.

Laughter is our gift from God. It pinpricks our misery until dark night is bathed in new light.

Old Ma Silver, true to form, exaggerated her mirth in response to Sophie's joke, while ranging through her brain for a suitable reply to build the sad, sweet joy that comes from love.

"We'll cut it up and put it on small pieces of toast," she said, the best she could come up with, "as an antipasto."

Ten minutes later, Sophie sought Old Ma Silver's hand as they walked along the pavement together on their way to the delicatessen. Old Ma Silver took Sophie's hand in hers, then used the contact to draw Sophie closer.

They walked in step, arms around each other, all the way to the delicatessen and back.

The Conference Begins

Ches worked wonders with the press. He had the knack. "I'm like one of those doormen you get out front of the best hotels," he said in his loud voice. "My job is to keep the press at bay, just like the doorman keeps the riffraff out of the hotel."

It was true in one regard. Ches stationed himself outside on the steps much of the time. But there the comparison fell down, for instead of a gruff dismissal of the 'riff-raff', Ches engaged with the press totally, charming them while feeding them carefully chosen segments of information.

"What do you say to them?" the cardinal asked.

"I tell them stories, mostly."

"You mean porky-pies?" Sid said, smiling at his own joke, pleased that a British expression had tumbled out without effort.

"Not at all," Ches replied seriously when the laughter died down, "actually strictly the truth only. 'Porky-time' always catches up with you, at least that is what my father drummed into us, although he didn't use such a quaint expression."

When pressed further, Ches admitted that he did two things in particular to control the press. "First, I tell them a lot of funny stories about things that have happened over the years. Working in drinks distribution all my life gives rise to some real good ones. Plus, my grandpa set the business up during prohibition and that always goes down well with an audience. It helps that I throw a few of my favourite jokes into the mix!"

Ches' second tactic impressed the delegates greatly. He explained that he took individual members of the press aside from time to time and gave them snippets of harmless information. "Each one thinks they are getting the intel straight from the centre of operations, yet no-one gets the complete picture, therefore no-one has preference over the others."

"So, let me see if I understand. Everybody is happy but nobody gets the full lowdown," Bill summarised, wondering where Fi had got to.

Recently, she had been disappearing at odd times.

Cardinal Forrundiker had set the date for the conference to start, choosing the second Thursday of Advent, but, in reality, the first few days were lost to preparation and organisation. These fell mainly on Ches, Fi, Sophie and Old Ma Silver. Everything from food to pens and paper, agendas and timetables had to be organised. The cardinal dropped in from time to time like an inspecting general. Mostly, he seemed to defy his age with an exhausting series of meetings and memos behind the scenes. In an effort to understand what was going on around her, Fi asked the cardinal directly on Friday evening. The reply came back vague, in a friendly way that told Fi little.

By 11 a.m. on Saturday, they had their first group meeting. The cardinal's seat was at the head of the table in the first-floor conference room. Old Ma Silver sat at the bottom and the others were ranged around the sides, alternating between Catholic and New Moderator.

"Welcome everyone," the cardinal started. "We've laid out the table this way in an attempt to make the process as collaborative as possible. I inherently disliked the original seating plan with the Catholics on one side and the 'new boys' on the other. Now is everyone here?"

Fi was late, had gone again to the bathroom. Tammy stood to go and find her but Sophie was already out of the door.

"She's like a jet engine on legs," Sid said. The cardinal smiled, made a joke about the younger generation being in a terrible hurry.

But he took pride in the daughter who had been brought up by someone else rather than him.

"All we want to discuss today is the general agenda and some rules of engagement." The cardinal brought the meeting to order. "Nothing too heavy for the first session." Hit them later, he thought. Wait until the cosiness had settled upon them like a thick blanket on the bed. Then he would launch his plan, not before.

Timing was everything and everything mattered with the stakes so high.

He savoured his plan a moment, examining the cleverness and inventiveness from different angles. He felt good and proper about it for what cardinal of the Holy Catholic Church would enter negotiations on the future of their own dear church without a whopping big plan for counter-attack?

And what ambitious cardinal would not seek a little advancement in the process?

They broke for lunch, Sophie's delicatessen providing a delicious salad washed down with the lightest of wines. The sun spread a sleepy warmth through the dining room windows; seeping like oil in an engine, easing the way. Differences merge with the correct amount of wine, something the cardinal had seen to. Outside, bare trees leaned over the back garden like skeletal policemen looking in on other people's business.

"Good Lord!" said Bill, suddenly. "Look at that bod in the tree."

"It's Harry Brine," said Ches, having become acquainted with most of the press members outside the walls to 14, Via Romulus. "He's with the National Enquirer out of Chicago. Another American, I'm afraid to say!" As he spoke, a second figure, clearly his photographer, climbed along the branch that came over the wall into Old Ma Silver's garden. They had selected the one evergreen available for disguise. And this evergreen, being supple with sap, was kind to the interlopers in another way. As the weight increased on the branch, it dipped slowly and sedately until the wall provided the support it needed and stopped it snapping. Both Harry and his photographer were left dangling from the branch. Harry was feet down, scrambling for a foothold on the lawn. His colleague was not so lucky; clearly his legs were stronger than the arms for he was hanging upside down, legs looped over the branch.

As all 19 inside the house stood watching from the window, the photographer gave up the fight to stay on the tree and tumbled to the ground. Physics stepped in but, strangely, in slow motion, or so it seemed. The branch, load lightened, started to rise again, leaving Harry springing into the air. He decided that the ground looked safer and let go, landing and rolling heavily like a badly-trained paratrooper.

True to form, Sophie was out in the garden first, followed by Ches, who felt responsibility for his press corps.

"You, my prisoner. Come quickly." Sophie's English lacked coherence but the dramatic message was plain.

"What?" Harry was lying on the ground, winded, no real pain.

"You, my prisoner!" Sophie sang triumphantly. With sudden inspiration, she whipped away the twine supporting a young apple tree and quickly tied his wrists together.

"Hey, what're you doing to my buddy?" the photographer called. Sophie looked up from her crouching position next to Harry. The photographer was bigger, un-winded and upright, making for a very different kind of captive.

"This man is my prisoner. I want you come too."

"Where to, lady?"

"Into the house." The photographer could not believe his luck, bent down to help Harry to his feet, then thought of his cameras and went to look for them. If they were damaged by the fall he would have to use his phone – provided this crazy lady did not confiscate it.

"I need full names." They were back through the French Doors now and into the dining room. Sophie had grabbed pen and paper and was trying to write while holding the paper in her hand.

"Do the honours, Mighty," Harry said, recovering from his fall, indicating towards Sophie. His photographer immediately got down on all fours, his back making a table. Sophie laughed, crouched down beside him and put both elbows heavily on his back.

"Ouch," he cried.

"I said full names, Ouch what?" Sophie repeated, but now found it hard not to let a big grin mask her severe countenance.

"Harry Brine, news reporter extraordinaire, at your service Senorita."

"Signorina not Senorita. This is Italy, not Spain. And your table friend?"

"Mighty Snappy."

"Like a crocodile?" The connection with photography, in English, was lost on Sophie.

"Yes, like a crocodile," Harry replied, "so watch your step around him."

"He is crocodile with wrinkly skin and what a smell!"

"Touché!" Mighty spoke in a loud voice but directed at the tiled floor. "Can I get up now please?"

"Only if you promise not to bite." Sophie was at her limit in terms of the English language, finding jocularity far harder than serious press interviews.

"Do you taste good?"

"How do I know, silly? I've never eaten me!"

"Okay, I promise not to bite you. But you have to know I'm making a big sacrifice."

There was no more work done that day, which suited the cardinal. Instead, Ches and Sophie showed the two pressmen around the house, allowing photographs of the key rooms. At Mighty's request, everyone posed around the conference table, smiling with that gingery grin of self-consciousness. Fi insisted on multiple takes, inspecting each one on the screen until she was satisfied.

"I think I've sat in every chair in the room," Bill sighed. But Fi was determined to get the right perspective. She was equally determined to be on the right of the cardinal, causing a rumpus with Ernest who thought that was his position. When he stormed out, Fi became much more willing to approve photographs, allowing a clutch through that had eighteen instead of nineteen delegates.

"He makes his own bed," she said through tightly clenched teeth, reflecting with distaste how she had sucked up to him earlier.

But this was business and she was here to win for her client.

At 4:30 p.m., the cardinal called everyone together, Sara coaxing her husband down from his vast bedroom suite. "I think we're done for today. Let's try and meet early on Monday, say 9 a.m.?" It was put as a suggestion, but most people wrote '9 a.m. Monday' on their notepads.

"Wait a minute," Ernest said. "What about tomorrow?"

"Tomorrow's Sunday," Tammy said.

"So?"

"A day of rest," Tammy replied, the cardinal secretly pleased at Tammy's understanding of the church.

That gave him an idea.

"Tomorrow is Sunday as Sister Mary John, I mean Miss Shroton, so kindly pointed out." His look of graciousness and condescension worked, for Tammy lowered her eyes to focus on the shiny table-top. "I intend tomorrow to hold Mass here in this room at 11 a.m. Everyone, of course, is invited."

"Impossible!" Ernest was triumphant. "I re-read the rules you all agreed upstairs in my room. It says no specific religious services in this house during the conference. Here," his voice rose in pitch and volume as he waved the papers in the air, "rule ten says it all."

"Far from impossible." The cardinal remained coldly calm, as if dealing with a minor irritation from an even more minor official. "I suggest, Mr Justice, that you read out rule fourteen."

"All these rules are community driven and can be changed by a two- thirds majority vote at any time following a proposal from any member of either delegation," Ernest read, spotting the trap as he finished the sentence. "But we'll vote it down!" he cried, an edge of triumph back in his voice.

"And rule 15?" the cardinal prompted.

"All votes to amend rules to be done by secret ballot."

Sophie jumped up to organise the secret ballot. Actually, there was not much organising to do. She tore two pieces of paper into sufficient ballot-sized slips and handed them out, making up the protocol as they went along. "Write 'Yes' if in favour of a rule change to allow religious services during the conference and 'No' for the rule to remain."

It was going to be no worse than a draw for the cardinal as every Catholic delegate would follow his lead without question. One better than a draw, in fact, for he had taken Old Ma Silver aside quietly while the ballot papers were being prepared. Her assurance of support was given and accepted.

But the real question in the cardinal's mind rested on Tammy and the small sub-group gathered around her now. His best guess was that Miles would go with Tammy, whichever way she voted. If Tammy supported the rule change, he knew his plan was home and dry.

"Got a minute, Cardinal?" Fi approached him and squatted next to his chair by the fire.

"For you, my dear…" but stopped, realising how pompous he sounded.

"I'll do you a trade," she said, peering around to check Ernest had not noticed her. "I'll give you my votes on this in return for something."

"How many votes do you bring?"

"Four. That's Bill, me, Tammy and Miles." That meant fourteen to five.

"What do you want in return?"

"I want a wild card."

"What do you mean?"

"I want to come to you with one reasonable request at some time during the conference and you grant my request regardless of your position on the matter."

"What if it breaks the rules of the church?"

"I said it would be a reasonable request, take it or leave it, Cardinal,"

"I'll take it." They shook on it, then Fi rose and re-joined Tammy at the table. She had no idea what she would ask for, but long experience in negotiations said it would be needed.

"And the result in the secret ballot for a change to rule ten to allow religious services at 14, Via Romulus during the conference is as follows." Sophie had elected herself as results announcer and was loving every minute. "The total votes cast was nineteen, giving a voter turnout of one hundred percent."

"That's obvious," Sid said, "can you get on with the results?"

"For the motion…17 votes. Against, two."

The cardinal's face darkened slightly as he did the calculations. He had not needed to give away the wild card. Without Fi's four votes it would have been thirteen to six, sufficient for the two-thirds majority required.

But the real question in his mind was whether Tammy would have voted for Mass if Fi had not already traded her vote. That would have been useful information to know given his plans.

Everyone else was wondering who had voted alongside Ernest. Sara saw all eyes on her and blushed, looking away.

There were two people in the room who had not had a vote. Harry was writing furiously, while Mighty snapped with equal ferocity.

"Motion is carried," Sophie said.

"I will be saying Mass at 11 a.m. tomorrow morning here in the conference room. Everyone is most welcome." His eyes rested on Ernest briefly. He looked away. Then the old cardinal looked at Fi, wondering what game she was up to. Would she have a trump card to surprise him or would his clever plan win the day for his church? "Father LaPetite, would you mind driving me back now. I feel quite exhausted."

"Of course, Your Eminence."

He would confide in his deputy that evening back in his rooms; see what Father LaPetite had to say about it.

Once the cardinal was away, people started drifting off. Sophie and Ches disappeared into the drawing room downstairs, coming back a few minutes later with two hand-written documents.

"Your passes," she said, handing them to Harry and Mighty with a grin, "so you can come back tomorrow and each day."

In the space of four hours they had gone from unwelcome interlopers to favoured press attendees.

And mostly this was because they had the cheeky spirit that appealed to Sophie.

And because Ches thought it high time they had some American pressmen in on the action. And owing him something for their attendance.

Sunday Worship

Humphrey considered it profane to use the Mass for earthly ends. Yet the other priests in the delegation, led by Father LaPetite, seemed fine with it, some even competing to support the cardinal in celebration of the Mass.

But Father LaPetite was too wise, too connected to some sense of dignity, to compete in such a manner. He claimed tiredness from the trip to America and allowed Father Ellsworthy and two other priests to stand alongside the cardinal.

In fact, the cardinal sat for much of the Mass, finding standing too difficult. Sophie placed the same throne-like chair at one end of the room, then moved a large side table there and draped a white linen tablecloth over it. Old Ma Silver added a crucifix from her bedroom wall and also rummaged around for something to act as a chalice for the wine and a plate for the bread.

Bill and Sid, with some help, moved the conference table to the far end of the room, out of the way. Then Fi organised the chairs in two semi-circles around the altar.

Everything was ready. The four priests were robing up in the study next door, so there should be 15 in the room. Fi counted heads. There were only twelve.

Twelve disciples crossed her mind.

Then she worked out who was missing. Both of the Justices, one, of course, to be expected. Sara might have discovered some distorted degree of loyalty to her husband that kept her away, despite his despicable behaviour in getting Tammy and Father Barrow arrested.

But the third person was Tammy, very much unexpected.

Fi left the room to determine where Tammy might be. As she came onto the first-floor landing, she heard her friend's southern drawl from the study where the priests were completing their robing. The door was half open, allowing Fi to see inside.

And Sara was with them.

She moved closer, meaning to break into the conversation and draw them into the conference room-turned-chapel.

She stopped in amazement as Tammy's words came to her.

"Please, Your Eminence. It would give me such joy to serve you."

Fi could not believe that Tammy was turning to the enemy.

"Your Eminence, I really don't think it would do any harm. After all, she trained as a nun." And Sara was backing her up. What was going on behind her back? Or, more likely, right in front of her? Was she losing her touch?

Fi quietly stepped away and returned to the conference room, lost in thought.

"Did you find them?" Bill asked. "What's the matter?"

"Nothing, Bill," she tried to say but, remembering it was her boyfriend who was asking, decided to tell. "It's Tammy, I think she's separately negotiating with the other side."

They discussed in whispers for a few minutes. Bill could not believe it, arguing that Fi must be mistaken in some way. Then Sophie set a disc of Segovia in the CD player and all fell quiet. Just before the priests entered, Sara slipped in and took a seat at the back near the door. But still no Tammy. What was she doing?

Everyone stood, most heads bowed, as the priests entered in a slow single-file procession, clearly speed governed by the hesitant steps of the cardinal. And then Fi got her questions answered. For just in front of the cardinal, carrying a large crucifix like a warrior on crusade, was Tammy, dressed as an altar girl in purple for Advent with a white smock over.

She walked sedately, head bowed, seemingly at peace. Then she raised her face to look at the crucifix she was carrying. Sophie had ensured the lighting was subdued to give the room more of a chapel feel. As Tammy approached the altar, the candles lit her face with a yellow glow, giving emphasis to her solemn features.

It was as Fi looked at her best friend that she realised exactly how she was going to use the wild card she had negotiated with the cardinal.

And it would not help the New Moderation's bid one jot.

Mass was lengthy and Miles wandered in his mind. He disliked seeing Tammy with the priests, dressed in purple and white and fitting in to the establishment. He thought about her on her porch on Bent Mountain, rocking slowly, long legs over the side of the chair; shorts, crop top and bare feet.

The girl he was in love with loved another and it was a decidedly uneven contest.

Later that afternoon, still despondent, not wanting to disturb Tammy in her prayers, he found himself walking towards the kitchen in an idle, kick-the-skirting-boards type of way. Afterwards, when he thought about it, he realised there were several centres of power in that house. They lurked just below the calm and genial surface, alligators biding their time before pouncing on their prey. He felt cynicism rise like dirty suds in a drain, realising that there was nothing cosy and warm about the conference; everybody was out for their own ends.

There was the cardinal, deep in quiet conversations, assuming authority as if God-endowed. He was centre of a flock of glossy black birds. Then there was Ernest with his semblance of authority, strutting like a prima donna on the boards, cocooned so he almost did not care whether he had followers or not. There was no overlap between his world and the real world.

Fi formed another power base. She, like the cardinal, had numbers on her side. There was Bill, of course, always by her. Then there were the lieutenants, Sid and Al, runner boys to do her bidding. Miles knew that Fi had Tammy's best wishes at heart, but he sensed a tendency to get carried away; to play the game for its own enjoyment rather than a means to an end.

Fi was a medieval hunter who lived for the chase through trees and undergrowth.

Finally, there was Old Ma Silver with Sophie by her side, sometimes Humphrey when he could get away. And, increasingly, Ches was there too. They seemed like spirits joined together by some bond; unassuming, thinking ahead and thinking of others. It was a powerbase that belonged to the kitchen, with its pale flagstones and warming fire, mugs of coffee at the ready.

Miles' feet were taking him to that kitchen-based band right now, acting in isolation, for his sulky brain told him to leave on the next flight, go back to the chip shop and never come back.

But the brain often loses out where the feet are concerned, for they have the knack of taking you exactly where you do not think you want to go. Miles had size 12 shoes, but they were rubber-soled, cheap affairs to last a year at best. They made no sound as they trod along the back passage and down the stairs to present Miles Standish to the company that congregated in the kitchen. He opened the door to see Ches and Old Ma Silver in two armchairs by the fire, Sophie sat at their feet on a cushion, legs drawn in and up to make a sleek black mountain of her long skirt. Miles realised that, increasingly, she was wearing black. It made such a contrast with her bubbling personality.

Miles could have blamed his feet. He could equally have said he had no-one to be with as Tammy was praying. But he did not as he was British. Instead, he apologised profusely for interrupting them and made to leave.

"Hold your horses," Ches called out. "It looks to me like you sure need a friendly shoulder to weep on."

He could not refuse. For half an hour as the sun prepared for sleep, he bared his soul. Fear danced with hope, despair with faith. He felt the better for telling his story.

"That's just like me," Sophie cried.

"What do you mean?" Miles could not see any connection. Sophie flirted with the priests, Father Humphrey in particular, but there was nothing serious about this yellow-topped butterfly. Soon, with the onset of winter, she would fold her lively wings one last time and become part of the dust in the corner of the room. How could she make comparison with his agony?

It took 20 minutes for Sophie to explain. In that twenty minutes the sun finally settled down, sending crazy paving patterns of light and shadow as it slid down the last segment of sky. Miles had drawn up a kitchen chair, straddling the back like a cowboy in a saloon. Old Ma Silver made a pot of tea and, remembering Miles' preference for it black and sweet, had pushed it gently into his hands, not wanting to disturb the story.

Sophie's story filled 20 minutes of that mid-December day. It was not drawn out but spaced in an elegant way, reinforcing Sophie's agony while building her dignity.

She spoke first of hate and frustration. The setting was 21st Century Rome, more specifically the Vatican where she worked. She spoke of the tedium of her job, suddenly understanding how unsuited she was to a secretarial life. She spoke of her boss, the cardinal, and how he would not give her the time of day.

"But you are such a favourite of his!" It was Miles' only interruption. Old Ma Silver's expression warned him towards patience.

Into Sophie's life had come Humphrey and nothing had been the same again. "At first, I hated him, for what I thought he had done to Sister Mary John. But then I read all his reports from that time and understood the truth about him. And then, somehow, I fell in love."

"Love and hate are two sides of the same coin." That was Ches' one interruption out of the way.

Then she told of the time in the attic room, when they had come close to breaking Humphrey's vow, a vow she had somehow made herself in a strange type of way. Old Ma Silver leaned forward in her armchair and took Sophie's hand in hers, transmitting strength into that determined body through her silent presence.

Afterwards, with the story complete and up-to-date, Old Ma Silver made her one contribution – a determined cheerfulness to fill the inevitable silence. It was kindly meant but like mall music to Miles who simply stared at Sophie with tears in his eyes.

Her story was the mirror image of his.

Multiple Bombshells

"Ladies and Gentlemen, let me call the meeting to order." The tempo had changed abruptly, the cardinal insisting on starting at 7 a.m. on Monday. "We have a lot to cover. Is everyone here?"

"No, Fi is absent," Sid replied.

"Go and find her then," the cardinal snapped. "We can't start the conference without a full quorum."

Bill, Sid and Al all scampered off; the entire D'Alianti power base in search of their leader.

Al found her coming out of the ladies' bathroom on the top floor, still buttoning her skirt, slightly flushed when she saw him.

"Hi, Fi, you okay?"

"Sure, why wouldn't I be?"

"We were sent to find you." Al avoided Fi's question.

"And you have, so let's get moving." As Fi passed, heading for the narrow staircase that led down to the main part of the house, Al glanced into the open bathroom, saw the pile of dirty towels in the laundry basket.

"Right," the cardinal started, "down to business. First item on the agenda is current status." He looked around the room from his large chair, pretending to fumble with papers, seeking the right moment for his announcement. This was the moment for his plan to spring into action.

But before he could speak further, Fi stood up. "I feel a need to explain my personal current status," she said.

At that moment, Bill knew he was going to be a father. And he felt the joy of parenthood as it swept over him like rough waves scraping the body clean on the gritty seashore.

Everyone erupted with congratulations, Tammy first and foremost, rushing to her friend and kissing and hugging her. She did not forget Bill, shaking his hand, feeling ridiculous so then hugging him. "I'm so happy for you, Bill."

"I'm so happy for myself," he laughed. It all made sense now; Fi being off alcohol, her frequent absences, her mood swings and erratic sleeping patterns. Al thought of the long periods Fi had been spending in the bathroom each morning, so glad that they signified something positive.

Only the cardinal looked displeased. Father Ellsworthy imagined he disapproved of a child outside marriage. He saw Father LaPetite looking carefully at the cardinal but thought nothing more it.

But Father LaPetite knew the cardinal and his secret. Moreover, the cardinal had taken him into his confidence the night before. He knew in outline that the plan had been to dominate proceedings from the start of play today. Hence the cardinal's frowns were not of disapproval but frustration; frustration that his secret agenda was turned inside out before it had even started.

The cardinal recognised the setback but it was just that. He racked his mind for a solution and then it came to him.

"My congratulations, Miss D'Alianti," he said, reverting to the formal address which put a slightly different connotation to his words. "It is a remarkable coincidence for I, too, have something to say concerning paternity. In fact, I am going to ask Father LaPetite to make the announcement as I am somewhat connected with the events." He looked at Father LaPetite, mixing plea with command. Father LaPetite understood immediately.

He understood but did not want to oblige. He sent his pleas back to the cardinal but they were refused at the gate. So, the big priest with the big heart hidden behind a girth of gruffness, rose from his seat, dominating his side of the table.

An observer of the scene in the conference room of 14, Via Romulus over the next 15 minutes, would have noted, above all else, the changes to young Sophie over that timeframe. But as to what changes each observer would recall, we cannot be sure, for there were so many. Some would have seen how her hands froze, fingers pointing up at her chin as if to say 'Who? Me?

Why me?' Others, like her close friends in the room, would have seen the reflection of her real father in her eyes; that is before they misted over like fog racing across the sea, swallowing up the boats upon the water. Sara remembered the changes in the colour of Sophie's face; from light tan to grey, then red, white and grey again, like someone going through the stages of life in a quarter-hour.

There was only one person who saw everything and he felt it just exactly like she felt it; every whizzed-up emotion see-sawing around that room. A third of the way in, Humphrey rose from his seat, walked around the table and whispered to Al to change places with him.

At the halfway point, Humphrey shuffled his chair close to hers. At ten into the 15 he first held her hand; a hand he found full of dignified beauty. He took it from its pointed-under-the-chin position and held it delicately at first but with increasing firmness as Father LaPetite's revelations wound on. He wondered how someone so young could have so much written in her hands; who she was and where she came from. Those hands revealed to him her inner emotions; he alone could feel the tremors that echoed the volcano within; he alone felt her skin and noted the hot flush, like she was developing a fever in double-quick time.

At 12 minutes in, she fell sideways in her shock, her confusion, and leaned her beautiful head against his chest. He smelled her perfume, just as he had done three months earlier in the lecture hall on the first day of the new term but mixed now with the smell of her emotions; her fear, her outrage, her exhaustion. He felt her hair against his cheek, wondering at its silky quality. Then he heard her sobs, coming from deep within.

This was raw, uncultured emotion. It was the great ship Sophie struck below the waterline and above the deck, holed everywhere and its sailors grasping to cope, to find something that still worked as it should.

Father LaPetite was done now, slumping back in his chair; his vast frame seemed much smaller, as if he had offered up his innards as an essential part of the tale. Now he sat as a depleted man.

And he sat and looked into the silence, as did everyone.

"Is it true?" Sophie spoke first.

"It is true," Humphrey replied. He felt her shake as she rose from her seat, then everyone watched her walk around the table to the cardinal.

"Papa," she said into that silent intake of breath. Even Humphrey could not tell where that single 'Papa' word was on the emotion-grid. Did it hover somewhere in between incredulity and love? Or was it closer to disgust and disdain at the bottom of the chart?

"My Sophie," he replied, not sure whether it was mother or child.

But the ploy worked, swinging attention back to the cardinal and away from the new moderators.

Now he had them where he wanted them.

Ready for his bombshell.

He kept them waiting for most of the day, gauging the latest time he could make his announcement without risking the momentum swinging away from him again. He seemed weary, very weary, but inside was a mass of action and plans, constantly amending and improving as the stuffy conference room ticked through the day.

This was his chance, the chance he had been waiting for ever since he first placed a cardinals hat on his head and realised that the ultimate was possible. If he could save his Church from ignominious takeover, he would be the natural moral leader, ready to take over when the Holy Father went Heaven-bound.

They had a working lunch, at the cardinal's insistence. There was nothing to be gained by letting the other side regroup, so they discussed minor differences in doctrine; long-established beliefs against the newly-sprung. But the cardinal expertly steered the discussion away from anything controversial or enlivening.

The afternoon wore on with a stillness that was unreal. It was hard to believe that they were debating the future of the Roman Catholic Church. Then the cardinal demanded a break, but not for the participants, more for Harry and Mighty, the resident pressmen, to get up to speed. He was happy for them to take over for a while, repeated positions for photographs and inane questions requiring soundbite answers. It filled the late afternoon and early evening and allowed the cardinal more time to think.

And to fine-tune his plan.

"I'm afraid we've not made much progress on the theological side." He seemed now to be wrapping it up. Father LaPetite knew he was up to something, knew the announcement was coming. He just could not see how it would be made. He looked around the table, saw blank faces and staring eyes. He could not grasp Cardinal Forrundiker's strategy; was he trying to bore the New Moderators into submission?

It was 6:30 p.m. on Monday, third week of Advent. "I do have one more announcement to make today." The cardinal watched the spark waking in each face, flitting back and forth. He cleared his throat and began.

"As you know, a key part of our defence against the takeover bid of the Roman Catholic Church is that the Church of New Moderation is not essentially a church, a religion, in its own right. It is more of a reform movement that, logically, fits within the Catholic Church. Hence, it has no rightful position as a 'bidder' for the church. As of now, it is decidedly outside our church. But it fits so well as a movement within the church. Accordingly, I am formally announcing a counter-takeover bid for the church of New Moderation. Put colloquially, we are turning the tables on 'you guys'."

There were gasps of amazement, spread pretty evenly around the table. Even Father LaPetite, knowing it was coming, had not seen how it would be delivered.

Fi was the first to recover, but her immediate response was feeble.

"What?"

"Simple, my dear, we are making a takeover bid for the New Moderation movement." It put everything on the throw of a dice. Yet, the cardinal had the dice marked in his favour.

He was bidding to save his church, so rules of fair play did not count anymore.

"But the protocols, the procedure. We did our bid properly through the authorities."

"We all know, Miss D'Alianti, that the 'protocols and procedures' you so slavishly followed were no more than a marketing gimmick. It never was a genuine takeover bid by the New Moderation movement, merely a cheap trick to take advantage of some short-term difficulties in the church and so gain maximum publicity for your firm." He sounded like a television drama barrister delivering a particularly eloquent summing up speech. But inside he was on fire with nerves, only his will for the ultimate office keeping him going.

But that will was powerful; reinforced by seventy years of increasing authority, culminating in the right hand of the Holy Father.

For a little longer.

Fi did not have an answer. The accusations were so outrageous, so incredible after the cosiness of recent days, that even her fine mind scrambled to address them.

"No, Your Eminence," Tammy sprang up, flustered in a way Miles had never seen before. "Forgive me, please, Your Eminence, but that is not what Fi was doing. She was helping me…Your Eminence." Tammy seemed to be trying to take the blame, such was the New Moderators' disarray, yet when Fi analysed it later, recognising how artful the cardinal had been, she did not see it as a case of blame at all. It was clever manoeuvring by the cardinal, no more and no less. The great financier of New York City had been outclassed by an old clergyman.

For her efforts, Tammy received a headmaster's stare that silenced her opposition. She plumped back into her chair with a sigh-like air escaping from a plastic bag.

"What does this mean?" Sid asked eventually.

"It means democracy will decide," Father Ellsworthy replied on behalf of the cardinal who was slumped in his chair, not seeming to be awake at all. Father Ellsworthy had suddenly clicked onto the message, understanding exactly what his boss was up to. "We'll have a vote," he continued.

"That will take months to organise. And when your bid is defeated we will still be back at square one. We'll still have the bid by New Moderation on the table." Sid wished this was just a common case of corporate raiding where dollars weighed in to make the final decision.

"You forget one thing," the cardinal said, slurring his words. He pushed a booklet across the table to Father Ellsworthy. "Read section 16, Ellsworthy."

Father Ellsworthy read the words that had been the basis of the cardinal's plan; they were the words that had given him the idea in the first place and why he had jumped at the chance for a conference.

"Section 16. Mergers with other religious institutions. Should any consideration be given to merging the Church of New Moderation with any other religion or religious establishment, the board of the church shall determine the merits and vote accordingly by show of hands. Such a vote will be final and binding on all members."

It was short and it was sweet, and it damned Fi's chances.

The vote took place later that evening. There were five voters, just sufficient under the rules for a quorum.

Fi asked for privacy for the vote but did not exclude herself from the meeting.

They sat in the conference room, just six people dotted around the large table. Fi took the cardinal's chair, leaving the five voters facing her like directors to their chairperson. Fi noted that the Justices sat as far apart as they could manage. In fact, it had been Sara's doing. Arriving after Ernest, she pretended not to see him patting the chair next to his, went instead to a position at the far end of the table where Sophie usually sat.

They debated first whether to hold a secret or public ballot. Ernest argued vehemently for a public vote, then switched to private, then back to public. Tammy offered little to the conversation, seeming to have an internal debate of her own, weighing up the arguments. Fi smiled at her whenever she raised her eyes, but it was not often. Tammy was wearing a black, almost ankle length, dress with a matching black scarf making a triangle over her pony-tailed hair.

Fi was certain that Ernest would back rejection of the bid, if only to keep his delusion of authority alive. He made for a strange ally for Fi, but in twenty years of takeovers Fi had known stranger.

The others were all unknown. It was likely that Sara would go against her husband but not certain. Someone had voted with Ernest for the rule change allowing religious services. Had that been Sara, secretly reverting to the loyalty that had been the salient feature of their long marriage?

Her eyes moved around the table, back to Tammy. Who could tell with Tammy? She had been all for the takeover bid of the Catholic Church, yet since the debate she was a different person. Fi remembered her face in the procession during Mass. There was excitement but also serenity. It was like someone had found their purpose. Yet what of her loyalties? Did she not owe something to Fi?

Fi had spoken to Tammy earlier, just before supper, urging her to vote to reject. Soon Fi would find out whether her arguments had won.

Close to Tammy sat Miles, yet not so close that Fi assumed he would back her regardless. The distance between them had been evident since the debate. It saddened Fi who had grown fond of her friend's lover. But now it might work to her advantage. Miles was the most recently appointed of the board members, elected in recognition of his idea for the takeover. He also seemed the least religious. Would he vote down his own unique idea?

Last around the table was Ches. As her sight moved on to him, he raised his eyes to look directly at her, winked and grinned, before looking down again.

She should have known that she would have one supporter guaranteed.

They settled finally on a public ballot. Fi's mind raced with the possibilities. She had taken the chair so was in charge. How should she ask for the votes? Should she go left to right or right to left? Or pick individuals regardless of their position around the table. She had to consider what influence early declarers would have on those voting later. There were so many conflicting threats and opportunities. This is what made her who she was. This is what she lived for. She loved the aggression, the suspense, the intensity, the victory.

"Okay, ladies and gentlemen," she said, raising her voice above the chatter of debate. That presented another consideration. There were three men and two women present as board members. How would that influence the vote?

Suddenly she had an idea. It was vintage D'Alianti.

"Rather than go straight into the vote now, I suggest we pause, take a break."

"Why?" Ernest sounded aggressive.

"To ensure we come up with the right answer, of course." Fi played a double here. As she answered Ernest she gave the slightest of winks, suggesting she was on his side, backing the leader of their church. But then she turned to Tammy, quite naturally repeating her words "to come up with the right answer", thus getting Tammy's support by promising to do what was right.

Both Tammy and Ernest were on their feet. Fi allowed Ernest his authority back for a moment.

"Back here in 30," he called as he made for the door.

This was the part Fi called the 'crunch point', a block of time, usually short, in any aggressive takeover, where the issues are concentrated and success or failure is on a knife edge. In retrospect, it seems all else was leading up to this crucial period. Fi remembered a past project where the white-haired founder of the target met her for the first time, seeing her intentions and starting to understand that there could be positives arising. Another time, it happened much later, when the contracts were ready for signing and someone tried a slippery move, thinking the others committed to the deal so they would not object to a quarter percent more. The result had been as if the parties were thrown into a tombola and jumbled up, coming out in unlikely pairs; foe and foe now joined in common endeavour.

A crunch point had happened at some stage in every takeover bid that Fi had been involved with.

Ernest had set the time of 30 minutes, but Fi recognised the knife-edge opportunity and knew it was up to her. She had 30 minutes. She reckoned on five minutes with each voter and five minutes at the end to go back to the waverers. She set about her project calmly.

After all, she was a professional.

"Ladies and gentlemen," Fi called them to order, "I trust you have all had time to reflect and also an opportunity to clarify any points that required clarification." Had the crunch point gone as planned? "I will now ask each person to vote, one at a time. When I call your name, please respond with a Yes if you want to reject the counter bid from the Catholic Church and No if you want to accept it."

"Wait a minute, should it not be the other way around?" Miles asked. But Fi was one step ahead of them all.

"No Miles, the motion before us is to reject the takeover bid and continue with our own bid. Hence a Yes vote backs the motion." Fi knew that people were slightly more likely to say 'yes' to any motion than 'no'. It might just help them.

"So, if there are no other questions, let's move on to the debate. Remember, as your name is called simply say yes or no. Ches, please keep a record of the votes for the minutes." She paused a moment, cleared her throat.

"Sara Justice."

"No," said very clearly and immediately. This was a blow for Fi. She had thought to lead with a reasonably strong card. Should she go for safety or put Miles in an awkward position of voting before he was sure what Tammy would say? There was time enough for that game later. She went with safety.

"Ernest Justice."

"Yes," said with a glare at his wife across the table.

They were one each now, equal after two votes.

"Ches Bloakes."

"Yes." They went ahead, but it came down to how Tammy would vote. Who would she be loyal to? But first she played her trick.

"Miles Standish."

No answer came.

"Miles Standish." Still no answer. He looked at Fi, then looked at Tammy. Tammy's face was serene, leaving him with no idea as to which way she might go. She was the reason he was on the board. He wanted to go with her. But which way would she go?

"Miles, we need an answer, unless you want to abstain." That presented more problems than it answered, not a good road for now.

Miles looked again at Tammy, willing her to give some indication, to come out in the world. She looked up briefly, saw the agony in his eyes and saw the love for her too.

"Miles will vote in a moment. In the meantime, I vote No," she said firmly and clearly, like a voice ringing off the trees and rocks of Bent Mountain.

"I vote No," Miles said at last.

"So, the motion to reject the Catholic Church's takeover bid has been denied. We are accepting the takeover?"

"We are," Ches said. "It seems we are." It was not the result he had voted for, but he could live with it. His concern was for Fi who had hoped to keep their bid alive by rejecting the counter-bid. She sat still, examining a blank piece of paper on the table. Then she looked at Ches for reinforcement, received it and turned her attention to Ernest, the other in the room showing disappointment.

But there was nothing elegant about the desperate way he worked his fingers through the New Moderation rule book, hoping to find some straw to clutch. Could his reign as life president be over before it had really started? What of the gold chains he had ordered?

Pressing Engagements

Dirty deals are best done behind closed doors. Many people go through their whole lives never getting near to one. Some wish afterwards that they had stayed away; perhaps an awkward phase of a vulnerable business or the temptation to hide something from the divorce courts.

And then there are a few who relish the surge of power. Ernest was one of these but with a difference. He had always done it through intermediaries. He was the one who would nod and wink, never saying what he meant but knowing that his agent knew exactly what to do. In the top circles he would get credit for a 'job that needed doing', plus a reputation for efficiency and reliability. He had first made partner in his law firm in this way. A wealthy client was getting divorced by her husband on the grounds of infidelity. A few bundles of cash later, not that Ernest ever touched a single note, and the jilted husband was fighting to save his own reputation. Ernest had negotiated a fee of 10% of everything his client got over half of the estate. The case settled on a 60 to 40 split and produced the biggest single income for the law firm that year.

And got Ernest his partnership.

Ernest had done a dirty deal with the ex-editor and ex-assistant editor of the Daily Witness. It was one of the types he had excelled at before retirement. There was no cash involved at all. It was favour for favour.

They got Tammy arrested so that Ernest could take over. In return, he promised them exclusivity on every bit of news, real or fake, emanating from the takeover bid.

It was a dream deal.

Except he had not allowed for Ches and Sophie getting in the way.

"Where are you going, dear?" Sara asked, unable to kick the endearment.

"Just for a walk. I've decided to go every evening. Now that I have so much responsibility and…" But Sara had closed her eyes, was back in Stratford upon Avon; eating paninis and drinking white wine with her new Massachusetts friends.

She would take up their invitation to visit them when this was all over. She could imagine long walks through the Cambridge streets, wading through piles of snow and drinking hot chocolate in one of the bistros off Harvard Square.

She would travel alone.

Ernest made his way to the prearranged meeting place in the old apple orchard that sided the house. The trees were bare, twigs like the fingers of old women, gnarled and twisted. A few windfalls lay where they landed, now host to a million insects. The moon was almost full, allowing Ernest to see without using the flashlight he had placed in his jacket pocket. A panel in the far fence was loose and easily moved allowing access to 12, Via Romulus, the empty house next door. There, peering through the darkness, were Brandywine and Bathurst, ready to grab the story and sell on to the highest bidder, provided, of course, it was not the Daily Witness.

Even they had their standards.

"What you got?"

"A lot, a whole damn lot!" Ernest grinned into the moonlit half-light, not realising that the moon only had so much power of illumination and could not do justice to the expressions he sent out into the night.

Eddie Bathurst, as the junior, got out his notebook and pen, ready to scribble. "Go on," he said, flashing a pencil torch onto his notebook, then resting it on a fencepost to aid his writing.

"Well, I'll begin at the beginning…"

"And end at the end, no doubt!" Ches' voice rang out through the pale gloom. Ernest turned quickly, more a jerk, knocked the torch from Eddie's hand. It fell to the ground and went out.

"What are you…?"

"You might well ask," Ches replied. "Maybe I'm out for an evening walk. Maybe I'm patrolling for burglars. Or maybe, just maybe, bearing in mind that my responsibilities cover the gentlemen and ladies of the press, I'm out here looking for infringements of our rigorous press rules. Not that you, Mr Justice, as president of our church, would ever deign to break our rules, of course."

Ernest's grin had been hidden by the night, but Ches' broad smile found passage with his words and shone like the stars missing from the sky, cutting into Ernest and causing Brandywine and Bathurst to withdraw quickly.

"That's funny," Ches was still grinning, "I could have sworn there were some bodies through that hole in the fence. Must have been mistaken." They stood together a few seconds, frustration looking enviously at triumph, the former trying to find the real-world version of a legal loophole.

But none came, so he turned back to the house. Thinking to save face, he mumbled something about doing an impromptu security check.

But Ches was ready for this. "Goodnight, sir," he called. "Don't worry, I'll fix this broken panel first thing in the morning."

"Good, it should never have been allowed in the first place." It was a lame attempt to grab back authority from the hands of the bigger man.

But Ches was not perfect. He was lying in bed early the next morning, turning his night-time adventure into another of his amusing stories; a little embellishment made a world of difference.

He was debating how much bigger and more aggressive Ernest was, perhaps even menacing; that way Ches' pluckiness came to the fore. There was a loud bang from the garden. He jumped out of bed, knowing it was the fence.

It was dark still, close now to the winter equinox, but Ches heard voices carrying across the orchard. There was anger and indignation in those voices. He pulled on some clothes and went down the back stairs and out into the garden.

He should have known Sophie would be there; wherever there was activity she was on the scene. He saw her first in the orange light from the terrace. She was suitably dressed for work at night: black cat-like suit, just lacking the ears and whiskers. Her yellow hair was loose and long, and it was moving through the night with vehemence.

"Stop right there. You are under arrest," she cried, lunging forward with a shotgun in her arms. Ches moved forwards instinctively, his big bulk flattening the long grass as he moved through it.

"Hold on, Sophie, no guns, definitely no guns," he cried, wondering if his big voice would carry through the night, across the garden and the orchard.

But the wind was in his favour, assisting his words across the forty yards that separated them. Sophie turned, opened her mouth. Then Ches stopped his heavy run, relief sweeping over him like medicine to calm a fast-beating heart.

It was not a gun, but a piece of drainpipe, torn from the wall.

She had meant it to be mistaken for a gun, such was the adventure that filled Sophie's life.

"Don't wave… that gun… around," Ches said, deciding to play along, catching his breath as he spoke. "Have you caught some interlopers?"

"We didn't mean any harm." That was the whining voice of Eddie Bathurst. He saw only a panther like figure, fully armed, with bright yellow hair.

"They're muscling in," Harry's voice came out of the shadows, caught Ches by surprise. There was quite a party down by the fence.

"They're in my sights, Ches," said Sophie, still waving her drainpipe dangerously.

"Don't fire, please don't fire," Marcus added his pleading tones to the mix.

"Just a minute," Sophie replied, "I know that voice." Ches had caught up with them now. Breathing heavily, he switched on the torch on his phone to illuminate two frightened faces.

"It's that nasty reporter from the debate. The one who was so awful to Tammy."

"Don't move gents and you won't get hurt." Ches was enjoying it now as much as Sophie. "What shall we do with them?" he wondered out loud.

"Easy, keep them prisoners," Sophie replied.

"Yes, of course. But where?"

"In the old coal cellar. It's just used for storage now. Have you got a handkerchief?" Ches did not, so Sophie passed the drainpipe to Ches. "It's cocked, Mr Bloakes, and ready to go." Then she took his jacket and Harry's too, tied them loosely over the interlopers' heads so that they were blindfolded. The drama appealed to her; it was high adventure done properly.

Ches inspected the cellar while Sophie marched them into the kitchen, jackets over their faces like convicted sex offenders hoping to ward off photographers. But Mighty still got a few, lifting the jackets to snap 'quickies' as he called them.

Ches felt a little sorry for them and failed to remove a crate of whisky from the back of the cellar. There was an old toilet down there that the gardeners had used in the house's heyday. He placed six slightly stale loaves of bread and a large slab of cheese that was nameless and forgotten, and then added four bars of chocolate. As he went up the steps and locked the door, they were squabbling over whose fault it was that they would now be the last to know. Sophie had promised to release them exactly two hours after the general press release was issued.

Marcus Brandywine and Eddie Bathurst exit our story at this point, drinking their sorrows away. Later, when quite drunk, Eddie started singing, actually quite tunefully. But Marcus threw the cheese at him, not because the noise offended him, but because the man did.

Actually, they have one final task to undertake. It doesn't bear much significance to the story but arises because of a suggestion that Sophie made when Ches and she discussed the role Ernest had played.

"It's only fair, after all Ernest made a commitment to communicate with them," Sophie said, as Ches unlocked the door and shoved Ernest Justice down the steps to be with his English buddies. Then locked the door carefully again.

Two Audiences with the Cardinal

Sophie was waiting for the cardinal on the landing later on Tuesday morning as the old man made his way back to the conference room for the start of the day's proceedings. Officially, he knew nothing of the vote by the board of the New Moderators the previous night. He had left as the general meeting had broken up and spent the night in sleep and prayer. But he knew in actual fact, at least with some certainty, because he had been driven in by Father Ellsworthy and his faithful priest had said he understood it to have gone their way.

"Your Eminence," Sophie said, too loud and slightly too shrill. She had used the term 'Papa' once, but that did not seem right now. Its use following the announcement by Father LaPetite had been in the heat of the moment; drama had played its part and, afterwards, Harry had scribbled energetically.

Now reality had played its hand and, with the light of a new day, had come her anger.

"Sophie," he said, understanding instinctively the need to step back from expressions indicating paternity.

"I need to speak to you privately."

"Of course. Let's go in here." He indicated the study where the priests had robed up 48 hours before. "We won't be disturbed in here."

They were not disturbed but caught quite an audience as their voices rocked through the whole of the first floor of 14, Via Romulus.

"How dare you!" Sophie started.

"What?" It was foolish for the cardinal to suggest innocence. He was clearly as guilty as sin. We are going to put aside the original carnal sin and the breaking of his vows and concern ourselves with the offence against Sophie.

"What do you think?" Sophie was already in a rage. "You knew all my life that you were my father and then you announce it in a public meeting."

"I thought it for the best, my dear. I realise my error now." He had moved from innocence to misjudgement in one quick step.

"Don't you 'my dear' me!" she shouted.

"I'm sorry, my…Sophie. I genuinely thought it was for the best, to get it out there."

"Liar," Sophie was holding back tears, her defences thrown sideways and upside down at the same time; somehow managing to hold, but only just.

But the cardinal had only one line of defence left. And he used it now.

"I promised your mother," he said, trying to twist a vice into a virtue, a self-indulgence into a sacred act.

"You promised my mother to spring it on me in a public meeting?"

"Well, not exactly. You see…"

"You're lying again."

In three short minutes his three defences were expended. He only had one place left to go.

He told her the truth.

The whole truth. He told of the meeting in his mind where fear and ambition united, becoming much more powerful combined than separate; following that odd rule that two plus two makes five.

"I was so scared that this crazy bid would succeed. At the same time, I saw opportunity."

"What do you mean opportunity? You have everything you ever wanted. You are a cardinal in case you had forgotten!"

"There is still one thing I have not yet achieved."

"You mean? You can't mean?" The shock was in Sophie's white face, the suddenly wobbly legs, the shortness of breath.

"I want to become the next pope." It was done. It was said. The cardinal's only living relation knew his secret ambition. "If I succeed in putting the bid down, saving our church, I will almost certainly become the next pope."

Sophie could not think what to say, so stooped down onto her haunches and silently took her father's hands. They remained in silence, one squatting, the other sitting, for some time. Both tremored with emotion, the young and the old, joined through clasped hands. Fear on the one side facing outrage on the other like soldiers staring across a hostile border.

Sophie could not settle her thoughts. Images went around her head like dancers in a drunken jig. But those dancers had little spare energy for anger so Sophie's wrath was put to one side carefully, where the dancers would not trip and stumble upon it. From there the wind picked it up and dispersed it gently, scattering tiny drops of rage amongst those that had gathered to watch.

Some would conclude that Sophie had too generous a nature not to forgive, hence was a model Christian. Father LaPetite would have snorted and said "Typical Sophie, the girl can't even hold on to her anger."

"Papa," she said at last, showing how all rage was dispersed, "I still don't understand why you had to announce that I am your daughter in such a public way."

"Two reasons, my love. First, I had to keep control of proceedings in order to have any chance of success in the negotiations. I don't think Miss D'Alianti's motive in telling us she was with child had any ulterior motive, but it took the limelight, hence control, away from me. I had to counter it with something equally dramatic. This was the first thing that came into my head."

"So, you used me to further your plans."

"Yes, I did." It was the best response. Sophie warmed to the straight-talking. There had been three attempts over the first three minutes at evasion and deceit, but now, rightly or wrongly, the cardinal had stumbled on the truth; the best and only sure way to assuage the rage in Sophie. And the thing that would most build respect in this young girl.

It was a lucky find for the cardinal, this thing called truth.

"And the second reason?"

"That is a little more embarrassing," he replied. "It seems my reputation needed a little adjustment…if I had a chance of becoming pope that is."

"Explain." The single word instruction was taken straight from Father LaPetite.

"Sophie, I have been a clinical priest all my life. I've said Mass and heard confession and conducted marriages of course; in fact, hundreds and hundreds of times. But when you look at the roles I've been allocated over the years, they are all about administration and policy. I've never worked in a deprived parish or a prison, for instance."

"But you've done great things with education."

"Yes, but strictly from a policy background. I've never taught anyone – not a single schoolchild, not even a seminarian. I've been working in the background, getting a name for myself as a very able administrator."

"So? I don't understand."

"Well, I thought I needed something to make my story stand out, something a little different and racy. I wanted something that made me human and frail and…"

"Likeable," Sophie finished her father's sentence for him. She tensed a moment; he could feel it through his fingers. She thought then of her own manipulation, spurred on by prejudice and mistaken hate. She felt herself no different. She relaxed in the company of a fellow sinner, her fingers transmitting the message of acceptance, appreciating the artfulness put in honest language.

The audience outside the robing-room sensed this turning and all were glad. Only perhaps Ernest would have felt different but, in his cellar-gaol, he heard not a word from two floors up.

"Your eyes," Sophie said, looking up now into her father's face.

"My eyes?"

"Yes, you've got my eyes." It came to her now, where she had seen his eyes before.

"Actually, you have it the wrong way around."

"How?"

"Well, you must have my eyes. I did come first, at least that much is certain!"

She kissed him on the forehead, stretching her bent legs to reach. Father LaPetite would have snorted a "typical Sophie". His comment would have been apt, for she could not hold onto her anger; rather it flooded the room, rushing here and there with its assumptions and prejudices, before dispelling suddenly like smoke in a fresh breeze. It was a part of who she was and now it flooded someone else with the most precious memories. For the cardinal saw his Sophie back again. She had his eyes for sure, but her faint freckles, her cheeky smile, her dimpled chin and her love of life were all straight from his Sophie, his lover and his daughter's mother.

And there was more.

Hatred and other bad things had been momentary items in his Sophie's life, moving on like smoke in the wind. And this was, undoubtedly, the greatest gift she had given to her daughter on her death bed.

"So, you thought a little spice in your past would make you more attractive?" It sounded ridiculously artificial to Sophie, but she could see why he would think that way.

And she loved her father in that moment. Not for what he had done to her, but for who he was, this hopelessly frail man who was wrapped in ambition so tightly it made a corset for his hopes and plans.

The second act came hard upon the first. Sophie left the room a few minutes after their final words, shining from the new communion with her father, empty of emotion and needing to give to others in order to top up her own. She remembered that lunch had to be organised and went to find Old Ma Silver to share her wonderous story as they walked, arm in arm, to the delicatessen.

How long, Tammy wondered, is a decent interval? Weighing up the emotions involved between father and daughter, she thought at least ten minutes and started counting the seconds, checking her speed of count frequently against the clock on the landing outside the robing-room.

After three minutes she could wait no longer. She knocked on the door and called out, timidly, that it was Tammy and could she please have a word with his eminence.

The audience, gathering in the conference room next door, heard not a word of the second act. Perhaps they should have angrily demanded their money back, only admission had been free, at least in terms of hard coinage. Harry went right up to the door and put a glass between door and ear but still heard just the odd word.

But Fi knew what was being said behind that door. She knew it word for word, as if she had written the script herself. She went to stand by Miles, found his hand and squeezed it.

Whichever way it went, he would need his friends around him.

"Your Eminence, I have been much troubled recently."

"I know, my child. It is written in your countenance. You are in the middle of a great struggle."

"How do you…?" But it was obvious to those around her with perception, obvious to the cardinal and to Fi next door. It might have passed by Ellsworthy, but both LaPetite and Barrow had commented to the cardinal on Tammy's two loves. Humphrey had put it succinctly, saying, "she seems torn between this world and the next; two great loves that appear irreconcilable. She will have to make a choice."

But Humphrey was far less perceptive in another way; he simply could not see that the same words could be applied to him. There could be a mirror placed in front of him and it would have reflected Tammy back.

The cardinal had agreed with Humphrey's observation at the time, then wondered if it would be of use to his own project. Now, with the love of his daughter flowing through him, he was not quite so sure he wanted to manipulate anyone else for his ends; ends that seemed so unimportant compared to the relationship with his daughter. And, he had to admit, for he knew something of his own bounds, a connection through her to the one he had loved to distraction and the reason for Sophie being there now.

"Do you want to confess?" His instincts were working perfectly. He was an observer to the scene; actually, more like the director, intimate with the script and determined to create the mood he had in mind.

"Yes, Father." She forgot his rank, it did not matter. She fell to her knees, smoothed her long grey woollen skirt and started on the familiar words.

"Forgive me, Father, for I have sinned. It has been…nine years since my last confession."

"What sins have you committed my child?" His hands went to Tammy's, just as his daughter's had gone to his before.

He now had strength and he gave it willingly to this troubled child of God.

Tammy was human, felt the reverence, but also embarrassment and fear of declaring her most venal sins to this old man. She had sought it, but held back for awkwardness, for lack of courage. She started, as humans do, with the innocuous, the easy to confess.

"Father, I have been impure in thought and deed. I have slept with someone outside wedlock and wanted it, loved it." Her voice trailed away. That was only the easy bit done.

"Go on, my dear." Grips tightened, two whole turns in the vice.

"I have hated His Church and sought to bring it down."

"Anything else, my child?" This was asked in matter-of-fact fashion, as if adding to a shopping list rather than an emptying of conscience.

But it was the fork in the road that we all face once or sometimes twice in our lives. One way, the Path of Truth, leads to a sweet stream next to a meadow where the sun shines and butterflies and bees busy themselves with their work. The other path takes one over bland, never-ending moorland, every feature seeming the same to drive one crazy with repetition.

But the Path of Truth had an obstacle at its start. A great yawning crevice that has to be jumped. The other choice was easy, starting with a gentle slope downwards and bright flowers along the way.

But looking down the second road, Tammy could see the flowers were plastic so as not to fade with time.

She leapt.

"I lied," she said, thus telling the truth.

"I lied," she repeated.

"Go on. What did you lie about?" The cardinal thought he knew but had to hear it from her.

"I lied about Father Davies raping me. I mean, he did rape me but I sort of…"

"Encouraged him?"

"Yes." She looked into the eyes that were the same brown as Sophie's and said it for herself. "I encouraged him. I wanted to see what it was like, making love I mean. Before my final vows, I wanted to know what I was giving up."

"You encouraged him but he still raped you?"

"Yes, I asked him…"

"Can you speak up, my child?"

She made a big effort then, throwing her voice across the room so that Harry, ear still to a glass at the door, heard every second word; sufficient to get the meaning.

"I asked him to stop, Your Eminence, I got frightened. I pleaded with him, but he would not stop. He went on and on…"

"That's enough, my dear. You have imparted enough for me to understand the sin. Now say the Hail Mary three times while I consider the matter."

"Hail Mary, full of grace…" The cardinal did not feel he had much grace remaining, having squandered it to ambition. Tammy's ambition had been fierce also, yet it seemed to be gone now, leaving an empty chamber for grace to move back in. Where exactly was his ambition? Did he want the thing he had wanted before?

No, that was not the right question. If he was selected as the next pope, would he act for the good or would the next level of aspiration kick in? Could ambition ever be satisfied? That was the question.

"The Lord is with Thee…" Who was the Lord with? Catholics or New Moderators? More to the point, was God with Tammy who had left the Church or with him who had stayed all his life in its folds? Did God take sides?

"Blessed are thou amongst women and blessed is the fruit of thy womb, Jesus…" He thought of the birth his Sophie had given; the little baby that came to them but was all grown up now. Blessed are all babies for they know only purity. It is when they learn the ways of man that corruption sets in. And where was his ambition on the scale of corruption?

"Holy Mary, Mother of God…" The cardinal closed his eyes at this point and Sophie came immediately into his vision; not the mother but the daughter, bouncing with life and ideas; such a joy to bring life into this world, such a blessing.

"Pray for us sinners now and at the hour of our death…" When had be last prayed for anything other than himself, his ambition?

"Amen." The third 'Amen' startled him with its finality, but by then he had worked out his response.

"My dear, it does you credit that you take these trivial misdemeanours so seriously. It shows dedication to God, whatever particular church or meeting house you attend. For your penance, I would like you to say the Stations of the Cross. Do you still have a rosary?"

"Yes, Father, but I told Miles I would not use it again. He took a dislike to me using it in prayer."

"Then we shall oblige him, Tammy, for you have given your word. For your revised penance I want you to go to Miles and tell him what you have told me – the whole of everything. And tell him how you feel about the Church. I want you to commit to Miles and try very hard to be happy. Then in six months' time I want to see you again. At that point we will make a decision as to your future."

"But the Church?"

"The Church can wait. It survived two millennia without you and I'm sure another six months won't break it! Go now, child, and come back in six months."

"Yes, Father." She had received her instructions and with them a great weight was lifted. She had been trying to drive a car with the handbrake locked on, realised her mistake and released it to move more easily forwards.

She rose, let his fingers go and made to leave the room. "Thank you, Your Eminence." Correct title remembered as the spell was broken.

As she opened the door something else broke. Harry's glass fell to the floor and smashed, glass splinters slithering across the wooden floor. Harry fell forwards also, his head hitting against the door frame and knocking him out so he slumped to the floor, making a hurdle for Tammy's exit.

But others were close and ready to help. Harry was lifted, the glass shards swept up and Tammy was free to look for Miles.

And, despite the bitter cold day, they walked together in the garden, oblivious to the rain, even oblivious to the drunken cries and squabble-noise arising from the coal cellar.

Soon it was another joining of hands. Except they held hands like the lovers they were.

The Wild Card

Old Ma Silver was alone in her kitchen. The conference was in its final stages upstairs, discussing the specifics of the takeover of the New Moderation Church by the Roman Catholic Church. Father LaPetite had put it aptly, saying they were 'returning to the fold'. Even Fi had become accepting, seeing the bright warmth on Tammy's face; understanding that it had been rejection from the young nun's chosen path that had fuelled her desire to hit out at her church. Although the takeover bid had been spectacularly turned on its head and would go down as a rare defeat for Fi, the financier felt strange satisfaction in the result.

She had confided as much to Old Ma Silver earlier that day, in the break of the new day. Normally Sophie would be there but she was upstairs, making her peace or otherwise with her birth father.

"The only thing that concerns me," Old Ma Silver had replied, "is young Miles and that relationship. It seems he has lost out to God."

"You mean it is a three-way marriage?" Fi, for all her perception and insight, had been largely blind to the struggles Tammy, her best friend, was facing.

She had left the kitchen at that point, resolving to talk to Tammy about it, guilt at her ignorance giving a harsh tint to her promise to 'talk some sense into that girl', without quite knowing what sense she would be putting into her.

But Tammy was, by then, in with the cardinal and Fi had to put her plans on hold.

Old Ma Silver had stayed in the kitchen when Fi departed. She felt that the conference had become too detailed, too involved, to warrant her presence. She could add homespun wisdom but nothing on the technicalities. Instead she had fired up the big black range that the servants had kept going in the old days and was heating a rum punch her grandfather had made on special occasions back in the England of her youth. It was to be their celebratory drink.

She wanted to give something to the event, not realising how much she had already given.

Harry, recovered from his fall and having no real pride or sensitivity, had been in the kitchen earlier with his photographic side-kick, Mighty Snapper. Following Harry's exploits with the glass to the door, they had been banned from the entire first floor during the final session. But, as the minutes ticked on, they had left the kitchen, bolstered by the rum punch tasters, inching their way back to the main scene and leaving Old Ma Silver alone with her thoughts.

Three months earlier she had barely known Sophie. Yet now she loved her like the daughter she had never had. As she stirred her grandfather's recipe, a tune from her childhood came to mind and she sang. Her voice was not fine, rather rusted and scarred with age, but the words to *A Wonderful Life* seemed to wrap everything up.

She felt tired but happy as she sat in the comfortable dog chair by the stove. Glass of punch in one hand, she hummed the last line over again. She tasted her grandfather's punch and it was the last thing she ever did on this earth.

Fi found her. She was coming to the kitchen more and more these days, sometimes Bill came with her. The conference was finally concluded and she wanted to tell Old Ma Silver. She planned the two of them to take the punch up together, seeking a part in the pageant.

She found instead the still body that had been Old Ma Silver. She knew immediately that she was dead. Afterwards, she thought it was the punch stains running down her front that told her. But it matters not how she knew, just that she did.

"The conference is over now, Old Ma Silver," she said to the dead body, then added, "I came to love you as everyone did." She stooped to kiss the still warm skin, then turned to find Bill there and dropped into his open arms.

They went together to tell the others. But first they sought out Sophie and took her down to the kitchen. They stood guard at the kitchen door, punch bubbling on the stove top, while Sophie had a final time with Old Ma Silver.

When everyone knew, Fi remembered the punch. Some had evaporated into the cavernous kitchen, but there was sufficient for everyone, Harry and Mighty included, to sip a half-glass in memory of its curator and preparer.

Except Fi, being with child, just wet her lips before pouring her half-glass into the cardinal's, thus bringing another type of communion between the two parties.

There were no words said over Old Ma Silver, not then anyway. There were no words that could be said for she had been so much to so many and in so many different ways.

It was either everyone talking or nobody at all and simple silence seemed the best way.

Even Harry remained in the room when he and Mighty should have been rushing to release the greatest coup of the decade – the inside story of the largest takeover bid ever and with twists enough to keep the most casual reader fully engaged. Time was against them, as Ches had promised them only two hours' head start. But they hung around, feeling keenly for the woman who had provided warmth, hospitality and love for their short acquaintance, yet sensed she had done similar for all of her 74 years.

But we are dwelling on the minor characters during a momentously sad occasion. Sophie felt the loss the most, if loss of a loved-one can be measured and put on a chart for all to see. It was the cardinal who gathered Sophie into his arms and made light and comforting talk, reminding her to always celebrate the person Old Ma Silver had been.

"Take comfort, my Sophie, in the certainty that she went straight to Heaven and is up there now looking down at us and smiling."

Fi came up to them, sitting next to them on the window seat looking over the Via Romulus below. She placed a hand at Sophie's face and was all tenderness for this girl she had become so fond of.

"Twenty years I went without a sniff of love," she said, so words were spoken after all. "Then in the space of a few short weeks, I get overwhelmed with it, hitting from every direction. I can't begin to think what it is like for you, Sophie, except to imagine that my Bill was gone and that is unthinkable."

It was dark now, wintery sharp weather beating against the windowpane and making strange distortions of the knot of press on the street below. Some were pointing up at the window. Others were snapping constantly, as if they were Mighty's disciples, determined to prove their worth to the master. None of them below knew of their loss. No-one understood why the press release was held up. They all knew that, somehow, Harry Brine of the National Enquirer had wriggled in and got an exclusive deal, but why was he still in the house and not strutting in front of them?

"We're going to have to keep to the original plan," Ches said, coming up to stand next to the trio. "I can't keep the press at bay much longer. We said 5 p.m. for the press release and it's already 5:25 p.m."

"Yes," the cardinal replied, readying to heave himself up.

"One minute, I need to see Your Eminence for a few minutes first," Fi said. "We won't be long."

"What's it about?" the cardinal asked, forgetting his promise to her.

"I'm playing my wild card," was Fi's reply. "But don't let it hold up the press release. That has been prepared since this morning and we discussed it endlessly this afternoon. My wild card will not affect the press release. It is rather bigger than that," she added mysteriously.

Ches went to issue the press release, thinking thirty minutes of delay was not bad given the momentous events of the last few days. He left the conference room with Father LaPetite and Tammy. The cardinal and Fi both rose to go to the robing room for some privacy. Humphrey moved into the spare spot vacated by the cardinal.

"Sophie?"

"Yes?"

"Old Ma Silver dying like that. It was such a shock. But it made me realise that I can't live without you."

"But your vows…"

"I'm going to ask to be released from my vows and then I am going to ask you to marry me."

"Humphrey, you cannot give all that up for me." Her English was at its limit, straining under the emotion of hope. Then that little flame flickered and died, snuffed out by her hand, the hand that had lit it. "It's not right," she said, staring at a crack in the plaster on the wall, the other side to Humphrey. "You give your vows for life not for convenience. It is like a…"

"Marriage? Yes, I know. But it is not quite the same. Since I met you I have felt like my whole life has been pointless and then you came into it. I can't live without you, Sophie, my darling. It's like I am in a sham marriage and need to stop before it gets even more grotesque."

She looked at him. Could her faith be stronger than his, yet he was a priest, the cream of their religion? It was only faith that prevented her throwing herself at him, feeling the beat of his heart, the rush of blood, the tenseness of body.

Sophie felt the knife edge she was riding cut into her skin, drawing blood like spilt wine spreading across the altar cloth. She loved him beyond anything, but could she take him outside what he was? Could she be the vehicle that drove him to be ordinary, not a chosen one of God? Would he later resent it? And could she be the instrument that cut him from God and the hope of everlasting life?

If only Old Ma Silver was there to guide her. She cried then, rubbing her tears on both sleeves of her purple dress so the soft velvet became stained and pushed the wrong way by her cheeks. He tried to take her head in his arms. She fought against it, then gave way.

Take a snapshot of a tender but grim Humphrey with Sophie buried into the side of him. Neither know which will win, just that it is not a fight between them, but between earthly love and divine responsibility. Both care desperately but are beholden to another. An observer might say it was love of God that kept them stubbornly apart. But Harry Brine, in his wisdom and desire for a scintillating story, had already written of indoctrination and rigid catechism as the real villains.

Follow, instead, the steps that Fi and the cardinal took to the study come robing room, across the landing from the conference room. Fi switched on a side light, leaving much of the room in the dark. Then she crossed the room and closed the curtains, something Old Ma Silver would have done on any other day. The cardinal took the chair he had taken for Sophie and Tammy, hardly believing that those meetings had been just nine hours earlier.

Fi checked the door was closed, turned the key in the lock, mouthed "unwanted guests" to the cardinal and got a smile in reply.

These battle-axes understood each other.

In every way.

"When you become pope," Fi started, indicating immediately how much she understood.

"If I become pope."

"When you become pope," Fi said again, "I want to invoke my wild card."

"Only when I become pope?"

"Only."

"And if I do not become pope?"

"You are shed of all responsibility to carry out this task."

It was the biggest gamble she had ever undertaken. And not a penny would change hands.

"And the wild card is?" The cardinal felt like reminding Fi that he had not, after all, needed her votes in the decision to give permission for Mass to be heard in the house. But he decided it would serve no purpose.

He had won everything else and there was little point in pressing for more advantage.

"I want your promise that when you become pope you will change the rules in two ways. You will allow female priests and you will allow all members of the clergy to get married."

They argued long into the evening. At first the cardinal refused point blank.

"It is against Catholic doctrine," he said, but she reminded him that rules were there to be changed when circumstances dictated.

"Otherwise you end up with a dinosaur for a rule book, completely out of touch. That is a far greater danger than being open from time to time to changing outdated regulations."

It was a logic he could not argue with. It reminded her of the memo Father LaPetite had written when asked to assess Sophie for higher office. Sophie's views, Father LaPetite had concluded, were modern but well-founded. It had convinced him to allow the promotion requested by Barrow. That seemed a lifetime ago now.

He decided to move on. "You are asking for two things and our agreement was only one wild card."

"You're splitting hairs."

He persisted in this argument so Fi changed her wild card to one single request. "I want you to provide for equality amongst the clergy along the lines of the New Moderation Movement whereby either sex is permitted to conduct all services and all clergy can get married." It was a neat way around his objection and from this point he knew he had a tough road to climb back.

The argument grew, voices raised, tones sharper, less regard for the other party. Luckily, there was no-one listening in; everyone else was attending the press conference taking place that moment on the steps of 14, Via Romulus. The two who most sought the limelight were the two absentees, caught up indoors in their private feud.

In many ways this was the real takeover bid.

Harry and Ches led that press conference, giving details of the settlement to a frenetic press. Harry wore a huge grin, secure in the knowledge that he had the inside story and his boss, the National Enquirer's chief editor, had promised him both promotion and a fat bonus. Now he could afford that divorce he so desperately wanted.

Someone else was also plotting divorce. Ernest's reunification with his wife on release from the cellar did not go as he had hoped. Sara's frostiness made no attempt to hide her disdain and her desire to be anywhere other than by his side.

"I've called some attorneys," she said. And nothing else, for what else was there to say?

"Where's Fi?" Bill asked.

"Still in with the cardinal," Sophie answered, thinking it weird to have a cardinal for a father.

"We need to find her. We're leaving in the morning. Al just told me of a big new potential deal. Apparently, she needs to be in New York yesterday!"

"That's not possible, for yesterday I mean. Oh, I see, it was a joke."

They found Fi in the robing room, still in discussion but a little calmer now. Both were so, having laid all their cards on the table, the time for positioning was gone. The cardinal could see Fi's strengths and weaknesses, and Fi could see those of the cardinal.

With all artfulness blown away by an honest wind, they were coming to an accommodation.

"I'm coming," she replied to Al's entreaties, then knelt and kissed the cardinal's hand. "You can brief me on this opportunity while I'm packing," she called through the locked door. "When do we leave for New York?" She was already back in her familiar world.

She had played her wild card and now was on to the next deal. Such was the life of a billionaire financier.

Some would say "no rest for the wicked" but then they did not know Fi.

Twelve Months Later

They all gathered together for the funeral of the cardinal. It was Sophie's idea to use 14, Via Romulus, and Old Ma Silver's son, the stockbroker, was happy to oblige, knowing what joy the conference members had brought his mother at the end. The house was in the middle of a major renovation project, yet her son proved almost as able a host as Old Ma Silver had been.

Ches and Sara arrived early to assist with bedroom allocations and catering requirements. For the latter, they took Sophie's shortcut and contracted with the delicatessen on the square where she lived.

Sophie was bereft to lose her remaining parent.

"I was so lucky to have four parents," she said to anyone she came across. Normally, this would have indicated multiple divorces and step-parents making up the numbers, but not in this case. "I had my birth mother and birth father. Then I had my surrogate father."

"And the fourth parent?"

"Old Ma Silver, of course!" she would say with a grin. Thus Sophie, true to her character, could find joy even in the depths of sorrow.

They persisted in calling him the cardinal because that is how they remembered him; ferocious, unbending, unwavering, like any able administrator of the largest religion on earth. Yet sometimes Sophie thought there was so much more to the father she had come to love so fully.

They persisted in calling him the cardinal because that was their habit, staying with them even when the electoral college sent the white smoke into the air to indicate they had selected a new pope.

From the first day, he broke ranks, albeit in a small way. He selected his name with care, but there was really only one contender.

"Sofia? Are you sure?" Father LaPetite asked.

"After St Sofia of Rome," he lied, "a sixth century saint."

"Appropriate, I suppose to take a female saint's name, given your agenda." Father LaPetite had been deeply involved in both his election and his plans.

It had been a pitifully short reign, lasting from 15 May 2035 to his death on 12 December, not quite making seven months.

But it had been seven months of furious activity. Pope Sofia went without an inauguration celebration, saying he had too much to get on with. It was as if he knew his reign was going to be months rather than years. Instead of an inauguration, he said a simple Mass on Trinity Sunday in St Peters. The next day, he took an hour to himself and said Mass at the gloomy San Cristobal on Sophie's square. He called it the Church of Light and Shadow, for the light in that church seemed to play games, illuminating patches and corners that did not exist and distorting the colours of the sun, making winter out of the bright spring. Yet it was Sophie's church and he loved it as such.

By then he had already announced what he called his Passing Synod. He argued that all rules of the church fell into one of two categories. There were those based directly on the Ten Commandments and the teachings of Jesus. These were fixed and could never change. They formed the central tenet of belief so necessary to be a Catholic. The second category he called the Passing Regulations. These were the rules that could and did, from time to time, change with changing morality. Father Barrow wrote a fascinating paper to support the proposition. It divided morality in similar fashion: a central core that would never alter and a periphery that could change as times change. His paper depicted it as a ball with a rigid centre wrapped in more flexible outer material.

The obvious example was slavery, at one time accepted across the civilised world, now universally condemned. According to Humphrey, a pope was infallible only when pronouncing on the former category. It stood to reason that infallibility was not appropriate where rules were based on matters of this earth and changed as the generations changed.

The paper effectively divided religion into a sphere dictated by God, mainly through His Son, Jesus Christ, and a sphere controlled by man based on the core theology but adaptable to changing times. In summary, it argued that this was a meeting of religion with humanism; a participatory religion in which man and woman played a part.

It also opened the way for serious reform.

The synod met in late June and ran for four weeks. It concentrated exclusively on female clergy and the ability for religious folk to marry. Father LaPetite, now the pope's righthand man, drafted and redrafted the new rules every night for presentation the following day. Pope Sofia bullied and cajoled from early morning to late at night. Finally, on 27 July 2035, the new rules came into effect.

Pope Sofia celebrated with a phone call to Fi, battling away on a project to buy a group of a hundred hospitals and make them profitable. It was a messy bid with vitriolic statements on all sides. She took the phone call immediately, breaking off a meeting that promised to be decisive.

There were a few things more important than making money, or, as Bill called it, this was the new Fi.

"Have you seen the news from the Vatican?" the familiar voice shouted down the phone.

"No, cardinal, I mean…"

"Cardinal is fine, my dear. Look online now." She did so and gasped with astonishment.

"You've done it! You've actually done it."

"Didn't I say I would?"

"Well, you didn't actually. If you remember we ended up with a stalemate. We'd gotten real close but didn't quite meet in the middle. You said you would do what was appropriate and I thought that you were backing down."

"It was tempting, but I prayed long and hard and it seemed the right thing to do. It was hard in the extreme to get everything through the Synod."

Pope Sofia rang off and went to bed early, exhausted from his efforts.

The following morning, 28 July, he had risen to say Mass, followed by a meeting with the implementation committee headed by a beaming Father LaPetite. Pope Sofia thought it odd because he had always understood Father LaPetite to be vehemently opposed to the ideas behind the changes. No matter, perhaps he too had met a shining light on the road to Damascus.

He had closed the meeting early that morning, feeling heavy in the head, like a bad cold. Later that day the splitting headaches started, pounding through his skull like a prisoner in solitary, deep in the mind, determined to have his protest heard.

Those headaches had stayed with him. Father LaPetite had called the doctor two days later. Several specialists later, they located the brain tumour. It was big already and growing bigger, pressing on some part of the brain. LaPetite forgot the name but remembered that it governed behaviour.

The last few months of Pope Sofia's life was an erratic and harrowing time for all involved, most especially for the pope himself. He might have a morning when he felt normal, reasonably content with the pain, able to converse. But it would be swiftly followed by retribution, a grim and menacing pain that overcame him and made him cry out, swearing and cursing as if born to it. He grew increasingly infirm. In late October, he went to bed one afternoon and never rose again. In lucid moments he would ask about the progress of his great reform, taking pride in the reversal of his position and the single-mindedness that had put the reform in place.

He knew, in those better moments, that he had been motivated to his reforms by two equal forces. On the one side stood a coalition of his faith with the reasoning of others like Fi, Humphrey and Sophie, aided by the constant but odd encouragement of Father LaPetite. On the other side sat his pride, quite alone but equal to any other force on the field.

He knew also that good things often come from bad motivations. He chose Humphrey Barrow for his final confessor and spent a relatively pleasant hour discussing such matters before the pain grew again, reminding him that the end was near.

Sophie came often to see her father. At first, he tried to cheer her with his bluff roughness, but soon she became a strength to him. "I love you, Papa," she would say as she leant over and kissed him on the cheek or forehead, rinsing the wet cloth to cool him in his agony, wiping away the hot sweat that seemed never to dry up.

Once she read to him a commentary on his great reform, thinking to cheer him up. It was late November and late afternoon; dark clouds sat in a dark sky but no rain, nothing sent down from Heaven to distract her while she read.

"Papa, it says here that the Roman Catholic Church has increased membership by almost six percent since your reforms came into being."

"What reforms, my dear?" It was then she knew that he was dying for certain. He lingered on for two more weeks, as if God could not decide whether to take him now or wait a little longer. Surely there was nothing else for this great man, her father, to do upon the earth?

Surely there was a place in Heaven for this wonderful man, who had changed His Church through his efforts?

She had been a direct beneficiary of his changes, but true to form, she made a drama out of their meeting at 14, Via Romulus after the funeral of the old pope.

They sat, for old time's sake, around the large table in the conference room. There were fewer of them now. The cardinal was gone to Heaven, Ernest was licking his wounds as life president of a church that no longer existed and several of the cardinal's lackeys had moved on to other posts.

And, of course, Old Ma Silver had gone on as well.

But Sophie felt cheerful as she controlled the meeting, much as her father would have controlled it if he had been there.

"I think we should go around the table and get an update from each of us in turn," she pronounced, relishing the game. She turned to her right. "We'll start with you, Fi."

Fi had a lot to tell. "I've bought three companies, sold two for a lot more than I paid for them and expanded into Singapore and Hong Kong. I now have two thousand associates in my firm." She made to sit down again, then her smile increased to treble size. "Oh, I almost forgot. In March I got married to Bill," she stopped and kissed her husband warmly, "and in August I gave birth to Alfonso D'Alianti Mannings." She shoved photographs of their son across the table. "Viewings this evening when I bring the little guy in."

Next along the table it was Father LaPetite. He stood up, looked at his watch deliberately, sighed and started to give a complete review of every meal he had eaten over the last twelve months, together with the wines he had swallowed alongside the food. He went into detail, describing the steak that was slightly too well cooked, the desert wine that was corked and the scrambled egg that was too runny. "I can't abide runny scrambled eggs," he said to shouts of 'how long is this going to take?' and 'shame on you, big man'.

The meals grew more bizarre as he moved through the days. Before he had even got to Christmas 2034, he was eating a whale stake and washing it down with buckets of brandy.

'You wish!" Miles called out, but the fat priest kept on and on, grinning as his voice rose louder above the throng.

It was Sophie who saved the day. She left the room and returned with a tray of cakes, delivered earlier from her delicatessen. She placed the tray in front of Father LaPetite but then slid it out of reach when he went for one. He reached further and she pushed it again. He was quiet now, playing the part to perfection.

"Cake, please," he said in a whisper. Everyone heard, such was the sudden silence in the room, most struggling to hold back their laughter.

"On one condition," Sophie said, teeth tightly clenched to keep the grin spreading.

"Anything, anything!"

"You have to keep quiet."

Instead of replying he put his finger to his mouth, then grabbed a cake with his left hand and jammed it in.

"Well, that's been sorted out," Sophie said, except there was as much noise from his audience as he had been making himself.

Next it was Tammy's turn. She stood up, but so also did Miles. "We're together," he explained, "so we might as well do it together."

There was no laughter as they told their story of the last twelve months. Miles started. "We returned to my fish and chip shop. Everything seemed okay, but I sensed that Tammy was trying too hard, that something was missing from her life. Then one day, it must have been early April, I read an article in the newspaper in the shop about nuns living in the real world rather than be cloistered alone. It had some catchy headline that I forget now but was written by a freelance newspaperman called Harry Brine!" Everyone turned to look at Harry who, despite not being a delegate to the original conference, had been invited to the reunion.

"That's correct, I left the National Enquirer when the editor reneged on his promise of a bonus and promotion. I wrote the book, of course." The story of his few days with the conference that changed everything had been told in '14, Via Romulus', a hastily pushed-out best seller. "Then I became a freelance journalist." It was a quick update from the rogue journalist inserted into Tammy's and Miles' time.

"I don't know why but I went upstairs to Tammy and read the article to her. It changed our lives."

Tammy took over then, describing the tearing feeling of loving two in equal measure, seeming to have to decide one or the other. "Remember, this was April, before the great reforms were even aired as a possibility, let alone a certainty. We flew to the States the next day. We went to see the Mother Superior of the Order of the Holy Cross. We thought it would be two days and we were there for two months. The Order, my Order, was sadly depleted, unrecognisable from ten years earlier."

She was correct as a short history of the Order of the Sisters of the Holy Cross will tell. Numbers had plummeted in the late 20s. There had been no new entrants since Sister Mary John in 2022. Several had left the Order, she thought due to the response from the previous Mother Superior who had sought to make the regime stricter, like someone concerned about their gums wearing away so brushing ever more vigorously, thus exacerbating the original wear. "When I started as a novice, there had been 30 in the Vigilance satellite and about 80 nuns in the home convent. When we returned in May 2035, there were four at Vigilance, two of whom are over 80, and 16 at the main convent. Everything was neglected and derelict. It was a sad sight indeed. In particular, the gardens at the home convent were in a real sorry state."

They had gone on to Vigilance, where an extraordinary thing was waiting for them. "Father Davies, the one who raped me, had set up shop in a part of the convent that was surplus to requirements, there being only four nuns in residence."

"What a cheek," said Fi. But Sophie had an inkling that the calmness exhibited by Tammy and Miles meant a better outcome. She remembered Father Davies. She had been determined to hate him for what he had done to Tammy but could not stop herself from liking him.

Miles then told how Father Davies had set up a residential clinic for the reform of rapists. "He begs and borrows money from wherever he can find it and actually pays rent to the nuns. This gives them a little income for food and necessities. And Father Davies' programme seems to be a great success, albeit run on a shoestring. He had 16 men in his programme when we were there in June."

"Seventeen," said Tammy, "including him."

It was Tammy's turn in this duo-told tale. They seemed to know when the other was scheduled to take over.

"Father Davies is a much-changed man," she started, shaking a vision of him on top of her ten years previously. "Physically, he is very different. He is much older and frailer, yet there is a sinewy quality about him which I did not see before. But the main difference is that he is a bad man turned good and the grace of God is back within him again." It might sound simplistic, even naive, yet nobody around the conference table had any such thought.

Most people are both good and bad in a hotchpotch, ever-changing. Often someone is selfless for the most selfish reasons, or arrogant with the best intentions. Sophie, with far more wisdom in her head than average for her age, considered it a moment, concluding this must be why God told people not to judge one another. It was far too complex a mix for humans. Hence, she put it aside and returned to her friends, Tammy and Miles.

"Did this lead you anywhere?" she asked, a question Father LaPetite would have been proud of.

"Yes," they both said together, looked at each other, then Miles sat down. This was Tammy's show after all.

"Yes," said Tammy again, "it led us to a whole new world and to an incredible easing of my mind. It was even better when the cardinal published his new rules at the end of July." She went on to explain that she had found happiness with both the loves of her life. "I am in the church but also I am married to Miles. I am a nun but married to the love of my life. I could not be happier."

Miles stood up. "Let me tell the next bit, my darling. We started a new sub-convent of the Order of the Holy Cross. We located it on Bent Mountain, Virginia, where Tammy has lived since leaving the Order in 2025. We took over a rambling old farmhouse, did it up and made it into our convent. We have six nuns and eight rapists wanting to reform. We had Father Davies up for three weeks in November to set us off in the right direction. He is Heaven-sent for this work, an absolute natural." The room was spellbound, as if watching the latest hit movie, engrossed to the ending credits. And they came next as Miles proudly announced that Tammy and he had got married in September. "And we are expecting our first child in May next year."

There was no applause as Tammy and Miles sat down, somewhat exhausted from their tale. There was equally no attempt at humour or discussion.

Applause or any other reaction would seem so out of place, Sophie thought, for it is a most beautiful story with goodness and love dropping out of every page.

"Okay, so we are all done. Let's go and relax awhile before supper," Sophie said after a decent interval.

"Hang on," Father LaPetite said, "aren't we forgetting someone, or rather some people?"

He was right. Sophie had omitted an update from her and from Humphrey. Whether that was deliberate or forgetfulness we will never know.

"Oh, of course," said Sophie, wondering how on earth she would give an update.

Everyone had taken the exact places they had occupied a year earlier for the conference. Hence, Humphrey was the other side of the table to Sophie, looking across at her. On instinct, he rose and came around the table, just as he had last year when Father LaPetite had told the conference of the relationship between Sophie and the cardinal.

"With your permission," he started, "I would like to copy the precedent of Tammy and Miles and give a joint update. And with your permission, Sophie, I will start first."

Sophie nodded her agreement, sensing something but not at all sure what.

"As you all know, I am a priest and take my role within the church very seriously indeed." Pompous or natural, how did he sound? Suddenly, he did not care anymore. It would just come out. "When I first came back to Rome in September of last year, I came to teach seminarians. I decided to try and be clever and change the lesson plans in order to spice them up a bit. The cardinal got word of this and sent Sophie LaNeve to spy…yes, spy…don't interrupt me, Sophie. He sent her to spy on me. I started my first lecture, meaning to make an impact and I chose the opening words:

Well, it has been quite a year and I think I can safely say that God is not bored any longer.

Sophie came into my life and I was smitten. I did not understand it at first and I sought to belittle her. I asked the cardinal for her as my secretary, even though, as Father LaPetite persistently pointed out between mouthfuls of clams and slugs of Frascati, she has a higher intellect than anyone in this room, proud me included." He paused while a light laughter filled the room, reminding Humphrey of the light white wines Father LaPetite and he had drunk in deep conversation.

About Sophie mostly.

"Sophie took exception to me because of a misunderstanding about my role with Tammy, or should I say Sister Mary John?"

"Sister Mary John is fine," she replied. "That is what I go by now."

"We fell in love. But we resisted it, mainly through Sophie's faith and strength which has been an inspiration to me.

Sophie has had quite a year indeed. This time last year she learned that her real father was the cardinal, soon to be our pope. At the same time, she lost her surrogate mother, Old Ma Silver, who we all remember with love. This was shortly after her surrogate father, Signor LaNeve, passed away. Throughout these terrible times, Sophie remained positive, loving and giving and, most particularly, full of fun. I can safely say I have never loved anyone as I love you, Sophie."

He stepped back and dropped onto one knee. "Sophie, the love of my life, will you marry me?"

"I will," came back the reply, short and sweet.

As they kissed, the applause came thick and fast.

And God certainly was not bored anymore.

THE END

18 Acres of England

"Could not put it down, not even for the Superbowl!"

Ben Franklin has a mind-numbing job as a White House security guard.

Dakota Jamieson is one quarter into a forty-year sentence for a crime she didn't commit.

Ben stumbles upon a secret so incredible it threatens to turn the western world in on itself, turning long friendly nations into enemies.

Did America ever really gain its independence? Or has it remained a secret vassal of the British Empire?

Fact, fiction, politics, slavery, imprisonment, redemption, romance and history all wrapped into a novel that will enthral the reader to the very last page.

"The author wisely blends facts with fiction, until the two are indistinguishable... Loved this book and highly recommend it to anyone looking for a thought-provoking plot twist in history."

The Stuff of Heroes

A 1960s Britain very different to the one we remember.

Georgia Nullgeben wore privilege like a badge of rank. Daughter of the sector commander, she was destined for great things.

Mark Smith was an English.

They should not have met.

But they did.

"Imagine if we'd just given up and rolled over and let the Nazis win the war, let them invade Britain and take control and make the English a second-class citizen."

The British had not bothered to develop the Spitfire, preferring to save the money and chance it. The War of 1940 was short and the occupation thorough; enough, they thought, to ensure that the British could never stand tall again.

All they had to hang their hopes on were the Beat Kids, music filtering in from America, played underground – literally. Would their spirit prove to be enough?

And what would Georgia make of those she was forced to be with?

The Stuff of Heroes is first in the Semblance of Order Trilogy, tender thrillers that look at the juxtaposition of chaos and order.

The Agent Within, 2nd in the trilogy, will be available in late 2020.

The Dorset Chronicles

"…an absolute page turner and perfect in every way."

Historical fiction from the forging of our modern nation

It's 1685, Charles II is dead and Britain is about to be turned upside down. The Duke of Monmouth lands in Lyme Regis, intent on taking the throne from his uncle, the hapless James II.

The Dorset Chronicles puts the reader right into the momentous events of the day through the eyes and experiences of ordinary people; Monmouth's rising leading to the Battle of Sedgemoor, The Glorious Rebellion, the Siege of Londonderry, the Battle of the Boyne and King William's War in faraway America.

The series reflects the personal, agonising and transformational journeys of each character in stories that weave together into a mass of emotion; whether love, hate, revenge, desperation or the sheer joy of being alive and at the threshold of the creation of our modern nation.

Book 1: A New Lease on Freedom
Book 2: It Takes a Rogue
Book 3: A Simple Mistake
Book 4: One Shot in the Storm.

Enter a tumultuous world of change, transition, resistance and revolution; new ideas sweeping out the old, bringing new hopes and new fears, and testing the resolution and courage of all those involved.

"A wonderful combination of fiction and history which kept me riveted"

"I dare not pick it up just yet for fear that I won't be able to put it down."